I0842999

Pluto II
Voyage to the Edge of the Universe

Written By

Paul D. Escudero

Director's Copy

WORKBOOK PRESS LLC
187 E Warm Springs Rd,
Suite B285 Las Vegas NV 89119 USA

Website: https://workbookpress.com/
Hotline: 1-888-818-4856
Email: admin@workbookpress.com

Ordering Information:
Quantity sales. Special discounts are available on quantity purchases by corporations, associations, and others. For details, contact the publisher at the address above.

Library of Congress Control Number:

ISBN-13:   978-1-963718-81-2   Paperback Version
                978-1-963718-82-9   Digital Version

REV. DATE: 05/02/2024

<u>EXT. CGI. ANIMATE SPACE FLYING TOWARDS SEQUENCES OF JWST IMAGES DURING VOICEOVER. 10 SECONDSD EACH SLIDE.</u>

Pluto II

VOICE OVER

It all started when scientists started making the claim they could see the edge of the universe. Certain people like Gregory Bissell had a logic based on faith, there could be no end to the universe and the Big Bang

Theory remained bogus to him. His faith in God left no room for the magic these scientists created that said the universe came out of something the size of a tip of a needle and expanded to what it is today.

However, to prove their Big Bang Theory, numerous brilliant scientists came up with calculations and cited that no light images could be seen beyond thirty-five billion light years from our planet.

Those observations didn't really impact Gregory Bissell because he had his own viewpoint that light traveling in space was no different than sound traveling in the ocean. Just like the Hubble Space Telescope can focus images very uniquely billions of light years away producing spectacular images. Sensors on American and competitor submarines could do the same thing with sound. And no matter how good the sensors were, the spherical and cylindrical spreading loss would eventually attenuate the sound energy until it could no longer be detected. Hence there was a range limit until new types of beamformers were designed.

In space the James Webb Space Telescope was already showing how better receivers can extend the range limit.

A really simple experiment in Gregory's mind was, hold a flashlight up to someone's face and it is very bright. Send that person a mile down the street and have them shine the light this way and it's significantly less bright because of the light spreading over the distance. When the light is a foot away, most of photons in a small cross-section arrive at the viewer's eyes. However, a mile away due to the spreading as the beam goes the distance, less than one hundredth of the photons reach the eye of the observer which gives the apparent attenuation.

People traveling on two-lane country highways at night deal with this factor all the time when some jerk doesn't dim his lights as they are passing.

The same thing works in space. Just like spherical spreading losses of sound in the ocean, spherical spreading of light in the universe undergoes the same spreading.

Light in fiber optics does the same thing resulting in modal distortion in a perfect medium which requires single mode fiber to transmit light over long distances.

Just like sound in the ocean has a "range" light in the universe also has a range. The red shifts and the blue shifts caused by Doppler are not reliable. New research indicates there is a light decay factor that causes shifts as well, especially at extreme distances.

Nothing much came of Greg's notions for a while until the great debate circled around academia where dissenting opinions created a curiosity that begat a need to try to get some answers. And technology was creeping along to a point where at last a solution could be engineered to allow the most extravagant experiment ever envisioned by mankind.

Nuclear rockets were nothing new. First developed in the 1950s to produce a fast rocket that could be launched at great distances to attack Soviet facilities, the technology produced some viable power plants. The Lawrence Radiation Laboratory (once headed by J. Robert Oppenheimer) was selected to do the study. The Radiation Laboratory eventually became the Lawrence Livermore National Laboratory.

Dr. Theodore Charles Merkle (any chance he's related to Germany's former PM?) stood up the project code named Project Pluto. The goal of the project was to develop ramjet engines by applying heat from nuclear reactors.

The nuclear ramjet operated by pushing air in through the front of the vehicle (ram effect) while in motion, a nuclear reactor super-heated the air, and then the hot air expanded at high speed out through a nozzle at the back, providing immense thrust from the plasma-like exhaust exiting at super velocities.

Scientists working on the new idea to send a spacecraft to the edge of the universe at ultra-high speed would fabricate it by assembling modules in space. And because there was no air to scoop in (or very little amount of hydrogen atoms until it reached light speed), large hydrogen tanks were to be installed to provide the feed through the nuclear reactor that would super-heat the hydrogen creating a plume traveling at light speed.

But because of the air scoop that could be opened once reaching light speed, the internal hydrogen would only be needed to accelerate and once reaching the theoretical limit where out in space a few hydrogen atoms per cubic feet multiplied by three hundred million meters per second passing the rocket engine nuclear reactor would sustain the push.

There was another theory added. Since there is little or no friction in space, the craft could continue to speed up beyond light speed where the intake of the sparse number of hydrogen atoms multiplied in a logarithmic amount.

As the ship got closer to the end of the universe photographs would be recorded in small rockets jettisoned out of the spaceship that had enough fuel to accelerate beyond light speed heading back towards earth to deliver the images for the sake of mankind.

This new program would operate under the code word Pluto II in honor of the men who created the SLAM (Supersonic Low-Altitude Missiles) design President Eisenhower decided not to build based on inputs from his liberal brother Milton, as there were fears the Soviets would counter and build their own SLAM which would make the world a much more dangerous place. Eisenhower's easy way out of the political firestorm he created with the contractors when he canceled SLAM was resolved.

The Submarine Launched Polaris Nuclear Missiles easily alleviated the need to go forward on building SLAM. Nevertheless, SLAM didn't need to be launched from a submarine, so Eisenhower gave up versatility over misguided advice.

Pluto II would be a rocket of gigantic size. Never had such a large spacecraft was conceived and constructed mainly to house the amount of hydrogen to get it accelerated. But also, scientists wanted a human aboard to send electronic logs back throughout the journey and with super sensitive video and telescopic ability, there was a good chance the rocket could pass by intelligent life forms or detect habitable planets. It would be a one-of-a-kind experiment ever attempted and never again since it.

Water was not a problem. Urine would be reprocessed and with the water tank initially filled, it was believed could sustain the astronaut indefinitely, though it was expected only twenty years was needed. This would be a one-way trip. The volunteer would know he's never coming back after the ship was long gone on its mission. In essence the poor bastard will not know he's been Shanghaied with no means to do anything about it other than commit suicide.

Scientists calculated minimal calories needed for twenty years and with a fudge factor that's how much special prepared food was carried for the mission. The food could be stretched way beyond the time limits required by sequencing the astronaut into periods of suspended animation by inducing a coma like sleep that would last a month at a time. In essence if the astronaut did suspended animation, the food would long outlast that person.

This would be a lonely mission with no thoughts of ever coming back. The volunteer would be provided cyanide pills to commit suicide if he felt he could no longer continue after a period of time.

The spacecraft Pluto II would travel in full autopilot with assistance with Artificial Intelligence and Sensor intercepts. But mission planners decided having a Human observer onboard was highly desirable.

However, after twenty years if that person decided to swallow the cyanide pills the craft would continue with its mission, utilizing the onboard humanoid Robot to shoot off a status missile preprogrammed approximately once a month until they were all expended. During the mission, if they encountered Aliens or a significant reporting event a message buoy missile would be launched immediately.

Gregory Bissell had no idea that such a space research development to resolve the issue surrounding the Big Bang Theory was going on as he was just a casual observer of a lot of the space development happening with the recent introduction of the UNITED STATES SPACE FORCE.

Gregory Bissell's own life went through oscillations and twists and turns, and as events changed his destiny, he was lucky, he was reaching and advanced age in life where all that was left is waiting for his time clock to run down and it all end. While he was pondering his future and the grim outlook on aging, the developers of Pluto II were trying to figure out, the best volunteer they could send out knowing they would be sending that person out to space in loneliness and eventual death. The key person would be an adult with no more than thirty expected years of life left, but in good physical condition with no known medical conditions requiring any form of medication.

The program managers worst nightmare would this person falling apart while within radio range of Earth. Once he was out traveling far out of the solar system and traveling at light speed, Earth would be spared of any grim news that came about prematurely in the mission. The backup plan centered on the humanoid Robot that could complete the mission's desired milestone, reaching the edge of the Universe to prove the theoretical limits were real or a farce.

The search for the astronaut was done in complete secrecy. Pluto II was only started when the researchers all agreed the entire project would remain top secret for the rest of their lives. Unless there was some compelling reason to broadcast any aspect of the mission to the public, such as an alien encounter that created a need to do so, Project Pluto II would remain in the shadows for all the current living inhabitants of this planet.

<u>EXT. DAY. MISSION BAY PARK, SKI BEACH, PARADISE COVE IMAGES INCLUDING HIGH SPEED BOAT RACES DONE THERE ONCE A YEAR.</u>

San Diego is such a unique climate, therefore a number of researchers working on Pluto II project, commuted from there to the San Francisco Bay area where the redesign of the spacecraft's nuclear reactor was ongoing. One such researcher, Dr. Robert (Bob) Moore, often exercised at the San Diego Ski Beach that had great year-round climate for runners and joggers except for the rare days it rained. In the numerous times Dr. Moore bumped into Gregory Bissell out there walking ten miles on any typical day and certainly did not look his age.

Finding the candidate to travel on Pluto II Rocketship to the edge of the universe would entail a complex recruiting process.

The Pluto II program managers had to find the person first then study him/her and then find out if such a possibility existed. In fact, some of the researchers felt they should give up on recruiting a person and go fully automated because who the hell would want to do such a mission where they would in a way be strapping on their burial casket in the form of a spaceship?

Because of the consistency of Gregory Bissell's workout ethics, it was expected Dr. Moore would see him running laps down at Ski Beach. Bob Moore never sought Gregory Bissell's out as a potential recruit because in the beginning it's the last thing Bob ever thought Greg would entertain.

People who work out together all the time often develop interpersonal relationships. It could be at the gym, golf course or some other venue. People tend to socialize with like minds. Gregory Bissell being somewhat of a computer geek, was the typical adult nerd with a degree of polish and an associate degree of barnacles.

Gregory Bissell's two sons were grown up, moved out and as far away from Dad as possible. It wasn't they had a bad relationship, it was just one of those things where peculiar interests led them off in directions and situations that slowly decayed the relationship people would assume normal in America where Grandad and Grandma would be bouncing their grandkids on their knees. But each son was a committed bachelor with no hope in sight for grandkids.

After retirement at an early age, Gregory Bissell's Japanese wife decided she wanted to move back to Japan.

Greg's wife wanted to grow old and die in Japan, her country and be buried with her relatives.

Suddenly Gregory Bissell was a loner with no desire for any relationship with another woman and in fact informed his departing wife he would never divorce her mainly so he could continue taking care of her even though she would be living far apart. She of course felt that strange pain of separation but knew she had married such an ideal man who cared so much for her he would continue providing for her even though in a sense she was deserting him during their golden years.

It wasn't that Dr. Moore was nosey, but when you become friends with people often things come out that you never expected.

<u>EXT. DAY. SAN DIEGO MISSION BAY PARK, SKI BEACH.</u>

GREG BISSELL

I will be taking my wife to the airport tomorrow and
she is not coming back any time soon.

DR. MOORE

Wow, I'm sorry to hear that.

GREG BISSELL

It was almost a shocking revelation, but I understand
why she wants to do it.

Gregory Bissell's wife certainly sealed the complexities of Gregory Bissell's life. All the years with his beautiful Japanese wife were great years.

DR. MOORE
I hope you adjust to the new circumstances soon.

GREG BISSELL

I have no regrets and understand why she is doing it as she misses her country terribly.
America was never her home. You could never take Japan out of her, living in eyesight of Mount Fuji and being able to see the cherry blossoms and experience Golden Week made her feel more serene.

DR. MOORE
Nothing to keep her here?

GREG BISSELL

No. Had our sons given her grandchildren she might not ever got home until her death, and she would have stipulated burial in Japan (in an urn).

Two things Dr. Moore understood about Gregory Bissell was his health was outstanding and he fit the criteria for the type of person they were looking for. Educated, computer savvy, meaning he would have no difficulty in observing and operating the systems which were in autopilot with a human supervising.

Dr. Moore knew how the recruiting process works. It was done to him, and he had recruited a number of associates. Because of the security aspect one had to be very subtle. The candidate had to be brought to a certain point before he learns fractions of the program.

Observing Gregory Bissell days after he took his wife to Japan Airlines terminal at San Diego's Lindberg Field, Dr. Moore was impressed that Greg's personal psychology appeared to handle it. At an opportune moment when they met at Ski Beach the initial conversations and recruitment began.

GREGORY BISSELL
Good morning, Bob.

Gregory Bissell seemed in a most cheerful manner or was it a poker face? Dr. Moore wondered.

DR. MOORE
I see you are out getting the miles in?

GREG BISSELL

Yeah, now that my wife is gone, and my sons are long ways off and never call, I can get the exercise done

which makes me feel a lot better. The only adjustment
I'll have to make is getting used to doing the laundry.

DR. MOORE
Greg, did you ever think about doing some consulting
work?

GREG BISSELL
Money's not a problem, I planned well.

DR. MOORE
Yeah, but now that you're practically single now, I'm
sure there are some companies that would value your
talents and experience.

GREG BISSELL
I suppose there are, perhaps one day I might consider
a consulting gig, it would certainly give me something
to do now that my wife is gone.

DR. MOORE
I bet there is something available you might enjoy.

GREG BISSELL
I could probably become a road warrior again, but I
got kind of sick of living in hotels.

DR. MOORE
I know how you feel.

GREG BISSELL
I wouldn't mind traveling and seeing the sights on
someone else's nickel, but I've already seen the sights!

DR. MOORE
I got an idea, this evening why don't we meet down in
Pacific Beach at one of the bar restaurants there, I have
some friends that might be looking for an experienced
guy like you in your circumstances.

GREG BISSELL
Sure, any suggestions?

DR. MOORE
I like the Flaming Flamingo, it has a nice clientele, the
prices are little higher, but it keeps the riff raff out of
there and lots of eye candy. Who knows, you might
meet some young lady there who needs a sugar daddy
you can spend all that consultant pay on.

GREG BISSELL

With as many STDs floating around these days, I would seriously have to know a woman well before I would consider any such action. Plus, all the women my age look like grandmas or old hags. I'm not sure I could handle a young dumb-shit broad who has no experience in life.

DR. MOORE

I know what you mean, men our age have a rough time meeting a suitable female partner.

GREG BISSELL

I'm sure women feel the same way.

DR. MOORE

I know I hear from them all the time.

GREG BISSELL

What's a good time?

DR. MOORE

How about 6:00 P.M., get there a little early to get a good seat.

GREG BISSELL

No problem. I got a guy on the block who's an Uber driver, so I can have a couple glasses of wine and enjoy the sights and not worry about dealing with the police.

DR. MOORE

Me too.

GREG BISSELL

See you then.

The men continued their exercises going their own way, and after ten miles, Gregory Bissell put his tired body in his car and drove home to Point Loma, where he had just spent the best twenty years of his life until his wife decided she needed to leave and move to her native country.

Gregory Bissell had been to Japan quite a few times. It's a lovely place and there are lovely people, but it's not America. And a lot of Japanese really do not speak English, so if a person moves there or stays for a long period of time if they can't speak Japanese, they are isolated. All the television is Japanese. Though for a hefty sum, you could get some American cable channels.

The other problem Gregory Bissell would face is all his Japanese contacts would continuously want to visit and provide sake and beer and pickle his liver.

After a nice shower, snack, and some internet surfing, reading a book then it was time to dress and meet up with Bob at the Flaming Flamingo.

Greg wasn't going to dress to impress, so he put on a typical Aloha Shirt and blue jeans. Another change in life he made was he liked running and walking shoes so much, nowadays that's all he ever wears. He didn't like sandals and his leather shoes stayed in the closet most of the time.

When he was ready, he called his Uber driver.

RODRIGUEZ
Hello, can I help you?

GREG BISSELL
Hi, Rodriguez, this is Gregory Bissell. Are you busy?
Can you give me a ride over to Pacific Beach?

RODRIGUEZ
Sure, when do you want to go?

GREG BISSELL
I'm ready now, so whenever you can get here.

RODRIGUEZ
I'll be there in five minutes.

GREG BISSELL
Thanks!

RODRIGUEZ
You are welcome, Greg.

Gregory Bissell looked in the mirror one last time. He looked okay. He was no longer a spring chick, but some old hag, out there somewhere, would love to get her hooks into me.

Then Greg thought, *I know it's awful soon after she left, am I making a mistake?*

Without remorse, Gret walked to the front door and left and walked out to the sidewalk knowing Rodriguez would drive up in his BMW soon.

Rodriguez was a handsome man, educated, good job, but San Diego real estate is so costly he had to do part-time work with Uber gigs to afford his house payment. He loved picking up Greg who always tipped him very well. And usually, it meant a round trip so later in the night he would call again and make some more decent coin. Which meant he would have to stay sober and not hit the tequila until later in the night.

Rodriguez pulled up and Gregory Bissell walked over and got into the front seat with him. They drove off.

> RODRIGUEZ
> Where to, boss?

> GREG BISSELL
> I want to go to the Flaming Flamingo in Pacific Beach.

> RODRIGUEZ
> You going there to chase some tail now with the missus
> gone?

> GREG BISSELL
> No, I'm not in the mood to let a woman latch onto me
> any time soon. Why complicate one's life?

> RODRIGUEZ
> You got that right; my girlfriend wants a little bambino
> now. I'm not ready financially to have her stop working
> if she gets pregnant.

> GREG BISSELL
> You know what you need to do about that. Make sure
> you wear overshoes every time and get one of those
> that have the extra spermicide in them, so you don't
> have an accident.

In due time they pulled up to the Flaming Flamingo, right on Pacific Beach Drive, in the surfer dude Mecca of Southern California. Gregory Bissell walked into the venue and was met by the most elegant and beautiful Maître d' he had seen in quite a while. Her attire was beautiful and did a great job of exposing a lot of cleavage. *No doubt she is high maintenance*, Greg thought.

Bob Moore apparently had not arrived and was nowhere to be seen.

Pacific Beach is the hotspot for San Diego. More action there than any place in town. And on nice summer evenings, it's a madhouse. Between the dopers, drunks, and dancers, an incredible dichotomy evolves.

The Flaming Flamingo would be crowded with young punks, but the drinks were expensive so that kept most of the trash out plus the Maître d' would have the bouncer escort someone out if they were not properly dressed as the sign outside said no swimsuits allowed and no shirts and no shoes, no services.

Inside the Flaming Flamingo, clientele appeared upward mobile that liked places like this that had good-looking waitresses not covered in tattoos and had a friendly atmosphere. Outside were flaming torches which accentuated the pink flamingo colored exterior. And of course, there were all kinds of flamingo artifacts and pictures to add to the ambience.

MAÎTRE D'
Can I help you, sir?

GREG
Yes, I'm here to meet a friend.

MAÎTRE D'
Would you like to wait for your friend at the bar?

GREG
Yes, thank you.

The Maître d' had a nametag that said Beverly on it. She took Greg Bissell to the bar.

MAÎTRE D'
Enjoy your evening.

GREG
Thank you, Beverly.

The bartender, a gentleman with a nametag stating Tio.

TIO
Can I get you a drink?

GREG
Yes, how about a glass of Cabernet?

The bartender handed Gregory Bissell a wine list which sold wine by the glass or the bottle.

GREG
I'll have Robert Mondavi.

TIO
Okay.

Moments later the bartender was pouring a large glass of wine in front of him. The typical process with Tio was he always poured the first glass full and if the dude was a good tipper, he got similar refills.
TIO
Want me to put that on your tab?

GREG
I will be eating dinner here, so let me just pay you now.

Greg reached into his billfold and pulled out a twenty-dollar bill.

GREG

Keep the change.

Tio was all smiles.

TIO
Thank you, sir.

Tio knew firsthand there were a lot of cheap Charlies that came in who didn't realize bartenders worked for tips too.

GREG
Can I get a glass of Sprite; I like to chase my wine.

TIO
Sure.

The bar was half empty and Tio didn't mind giving Greg the chaser for free after his nice tip.

RECRUITMENT

After a couple sips of wine and the chaser, Dr. Moore came to the bar and quickly recognized Greg and approached him.

BOB MOORE
Hello, Greg.

GREG
Hello, Bob. How's it going?

BOB MOORE
After the run and a nap, I feel like a new man.

GREG
Good to hear.

BOB MOORE
Do you want to sit here or get a table?

Greg, remembering his road warrior days where he ate all his meals at the bar, replied,

GREG
Why not just stay here.

BOB MOORE
Sure, if that's what you want.

TIO
Sir, what would you like to drink?

BOB MOORE
I'll have a wine like his.

TIO
Cabernet, okay?

BOB MOORE
Sure.

After a couple sips of their wine, Bob started recruiting Greg.

BOB MOORE
You know after we met today, I called up one of my associates up North and mentioned I had a friend who did electronics and recently retired, somewhat early and might consider a job as a consultant.

GREG
Alright.

BOB MOORE
Because of some of the projects you worked on in the past, it's probably something you can handle, he wants to send you a round trip plane ticket and go up to Livermore, California, for a job interview.

GREG
Interesting.

BOB MOORE
You would not have to move; they would provide your commute fees.

GREG
Does that mean I come home every day?

BOB MOORE
Only if you want. I would think after you get into the swing of things, you would want to stay there Monday through Friday, come home Friday afternoons so you can be at the park Saturday to work out, and staying up there you would save enough time to be able to do some of your workout up there.

GREG
I'm kind of an old geezer now, why the hell would they want me?

Bob knew he couldn't pitch Greg space flight in front of Tio or anyone else in this restaurant, responded smiling:

BOB MOORE

You never know what people are looking for in a project.

GREG
Sure. I'll talk to the guy. When does he want me to go up there?

BOB MOORE
Monday morning.

GREG
That soon?

BOB MOORE
Yep, they are looking hard for someone to fill this position.

GREG
I suppose I could. Do I need to go up there in a shirt and tie?

BOB MOORE
No, the interview would be low key, dress comfortable like you are now.

GREG
How will he get ahold of me?

BOB MOORE
With your permission, I'll text him your phone number and he'll text you all your itinerary as soon as he gets it.

GREG
Alright.

Moments later, the man who would change Gregory Bissell's life had his phone number and before Greg made it out of the bar/restaurant, his itinerary was texted to him including his airline *eticket* and rental car information. Oddly they also reserved him a hotel room for several days so that he would have a place to stay if there needed to be any serious discussions.

BOB MOORE
Shall we order something to eat?

GREG
Why not?

The two men ordered off the bar menu which has a partial list because of the lack of space at the bar they could only do so much. Both men settled on the New York Strip steak sandwich. It came sliced and had French fries and some toss away veggie on the plate.

BOB MOORE
The Chef knows his business; this steak is great.

No sooner than the plates were cleaned off a couple very good-looking Asian ladies came into the bar and sat down on the barstools right next to Gregory Bissell. They were a sight for sore eyes. Incredibly beautiful.

After a while there was some introductions as the lady closest to Gregory Bissell appeared to be very sociable.

MONICA CHEUNG
I'm Monica Cheung and this is my friend Betty Li.

GREG
I'm Gregory Bissell and this is Dr. Robert Moore.

MONICA CHEUNG
Pleased to meet you, Gregory.

GREG
Just call me Greg.

MONICA CHEUNG
Sure Greg.

Monica was on the lookout for special men. The conversation was being recorded. Monica worked for the MSS, Communist China's Ministry of State Security. She was a deep plant mole recruited out of Hong Kong. She had no special allegiance to the Communist Government, but she liked money, travel, and the suspense of manipulating the little heads of most men.

Monica had no idea who these two men were, but her business practice was to network out because eventually she met someone who knows someone she wanted to get to know. She was just out for a good time with her friend Betty Li who was a contractor for the Chinese Consulate in Los Angeles. But Betty had to come down to San Diego quite often as they did business with a lot of San Diego concerns.

Betty Li had no idea Monica Cheung was an MSS spy, nor would she ever know. When the Chinese insert a mole, they work hard to penetrate them without giving the slightest indication to anyone what their true intentions are. As such Monica had a commercial venue, she was attached to that provided her a cover story, as the chief investment officer for the company that arranged for Chinese ownership of American corporations or vice versa.

As the chief investment officer gave Monica Cheung the ability to dish out business cards as part of her networking. Once she spotted a viable candidate, the system would kick into high gear and espionage would beget the target of their interest. Monica Cheung handed Greg one of her business cards and nonchalantly and offered.

MONICA CHEUNG
Call me sometime, perhaps we can have lunch.

As Greg looked at Monica's business card, he had a sudden thought, *If she looks this good in casual clothes, I bet she looked incredible in a Jenny Business Suit.* Then he remembered from his time in Hong Kong of the number of great tailors they had there. He also had a flash about Korea where they also had tailors who made outstanding business suits. It's been a while since he's been to Korea, and he wondered if business suit tailoring was still thriving.

MONICA CHEUNG
Greg, what do you do for a living?

Monica asked that question in the most unassuming way, with no prejudgment since he looked sophisticated, and San Diego was a high-tech location with a lot of defense contractors making a lot of systems her sponsors wished to learn more about.

GREG
I'm retired now. My job is to walk ten miles every day
and attempt to eat a healthy diet.

MONICA CHEUNG
Are you married or single?

Wow, she really gets to the point fast, must be another gold digger, or someone to help her get a green card, Greg thought for a while before he answered.

GREG
I'm married, but my wife has moved to Japan
permanently. She wants to spend her final days there
near her family and relatives and experience Japan as
much as she can since she's growing older.

MONICA CHEUNG
You didn't want to go with her?

GREG
I've been to Japan quite a few times with her. It's a nice
country, but the city where she lives about the same
size as San Diego, is mostly Japanese-speaking people.
It's rare that you come across someone who can speak
English efficiently. All the television is in Japanese, and
I don't really are to watch any more Samurai movies.

MONICA CHEUNG
Do you go visit her or does she come to visit you?

GREG

I don't care to fly to Asia too often. It's a twelve-hour flight and upon arrival there the only thing, I think about most of the time is how soon I get to come home.

MONICA CHEUNG
Is moving to Japan out of the question?

GREG
Most definitely, I could visit now and then but I'm sure as time passes, I'll reach the point where I say to myself, What's the point?

MONICA CHEUNG
You don't have any romance left in your marriage?

GREG
The romance part was fine. It was great up to five minutes before she departed, but the reality is she went there to spend the rest of her life there and has no intentions of ever coming back.

MONICA CHEUNG
Do you miss her?

GREG
One can never erase the memories. I fell madly in love with her, and she was a fantastic wife every single day, until the day she departed.

MONICA CHEUNG
Are you angry about her leaving?

GREG
No, I sense her feelings. I feel happy for her that she can experience her country and her relatives for a few more years as we grow older.

MONICA CHEUNG
And you are good with that?

GREG
If it brings her happiness, then yes. It's no different than when a person has a pet bird who doesn't like to live in a cage one day walks to the door of his home carrying the pet bird and when he opens the door throws it up into the air. Most likely the bird will fly away and never come back. The satisfaction of watching the bird fly away happy to be free, is a pleasant sight.

MONICA CHEUNG

Most men would not think the way you do.

GREG

I can't speak for other men. My wife was my beautiful pet bird all those years and when I took her to the airport, I set her free. That is an act of love, knowing that I can make her happy in a unique manner.

MONICA CHEUNG

Are you interested in meeting a woman to give you some company since she's going to be gone forever?

GREG

I take it one day at a time. My focus is exercise, maintaining my health, reading, writing, and exploring the universe in my studies of what begets mankind with all the new discoveries we learn almost every day about the universe.

MONICA CHEUNG

You are a good-looking guy; you should easily be able to find a very pretty girl who wants some company.

GREG

I suppose I could but it's not my priority right now.

MONICA CHEUNG

You got my business card, if you ever want someone to have dinner with or someone to talk with, please give me a call.

GREG

Thank you, Monica. Perhaps one day I will.

All four sat at the Flaming Flamingo Bar for a while longer, had a couple more drinks and it was time to call it a night. The two men shook the ladies' hands and departed.

BOB MOORE
Do you need a ride home, Greg?

GREG

I'm going to call my Uber driver friend, he's all set to come pick me up.

BOB MOORE
I could give you a ride home.

GREG
How far from here do you live?

BOB MOORE
Just a few blocks.

GREG
It's less likely you'll get a DUI if you just drive home. I
prefer to take the Uber because I wouldn't want you to
drive very far after you have been drinking.

MOORE
Sure, no problem.

The two men shook hands and Dr. Moore, walked a short distance, and paid the valet who had his car waiting for him, and away he went.

Within minutes Rodriguez arrived and took Gregory Bissell home where he contemplated his future in his empty and quiet home. Oh, how did he miss his wife watching Japanese TV all the time. The noise gives a sense of life and in the past when she took her separate trips to Japan for business or visiting her family, sometimes Greg turned on the TV to the Japanese channels just to make the familiar noise.

His greatest pleasure was when she came home. She was always positive and sweet, never any arguments, though she could lose her temper occasionally.

Greg's wife was a very straight woman. She never deviated and kept it simple. She successfully started and ran three companies. Her life orbited around her business and all the contacts she had, as she was networked out extensively but, when her sudden desires to experience Japan and close her business, had a huge impact on her psychology. Ending her business relations with friendly people and her multitude of customers left a huge gash in her emotions. She didn't realize the extent of leaving behind such an extended family meant until it was too late, and she was merely hours away from the airport. She said she could always change her mind and one day come back, but deep in Greg's heart he knew this was her final passage, she begged to feel her Japanese culture once again and not just observe it on Japanese TV.

Japanese TV does wonderful reports of travel around Japan as well as around the world. It's one of the best learning experiences a person can get for low cost. And at the same time, it can have a huge impact on home sickness. Japanese people love their country, their home, and their culture. She was returning to her past where she would experience Japan every day for the rest of her life. If Greg wanted to immigrate to Japan and move there, she would not mind that at all, but at the same token, she knew just like on their numerous trips to Japan, it would be like putting Greg into a birdcage, just like the one she just escaped.

Greg's future handlers were quickly learning much about him. Monica's question-and-answering session could be heard a short distance away. These details would soon be typed up into a report by Dr. Moore and sent to Lawrence Livermore where people of interest would slowly accumulate a database on their subject as they vetted him for the project. His arrangement with his wife that appeared to be a permanent breakup with no animosity or extracurricular marital events, placed no shadow of a doubt of the authenticity of the reasonable expectations their candidate would adhere to. The distance to his two sons, which were a void too far to be filled, cleared that mine field as well.

By all appearances, it was the psychological condition of the subject that would determine his suitability for this once-in-a-lifetime experiment. Since the scientists would in fact be ultimately killing their subject of the experiment, it would be unlikely permissions would ever be granted again to conduct such and effort. Therefore, they had to make the most of it. This was their one shot to clarify what science thought the universe was made of and why we couldn't see beyond approximately thirty-five billion light years.

In the separation Greg and his wife communicated weekly that slipped into monthly that soon slipped into rarity. In all these months as time passed by, the researchers predicted communication between the two would ultimately cease. Money and financial support were sent monthly automatically by the bank.

Greg's wife would never expect anything to change and since she rarely called, Greg would be long gone before she ever suspected something was up. If his two sons ever had a change of heart and sought out a relationship with their dad, it would be too late. They missed their chance. Whatever it was that drove them far away would be a thing of the past, just like their memories of him.

In Greg's experiences he had gone on trips halfway around the world on a day's notice. Finding out Saturday he had an itinerary for Monday was no big deal for him. And taking the advice from Bob, he wasn't going to dress to impress because he really didn't need the job and he was going to show up dressed casually.

Greg Bissell's days of worrying about stuffy people from the Beltway were long over. Back in the days when he traveled often to Crystal City for meetings with GOV Guys and Beltway Bandits, if he didn't show up with a suit coat and tie on, he would certainly be the odd duck out. A lot of that has to do with the Beltway Boys in how they hustled the work. A lot of conniving went on and you had to present yourself as a respectable and competent person, or some other *son of a bitch* was going to eat your lunch.

<u>EXT. DAY. OAKLAND AIRPORT SHORT PLANE SCENE AND GREG LEAVING THE TERMINAL HEADING TO RENTAL CAR AGENCY ON SHUTTLE BUS.</u>

Flying up to Oakland Airport with no care in the world and getting a rental car there was just like old times back in the days when he often had to go there for projects. However, he had never been sent to the Livermore Lab.

<u>EXT DAY SHOT GREG IN RENTAL CAR DRIVING EAST OF LAKE HAUSSMAN ON THE N INNER LOOP DOWN TO THE S INNER LOOP.</u>

Greg enjoyed the landscaping and the map page sent to him identified Lake Haussman as a landmark to key on to find building 140 where the interview would take place.

<u>EXT. DAY. DRIVING INTO LAWRENCE LIVERMORE LAB FACILITY IN RENTAL CAR AND PARKING AT A RESERVED PARKING SPOT FOR GREGORY BISSELL.</u>

Because of the security surrounding the project he was escorted into the facility and marched into a conference room. It was good he dressed casually because he would have stuck out like a sore thumb if he was dressed for Crystal City.

<u>INT. DAY. LIVERMORE LAB PROJECT PLUTO II BUILDING 140</u>

In some ways Lawrence Livermore Lab had a park like atmosphere but there were industrial and office buildings spread around the campus as if there was no planning or thought process into the arrangement. This had been a Naval Air Station during WW2 so some of the layout was due to the way the Navy initially laid it out.

Driving by Lake Haussman in the middle of the facility, Greg wondered if that was actually a cooling pond for some nuclear research. It was at this very location that Edward Teller created the fusion reaction and hence the genesis of the hydrogen bomb.

Ironically Edward Teller was also put in charge of a lot of activity at Area 51. Various people have claimed Edward Teller oversaw the Alien UFO re-engineering program where scientists disassembled Alien UFOs to glean technology associated with propulsion systems including anti-gravity devices.

Inside a building that had no flare or grandeur, and most likely a leftover WW2 building rebuilt and reconditioned, the conference room Greg was led into by his escort sat two men. The first had his badge on a lanyard around his neck and Greg could clearly see it stated, Walter Bissonnette. The other man had no badge or identity and the vibes Greg got from that man were almost chilling. If you could ever spot evil this man, had it written all over his persona. All during the interview he sat there and did not introduce himself, it's likely he wasn't allowed to.

Walter Bissonnette had a very thick folder with numerous pages. The man wearing his security badge on a lanyard introduced himself.

WALTER BISSONNETTE
Hello Mr. Bissell, I'm Walter Bissonnette. I'm the project manager for the program we have taken interest in recruiting you for.

There were no handshakes or any social transcendence as these guys were all business. And business started abruptly. Greg was somewhat mystified why the other man kept quiet and just looked on. He certainly had a piercing look.

WALTER BISSONNETTE
Please have a seat.

GREG
Thank you.

Walter Bissonnette opened the binder up and made no hesitance to cover up any of the information. He knew that Greg could see what he was looking at. These guys don't mess around. They built a rap sheet like there is no tomorrow. Just before his eyes he could see there had been substantial surveillance on him. In his past profession dealing with various projects, no doubt he was vetted to an extent he never realized possible.

WALTER BISSONNETTE
What we have in mind for you is one of the most guarded secrets this nation has ever undertaken when we found you. Since you didn't find us that's the way we prefer it.

GREG
I see.

WALTER BISSONNETTE
You don't have any problem going back to work?

GREG
As a contractor/consultant?

WALTER BISSONNETTE
That's correct. We know your life story. Since you had a lot of involvement with the government in the past, we were able to obtain all your personnel files and study you for some time to conclude you might fit in the role we invasion for you.

GREG
What kind of roles do you have in mind?

WALTER BISSONNETTE

This will be an evolving process. We'll put you on the team and have you help us develop the products and then when the time comes to deploy, you may be given the option to get operationally involved.

GREG

Would I be some sort of spy or mercenary?

WALTER BISSONNETTE

In a sense. However, you would not be facing any enemies that you are accustomed to. The operational phases are a few years down the road from now, but for now, we value someone like you that has lived a life of troubleshooting in extremely stressful conditions that have severe time limits.

GREG

What makes you think I can handle it?

WALTER BISSONNETTE

We know a lot about the special compartmentalized missions you supported in the past and what the outcomes were.

GREG

That's interesting.

WALTER BISSONNETTE

Because of your past dealings with special people, we think you understand that with extremely important matters there can be no tolerance of allowing failure.

GREG

Okay, suppose I agree to work for you, my friend Bob said something to the effect you would allow me to commute from San Diego and not have to move up here.

WALTER BISSONNETTE

Yes, we'll pay for your commute if you agree to work for us, but if you decide you want to spend days here and not have to travel back and forth to San Diego, that's fine too. We'll find you decent lodging here, so you don't have to stay in a hotel.

GREG

I appreciate that.

WALTER BISSONNETTE
You are quite welcome. Now what we need to do is tell you that all this is compartmentalized.

GREG
Alright. What's the project?

WALTER BISSONNETTE
You will not know the entire project. You will only know portions of it which we engage you in.

GREG
That's understandable.

WALTER BISSONNETTE
As time evolves, when we think we need to involve you in other portions of the project we will transfer you there and you will continue expanding your involvement into other areas.

GREG
You are not concerned about my age?

WALTER BISSONNETTE
No, in fact you were handpicked because of your age. If you continue with the process and evolve as we think you will, you will be the perfect age for project termination when it comes to it.

GREG
I see.

WALTER BISSONNETTE
We set aside a few days as part of this check-in process to have you evaluated by some professionals. We have no doubt about your technical skills and are not concerned about them. This is for other reasons. We realize we must train you to be able to do your job efficiently and you will work directly with PhDs who will explain systems to you that you will master and become the Subject Matter Expert.

GREG
So, you want to indoctrinate me here over the next few days?

WALTER BISSONNETTE
That's correct.

GREG

When will I know I've been selected for the job?

WALTER BISSONNETTE

You have already been selected. The main purpose of this indoctrination is to learn more about you so we can determine the best way to facilitate you obtaining Subject Matter Expert (SME) expertise in the shortest time possible and not set you up for failure.

GREG

Okay, what's in the indoctrination?

WALTER BISSONNETTE

After we get some preliminaries out of the way, you will be briefed shortly by security personnel as to requirements and you'll sign some nondisclosure forms and be briefed on how to handle situations that may come up in the event any information about this project is compromised in any way that you take steps to contact your controller who will be introduced shortly and report any breaches so we can plug them.

GREG

May I ask what the project is?

WALTER BISSONNETTE

The classified code word for this project is Pluto II.

GREG

Is this a reconfiguration of Pluto I, or is that just a cover acronym?

WALTER BISSONNETTE

In your indoctrination we'll tell you about Pluto I, but it has barely anything to do with Pluto II, even though we did obtain some technology developed for the Pluto I program.

GREG

I see.

WALTER BISSONNETTE

This gentleman here will now start your security briefing and when he's done with you, others will come in and do their part.

GREG

Alright.

Walter Bissonnette stood up, didn't offer a hand, in a semi-cold manner walked right out the door.

C.U. GREG
VOICE OVER
Then it was just me and the Devil facing me.

In the next couple of hours Greg signed more documents than he ever did working on classified projects in the past. The non-disclosure forms stated the term was for life. Greg could not divulge any Project Pluto II information to anyone not cleared in the program and had the need to know. He also discovered he now had a controller.

SECURITY OFFICER
Your controller is a gentleman by the name of Mr.
Black. The rules are you will never be allowed to
physically meet Mr. Black.

GREG
Alright.

SECURITY OFFICER
You also now have a personal telephone or electronics
media coordinator, and that person's phone number is
on the back of this badge.

The Devil handed Greg's new badge to him. It had a magnetic strip on it and a computer chip.

SECURITY OFFICER
You keep your badge in your billfold. All our scanners
can read it, so you never have to remove it. You must
memorize that telephone number on your ID card in
case it's lost so we can immediately deactivate it, no
matter where you are any time of the day.

GREG
How do I get ahold of Mr. Black in case I need to talk
to him?

SECURITY OFFICER
If you need to talk with Mr. Black, call your media
coordinator and they will inform Mr. Black you need to
talk to him. He will reach out to you wherever you are.

Then a discussion about the legal ramifications in case Greg violated the rules. Greg was suddenly made aware the government could take him anywhere they wanted and because of the statutes involved in this project under the 1954 Espionage Act, Greg could simply disappear, they would not be compelled to divulge what happened to him. Greg read through the lines, Greg would simply disappear, and life would then suck.

The other uncomfortable part of this recruitment is it was now rather apparent Greg had gone past the point of no return and these bruisers could make his life suck really bad if he thought he could walk away from it now.

Greg probably had his chance to turn down the offer while Walter Bissonnette was still in the room before he signed the documents. Now it was too late. His cover story was he worked with AEROM doing logistics support (box kicker), formerly associated with EG&G who built the first nuclear triggers for America's first atomic bombs. They also did the high-speed photography that allowed much of the Manhattan Project to proceed successfully.

Greg reconciled since his wife had abandoned him so she could live out her life in Japan, he didn't really have any pressing things to do, and they haven't even discussed pay!

But that came soon. And soon he had a benefits adviser talking to him.

BENEFITS ADVISER

Greg, you are working on a very important project and your compensation will be more than you are used to getting paid. That's due to secrecy and possible risk to you. Your compensation is classified TOP SECRET and it's nobody else's business. Do not discuss it with anyone.

Greg no doubt was being paid by BLACK MONEY via a BLACK PROGRAM, most likely his sponsors were CIA, and he would find out eventually. His eyes just about bugged out when he saw the $$$$$$$.

BENEFITS ADVISER

Greg, A special division of the IRS will handle your taxes including automatically filing them. One of your benefits is we pay them to file your taxes for you via Efile because there may be a period of time you could be deployed and not able to file. They have access to all your financial institutions' records and your annuities.

Greg would no longer be able to use his lifelong accountant, Sal.

That was the last briefing and indoctrination for the day. Greg was then ushered out to his rental car and then he went to a La Quinta Inn where he checked in. The place was nice and clean and smelled nice too. And he was not far from places Greg could eat he could walk to and get some exercise.

Shortly after checking into the hotel Greg changed into shorts and a Polo Shirt and left the hotel, walking down the street in the direction the hotel clerk mentioned was some good places to eat.

It took a while to get there, but Greg was walking on purpose for exercise which he wouldn't get a lot of over the next few days. He came up on a place called "Cattleman's."

Thinking about the dollar signs on his compensation package he decided if Cattleman's had a Porterhouse Steak, that would be just the ticket.

INT. DAY. CATTLEMAN'S RESTAURANT.

AMI

The plan worked out well until his waitress came over to his table. He almost felt like he saw a ghost. A Japanese lady who looked identical to his wife twenty years ago. *Is God torturing me?* he wondered.

The waitress seemed irked quick and snapped.

C.U. AMI (with alias Cindy name tag)

AMI (a.k.a. Cindy)
Why are you staring at me, sir?

Ami was sick and tired of being eye candy to a bunch of horny assholes that come up for a few days each week to work at Livermore.

GREG
Would you mind if I showed you a picture of my
recently departed wife?

At first Ami was obviously incensed. Greg wasted no time and pulled out a picture of her twenty years ago. The picture was only slightly faded but the image appeared stunningly identical. Ami was upset for a few minutes.

AMI (a.k.a. Cindy)
Is this some kind of stupid joke?

GREG
No, in all due sincerity, I was awestruck how closely
you look like my wife.

Ami sized Greg up and realized she had been nasty to the customer and her words had been unjustifiable and responded.

AMI
I'm sorry, I've had a rough day.

GREG
Please don't worry about it and thank you for being
here because seeing you lifted my heart a notch or two.

The waitress Ami realized Greg was all sincere and had tears forming at the corner of her eyes and handed him back the picture.

AMI

I'll be back in a moment with a glass of water for you,
here's the menu.

The waitress walked away and went back to the kitchen area where they had an employee restroom and went in and shuddered for a few moments. The gentleman had spiked her emotions. And he was just another gentle soul. The waitress had a nametag that said Cindy, but that was a lie, her real name was Ami Suzuki. A woman who desired to be put on the movie screen one day. But working on these God-awful jobs while she finished her college wasn't cutting it.

After Ami (a.k.a. Cindy) regained her composure, she went back out and gave the customer his water.

AMI

Would you like something to drink?

GREG

Yes, how about a glass of cabernet, just give me the
house wine.

AMI

Certainly, I'll be right back with your drink.

Greg noticed a subtle change of demure in Cindy. In due time, Greg had a sixteen-ounce Porterhouse Steak in front of him with a nice baked potato on the side fully loaded. The first glass of wine went down easily, and it tasted very nice.

Little did Greg know, Cindy (a.k.a. AMI), feeling bad about the way she had treated Greg told the bartender to give him the best cabernet they had. She charged a regular price for it. Greg didn't know he received a special deal and had another.

Dessert was out of the question after that big steak, and as AMI cashed out Greg, he gave her a $40 tip.

GREG

That's for bringing back nice memories for me for a
few minutes.

Ami acted awestruck for a few moments, because the stranger turned out to be very pleasant, and there were a lot of cheap Charlies who came in there who didn't tip worth a damn.

Greg left Cattleman's restaurant and walked back to his hotel. Greg kicked back and did something he rarely did; watched TV.

<u>INT. DAY. GREG'S HOTEL ROOM IN LIVERMORE CALIFORNIA</u>

In due time Greg was in bed having dreams that were modulated by his past.

Morning came too quickly, and Greg was back over at Lawrence Livermore Lab, back in the same conference room facing three people. Two men and a woman. Turns out these people were Psychiatrists and Psychologists.

Before Greg settled down, the three people began asking very crazy questions and how he felt about some bizarre things. Some of their questions probed his sexual activities such as whether he still had any and with whom and how. They knew his wife was in Japan. It's obvious to Greg, his new Employer who he assumed was Lawrence Livermore Labs, had done their homework on him.

MALE PSYCHIATRIST
Tell us, Greg, how do you feel about your wife living in Japan away from you?

GREG
I can say that all these years my love for her never wavered. It was a long-standing fresh relationship. We never argued, she was mild and accommodative. If living back in Japan makes her happy, it's the least I can do for her to reward her for all she has done for me.

FEMALE PSYCHIATRIST
What if something came up where you could never see her again?

GREG
Right now, it appears that we will probably not see much of each other in the future.

FEMALE PSYCHIATRIST
How do you feel about that?

GREG
I'm a practical man. It is what it is, and I understand how my wife feels. She doesn't have that much time left in her life and she terribly missed Japan.

FEMALE PSYCHIATRIST
So, if something happened to you or happened to her and you absolutely could never see each other again, you are okay with that?

GREG
I'm already resigned to the fact we will see little of each other in the future. I have no desire to live in Japan and she has no desire to live in America.

MALE PSYCHIATRIST
Do you financially support her?

GREG

Yes, that part will not change, it's the least I can do for her for providing me so many wonderful years together.

MALE PSYCHIATRIST

Do you have a contingency drawn up in case something happens to you?

GREG

Yes, she gets ninety percent of my estate, the other ten percent goes to my sons.

FEMALE PSYCHIATRIST

Even though you are separated forever, are you still willing to give her all that?

GREG

There is nothing that says she will outlive me. We don't know where life takes us until we get there.

FEMALE PSYCHIATRIST

That's true and most people do not realize it until it's too late.

GREG

For now, it's the least I can do for her so she can continue living well and not have to suffer.

FEMALE PSYCHIATRIST

That's very generous of you.

C.U. DR. SHIRLEY EXPOSING THE NAME TAG.

The attractive psychiatrist had aqua blue marine eyes, blonde hair and was well built. Greg noticed her name tag identified her as "Dr. Shirley."

GREG

I just consider it my responsibility.

After more probing questions they gave Greg a test to take. The test was rather odd. But Greg could tell it was sort of a psychological test.

The next phase of Greg's indoctrination included an unusual series of tests brought into the conference room on a laptop. The person who brought in the laptop, Mr. Barnes, explained.

MR. BARNES
We have looked at your school transcripts and unfortunately most of your higher education ended several decades ago. We are not saying you are obsolete, because you have worked your adult life in high technology, but we need to know what your weak areas are so we can beef them up.

GREG
Alright.

MR. BARNES
You will see the test is on a formatted Word document and you just fill in the blanks. Half the questions are essay questions where you describe what you know about the subject matter. If you feel you have weakness in this area, instead of attempting to answer the question with not enough level of knowledge, just click on the icon by the question that will auto-fill "I need more study in this area.

GREG
What's the time duration of this test?

MR. BARNES
We are not measuring you in a quantitative manner like schools normally do to measure proficiency and expertise, so the time restriction is not necessary. Take as much time as you want on each question and the document is of course unlimited in size, thus you can articulate as much as you desire to explain your answers. We'll evaluate your answers and program your future training around your test results.

GREG
Do you have any examples of how much time this test requires from other individuals?

MR. BARNES
Yes, it has taken anywhere from two hours to eight hours for various individuals.

GREG
What if I'm not finished by late in the day?

MR. BARNES
That's okay, someone will be here with you as long as it takes. We want you to finish the test today. We see no reason why you could not be done by dinnertime.

GREG
Okay, thanks.

Greg commenced answering the questions. It should not have surprised him that a test like this would be unlike anything he had ever taken in his lifetime. It certainly seemed like it was tailored for specifics that probably relate to the task at hand.

The first section of the test had significant chemistry and nuclear physics content. It was obvious they wanted someone who could handle aspects associated with nuclear physics and chemistry.

The next series of questions had some very interesting Macro's deployed in answering the question. As the information was answered, pop-up dialog boxes presented a graphic associated with a mathematical question such as problems associated with limit theory, differential equations, and integrals. It was apparent his strength was more so in integrals, since his lifetime experience with FFT, Laplace, and Z transforms fit right in well with the test.

In later years as Greg reflected on this day, the sum of the questions was orientated towards technology and insights relating to aerospace and nuclear physics. Humanities such as literature, history, and factors relating to society were not asked. This test was tailored towards technology and possibly space-related issues.

At the conclusion of the test Greg felt dumb and devastated. Many questions were difficult and poignantly directed at a process or a theory that most likely pertained to his future tasks. He thought for a while his poor performance on the test would most likely result in his dismissal and wondering what the hell Pluto II was all about.

The proctor for the test, Mr. Barnes, stayed in the room with Greg and patiently waited while the test was in progress. He was obviously observing Greg, possibly part of an evaluation of the candidate for reasons he would never understand.

And as advertised Greg wrapped up the test around dinnertime. Mr. Barnes walked over, closed the laptop, and said he would escort him to the front entrance and to come back in the morning to continue his check-in.

What Greg didn't know was that thanks to the wireless router, others in remote locations observed his test questions just as quickly as he answered them. Some of those evaluating the answers were professors at UC Berkeley under government contract to evaluate the answers and make recommendations as to what training he needed to certify him as an SME (Subject Matter Expert) for the Pluto II project. The professors didn't know Pluto II existed and were fully shielded from student number 2576.

These professional educator evaluations ongoing in parallel for almost six hours completed around the same time Greg left the building and headed for his hotel room.

Greg felt that nothing can improve disposition better than a hot *Hollywood Shower*. Greg then took a hot shower, then dressed and headed out to go have dinner. The restaurant Greg experienced the night before was not far from a Thai Restaurant. *Pad Thai might not be a bad choice tonight,* Greg thought.

The Thai restaurant had some very attractive young ladies working there. It was a cheerful environment and to get started he ordered Thai Iced Tea, which is sweet and has cream in it. He started out with Thai fish soup, that has a lemon taste to it and with appropriate amount of Siracha sauce can make it very pleasant. Topped off by Chicken Pad Thai and later Thai ice cream, the meal was very pleasant. No doubt he would be coming back here multiple times. The waitress eyes about bugged out when she saw her tip. With his salary and his current life savings, he could more than afford to tip them well to demonstrate how important they are to his life, treating him well and making his dining experience very enjoyable.

The following morning Greg was back in the conference room. Mr. Barnes was back with another laptop, not for a test but to show him the recommended training he would receive going forward.

Walter Bissonnette arrived shortly and sat down at the table next to Mr. Barnes facing Greg. Walter waited patiently while Mr. Barnes finished his briefing on what areas of training they would enhance but did not give many details in how it was going to be accomplished.

Finally, as it seemed he had completed his briefing Mr. Barnes stood up and closed the laptop and exited the room. After he was gone Walter Bissonnette continued with what he wanted to discuss.

WALTER BISSONNETTE

In case you are wondering how well you did on the test, I'm going to let you know that had you not done as well as you did, we would be sending you back to San Diego with a message that your services were no longer necessary.

GREG

Okay, but to be honest with you, I didn't think I did that well and figured I failed the exam.

WALTER BISSONNETTE

Greg, every section of your exam was graded by a Professor with a PhD, or one of our principal researchers here at the lab with much higher levels of education than the professors.

GREG

I appreciate that.

WALTER BISSONNETTE

In due time as you receive your training, they will go over with you portions of the exam they were responsible for and critique you and explain what learning objectives are scheduled in your training curriculum.

GREG
I appreciate that.

WALTER BISSONNETTE
Greg, you have some more indoctrination that will follow, by now you can probably guess we are very committed and passionate about the project.

GREG
Sure. I understand.

WALTER BISSONNETTE
There is maximum effort being put forth by everyone on the team. We realize we are not going to complete the project overnight and this will take a while.

GREG
Big projects usually take a while.

WALTER BISSONNETTE
Greg, that's true, but at the same token we understand the political reality the subsequent administration three years from now when they get briefed on the project may decide to cancel it and cut all funding abruptly.

GREG
I've seen that happen in my past experiences with government contracts.

WALTER BISSONNETTE
Greg, therefore, we must have mission success before the next President is sworn into office.

GREG
I understand.

WALTER BISSONNETTE
At times you may feel we are putting pressure on you but be advised we are also putting plenty of pressure on ourselves because in a development sense, three years from now is not a lot of time for the size and scale of this project.

GREG
I've worked on many high-pressure projects in the past.

WALTER BISSONNETTE
Yes, we are aware of your work history, and we've had several conversations with your former sponsors in Crystal City. This room isn't a SKIF so we can't discuss what you did, but we know all about it.

GREG
Alright, what's next?

WALTER BISSONNETTE
You have some more indoctrination, then when you finish you will be permitted to fly back to San Diego for the weekend.

GREG
When do I start working on the project?

WALTER BISSONNETTE
We will text you the itinerary for you next week. You will fly up here on Monday and we'll start moving you into activities we want you to experience, and you will then start receiving training and becoming part of the team.

GREG
Alright.

WALTER BISSONNETTE
I want to remind you, under no circumstances are you to mention Project Pluto II or even the title of the project to anyone who is not cleared and part of the organization. Other people working at the Lab have no need to know what you really do.

GREG
No doubt in my travels, people will ask me what I do for a living. What do I tell them?

WALTER BISSONNETTE
Your cover story is you do logistics for AEROM, and you are not authorized to discuss your work to anyone outside the company.

GREG
Understand, I will keep my lips zipped.

WALTER BISSONNETTE
So far you have done well. Dr. Moore is a good judge of character. He did rather well to introduce you to us.

GREG
Does Dr. Moore work on Project Pluto II?

WALTER BISSONNETTE
No. Dr. Moore works for a contractor providing special sciences that derive equipment the lab needs for various projects.

The conversation soon ended, and Walter Bissonnette stood up.

WALTER BISSONNETTE
Another person will be arriving soon for more introduction. If you need a restroom break, I suggest you take it now as that person will be here shortly.

GREG
Thank you, I'll take you up on that opportunity.

No sooner than Greg finished his business and was sitting quietly in the room, a very pretty blonde lady walked in the room. She wore white shirt and beige slacks obviously designed by some Couture Designer. *No doubt she distracts a lot of men,* Greg thought.

The woman's nametag said her name indicated Meghan Sparks. *No doubt her boyfriend calls her Sparky,* Greg thought.

Meghan spent several hours going over procedures and policy. These are the sorts of things he needed to know so that he could function as part of the team. There was nothing out of the ordinary, but each new company or new job always brings with it a different approach and various managers have their own style. Some of it seemed a little overhanded or harsh, but as Greg got closer to the truth, it started making perfect sense to him.

Part of Greg's training set up in modules was self-paced, but they obviously would put pressure on him to complete the requirements promptly. At first since he didn't know much about anything in the project, his focus was going to be training, splashed with some exposure to the systems he would later become responsible for. Based on all he was being spoon fed, his impression was as a SME, he was like ISEAs (In-Service Engineering Activity) people who are tasked with detecting and resolving system deficiencies and writing engineering instructions to complete the task. From his experience the ISEA often had the responsibility of determining appropriate materials, methods, and procedures to deal with a myriad of issues a large system often incurred.

The growing pains for new systems often took fifteen years to fully work out. Of course, there were situations where the defect would not prevent the deployed asset to complete the mission, but people going in harm's way always want their systems fully functional as designed. But the facts of life, the users had no choice but to live with inherent issues derived from short circuiting the development time just so some program manager could be seen as a super achiever by meeting all schedules on or ahead of schedule.

Schedules mean money and when you amortize the cost of a system of the life cycle it becomes apparently significant how much money is wasted such as, the amortized cost of keeping a hull tied to the pier or plane out of the skies, if factored out in the real cost of the program.

As an example: say a ship or submarine costs one billion dollars to build and equip, if it's stuck pier side for three months because of some defective equipment due to poor design, you are losing over one million dollars a day that it stays tied up to the pier. Also, there is a tactical lifespan of extremely costly devices such as ships, submarines, and aircraft.

Greg knew the first hand from involvement in tactical systems, there is another factor that is far more glaring. What if in the middle of the mission the critical system fails, and no spare parts are available to do corrective maintenance? Should the tactical ability of that hull be diminished fifty percent by the loss of a key system, it may result in aborting the mission so the crew can get it back to some safe harbor for emergency repairs.

The ISEA and the SME that Greg will become are the key people to prevent such scenarios. And when they do happen, the program manager is likely to get a red ass (as they say in the business).

Not knowing anything about the "gadget" Greg would be involved, he had no idea the stress level to expect or to what degree of failure tolerance was built into the device.

Fault tolerant software and fault tolerant hardware are not as simple as people would think. Because until you shake out the bugs in operational testing, you have no idea for sure, what is probably going to fail.

Meghan Sparks might have been a head turner, but she knew her business. *She probably graduated from Cal Tech, Berkeley, MIT, or Stanford*, Greg thought.

Time flies when you are being schooled by a head turner like Meghan Sparks. The interaction was genuine and productive. Meghan appreciated Greg's ability to assimilate all the information as fast as she was dishing it out. She knew by the end of the day, he was a fast learner and behaved nothing like his real age, nor did he look more than ten years younger than his real age. Meghan could sense some subtle attraction to the man. If there was a man at Livermore that could possibly create incentives, it no doubt was Greg, Meghan thought.

The day ended and they went their separate ways and Greg did his ritual, having a hot shower, then head out walking a distance to his dinner. If he had to walk three miles round trip to get there it didn't bother him, and it would take about an hour at his pace. His best times were typically four point five miles per hour or even faster if he hustled enough. Three point five miles an hour was comfortable for him. Greg had walked twenty-one miles in a day and could have gone more but he said to himself, What's the point?

After several more days of probing and discussions, this intense introduction to his new world came to an end and Greg found himself on an airplane heading to San Diego.

Greg was sitting next to a lovely woman from Pakistan, a PhD from UCSD. The woman was very sociable and conveyed a desire for a future meeting and handed Greg a business card and asked he call her and if wasn't busy perhaps they could go to dinner or the symphony real soon.

When Greg arrived home, he sent a text to his buddy Alex up in Minnesota about the woman. Alex having former involvement in government contracts advised Greg to discard her business card and never call her because, "You will end up on a watch list."

Having just received some heavy-duty security training, the business card was immediately fed into Greg's personal shredder.

On the weekend, Greg met Bob at the beach exercising again. Bob already knew a lot that went on with Greg, because Walter Bissonnette didn't really think it would be in Greg's best interest to know the extensive amount of surveillance that went on him and how much Bob was involved.

It would not be until near the launch date that Greg understood who Bob really was. Greg had been recruited by someone very near the top of the food chain by mere accident. This was good for the program because Bob knew just about everything in Greg's life and that's what enabled him to find that special man who had the life span right in the "green zone" they needed for this mission.

The heads of the program wanted someone approaching the end of their lives who was healthy and functional enough to be that soul venturing out into the universe to help answer the biggest question that ever-faced mankind.

If the fact scientists were wrong about the Big Bang Theory and they merely were experiencing Spherical and Cylindrical spreading loss as the photons diffused in space, once Gregory Bissell reached the edge of the universe, he would discover whether it existed or simply the scientists were duped by their own calculations and mistaken physics that were seriously flawed.

It also meant one other thing that would cause extreme soul searching within Gregory Bissell because if the universe is endless, what does that make God? Size and scale could not be imagined. A God that never ends. A thought that is rather incredible for what Greg and would further his viewpoint humans could be nothing more than cosmic cockroaches.

These ideas were flooding Greg's thoughts as he had a chance encounter with Dr. Moore at Ski Beach.

DR. MOORE

Hello Greg. How did you enjoy your time up in Livermore?

GREG

Well, it wasn't quite what I expected.

DR. MOORE
I can imagine. Are you going to continue working
there? Has the determination been made?

GREG
I decided that since I don't have anything better to do,
that I might as well help them if I can.

DR. MOORE
They would not have hired you if they didn't believe
you couldn't do the job.

GREG
Well, thank you for the kind comments. I hope I do not
let them down."

DR. MOORE
How's the hotel situation working out for you?

GREG
I think after I get settled in good, I will probably stay
up there during the week because commuting back
to San Diego during the week would kill any exercise
time, I might have available. Plus, I don't like walking
after dark.

The two men went their separate directions as they had different exercise regiments. Shortly after noon, Gregory Bissell finished his ten miles and headed for home. It wasn't the same going home to an empty house. The noise that used to be here was sadly missed.

Greg's sons, his wife, they were all long gone. The quiet was so dissatisfying. Kids screaming, wife's TV blasting, the cacophony of life was missing. If it were not for the desire to get to Ski Beach on the weekends and get a good walk in and throw a few hotdogs at the seagulls and black birds while the park rangers were not watching, there would be no point in even coming home on the weekend.

After a shower and a nice meal from premade food at his favorite store Baron's Market, he settled down to his laptop to check his email. It would be nice if his wife sent him an email now and then, or his son. But as usual no such emails existed. But there were probably forty-five waiting in his in basket from internet friends, some of which he had met in person. They were all good people of similar political and moral likeliness.

The NSA had long ago tracked down Greg's internet friends. They too were observed because studying them also helped derive the profile of Gregory Bissell. All his internet friends were high-caliber people and many of them were very successful in life or appeared to be pillars of society.

Just like most internet acquaintances, they send out a lot of links, pictures, and political rantings that are a waste of time to drill down in all of them. Greg often did not open the links and relied on comments of others in the group to vet them and determine if they were even worth opening.

Sometimes Greg gets into a hurry and starts deleting emails that were some people that always put out boring and ridiculous crap. He was quickly deleting them and just about deleted an email he needed to keep.

It was from his new Employer, AEROM. For some projects the Lab used AEROM as a front and an interface. His pay and a lot of training materials would come via AEROM.

AEROM had an attachment that was a training module in a fast-paced course on nuclear physics.

Greg put on his headphones and started playing a Brahms piano concerto by the incredibly sexy Yuja Wang and proceeded to dig into the online course that had regular college lectures, developed for online courses sprinkled with quizzes and other surprises. These were closed-caption videos so that a deaf person could take them. That made it nice since Greg could listen to the music while reading the course material.

Lawrence Livermore Lab developed fusion without the rest of the world knowing much about it. The most closely guarded secrets associated with fusion power and the hydrogen bomb were quickly stolen and sold to the Soviets.

The chief perpetrator was put to death in an electric chair. J. Robert Oppenheimer didn't want to build the hydrogen bomb because he knew you cannot keep secrets like this for long.

As a brilliant scientist and former director of the Radiation Lab, J. Robert Oppenheimer resisted Edward Teller and Senator Lewis Strauss in building the hydrogen bomb.

Senator Strauss was the driving force in the U.S. Atomic Energy Commission Personnel Security Board controversial hearings, which revoked J. Robert Oppenheimer's security clearance in 1954. Strauss also attempted to remove Oppenheimer as the director of the center for advanced study in Princeton University.

President Dwight D. Eisenhower's nomination of Strauss to become U.S. Secretary of Commerce in 1959 was not confirmed by the Senate. Scientists around the nation bitterly opposed Teller and Strauss for their treatment of Oppenheimer.

As a strange twist, it was Edward Teller in his hotel room in Sweden who told the Russians what they were doing wrong and why they couldn't detonate an atomic bomb. So it should have been Teller instead of Oppenheimer losing his security clearance.

The Russians thought they didn't have pure enough Uranium. They even stole samples of the American Uranium and tested it and determined it was not nearly as pure as Russian Uranium so they were dumbfounded why they could not obtain the nuclear detonation.

Teller set them straight about the triggering mechanism and in short order the Soviet Union detonated their first atomic bomb in 1949. Did Edward Teller do this evil act to force Oppenheimer's hand in allowing him to build the hydrogen bomb?

That personal quarrel went all the way back to the start of the Manhattan project when Teller wanted to do a fusion based hydrogen bomb vice the fission based atomic bomb. All these thoughts were swirling though Greg's mind as he delved into nuclear physics as he had read Oppenheimer's biography.

The copy of the *Bhagavad Gita* sitting on Greg's coffee table was purchased mainly because he was curious why Oppenheimer read the *Bhagavad Gita* every day of his adult life after he started graduate studies in Europe.

Greg concluded what struck Oppenheimer is the *Bhagavad Gita* stated, "There is life throughout planets scattered throughout the Universe with life on them."

Oppenheimer's most famous quote after the experiment at the Bikini Atoll detonation of our first hydrogen bomb was: "Now I am become Death, the destroyer of worlds," which is taken right out of the *Bhagavad Gita* based on information about powerful weapons written some 6,000 years ago.

When Greg read the *Bhagavad Gita*, he noted the wonderful writing skills. The English version of the *Bhagavad Gita* is clearly written by a brilliant person in command of the English language.

C.U. BHAGAVAD GITA ON GREGS COFFEE TABLE.

Greg wasn't expected to spend long hours on his weekend studying his learning modules, but he was tracked by his controller. The quizzes imbedded into the coursework did a good check on the efficacy of the training. The statistics used to measure the progress of the student Greg Bissel demonstrated what they already figured out about Gregory Bissell.

Gregory Bissell had a high IQ and had superior study habits and grasped the concepts very quickly even though some of it was a refresher.

Greg's controller had estimated times for each milestone, none of which Greg knew was going on. His every movement was monitored. Observation on him eclipsed that of any NASA Astronaut or Area 51 Test Pilot, especially those flying the TR-3B and the new TR4B now in the test phase.

Lawrence Livermore Lab officials involved in Project Pluto II became aware that when Greg reported to work on Monday, he had completed a large chunk of his Nuclear Physics Module.

Greg was already way ahead of their estimations including a planned meeting with a Physics professor in the conference room and going over some various applications and aspects of nuclear physics.

One hour with the professor one on one was equivalent to several weeks in a classroom. Those face-to-face meetings cemented the overall understanding of their prospective Astronaut. Greg was a special dude who could accomplish the mission when the time came, even if they had to go so far as to give Greg an unpleasant ultimatum.

Walter Bissonnette didn't like to have to coerce someone the way they would Gregory Bissell, but with as much as they had already invested in him and no other suitable candidate was identified that could be prepared in time, hence as ugly as it would get, Pluto II mission had to happen before they hit that three year deadline. Otherwise, it was quite possible the next President might cancel Pluto II mission and the program would be scrubbed and all that effort wasted.

Pluto II management would not have to cross that bridge of such an unpleasant meeting with Greg, until almost three years in the future. The current plan included a humanoid Robot aboard Pluto II that would deal with Gregory Bissell long after the spacecraft left the solar system above light speed and too late for him to do anything about it. Since the craft would navigate in autopilot exclusively, there was nothing Greg could do about it.

Based on Gregs amazing weekend progress, the physics professor Chunhua Liu brought in to the conference room after lunch to start and put the final touches on Gregory Bissell's nuclear physics refresher training.

Chunhua Liu appeared so youthful, she would most likely never be viewed as a nuclear physics professor. At best the young small thin Chinese woman appeared almost like a high school graduate, but Chunhua Liu actually was quite a few years older than her youthful appearance.

Greg was slightly intrigued as Chunhua Liu, very pleasant looking and smelled very nice by her selection of an expensive French perfume. The brilliant Chunhua Liu was all business and had gone through Gregory Bissell's learning modules and adequately identified areas she needed to boost up, which she did over the next couple of weeks.

In Chunhua Liu's final report concerning her student Gregory Bissell, she cited his quick learning and his diligence in the coursework.

Walter Bissonette quickly focused on one statement in Chunhua Liu's evaluation of Greg: *If she had a couple students in her Berkeley classes that had the same work ethics as Gregory Bissell, she thought she could create another J. Robert Oppenheimer.*

That was quite a compliment coming from a woman who finished college at seventeen and received her PhD at the age of twenty-one.

The following week Greg was in for a big surprise. His days in the conference room were finished.

On his subsequent trips, he was directed to an office building that had facial recognition and armed guards and he was taken to his new private office. There was generally very little contact with individuals who had offices on the second-floor wing that housed his office. Most of the time many of them were away on official travel somewhere else. And because of the security surrounding their assignments they had no benefits by socializing with others stuck in the same building wing.

All the amenities of a modern office of a business executive were available in his private office including a change room and a private bathroom with a shower. If Greg decided to take a jog around Lake Haussman in the center of the facility and work up a sweat in gym clothes he could come back, take a quick shower and put back on his street clothes.

Greg's next learning module was unexpected: *The Theory of Robotics.*

There was a package sitting on Greg's new desk he noticed as he was escorted and entered his new office and shown all the features and materials and equipment available to him.

After the escort left Greg by himself, he opened the package which had a note from Walter Bissonnette:

This is your required reading. Spend the next few days reading it on company time.

C.U. on robotics book:

It would help if a person had a mechanical and electrical engineering degree. Soon Greg would learn advanced humanoid Robots were being developed at Livermore.

The main reason for Lawrence Livermore Labs developing humanoid looking robots stemmed from the public would never accept commercial passenger planes or military jets flying with nuclear payloads flown in autopilot with no humans aboard. The idea was to create a humanoid Robot that looked so real that sitting in the cockpit of aircraft so that airline passengers as well as the Air Force crews would not know it wasn't human.

Greg advanced rapidly through nuclear physics, but Robotics was another exquisite study. As Greg studied the *Screw Theory in Robotics* book and read information sent to him from his controller, he discovered the huge Robot race between Japan, China, and America. China desperately needed Robots because their one child policy for over thirty years had created an artificial aging population.

There would not be enough younger people in China to care for the elderly in just ten more years. China was now undergoing a crash program on the advancement of Robotics to bridge the gap. Elderly Chinese would be assisted by humanoid robots and AI.

Stolen technology from Silicon Valley and Akihabara Japan had advanced Chinese Robot designers in Guangzhou very rapidly. Chinese robotics designers were now a short distance behind the top Robot designers in the world: Japan.

Thanks to relaxed travel restrictions, more and more Chinese Tourists were traveling to California and Hawaii. Some of them arriving didn't want to go back to China and had relatives in America. A few Chinese Engineers had pirated the top Chinese Robot technology and brought it with them to America and these well-educated Chinese that spoke English quite well didn't take much time to hunt down talent headhunters in Silicon Valley.

Through Lawrence Livermore Lab's nefarious activities, a few of the Chinese robot designers were granted green cards and given the opportunity for permanent residency in a quid-pro-quo scenario by handing over the thumb drives loaded with essential robotics research.

Japanese robotics companies in hot competition would be appalled if they knew how much technology Americans received which put them back up near the top in Robotics' research again very quickly. Some of that super-advanced Chinese Robot Technology made its way to the Livermore Labs and as a consequence was now slowly integrated into Robotic nuclear bomber pilots.

AREA 51

The Robotic technology course was difficult but not impossible. A person with good work ethics and habits will work harder when the challenges get greater. That's exactly what Greg did.

Greg appeared to be advancing very rapidly in Robotics' theory and had just arrived again on a Monday morning and was soon prompted in a popup inter-office chat box on the company computer he used in the office.

Your robotics studies are curtailed for the day. Meet Walter Bissonnette down at the front entrance lobby at 09:00.

Gregory Bissell wondered what that was all about but made no assumptions. About 08:55 Greg left his office and walked a sort while to a stairway and took it to the bottom floor and out in to the lobby through a security door that would be unlocked by security code or the armed guards to enter.

Gregory Bissell walked out into the lobby and exactly at 09:00. Walter Bissonnette walked in the front entrance all smiles and walked over to his quickly advancing future astronaut.

WALTER BISSONNETTE
We are going for a little field trip.

GREG
Alright.

Walter Bissonnette led Gregory Bissell out the front entrance to a golf cart waiting for them with a driver. They hopped on the four-seat golf cart which drove them over to parking lot 6E where an SUV waited for them.

Greg got in the SUV with Walter Bissonnet, not having any clue about where he was going or what they were doing. The vehicle had a driver, the air conditioner was running, and the SUV comfortable and had a fresh smell to it.

The unmarked SUV made its way to Interstate-580 a short distance away and headed West until it came up to Highway 84 it got off at and turned south towards the Livermore Municipal Airport which they turned into. The SUV went past an airport security gate and checkpoint after the driver showed the airport security personnel his access badge and continued to an area north of the runways where aircraft were parked and pulled up to a Gulfstream 650 jet. It looked brand new, and a flight attendant was waiting at the steps of the jet.

WALTER BISSONNETTE
As you can see, Greg, we are going for a little ride.

<u>EXT. DAY LAWRENCE LIVERMORE AIRPORT SUV NEXT TO THE GS650</u>

Gregory Bissell was amused and since nobody had any luggage, he assumed it would be a short trip. He had never been on a Gulfstream before, so this was kind of a novel experience.

As soon as they were climbing the stairs onto the GS650 Jet.

The flight attendant followed them up and closed the door while the SUV drove away, ostensibly back to the Lawrence Livermore Lab.

The flight attendant walked up to the cockpit and informed the two pilots.

FLIGHT ATTENDENT
Passengers are onboard, we are ready to leave.

Soon Greg could hear the jet engines turning over and within moments the plane nudged forward and was soon out on runway 7L and promptly took to the skies.

With no luggage and only a few passengers the plane was very light, just like the way the disgruntled former Air Force Jet Jockeys liked it. Their angle of attack could be much higher with little weight, relatively speaking.

WALTER BISSONNETTE

Greg, this is a classified trip, assume every aspect of it is top secret and not to be repeated to anyone. It's covered under your non-disclosure agreement.

GREG
Understand, Mr. Bissonnette.

WALTER BISSONNETTE
Greg, please call me Walt.

GREG
Okay, Walt.

Greg had nothing to do but look out the window. One thing he knew is they were flying East based on the angle to the sun and the fact they were flying over the central valley and he could recognize from the air some of the landmarks he was familiar with. Greg didn't know if they did it for him, but the plane flew over Yosemite.

PLANE CAPTAIN (INTERCOM)

For you Passengers in the cabin, I'm banking the aircraft so you can get a look at Yosemite.

The pilot banked the plane on both wing tips so the passengers could see it from their side of the plane.

It didn't seem much longer, perhaps twenty minutes, and the GS650 started reducing altitude over a desert area and the plane went over some type of industrial complex with a long runway and a dry lakebed. The pilot did a U-turn near the end of the runway and Greg could see it was runway 32 and they were soon landing heading Northwest.

The plane taxied over to some hangers and stopped, and the jet engines soon wound down. Moments later the flight attendant opened the GS650 jet door.

FLIGHT ATTENDANT

Gentlemen, you may now exit the aircraft.

Walt and Greg were both in shirtsleeves dressed casually. The heat from the desert hit them as they walked down the plane and met a couple of civilians and several military personnel wearing wings, obvious pilots. There were a couple SUVs there which they were all invited over to.

The SUV drove over to a large hangar with the number 28 painted on its corner. The SUVs stopped in parking spots adjacent to the hangers. These people were obviously expecting them.

An Area 51 Rep wearing shirt and tie and pilot's sunglasses approached Walt and Greg.

AREA 51 REP

Follow us, gentlemen.

<u>INT. DAY. AREA 51 HANGER BUILDING 28.</u>

The Area 51 Rep escorted Greg and Walt into the side entrance of the hangar after he keyed in a security code on the electric lock keypad. A solenoid clicked and the Rep opened the door and led Greg and Walt into the lit-up hangar.

Right in the middle of the hangar was a strange-looking black aircraft, unlike anything Greg had ever seen in his lifetime.

The group walked over to the aircraft where Walt explained to Greg why they were at Area 51.

WALTER BISSINETTE
Greg, in your assignments, you will most likely spend some time in space.

Greg suddenly had a psychological transcendence. This new job suddenly was taking on dimensions he never would have assumed. Greg was now utterly stunned. Pluto II now started to seem like a much bigger deal than he could imagine. There wasn't much Greg could say since there was still a lot of unknown and discovery, he knew he would experience.

GREG
Alright.

WALTER BISSINETTE
This aircraft is a United States Space Force TR-4 capable of flying out into space. I've arranged for you to get a ride as a passenger so that you can get a feel what it's like being in space.

GREG
Alright.

WALTER BISSINETTE
We need to know now if you are mentally ready for such assignments before you go further in the training program.

GREG
This should be interesting.

WALTER BISSINETTE
This is one of your checkoffs that are mandatory to proceed with the project. You will be gone for a couple hours; the craft will come back here, and land and I'll fly you back to Livermore at that time.

GREG
I never thought I would ever travel in space.

Greg suddenly started sensing an awareness like he never experienced in his lifetime. He really didn't quite know what his job was going to be, but this space ride peeled back one more layer on the onion. Greg privately speculated he was training to become some kind of spook that goes out into space. Maybe he was getting into the space satellite repair business?

Nuclear Physics, Robotics, and now a trip out into space. All this exposure tied together started feeling bigger than life as to what he was going to be doing in Greg's future.

The United States Space Force had just stood up and was operational and had already launched ninety-one missions in space. It was now a rather complex situation why the hell Lawrence Livermore Lab would pick an old geezer like him, but Greg knew he was in really great shape compared to his peers.

Greg wondered that since America has an entire space force, why couldn't a younger man do what he was going to be tasked with? The only thing that made sense was he was picked for his age to be expendable if necessary.

AIR FORCE PILOT
The TR-4 is a brand-new prototype. We have flown it out into space a few times, and the technology is proven.

WALTER BISONETTE
Major Blackburn, I appreciate your assistance in this mission.

AIR FORCE PILOT
Not a problem, Mr. Bissonnet, we appreciate all the help the lab provided in the design of the power planet for the TR-4.

Major Blackburn had been briefed ahead of time that Greg Bissell would be the passenger. Greg's picture taken by security monitors was sent to Space Force mission planners and forwarded to Major Blackburn a few days before.

WALTER BISONETTE
Major Blackburn, let me introduce you to your passenger Greg Bissell.

AIR FORCE PILOT (Major Blackburn)
Pleased to meet you Greg.

GREG.
Thank you Major. Will I be issued some type of space suit?

AIR FORCE PILOT (Major Blackburn)
Greg, because of the unique design of the craft you will not require a pressure suit, or any special clothing prior jets required. All you need to do is follow us up into the aircraft and you will be strapped in one of the mission specialists' seats.

Greg was soon led up the ladder into the TR-4 to a mission specialist seat where the crew assisted him latching in the safety harness.

AIR FORCE PILOT (Major Blackburn)

Greg, don't touch any buttons or switches or anything,
just sit back and enjoy the ride. You will not have a
window to look out. All our vision is via video as this
is a windowless aircraft. Cameras are our eyes. And we
have a lot of cameras so we can see in a lot of directions
at the same time.

The TR-4B he had a large video monitor in front of Greg that had some type of test pattern on it.

AIR FORCE PILOT (Major Blackburn)

When we get out of the hangar and over to the runway,
your video on that large flatscreen will start showing
you multiple views simultaneously so you can observe
everything we can see up in front.

<u>EXT. CGI/AI. DAY HANGER BUILDING 28 DOORS SLIDE SIDEWAYS OPEN AND THE TR-4 COMES OUT OF THE HANGER THEN GOES VERTICAL.</u>

Greg could not see outside yet as the video wasn't displaying anything, but he could suddenly feel movement, but virtually no sound. The pilots gave Greg a set of headphones so he could listen in on the pilot and when the pilot wanted to tell him something.

Suddenly, Greg saw video on the large flat screen and felt some strange vibration unlike anything he felt in his lifetime. On one corner of the big screen was an image that was apparently what the pilots were seeing dead ahead in front of them.

The TR-4 seemed to stop momentarily. Then after a couple minutes he could feel movement and looking at the video monitor could see they were indeed traveling down the runway somewhat slowly, probably thirty miles per hour.

Suddenly the TR-4 started rising in the air gaining altitude after slowly lifting off the ground. More and more displays suddenly showed up on the large screen video. The video seemed to suggest they were one hundred feet in the air but traveling towards runway-32 which he came in on. The craft then pointed down to the end of the runway but stopped and hovered at one hundred feet in the air!

Then suddenly the TR-4 started moving forward and the velocity increased rapidly but Greg did not feel any movement. By the time they were at the other end of the runway, they were going very fast then slowly started pitching upwards. Based on the video he was watching it appeared they were traveling straight up in the air and not making a lot of sound.

Greg had a very eerie feeling. According to the monitors the distance below them grew rapidly and soon it appeared like they were already up to 30,000 feet like on an airliner, six miles above earth with velocity increasing. Up on what appeared to be a heads-up display in the center of the screen Greg started noticing indicators including speed, attitude, and heading. The TR-4 indeed was going straight up in the air, and velocity was already 2500 miles per hour!

In total astonishment Greg watched the speed climb. In another minute, they were doing 7,000 miles per hour and he could see the sky was getting darker and it appeared Greg could see the circular shape of the planet on the horizon.

In another couple minutes the velocity indicated 14,000 miles per hour. This was totally amazing, and again no real vibrations or loud noise. Greg felt incredible inspiration!

The large flatscreen display installed for mission specialists showed they continued to speed up and within ten minutes they were doing 50,000 miles per hour and still accelerating. The monitors showed clearly the sky was dark and the stars were far brighter than he had ever seen in his lifetime. But they kept accelerating! In fifteen minutes later the craft was doing 350,000 miles per hour and the ship had maneuvered and right in front of them was a bright spot.

TR-4 PILOT (via headset audio)
Mr. Bissell, do you recognize what's in front of us?

Greg replied via his headphone microphone.

GREG
Not really.

TR-4 PILOT (via headset audio)
I need to put on a light filter, it's very bright now, let's
see what this does.

Moments later the glare of the image reduced and to Greg's astonishment it was a view of the moon about the size of a basketball on the screen.

GREG
It looks like the moon.

TR-4 PILOT (via headset audio)
How many men do you think went to the moon
before us?

GREG
Not many.

TR-4 PILOT (via headset audio)
You are right about that. This is our third trip to the
moon doing a checkout.

GREG
Did you guys ever land up there and get out of the
craft?

> TR-4 PILOT (via headset audio)
> Not yet, but it certainly is in our planning for the
> future. We figure we could get rich bootlegging moon
> rocks back to the planet.

Going at 350,000 miles per hour it didn't take long for the craft to reach the moon and they came close to it and used the Moon's gravity to help sling them back around to head for Earth. During that maneuver, Greg could feel what felt like a slight sensation of gravity. They passed within a mile of the planet, the view of the back side of the moon that was now partially bathed in sunlight was a sight few people on earth would ever get to see except via NASA pictures.

Greg took it all in feeling exhilarated he had got to see and do something very few people in life would ever get to do. This TR-4 aircraft was super amazing. However, just like Walter had stated, the entire mission was Top Secret meaning it was also compartmentalized.

Greg could never tell a soul about it. However, what he didn't know is his friend Dr. (Bob) Moore knew what he was doing on the TR-4.

On the way back to Earth thanks to being slung back by the maneuver around the moon, the TR-4 reached a velocity of 400,000 miles per hour. Now the Earth was center on the flat screen and Greg could see it slowly growing.

As the TR-4 approached the Earth it went into orbit and made loops around the planet as they were slowing down. The speed seemed to bleed off quickly and when the velocity indicated 14,000 miles per hour as they seemed to have been breaking somehow, the ship reoriented downwards and headed down towards a large ocean area and before long they were traveling east as indicated on the heads-up display and soon over land with an altitude of 100,000 feet.

Continuing downwards the TR-4 were approached a desert area and soon Greg could make out a dry lakebed and a large dark line running through it and when they got closer it was obviously a runway. True to their word, they were back landing at the facility in two hours.

What an experience of a lifetime, Greg thought.

The plane did not land on the runway, but it followed it at 100 feet until it got down near the hangers then it slowly dropped down on the runway and taxied over to building 28 that had the very large doors open and the plane pulled in and the doors slowly started closing.

The crew came out of the cockpit and walked back and unstrapped Greg.

> AIR FORCE PILOT (Major Blackburn)
> You can get off the plane now with us. We hope you
> enjoyed your ride.

GREG
Best ride of my lifetime.

AIR FORCE PILOT (Major Blackburn)
Glad to hear it.

Major Blackburn knew Greg knowing truly this dude was one of the lucky ones to experience something like that. But he also knew that when spooks come out and go through various training, they will soon be going on a mission they can't talk about that is probably full of serious danger. Many of them do not come back alive.

As soon as Greg stepped down on the floor of the hangar which also happened to be an oversized elevator, Walt was there.

WALTER BISONETTE
There is an SUV outside to take us to our aircraft
waiting for us.

Walt and Greg exited the hangar through the same door they came in and got in the SUV that took them back to the Gulfstream parked about a mile away.

The crew was waiting for them and as soon as they were onboard and the door shut and strapped in, the plane was rolling for runway 32 North to head back to Livermore.

Back on the plane, Walt was sitting in front of Greg and knew he just had the experience of a lifetime. Walt had never gone on such a trip and envied the visual that Greg had just experienced, but this was necessary to gauge deeper into his psyche and determine how he reacted to the event and how it would affect him going forward. A short trip out in space is nothing like spending your life out in space and dying alone, but it would give an indication of how efficiently he would start the mission.

Once Greg's mission aboard Pluto II began, interlocks in the software prevented Greg from turning the ship around and returning to Earth. The flight control system including inertial navigation and star charting would keep the spaceship pointed towards the destination that included one of the darker areas in space that meant a better chance of avoiding collision with a planet or a star.

After the mission got underway, it was believed by psychologists that Greg would psychologically handle the early phase of the mission just fine, but after a year or two in space is when the breakdown would occur if it did. Putting the humanoid Robot aboard for the flight would give him a psychological outlet to fill some of the void manifested by being alone for such an extended period of time. The Robot would be like a service dog as well as assist in operations.

WALTER BISONETTE
Greg, I wanted to remind you that everything you experienced from the time you left Livermore until you arrived back at your office is Top Secret SCI information that falls under the SAP program. You cannot discuss it for the rest of your life.

GREG
I understand, Walt.

WALTER BISONETTE
Greg, what you have just experienced is more than almost any human that has ever lived. Even though it may seem larger than life, we must protect the secrets associated with how you went to where they took you. Our national survival may depend on keeping that technology protected.

GREG
I realize that, Walt.

WALTER BISONETTE
Good. When you get back to your office you will have a visitor who will debrief you. The person Colonel Schneider will have on a military uniform and is read into the project. He will ask you some questions about your experience as part of the process.

GREG
Alright.

In what seemed like a short time the jet arrived back at Livermore Municipal Airport. As soon as they stepped off the plane, an SUV was there waiting for them. In a brief period of time the SUV made its way back on the freeway that was slightly congested with commuter traffic, but they were able to be back at the Livermore Lab in thirty minutes. The SUV pulled up to the building where Greg had his office, and he was let out. Walt and the driver continued to the destination where they most likely split up.

By now the facial recognition software and the familiarity of the security people allowed Greg to walk right up to the security door where the solenoid was activated and the green "Enter" light lit up. Greg walked up a flight of steps and down the hallway and put his hand on the palm print device that unlocked the door to his office. He walked in the room where his laptop sat on the desk in a most austere surrounding. There were no pictures or mementos. The room was totally sterile.

Within five minutes of Greg's arrival, there was a knock on the door. It was the expected Air Force officer.

COLONEL SCHNEIDER
Are you Gregory Bissell?

GREG
Yes, sir, come on in, I was expecting you.

COLONEL SCHNEIDER
Thank you.

Greg walked back behind his desk and sat down facing his laptop that was currently shut down so he closed the lid.

> COLONEL SCHNEIDER
> Greg, I'm Colonel Schneider. I supervise several flight surgeons for the Air Force, but I also lend a hand to Lawrence Livermore, CIA, NSA, and a variety of military activities.

> GREG
> Pleased to meet you, Colonel Schneider.

Greg stood up and held out his hand to shake the Colonel's hand to show some respect for a man who probably had an extraordinary history being a full Bird Colonel in the Air Force.

> COLONEL SCHNEIDER
> Greg, by now you have probably figured out you may be called upon to spend some time in space on classified missions. I'll come right to the point and explain a few things so that you will realize what I have to tell you is something you can trust. I will always be available to help you as much as humanly possible.

> GREG
> I appreciate your concern.

> COLONEL SCHNEIDER
> As a flight surgeon, I also have a second degree and license in Psychology. I'm a board-certified Psychiatrist and an internal doctor specializing in men's health.

> GREG
> Is this some kind of psychology examination?

> COLONEL SCHNEIDER
> Even though you are not a pilot who has to get a flight certification like a regular Air Force pilot, since we are potentially putting you in a dangerous environment at times, we want to give you the same certifications that a pilot would have.

> GREG
> Okay.

> COLONEL SCHNEIDER
> I'll be frank with you. You are much older than a pilot we would normally certify. That in part was a

decision made that because there is an element of risk involved, you were picked because of your age so that if something happens to you in the line of duty, you have already had a chance to live and experience life.

GREG

What you are indicating is that I'm expendable due to my age, is that right?

COLONEL SCHNEIDER

I'm not saying you are expendable, and in the end you will have the final decision whether or not you are willing to complete certain missions, but as long as you are willing to accept those assignments, we have to make sure you are medically and mentally ready for the challenges.

GREG

I appreciate that.

COLONEL SCHNEIDER

Over the next few days, you will get blood drawn, do urinalysis, and go through a series of diagnostics. We don't expect you to be in perfect health. We know based on your records you had submarine physicals in the past where there were certain criteria that would disqualify you from serving on submarines.

GREG

What does that mean?

COLONEL SCHNEIDER

Based on your exercise routine and your medical files from you routing physicals which we have access to, we already know you are a lot better fit than most people your age.

GREG

I do not feel like a lot of people my age.

COLONEL SCHNEIDER

We concur you look good for our age, but we hope to improve that a few notches.

GREG

I'm okay with that.

COLONEL SCHNEIDER
I'm sure you know from your prior employment where you underwent intensive surveillance to clear you for those programs that a person being put in a position of responsibility like you are now, we have to be certain in all respects.

GREG
Yes, I get it.

COLONEL SCHNEIDER
You have been under a lot of surveillance at the park doing your exercises and walking two or three miles one way to restaurants here to get exercise.

GREG
I like to try to stay in shape.

COLONEL SCHNEIDER
Your pace and your efforts demonstrate a man in good health especially for your age.

GREG
I see a lot of men my age that appear in terrible shape.

COLONEL SCHNEIDER
We think the fact you look ten to fifteen years younger or more than men your age is attributed to your workout ethics.

GREG
Thank you, I appreciate your kind words.

COLONEL SCHNEIDER
If you will please turn on your laptop now you will see I sent you an email with a link.

GREG
Okay.

COLONEL SCHNEIDER
Click on that link. It will automatically record our conversation so that I can get a transcript of your answers to some questions I have.

Greg booted up his very fast laptop the Lab provided him for his office and a moment later he pulled up Colonel Schneider's email and clicked on the link.

To Greg's surprise there was a video showing six boxes showing what appears to be camera views of him and some of the various interior and exterior cameras recapping his TR-4 experience. The video stream all started from approximately when they left the hangar and he first saw the screens showing the visual representation of what was around him.

COLONEL SCHNEIDER
Greg, we know you did not know the destination of where they were taking you or what it would be like.

GREG
That's correct.

COLONEL SCHNEIDER
What were you thinking and feeling at this time?

GREG
Well, to be honest, I've never flown on a private jet like that before and when the pilot flew over Yosemite and banked the plane so we could see it from above I felt privileged.

COLONEL SCHNEIDER
What else were you feeling when you were on the TR-4?

GREG
I felt quite a level of appreciation that I was being given a ride on this special TR-4 aircraft the world does not know about.

COLONEL SCHNEIDER
Did you have any fear or anxiety at this time?

GREG
Those Air Force pilots appeared to know what they were doing. I felt secure with them. I will say that I was hoping they would not go on a joy ride to shake me up, because I know of stories how F14 and F15 Pilots took VIPs on rides and scared the hell out of them. I appreciated the fact they were very gentle with me.

COLONEL SCHNEIDER
Did you think you would be going out in space at the start of all this?

GREG
No, I thought they would fly around and give me some sort of dog and pony show and take me back to the facility.

COLONEL SCHNEIDER
Do you know where you were?

GREG
No, I've never seen the place before or have any idea what it is.

COLONEL SCHNEIDER
Since you will be going there again in the future, you might as well know you were at Area 51.

GREG
No kidding.

COLONEL SCHNEIDER
By the way, I want to remind you of what Walt said to you on the jet on the way home. The fact you were at Area 51 and took a ride on the TR-4B, you are not allowed to divulge for the rest of your life.

GREG
Understand all.

COLONEL SCHNEIDER
At this point in time, you are now up about one hundred feet over the taxiway heading out to the runway. How did you feel about that?

GREG
Well, for starters I was totally amazed because there was virtually no sound. I've been on a lot of airplanes, and they are all noisy. I made a mental note, I was not hearing any sound at all.

COLONEL SCHNEIDER
The TR-4B accelerated down the runway quickly. Have you ever experienced that speed before?

GREG
The only time I felt or experienced speed like that was riding the Shinkansen Bullet train in Japan.

COLONEL SCHNEIDER
At the end of the runway, the TR-4B went vertical. Did you feel any gravity?

GREG
No, none whatsoever which surprised me.

COLONEL SCHNEIDER
See the image of your plane in the right corner box?"

GREG
Yes.

COLONEL SCHNEIDER
Notice the orange-colored orbs that are on the corners and the large one that started in the midsection of the craft?

GREG
Yes, that's quite interesting. Did that really happen?

COLONEL SCHNEIDER
Of course, those are images of the craft when you were on board going vertical.

GREG
What's causing the orange orbs?

COLONEL SCHNEIDER
Those are created by antigravity waves. That's why you didn't feel gravity. Did you feel any sensations at all?

GREG
Yes, I felt some kind of buzzing that initially got strong and slowly tailed off.

COLONEL SCHNEIDER
Those were gravity waves piercing your body in high intensity.

GREG
Any health risks associated with those gravity waves?

COLONEL SCHNEIDER
We really do not know yet. We haven't had enough time to see if there is any long-term impact.

GREG
I see.

Greg then thought, *I'm not a young guy so I don't have a lot of years to worry about it.*

COLONEL SCHNEIDER
At this point in time you were looking directly at the heads up display we put up there for you. What were your main observations?

GREG
I focused on the speed and saw how fast we were accelerating, and I was totally in awe.

COLONEL SCHNEIDER
Right about now you started looking at some of the other displays as it appeared the atmosphere was getting darker, what were your thoughts then?

GREG
The heads-up display had an attitude indicator. I knew we were going straight up and now going very fast. I realized we were leaving the atmosphere.

COLONEL SCHNEIDER
How soon did you figure out you were heading out into space?

GREG
I started thinking about that time looking at some of the camera video panning back towards Earth we were at the edge of space.

COLONEL SCHNEIDER
You surmised you were heading out to space?

GREG
Yes.

COLONEL SCHNEIDER
What did you think about that?

GREG
To be honest I was totally amazed. I had no idea America had such capability. I was led to believe we need a huge chemical rocket blasting out to space and the world would know about it. But instead, there were no rockets nor any public knowledge and we simply went into space.

COLONEL SCHNEIDER
The pilot shifted course and pointed the moon which you couldn't recognize until he filtered it. Once you realized you were looking at the moon, how did you feel?

GREG
Again, I was in total awe, just incredible.

COLONEL SCHNEIDER
You were not scared?

GREG
No, I assumed these pilots knew what they were doing and when we left the hangar, they appeared to be so casual. They displayed no concern whatsoever. I had complete faith in they knew their business.

COLONEL SCHNEIDER
You were not afraid of some kind of a mishap?

GREG
By this time, I had figured out this was probably routine stuff for the pilots and the public had no idea what goes on.

Colonel Schneider smiled a wicked grin and he knew exactly how Greg felt about it. It truly was an amazing advancement for mankind.

COLONEL SCHNEIDER
At this point in time, other than the awe associated with looking at such a huge magnification of the moon, what other thoughts did you have?

GREG
I was watching the speed indicator climb and it truly amazed me. I knew I was going faster than anyone in the world ever experienced. It was incredible.

COLONEL SCHNEIDER
You saw you were heading right to the moon; how did you feel about it?

GREG
I felt extremely privileged. I was seeing something very few people ever had a chance to see firsthand.

COLONEL SCHNEIDER
How do you rate your trip overall?

GREG

This is beyond words. I can't explain the exhilaration I felt especially when we passed close to the far side of the moon.

COLONEL SCHNEIDER
Were you scared?

GREG

No, I had complete faith in the pilots. Everything had gone on very smoothly and my greatest emotions were gratitude for being offered such an extraordinary opportunity.

COLONEL SCHNEIDER

Was this ride on the TR-4 to the moon a good experience?

GREG

Much better than good. It's something I never expected to experience in my lifetime.

COLONEL SCHNEIDER
How did you feel coming back to Earth?

GREG

To be honest it was anti-climactic. After observing the far side of the moon at a short distance which very few people will ever see, coming back to earth didn't feel quite as exhilarating. I had faith in the pilots knew their business and I felt secure knowing this was probably not their first rodeo. I will say this, based on watching TV and movies, I was expecting a rough reentry. The fact it was a soft reentry surprised me.

COLONEL SCHNEIDER

Would you be willing to go back again if you had the chance?

GREG
Definitely.

COLONEL SCHNEIDER

GREG
How about a trip to Mars?

GREG
If you can arrange it, I'll want to go.

COLONEL SCHNEIDER
How about somewhere else but further away?

GREG
If it turns out like this, why not?

COLONEL SCHNEIDER
See the little planet rotating on the bottom of the screen?

GREG
Yes.

COLONEL SCHNEIDER
Click on it.

Greg clicked on the planet and all of a sudden, the planet speeded up, the video went away, and a message said, "Keys erased." A series of musical tones suddenly occurred, and the laptop shut down.

COLONEL SCHNEIDER
Greg, the computer had to shut down to wipe the memory as a security precaution to downgrade the posture of the laptop to a lower and safer security condition. When it boots back up you will also discover my email has been deleted and no longer available.

GREG
Understand.

COLONEL SCHNEIDER
That will be all for today, if you are ready to go home, I'll walk you to the front entrance.

GREG
Sure, thanks.

COLONEL SCHNEIDER
My pleasure.

For security reasons, Colonel Schneider didn't know what Greg's mission would be. Very few did. But what he was briefed on was this was a very risky mission with a high probability Greg would not be coming home alive. He also knew he was picked not only for his skillset, but also because he was picked specifically for his age because they didn't want to send a younger man to his grave who had not had the chance to live.

This also meant Greg was a special person who probably understood he was in a dangerous business and would give great personal sacrifice if required. To Colonel Schneider it was a rare opportunity to meet and work with such an extraordinary person. Air Force pilots he cleared always thought they were coming home. None of the believed they would be killed on the next mission. He didn't know to what levels Greg had been briefed or what it was about, but he certainly knew this was not a fool and understood risk management and was showing extraordinary dedication, especially if he carried out the mission.

Every aspect of Greg's life was programmed Monday through Friday. They let him go home on weekends, mainly to help him maintain a healthy psychology and of course continue with his physical workouts that went a long way to maintain his physiology.

On the spacecraft, he would have a bicycle, but instead of wasting the effort, he would charge batteries that helped put energy back into the storage racks. Every five miles of a bicycle ride on the spacecraft would create enough energy to save a small amount of hydrogen used in the fuel cells used to charge the batteries and could extend the mission quite a few years if he diligently rode his bicycle every day.

Greg hopped in his rental car and drove back to his hotel where he took a shower and changed clothes into shorts, an aloha shirt and his walking shoes with lowcut socks. He was starting to feel hungry because he realized he had missed lunch. So, he walked the long distance to Cattleman's and to his pleasant surprise, Ami (aka Cindy) was there in all smiles. She had taken a liking to this kind man who seemed to be beaming today. If she only knew he was one of the few men in history that ever flew around the moon, she would realize why he was in such a happy mood.

To Greg, there was a bonus. Ami looked so much like his wife twenty or thirty years ago, it was like through the grace of God, Greg traveled back in time and could see her again as she looked back then.

The service was great, the food was exceptional, and Greg had a tremendous sense of satisfaction as he left the restaurant. The surveillance people who followed him into the restaurant gave a full report later. Greg was very predictable, and his polite manners were noted. The staff enjoyed seeing him every time and he and the Maitra d' had an understanding to make sure she gave him a table in Ami's section.

On one trip there she was upset that she had just seated a couple taking up the last booth in Ami's responsible area but Greg, being the nice guy he was had a surprise for the Maitra d'.

GREG
Let me see your hand for a second.

He then grabbed the Maitra d's hand and was obviously passing something to her, a $20 bill.

GREG
I'll be very happy to sit over here and have a glass of
wine and wait until one of the tables is open, I like to
sit at.

MAITRA D'
No problem, Greg.

By then she and Ami and a few others knew his first name. Greg was also informed Greg that Cindy's real name is Ami.

Greg's observers knew he never hinted at any extra circular activities. Not that they would mind, but it could complicate things a bit. As long as Greg's affiliation with project Pluto II was never revealed they didn't care if he took care of his sexual needs through normal human intercourse.

Greg already had a lot of money, and a gold-plated pension, and now a salary that a lot of corporate execs would be jealous of, therefore a $40 tip to Ami was trivial to him.

One night Ami confronted Greg about his tipping.

AMI
Listen, Greg, your tips are more than the cost of your
meal. You don't need to do that.

GREG
Ami, don't worry about it, I got plenty of money.

Then one day, he was lucky, his trailers were not around to record the conversation, Ami asked a question, she was curious.

AMI
Greg, what part of town do you live in?

GREG
I live in Point Loma down in San Diego.

AMI
How could that be? You are here all the time.

GREG
I'm currently staying at a hotel located a couple miles
down the street, but my sponsors are finding me a nice
condo to move in so I can feel more comfortable and
have more privacy.

AMI
What do you do that brings you up here all the time?

GREG
I'm a logistics consultant for a company that does
business here.

AMI

Must be an important job if you come up here every week, I assume you fly up?

GREG

I fly up most of the time, but now and then I drive up on Sunday just so I can drive up CA99 so I can get in some train watching along the way.

AMI

You like trains?

GREG

Yes, I'm a big train buff, I love trains.

AMI

I've been wanting to go on a train ride for a while.

GREG

If you are interested, I would be happy to take you up to Reno on the train. We can spend the night there and come back the next day. I'll get you your own hotel room so you will have privacy.

AMI

You would do that for me?

GREG

Why not, I love trains and to have a nice lady like you going with me would be a nice experience.

AMI

Okay, maybe one of these days, I'll take you up on the train ride. What if I bring my girlfriend along as a chaperone?

GREG

Sure, bring her along. It's more fun traveling with a group.

AMI

What if it's a guy?

GREG

That's good too, as long as he's not your boyfriend.

Ami busted out laughing knowing Greg was joking. Ami looked at Greg with an evil grin.

AMI

Touché!

The truth of the matter, Ami was thinking about her roommate Hikaru. Her only fear of taking Hikaru along is she loved sex and always wanted to do a threesome with her and a gentleman. Greg would fit the exact profile she wanted, a clean wealthy guy who would protect her privacy and do what she wanted. But she really didn't know that much about Greg. She would feel uncomfortable traveling alone with him. *What if he tried to have sex with me?*

<u>INT. DAY ROBOT LAB AT LAWRENCE LIVERMORE.</u>

C.U. Humanoid Robot (later to be named Tiāncái)

VOICE OVER

Greg went about his life unassuming and lately he was bogged down with Robotics which didn't seem to have anything to do with space travel, so he was amused they were having him spend so much time on it. Then one day it all hit home at once. He was informed by his instructors that as part of his assignments in the future, he might be required to use a Robot and he would be fully responsible for the service and repair of the Robot. Hence, he had to become a Robot doctor!

As time passed, his experience of Robotic maintenance and design slowly turned Greg into a subject matter expert (SME) for a specific type of Robot that was designed with the appearance of a human. As each month passed the modifications to the humanoid Robot seemed astonishing as it slowly evolved into the appearance of a real human with the exception, the eyes looked fake. The Robot's eyes were independent cameras with range-finding ability. Another neat feature of this Robot was it had a tactical link to his laptop where Greg could look at a dashboard and view numerous status panels any time he wanted.

The Robot's diagnostic health check system showed a series of colorized rectangular functional block diagrams that Greg could drill down into. When he clicked on one of the functional blocks it expanded into sub boxes, and he could drill down and see statistics and system notes over a variety of factors. In essence this electronic tech manual obliviated the notion of paper tech manuals by a quantum leap. It utilized artificial intelligence that took vast amounts of information and converted it to simple language people could understand. In essence it was like a query to a database that you didn't know the question for. It figured out the question for you and presented information in real time that was meaningful, and in a way, you could act on.

Some of the technology for the Robot derived from the stolen Chinese Robotics, but some of the numerical processing was designed at this lab, whereas a lot of other features were in fact designed at Silicon Valley, pirated from a dozen different companies.

Project Pluto developers could get away with stealing a lot of technology because this Robot would never see the light of day in public. The final product which Greg would check out personally would only be used in one place, accompanying Greg to the edge of the universe, a mission to which he had not been informed of.

While some of the Robot activity was going on, Greg could not travel back to San Diego for the weekend. He knew that if he left, it would take him a day to get back to the point he was, so by staying and working through the weekend, he avoided having to restart up and get back to where he needed to be to make progress. The Robot engineers and instructors were happy he unilaterally made the decision, which underscored his level of dedication to the project. He truly was a team player and was concerned about the outcome.

By helping to bring this Robot to life had a strange feeling to it. In a way Greg was already bonding to the Robot who already had speech capability. The Robot's artificial intelligence was breathtaking. A few computer science professors at UC Berkeley were designing artificial intelligence (AI) and machine learning (ML) algorithms so that eventually the Robot could learn on its own. These AI designer's ultimate goal was to teach the Robot a series of prime directives it would use to guide itself in self-learning. Vast amounts of information were made available to it via twenty-five Gigahertz links to an all-optical supercomputer built by Big Blue.

The information could be demanded from the Robot to the supercomputer via its high-speed wireless link to the optical computer, so it could be anywhere in the design lab and get what it needed. That optical supercomputer would also be part of the computational resources installed on Pluto II.

<u>INT. DAY CATTLEMAN'S RESTAURANT, LIVERMORE CALIFORNIA.</u>

C.U. HIKARU

This weekend, Ami was surprised to see Greg. She never saw him on a Saturday. And to make matters worse, Hikaru, who is Ami's horny bitch roommate was sitting in one of the booths in her section having lunch.

Ami was a little conniving herself and while Greg wasn't looking, she snapped a couple pictures with her cell phone and later showed Hikaru the tipster who made it possible to give Hikaru free meals like today. Hikaru of course viewed Ami as a wonderful roommate and her best friend.

Hikaru was munching down on a Chicken Caesar Salad when the Maître d' brought Greg to the next table.

MAÎTRE D'
Ami will be right here to take your order, Greg.

GREG
Thanks.

Those words got Hikaru's attention and she wondered if this could be the mystery man and she then started thinking he looked like the pictures Ami showed him.

Ami came out with an order for a person at another table and served him then spotted Greg and came over to his table.

AMI
I'm surprised to see you today, Greg. You didn't go to San Diego?

GREG
No, I had some things at work I wanted to get done, so I canceled my trip home and stayed so I can get things done this weekend, so I don't get set back next week.

AMI
I see.

Ami looked over at Hikaru who had that inquisitive look on her face, and she knew exactly what Hikaru wanted, confirmation this was Mr. Money Bags.

Ami knew she couldn't avoid it and didn't think much harm would come to it so she reluctantly introduced Hikaru to Greg.

AMI
Greg, this is my roommate Hikaru.

AMI then held her hand out towards Hikaru who then stood up and came around standing next to Ami.

HIKARU
Hello Greg, it's so nice to meet you.

Hikaru held out her hand. Greg shook Hikaru's hand and mentally noted Hikaru was built like *a beautiful brick shit house* (colloquialism for red necks meaning meets all requirements in a superb way).

GREG
Nice to meet you as well.

Ami was semi-flat-chested but made up for it by her beautiful face, hair, legs, and hips. Ami could instantly smell trouble. Where there is smoke there is usually fire and this could end up getting rather dicey especially if Hikaru propositioned Greg, which would not be out of the question, because Hikaru was a cross between a scorpion and a barracuda. Brilliant, Beautiful, and Bitchy, but with a sexual appetite and loved older men who were far more experienced.

As it was Hikaru was very polite and in due time returned to her seat, finished her salad. In a few minutes Hikaru stood up and approached Greg.

HIKARU

It was a pleasure to meet you. Ami says a lot of nice
things about you.

GREG

The pleasure is mine.

Hikaru walked over to the Maître' d to pay for her meal but she informed Hikaru.

MAÎTRE' D

Ami bought your dinner, so you can leave when you
want.

HIKARU

That's nice of Ami.

About that time Ami came out of the kitchen with a serving for another customer and saw Hikaru standing by the Maître' d and walked over to her.

HIKARU

I'm going home now, Ami, thank you so much for
dinner.

Then Hikaru gave Ami a hug and then she left the restaurant.

Thank God everything was calm here tonight, Ami said to herself.
The night passed by and Greg walked several miles home getting more exercise on the way. Some of the supplements that Colonel Schneider was giving him to help improve his health and give him the ability to work out longer and harder each day, seemed to influence him in that the miles were becoming easier to do. Greg felt the best he had in years. All the probing of his body by the medical team slowly revealed the obvious. Greg was healthier than a lot of people twenty years younger. The indoctrination and training were proceeding better than Walt had predicted and he reported to Dr. Moore he must have had keen awareness to spot this extraordinary individual that was working out a lot better than they imagined.

<u>INT. DAY ROBOT LAB LAWRENCE LIVERMORE FACILITY</u>

C.U. TIĀNCÁI (天才) SHOWING GREG INTERACTING WITH THE ROBOT.

VOICE OVER
DURING GREG'S INTERACTION WITH TIĀNCÁI
Part of the development of the Robot required identification. The robotics chief designer, Dr. Hudson had some limited knowledge of the role his Robot TIĀNCÁI would do going into harm's way with Greg, thus decided he would allow Greg to name the Robot.

Greg being fond of Chinese literature easily came up with a unique name that fit this Robot well: Tiāncái (天才).

Tiāncái (天才) is the Chinese word for genius. The Chinese would be proud since without their stolen technology it's unlikely the Pluto II team could have assembled the Robot Tiāncái so quickly. The Chinese would be horrified to learn the tables had turned. Americans were now doing industrial espionage against them saving years of development time to catch up.

Greg assisted in setting up a robot obstacle course which tested numerous tasks for Tiāncái.

A big surprise for Greg happened the following day when Walt walked into the Robot lab and approached Greg.

WALTER BISONETTE
Greg, tomorrow, I'm going to take you and Tiāncái to some place special. Do you think he's ready to try some complicated tasks?

GREG
I think we should give it a try. Tiāncái's done some amazing things at the Robot obstacle course.

WALTER BISONETTE
Yes, I read your report. Tiāncái's problem solving ability is truly amazing.

The next day, a golf cart picked up the chief Robot engineer, Greg, and Tiāncái and took them to another building where Walt was standing next to a waiting SUV.

Everyone got into the car and by now Tiāncái understood to take commands from the Robot Engineer Hudson or Greg or whoever Greg directed him to obey. Greg could also rescind the obeyance if he thought it was appropriate.

The Limo was hitting some of the commuter traffic, so it took them thirty minutes to reach Livermore Municipal Airport, where a new GS650 jet aircraft was waiting for them with two pilots and a female flight attendant.

Everyone got into the GS650 and Tiāncái observing Greg copied his movements and climbed up into the aircraft. An observer fifty feet away would not know Tiāncái was a robot, who was dressed in jeans, Polo shirt and tennis shoes, and wore sunglasses to hide the imperfections in his eye appearance. Even the flight attendant did not know Tiāncái was a robot.

The GS650 jet aircraft took off and headed East. Greg assumed they were heading back to Area 51. His assumption was wrong.

Instead, they flew When they landed there an SUV shuttled them over to a decent-size building without a lot of windows in it. They were soon led inside and discovered they were inside one of the most complicated flight simulators in the world. They could fly a mission anywhere in the world at this location.

Furthermore, the Air Force thinks ahead, and their systems engineering is very prudent, possibly from lessons learned from World War II when America built 270,000 new aircraft and trained 10,000 pilots a month for several years.

To be able to train many men to fly different types of aircraft, the Air Force designs the flight controls to cross deck to other aircraft type. For basic flying the pilot's glass in later models of F16s flew like F22s and F35s flight controls and indications. Hence if you learn one aircraft you can quickly master the others with some extra training to consider some of the differences in some of the aircraft versus the other.

As part of this systems engineer brilliance, the TR-4B, the super-duper outer space capable craft that was going to replace the TR-3B in a few years, had the same "glass" as an F22. An F22 pilot could climb into a TR-4B and safely fly it just as if it were an F22. But there was a big difference. The F22 doesn't have the artificial gravity which makes flight controls even easier.

In essence a TR-4B pilot simply flies it as if it were an F22 except they are trained to know the performance is extraordinarily different. Artificial intelligence essentially takes the F22 emulator and converts it to TR-4B flight controls. All the pilot needs to know is the artificial intelligence will keep him out of trouble and make all the corrections and modifications to flight controls to keep it safe. But a pilot must know if he points the TR4B directly upwards and pushes the throttle forward, in about ten minutes he'll be out in outer space.

Taking a space joy ride is the worst thing a pilot could do because NORAD would personally see that he is permanently grounded and never allowed to get near a TR-4B again.

For this simulation the Air Force Guys in the room were cleared for TR-3B and TR-4B because this simulator could do those aircraft types simply by running another APP. However, to do so they would have to take a half-dozen very large SSD drives out of the

TOP-SECRET SCI safe and load it up in the mainframe computer which up postured this portion of the building during the training session.

Since this training schedule had been planned for about a month, the Air Force personnel had loaded the software up, postured the simulator and had facial recognition verification of everyone including Tiāncái.

Tiāncái had plug-in modules that allowed the team to load up tech manuals, operational guidelines, and flight training manuals via wireless.

All of this had been done in advance and while Greg was not around, the design team did "virtual" simulator using their own super computers wired up to Tiāncái who took various missions and carried them out as directed by the scenario lists and objectives.

It's one thing to do a virtual simulator verse operating a real simulator that transcended into actual flight controls that moved the simulator in 360 degrees on the horizon and the vertical. Training in the TR-4B was not ideal because the crew never feels gravity. Therefore, to simulate gravity free movement, it simply didn't physically move, but the simulator projections moved as it would for a regular jet giving the sensation it was almost like being in a TR-4B.

However, in a TR-4B, the gravity waves were complex and slightly dynamic so a person could feel lighter from time to time as the processing and creation of gravity waves were adjusted in milliseconds to create the artificial gravity environment. In the simulator the gravity was constant as the craft didn't really move and a person never felt that lighter situation experienced in real flying.

<u>INT. DAY TR-4 SIMULATOR NELLIS AIR FORCE BASE.</u>

WALTER BISONETTE

Greg, have Tiāncái sit in the pilot's seat, and you go
ahead and sit in the copilot seat while we run through
a few scenarios.

GREG

Tiāncái, please sit in the pilot's seat and get ready to
control the TR-4B in scenarios.

Tiāncái could quickly access his TR-4B files thus quickly knew which was the pilot's seat as well as all the controls. He sat in the Pilot's seat and connected his seat belt and safety harness just like he would if he were flying a real TR-4B.

TIĀNCÁI

All right Greg, I'm ready to proceed.

For the next four hours, Tiāncái went through a half-dozen scenarios that included taking the TR-4B out of the hangar, taxying to the end of the runway and taking off. In a few of them they went out into space and the trainer has dynamic spacing meaning in real life it would take a craft maybe an hour to fly to the moon going almost 300,000 miles per hour, but to not waste valuable training time there is a time jump which everyone is advised so you cut out a lot of the transit time and deal with the dynamics of planetary entry or surveillance desired.

Greg sat there totally amazed. Tiāncái appeared to operate just as effectively as the two Air Force pilots who had taken him to the moon and back.

During the scenarios, Tiāncái was asked to vocalize everything he did and why he was doing it. He had interactions with the control tower and did everything a pilot would do and appeared to understand and take action on everything air traffic controllers directed him.

After the scenarios were completed, they all piled back in the SUV who took them over to the runway where they boarded the jet and flew back to Livermore.

As Walt dropped Greg off at his office, he announced their plans for tomorrow.

WALTER BISSONNETTE
We are going on another trip tomorrow at about the
same time in the morning.

GREG
I'll be ready.

The Robot chief engineer Dr. Hudson and Walt took Tiāncái back to the Robot lab and directed him to sit in front of a laptop and produce a report on all his experiences during the day.

Tiāncái could type about three hundred eighty words per minute with no errors. It was like watching the fingers of the great Concert Pianist Yuja Wang perform compositions like Chopin, Liszt, or Saint-Saëns Piano Concerto No. Two during portions of their music.

Since Tiāncái recorded everything, nothing was lost, and within hours while he was charging up his batteries for tomorrows event, the 3,000-page report slowly came together including several critiques of the flight simulator where they needed to add improvement since it didn't fully match the operational guidelines and emergency procedures seriously needed beefed up.

The report was sent over to Nellis the next day for comment, and an Air Force General over there was red faced by the end of the day. If he knew that it was a robot that had picked his organization apart, he would be even more humble. So, in effect, Tiāncái did more in one night to lay out improvements they needed to make for the simulator than Air Force systems engineers and their contractors had done in over a year.

Over the next few weeks as Walt and the Robot Chief Engineer digested Tiāncái's report, they saw the enormity of it all. Artificial Intelligence had a surreal effect, and this was just the beginning.

As promised the next day, the group was shuttled back to Livermore Municipal Airport and the GS650 headed east again, but instead of continuing to Nellis, it stopped early and went to Area 51.

Now another milestone in Gregory Bissell's indoctrination would bring to light just how far along he would go along with things. This would be a true test of his bravery as well as his commitment to risk. Today would in effect be one of those make-or-break moments as they all entered the hangar and there were no pilots.

<u>INT. DAY. TR-4B HANGER AT AREA-51</u>

At first Gregory Bissell was slightly confused when Walt made the unexpected announcement.

WALTER BISSONNETTE

Greg, you and Tiāncái are going to be the only individuals on the TR-4B today.

GREG
What does that mean?

WALTER BISSONNETTE

First of all, I want you to know we can fly this TR-4B from the ground using remote control via satellites. Therefore, you will have a backup in case something goes wrong. Tiāncái will be flying the TR-4B today, and you will be his passenger.

GREG
Alright

This was one of those moments where events challenged every moral and ethical fiber in Greg's soul as he stood there dumb founded. It seemed so surreal.

WALTER BISSONNETTE
Would you like to tell me what is our destination?

GREG
That would be nice to know.

WALTER BISSONNETTE

When you got your joy ride to the moon and back, you didn't know this craft can go a lot faster. We didn't need the speed to get there quickly, nor did we want to take on any risks more than we had to at that phase of the development.

GREG

I admit a conservative approach is more comfortable for me.

WALTER BISSONNETTE
Since then, this craft has gone a lot of further distances
and at a more rapid pace.

GREG
How long will we be gone?

WALTER BISSONNETTE
Where you are going today will take eight hours.

GREG
What if I suddenly need to use the toilet?

WALTER BISSONNETTE
On the TR-4B is drinks, snacks, and a portable toilet.
If you must use the toilet, disconnect the plastic bottle
attached to it and put a cap on it that's attached to it via
a lanyard so none of it spills on the plane.

GREG
What if I suddenly need to poop?

WALTER BISSONNETTE
The portable toilet is set up for that. After you wipe,
tuck the toilet paper in the bottle with your bowel
movement and be sure and put the cap on it. There is
a box of spare bottles for the toilet attached to it via
Velcro straps in case you need to do it more than once.

Greg wasn't pleased to have to do this. But climbing aboard a 594-class nuclear submarine to go out on sea trials and take it to test depth was probably just as dangerous. One thing a lot of submarine sailors knew, we lost the Thresher SSN-593 doing sea trials.

But riding 594 class submarines doing at-sea tests was a long time ago, when Greg had a lot longer life to live. This will be like taking the Parche to test depth after the conversion. There were a lot of scared people on that run when the boat came close to capsizing due to an emergency surface test (EMBT blow) that didn't work too well causing an 85-degree roll and almost capsizing. Several men on that EMBT blow had to change their underwear.

This felt just as bad as riding the Louisville to sea with an asshole captain and a crew Greg didn't feel safe with. But were any of them safe?

It was too late for Greg to back out now. Greg should have quit a long time ago. He was stuck whether he liked it or not. Greg's participation in creating Tiāncái was going to now make him pay for his sins or bless him with success.

GREG

Would it be possible for you to tell me now where Tiāncái is taking me?

WALTER BISSONNETTE

He's taking you to Mars and back.

GREG

Just like that, back in eight hours?

WALTER BISSONNETTE

That's how much time we calculated based on the flight plan we loaded in Tiāncái.

GREG

I suppose this is why you pay me the big bucks.

WALTER BISSONNETTE

You have already earned your pay many times over and don't know it yet. We do appreciate what you have done for the program. Some of our research assistants seemed to be dithering and lacked Esprit de Corps until you showed up and your interactions with them and all you do has uplifted them.

GREG

I'm glad to help.

WALTER BISSONNETTE

We've gotten about five times as much production of them since you showed up and gave them a reason to focus on their work and participate in this project.

GREG

Well, thanks for the kind words. I'm ready to go. Tiāncái, please follow me into the aircraft and sit in the pilot's seat as you are the designated pilot for this trip.

Tiāncái responded in the adaptable personality that was slowly evolving designed to better mesh with Greg's nuances and peculiarities.

TIĀNCÁI

Please lead the way, Greg,

INT. DAY INSIDE TR-4 GREG AND TIÃNCÁI

VOICE OVER
(DURING GREG AND TIÃNCÁI STRAPPING IN THEIR SEATS AND TIÃNCÁI TURNING ON THE TR-4 AND INITIATING PRE-FLIGHT CHECKOFFS.)

Tiãncái didn't need a checkoff sheet since it was in his memory storage already.

As part of Tiãncái's training, while Greg wasn't around all night long, computer scientists programmed Tiãncái with every detail in Greg's life that they were briefed about.

Tiãncái had a huge built-in memory designed by Sandia National Lab's located south of Livermore's facility. No other memory storage existed anywhere else in the world. The storage density was about ten times larger than any similar sized devices, enclosed in a radiation hardened module to protect it from cosmic rays.

Tiãncái had great amounts of psychology science programmed in him and many hours of one on one with some of the world's top psychologists from University of Washington and Berkeley, some of which were on contract to help our special forces who needed advanced theory on how to best cope with extraordinary challenges.

Special forces and CIA operatives sent behind enemy lines were taught advanced meditation techniques and at very secure locations, experts from the Monroe Institute were brought in to help them develop the Hemi-Sync techniques. Greg would be indoctrinated in Hemi-Sync. But he would also have his own personal psychiatrist Tiãncái.

The artificial intelligence in Tiãncái had advanced to the point where some of the researchers at the lab feared the day if they were ever mass produced. Hence, Tiãncái was treated as a TOP-SECRET-SCI asset, always guarded by highly cleared individuals.

The robot scientists were coddled and told, Tiãncái will be going on a mission away from the Earth and will never return. Therefore, you don't have to worry about proliferation issues.

Researchers concluded proliferated mass production of Tiāncái copies would be equivalent to proliferating hydrogen bombs if a despot got ahold of the technology and programmed them for nefarious activities. A fear existed such as nefarious special operations and missions they could perform better than Green Beret or Seals.

Tiāncái's eyeball ranging and special hearing capability could make him a very dangerous weapon. Tiāncái clones could be trained to do anything a human could including assassinating people.

Researchers were arrogant in showing off their talents designing and building Tiāncái with all the stolen parts from around the world but were pleased to know this Frankenstein Monster they had created would soon be leaving on a mission and would never come back to Earth where it could be proliferated.

Also, once the Pluto II mission was underway, all the information the researchers had serialized, and equipment utilized in Tiāncái's design would be destroyed.

Researchers like Dr. Hudson had created a monster but thank God that monster was going away. Robotic researchers didn't want to feel like Oppenheimer for the rest of his life, "The Destroyer of Planets."

After they were all strapped in and Tiāncái went through the check list programmed in his memory and verified at Livermore remotely and the Airforce special assistants verified Tiāncái correctly complied with all orders and directives. It was suddenly time for the big event.

Greg daydreamed when he was walking down the pier at Pearl Harbor with travel bag in hand how crappy he felt as he went to the torpedo retriever moored over by the BOQ at SUBASE in Pearl Harbor. And as he expected, he had a confrontation with the captain underway who was a flaming asshole and the CO was absolutely wrong. It really sucks when you are trying to help someone and their ego gets in the way.

At the precise moment, the huge doors of hangar building 28 slid open under electric power. As soon as they were fully open the ground controllers signaled Tiāncái via his temporary call sign.

GROUND CONTROLLERS
Red Barron please proceed out of the hangar and to the runway.

There was no jet blast. This was all gravity powered. The gravity waves were in effect working like magnets in a maglev train, pushing the TR-4 forward. It also had a jet-like engine that had no rotating parts designed around the technology of the Tesla Turbine. [Tesla turbine - Wikipedia]

All this movement was programmed in Tiāncái who could move the human controls as he did to give a psychological soothing to Greg. But instead, Tiāncái could simply give the craft the same exact controls via his wireless network without moving any his body parts.

Since Tiāncái's artificial intelligence knew the importance of psychological accommodation for Greg, he would do all the mechanical movements to simulate a real pilot to give Greg a better feeling about all this. Psychologists knew the extraordinary stress going out to space with a robot as the pilot could put on any human.

However, most people living today are unaware, there were no computers on the Mercury Space Program Rockets. NASA mainframe computers controlled them from the ground. The first computers ever installed on a manned spacecraft (that NASA will admit to) were the Gemini launches.

Greg and Tiāncái were not looking out windows. They were looking at flat screens that had video provided by cameras that gave the pilot the same visibility as if he had real windows.

The big advantage is that during night flying those video screens could have infrared and other technology to help them FLY in the dark. The ultraviolet systems were even better because it was as if you were giving the craft headlights that worked far better than landing lights.

At approximately fifty yards from the hangar, the tower radio communicated to the TR-4B.

HOMEY AIRPORT ATC TOWER
Red Barron, proceed to altitude one hundred feet and
proceed to the runway 32R (North).

TIĀNCÁI
Tower, this is Red Barron, understand proceed to
runway 32R at 100 feet.

As part of the design, they had to give the Robot a voice and since it was most important how Greg would like it since he would be stuck with it for the rest of his life, he was given the choice to pick any voice he wanted, provided there was ample recordings of it that could be digitized. Greg selected the Movie Star from the 40s to the 60s who was a major actor named Clark Gable.

Hence when Tiāncái responded he did with that classic Clark Gable sound. The tower operator would no doubt be too young to recognize the voice but if there were some older radio buffs out there who tried to pick up Area 51 communications and heard the voice, they would scratch their heads and say, "He sure as hell sounded like Clark Gable."

<u>EXT. CGI. AREA-51. TR-4 GOES VERTICAL TO 100 FEET TO TAXI TO END OF RUNWAY 32R.</u>

The TR-4 spacecraft made it down to the end of the runway and the ATC Tower called again.

HOMEY AIRPORT ATC TOWER
Red Barron, you have permission to take off IAW flight
plan Alpha-Gama.

TIĀNCÁI
Tower, this is Red Barron, understand take off in
accordance with flight plan Alpha-Gama.

Translated, flight plan Alpha-Gama means straight up. There was no dilly dallying down the runway like the last time planned to not shake up Greg too badly. Greg knew by now what the craft could do because they did this exact scenario in the trainer over at Nellis just the day before.

Tiāncái moved the throttle forward and artificial gravity to maximum and a very short time pulled back on the stick and the nose of the aircraft pitched straight up.

Speed quickly indicated three hundred miles per hour and a minute later was 600 miles per hour gaining velocity quickly. After two additional minutes passed and the TR-4B flew 2000 miles per hour going straight up leaving behind a good sonic boom heard for 100 miles. The speed continued increasing and Greg felt no gravity shift. But he did feel the strange buzzing sensation again. Greg but knew that buzzing sensation was caused by anti-gravity waves from three corners of the angle shaped TR-4. No doubt the TR-4 had orange orbs on the three corners and a very large orange orb around the middle of the craft. It did not take long before the daylight turned into darkness.

<u>INT. TR-4 GOING INTO SPACE SHOWING GREG AND TIĀNCÁI AND COCKPIT INDICATORS.</u>

It almost appeared like they were heading for the moon again, but there was a bright light offset not far from the moon that appeared like a bright star at first until Tiāncái explained.

TIĀNCÁI
Greg, do you see what appears to be the bright star
offset above and to the right of the moon?

GREG
Yes.

TIĀNCÁI
That's Mars.

GREG
Interesting.

Greg watched the speed build up and it almost appeared like they were flying at the moon. In effect they were just like in the trainer yesterday. The idea was to use the moon's gravity to help propel the TR-4 but instead of curving around it and heading back to Earth they would maneuver and head directly to Mars. The TR-4 continued gathering speed and by the time it shot past the moon it was already doing two million miles per hour.

TIĀNCÁI
In accordance with my instructions, we are now in radio silence. We are no longer allowed to attempt to communicate with the Earth.

GREG
I suppose that's for security reasons.

The TR-4 spacecraft continued to accelerate. Greg was in awe and surprised as he watched the velocity peak over fifteen million miles per hour.

GREG
How fast are we speeding up to?

TIĀNCÁI
We will stop accelerating at thirty million miles per hour.

GREG
Why so fast?

TIĀNCÁI
Flight plan Alpha Gama indicates we will attempt to be back at Area 51 in eight hours.

Thirty minutes after takeoff the TR-4 cockpit displays indicated the spaceship was traveling at thirty million miles per hour.

GREG
We sure accelerated fast.

TIĀNCÁI
The gravity waves give the TR-4 good traction since we are propelling against the sun using inverse gravity.

GREG

This thing must have a hell of a lot of horsepower.

TIĀNCÁI

It has a lot of horsepower, however, not as much as you think.

GREG

Then how does it accelerate so effectively?

TIĀNCÁI

We are in a vacuum here where there is only one hydrogen atom per 10 cubic meters. There is no skin friction or resistance or gravity because we created inverse gravity with the propulsion.

GREG

How can we obtain such speeds without a lot of thrust?

TIĀNCÁI

Since there is nothing to slow us down and we have constant power output pushing us along until we cut back the propulsion to maintain thirty million miles per hour, the speed increase becomes exponential. We could probably make it outside the galaxy and back a lot quicker than you imagine.

GREG

That's amazing.

The four hours getting to Mars were full of excitement and interest and as they got closer it appeared less white and more red. Fifteen minutes before they slid into an elliptical orbit around the planet, it had grown to huge proportions.

The bird's-eye view of the planet affected Greg in quite a few ways. It was a spiritual sensation. The public had no idea they had the means to get to Mars and back in eight hours or less.

EXT. CGI. SPACE. VIEW OF APPROACHING MARS.

Getting pulled closer to Mars by gravity, then travel around the planet helped increase the speed and as their track straightened out back towards Earth, they were coasting along at thirty-five million miles per hour, but within fifteen minutes were back down to thirty million miles per hour. At this distance Earth was just a little tiny spec in the sky and the moon was not even observable.

EXT. CGI. SPACE. VIEW OF APPROACHING EARTH.

It almost seemed anticlimactic now after observing Mars up close, then heading for home. It truly was an extraordinary moment in Greg's life. It also sent a chill down his spine as he realized if we could do it so could Aliens not from our planet. That suddenly made him appreciate many of the people who report and claim they observed UFOs. They probably did see them, but half of them were probably TR-3Bs, TR-4s, or B2 bombers that looked like UFOs.

The Earth slowly grew in size and a little white spec on it turned out to be the moon as they came in closer. As they passed by the moon, they were slowing at a rapid pace. They went from thirty million miles per hour down to one million miles per hour in ten minutes and Greg felt no slowing. It's as if the artificial gravity inside the aircraft was isolated from the external gravity by this ingenious machine. The TR-4 continued slowing and by the time they hit the atmosphere they were down to 18,000 miles per hour still slowing. Just like before they were over a huge body of water and those little islands below them were the Hawaiian chain of islands. Before long they were passing over land and looking at the bottom view, they were clearly flying over San Francisco Bay area heading East. They continued to lose altitude.

At 10 miles from Area 51 Homey Airport ATC Tower Tiāncái contacted the air traffic controllers via UHF RADIO.

TIĀNCÁI
Homey Tower, this is Red Baron, we are ten miles from
touch down, heading on a course of 105 degrees.

HOMEY AIRPORT ATC TOWER
Red Baron, this is Homey ATC, commence Event
Charlie.
TIĀNCÁI
Homey Tower, Event Charlie in progress.

Event Charlie was a preprogrammed air traffic control guide specifically for this mission. Simply put it meant at the outer marker change course to three hundred forty-five degrees and proceed to runway 32R North. They would come down and land like a traditional aircraft to throw off some surveillance by radio hobbyists and foreign intelligence services.

It was a very smooth landing because the Robot Tiāncái was at the controls inputting steering commands directly via wireless to the inertia navigation system.

<u>EXT. EVENING AREA 51 HANGER BUILDING 28.</u>

The TR-4 pulled up to the hangar, building 28 with doors wide open and slipped in it, then the big doors shut. Following his check list, Tiāncái shut down the TR-4 and Air Force personnel opened the aircraft door, and invited them to disembark to their guests waiting for them.

Walt seemed very pleased and would have a full report in a few minutes including all the video taken during the trip. They all hopped in the SUV that took them to the GS650 parked 1000 feet down the runway, ready to take off as soon as they boarded.

A major milestone in the project was reached. The artificial intelligence people were amazed at their creation.

There were some who thought Tiāncái could go by himself and not waste Greg's life, but Dr. Moore and Walter Bissonnette had rationalized it was best to have a human on board in case they encountered Aliens.

The first impression is very important. Meeting a machine first might not be a good thing.

Greg was feeling quite expansive having been only the second living person to pass this close to Mars. A previous mission flown by an Air Force officer for a dry run had been the only other time, partly due to the fact TR4 had just started flying six months prior. In essence the mission Greg flew had two areas of risk, first the reliability of the technology. And secondly it takes several years to work out all the bugs on a new airframe, especially one so complicated it could fly out into space and return and land on a runway.

The other remarkable aspect of the mission was Greg flew in his street clothes. Tiāncái also dressed in street clothes wearing sunglasses by all appearance made the cockpit appear like two civilians flying.

Greg's exhilaration for this trip to Mars and back was only eclipsed by an event that evening as he walked several miles to Cattleman's for dinner after taking a Hollywood Shower.

About a quarter mile away from his destination, his trailers knew exactly where he was going, so they also pulled into Cattlemen's to be in place to observe and report.

Greg's surveillance watchers reports never included anything to be worried about. Anyone in Greg's position would have this detail of surveillance. There was a lot at stake. Their investment in him and the timeline left nothing to chance. These well-armed men would be in position to intervein and protect their objective. But at the same time leaks of information could become quite serious, especially since half the town knew a lot of strange things went on over at the Livermore Lab and they were used to having an abundance of strangeness around them.

Ami and Hikaru by now had several discussions about Greg back at their apartment.

<u>INT. EVENING AMI'S CONDO</u>

> HIKARU
> He seems like a real nice guy; he must really like you to
> give you all those big tips.

> AMI
> Yes, I know he likes me and I know why.

> HIKARU
> Why is that?

> AMI
> He showed me a picture of his wife taken some twenty
> years ago. We look amazingly alike. I could be her twin
> sister.

> HIKARU
> He's married?

> AMI
> Sort of.

HIKARU
What does *sort of* mean?

AMI
His wife has moved to Japan; they are permanently separated.

HIKARU
Did their marriage fail?

AMI
No, they are still married, he said he would never divorce her, he still provides her financial support. She just wants to live the rest of her life in Japan in her home country. Greg has no desire to move to Japan and wants to stay in San Diego where the climate agrees with him and can take long walks at the beach any time of year.

HIKARU
How can he live in San Diego, he's here all the time?

AMI
He commutes to work here and now only goes home on the weekends.

HIKARU
Where does he live while he's here?

AMI
He has moved into a nice condo which he can walk to work and walk to nearby restaurants like here.

HIKARU
Does he have a girlfriend or someone to make up for his distant relationship with his wife?

AMI
No, he's not that kind of man, he's pretty straight.

HIKARU
What does he like to do for kicks besides exercising?

AMI
He's a train buff.

HIKARU
What does that mean?

AMI

He loves trains. He's always going to train museums in his spare time and doing train watching when he can.

HIKARU

That sounds boring.

AMI

We were talking about it the other day and he invited me to go with him on the train to Reno and spend the night.

HIKARU

Sounds like he wants to get in your pants!

AMI

No, he's not that kind of guy. Plus, I told him I would have to bring along a chaperone.

HIKARU

How did he reply to that?

AMI

He said that would be okay.

HIKARU

And did you agree?

AMI

I asked him, what if it were a guy? He said if the person wasn't my boyfriend, it would be okay.

The two ladies began laughing and giggling.

HIKARU

At least he has a sense of humor!

HIKARU

When are you going to go to Reno?

AMI

I've never told him I'm ready to go.

HIKARU

Do it, stupid, I'll go with you.

AMI

As long as you don't try to get us into ménage à trois.

                          HIKARU
                 I would never try to do that.

Hikaru winked and smiled.

                            AMI
        If he brings up trains again, I might just say yes to him.

<u>EXT. EVENING CATTLEMAN'S RSTAURANT, LIVERMORE CALIFORNIA.</u>

The evening of the Mars mission when Greg was feeling "in orbit" after observing all those celestial treats, he was beaming as he walked into Cattleman's. The Maître d was dressed beautifully that night. Greg thought, *If I were a younger man, I would pursue her.* Her exquisite beauty enthralled him.

Greg was promptly ushered to his favorite dining table right under the air-conditioning outlet where this booth was a lot cooler than the rest of the restaurant, which was highly desirable especially on nights when the place was packed. And if the booth wasn't available, he would wait for it if the Maître d indicated it would be available soon.

Just like clockwork he was at his favorite booth and Ami approached him with a menu. He already knew what he wanted the menu wasn't important. First a nice green salad, then a Porterhouse steak and corn on the cob. He also knew that Ami would instruct the chef to chop the corn on the cob into a half-dozen slices to make it much easier to eat.

The Porterhouse loaded with A1 steak sauce with fried onions and mushrooms on top was about as good as it could get. He would wash it down with two or three glasses of Robert Mondavi 2015 Cabernet Sauvignon.

That night the restaurant was half empty as Greg had arrived about an hour after the core evening dinner hours. He was uncharacteristically late and Ami assumed he went somewhere else that night.

The lack of a restaurant full of people helped the acoustics so the spooks sitting just a few tables away were able to get good recordings of the conversation. One thing was evident, Greg never talked shop and Ami never pried. Greg never went to this restaurant with any work associates. In essence he was an enigma.

After serving Greg's salad, Ami brought up the subject.

                            AMI
          Greg, I've been thinking about your offer for the train
          ride over to Reno.

                           GREG
                     It would be fun.

                    AMI
I would like to bring along Hikaru if you don't mind.

                    GREG
Absolutely, how soon would you like to go?

                    AMI
I have this weekend off.

                    GREG
Alright, would you be able to leave Saturday morning?

                    AMI
About what time?

                    GREG
We would need to be at the Oakland train station around 9:00 to get our tickets and catch the train to Sacramento. The Amtrak Train that leaves Sacramento at 11:00 A.M. We can walk around Sacramento Old Town for a while waiting for our next train.

                    AMI
What time would we have to leave Livermore?

                    GREG
I have this psychological condition about showing up late, I like to always arrive a little early.

                    AMI
What caused that?

                    GREG
My family always showed up for church late and I was forced to sit up front where everyone could watch me sing. I hated it.

Ami chuckled a bit,

                    AMI
I know how you feel. I'm sure we could be ready by 8:00.

                    GREG
Good. Text me your address and I'll swing by in a cab and pick you girls up around 8:00 in case we have bad traffic.

AMI
Alright.

GREG,
Ami, can you give me a piece of paper so I can write
down my phone number.

AMI
Here's a blank customer order sheet you can write on.

GREG
Thanks.

AMI
The train trip sounds fun.

After Greg finished dinner and left the restaurant and walked back to his condo and quickly received a text message with Ami's address.

Greg then went online and booked three seats on a commuter train to Sacramento then and a private cabin on Amtrak from Sacramento to Reno. He then booked two hotel rooms in Reno at Harrah's Reno. He would be traveling light. If he needed anything, he would buy it in Reno, a city that never sleeps.

Greg almost felt giddy knowing he would be in the company of two beautiful women. He only saw Ami in her uniform at work, he had no idea how well she could clean up. He knew that Hikaru could dress up like a sex kitten. She had outstanding features and a very pretty face.

Saturday morning Greg had his alarm set for 6:00 A.M., which was his typical morning if not 05:30 most of the time, as he always woke up about then needing to urinate.

Thanks to the three glasses of Robert Mondavi Cabernet Sauvignon and the melatonin chewable, he was drowsy and laid down and had the most peaceful rest he had in a long time. The thought of him spending the day with a pretty woman who could be his wife's twin sister, made him extra joyful. In a way it allowed him to relive the romantic period when his wife was a fresh peach, and he was a horny road warrior looking for that life's companion.

RENO, NEVADA, TRAIN RIDE

6:00 A.M. came earlier than Greg expected. He woke up and did his morning routine. First thing he ate a banana followed by a grapefruit and two boiled eggs. That combination seemed to always hit his gut real good allowing him to empty out his bowels which prevented the need to visit the toilet during the day.

After he S/S/S (includes a Hollywood shower) and bushed his teeth, Greg then dressed in slacks, a nice Hawaiian shirt, and black walking shoes.

Greg called a taxi who said he would be there in five minutes. By the time he hopped in the taxi it was 07:45. He gave the taxi driver the address who then plugged it into his Google Maps, and they proceeded over to Ami's apartment.

Standing out in front were the two delicious Japanese ladies wearing their "come get me quick" outfits along with expert makeup jobs and new wave Japanese hair styles seen with many top Japanese female singers.

EXT. DAY. TAXI AT AMI'S RESIDENCE

Greg hopped out of the taxi then gestured for the ladies to get in which they complied and hopped in the taxi followed by Greg who shut the door and informed the taxi driver to take them to the Oakland Train station.

The taxi driver could look up in the rearview mirror directly back at Greg and shook his head with a smile conveying, *You lucky dog.*

Ami and Hikaru each wore exotic perfume. One might get the impression they were two of the best-looking-and-smelling hookers on the planet. But in reality, Ami and Hikaru were just two clean-cut Japanese ladies struggling but slowly getting their way through a good university at an age several years older than most of their classmates.

These were not virgins; they had enough life experiences of their own. But they also were not *fools*. They read Greg and knew exactly what kind of gentleman he was.

Ami had a lot of exposure to Greg. He was kind, gentle and never assuming. Ami knew, however, Hikaru loved sex and if she wanted it bad enough would pursue Greg. In a way she felt this would be a good test for Greg to see how much willpower he had to turn down an extraordinary woman like Hikaru who would use him and drain him as she fulfilled her lust and her schemes. Rich men had an attraction for Hikaru. By all accounts and his generosity, it was obvious Greg had money. Ami was not too far off the mark.

Greg lived a frugal life. He bought a new car every ten years only because it was time to toss it aside for new reliable transportation. He didn't envy people with fancy cars. To them it was an object of wealth and a projection. To Greg it was merely transportation. Greg lived very close to a lot of millionaires in Point Loma, but his home was far more modest. And with his wife and sons gone, it was now simply a place to stay that afforded him quick access to Ski Beach, his favorite, or Ocean Beach from time to time.

Ami and Hikaru were caught up in a conversation they had started before the cab arrived and seemed excited to go on the trip.

EXT. DAY OAKLAND CALIFORNIA AMTRAK STATION.

They arrived at the Oakland Train station with plenty of time to spare, just the way Greg liked to travel. He paid the taxi and gave him a very generous tip. The taxi driver liked his passenger and knew this guy must be special having the two chicks with him going to Reno for the night as Hikaru had blurted out when he asked them where they were taking the train to. The taxi driver knew Reno was just like Vegas. *What happens in Vegas stays in Vegas.* Hence the Taxi driver had intriguing thoughts as he smiled at Greg leaving with the two women showing fabulous posteriors as they walked towards the ticket agent area of the train station not far from the passenger drop-off area.

After Greg and the women were gone and walking away on the sidewalk exposing and the nice image of two women with posteriors to remember, the taxi driver said softly to himself as he smiled at his tip:

TAXI DRIVER
You lucky son of a bitch.

The perfume scent they left behind in the TAXI added to surreal notions evoked in the Taxi driver. He breathed it in with a modest ahhhh.

In due time Greg, Ami, and Hikaru were in comfortable seats on the train facing each other. Greg sat on the seat directly across from Ami and Hikaru.

<u>INT. DAY CALTRAIN COMMUTER TRAIN TO SACRAMENTO.</u>

The commuter train they took to Sacramento had a few stops on the way, but it got up to speed quickly and on the flat area running from Fairfield to Davis, it was doing around 90 miles per hour. After the stop at Davis, it went to Sacramento without further stops until it arrived at the Sacramento train station.

Greg picked this train to give them a brief stopover in Sacramento where he wanted to go to old down for a bit.

The train made good time and they had forty-five minutes to kill so Greg suggested:

GREG
We are a block away from Sacramento's old town that
has the museum and a few other things, want to go
over there for a few minutes?

AMI
Sure, why not?

None of the three had luggage; they were traveling light. Hikaru was carrying a backpack that had a few items in it for Ami as well. They would share carrying the backpack.

It took them no more than five minutes to walk from the train station to right by the museum.

GREG
If you want, we can go in here for twenty or thirty
minutes and be back in time to catch our AMTRAK
train."

AMI
Okay.

97

<u>INT. DAY. CALIFORNIA STATE RAILROAD MUSEUM, SACRAMENTO CALIFORNIA.</u>

Greg bought them three thickets and they went in the famous State of California Railroad Museum where they have some beautiful trains inside. Greg was very familiar with this place and had taken his wife through it the last time when he deposited his son at UC Berkeley on a short trip then.

Greg knew they didn't have much time, so he quickly took them through all the main exhibits, which took about twenty-five minutes as he was watching his watch keeping track of the time.

The main exhibit area in the center of the State of California Railroad Museum has some very old trains that have been painted and restored and look fabulous.

Ami and Hikaru were snapping a lot of photos with their cell phones. Ami requested a couple photographs of Greg and her together. Hikaru had to have her fair share as well. Soon it was time, they needed to get back to the train station.

GREG

We must leave now. Our train will be arriving real soon.

Greg escorted Ami and Hikaru from the California State Railroad Museum and promptly walked over to the Amtrak train station a block away.

They were standing on the platform when the Amtrak train pulled in. It had three new locomotives on the front and seven large two-level passenger cars and a couple baggage cars and what appeared to be a few Amtrak Box Cars and Road Railer cars behind them.

<u>EXT. DAY SACRAMENTO TRAIN STATION.</u>

The three locomotives on the front of the train were the new Siemens Mobility's Charger locomotives. These new locomotives have the latest safety systems including Crash Energy Management and Positive Train Control. These locomotives have 4,400 horsepower using 16-cylinder Cummins QSK95 diesel engines. The traction motors on the wheels have modern control systems and Alternating Current (AC) propulsion. Even though it will not go at the design speeds it's capable of, those locomotives were designed to run at speeds up to 125 MPH. The Cummins QSK95 diesel engines are equipped with the latest Tier-4 emissions technology, reducing nitrogen oxide by over eighty-nine percent and particulate matter by ninety-five percent, and provide an average of ten-percent savings in diesel fuel consumption.

This type of locomotive currently operated out of San Diego and Los Angeles; hence Greg had observed them a few times already. There were track segments between San Diego and Los Angeles along Camp Pendleton where trains typically ran 105 miles per hour which greatly allowed them to make up for lost time on the slower track segments. I wonder if they are allowed to go faster by Camp Pendleton now?

Greg had reserved them a nice cabin in the middle of the two-level passenger car for this leg of the trip. They would have privacy as well as a first call to the dining car because of that. He wanted to make sure the two women enjoyed the view in the dining car because first serving coincided with the portion of the trip climbing through the mountains and they would be sitting there observing Donner Lake as they passed by. Some of the most picturesque landscape one could ever imagine. Plus, on a lot of the segments, there were no roads. The only way you could see a lot of the landscape they would observe would be either through hiking or on the train.

<u>INT. DAY PRIVATE ROOM ON AMTRAK CALIFORNIA ZEPHYR HEADING TO DENVER VIA RENO AND SALT LAKE CITY.</u>

Ami and Hikaru seemed thrilled they had a private cabin, which added nicely to the trip. They could talk without others hearing them. And part of the conversation they shifted into Japanese, which Greg didn't mind because he understood much of what they were saying. It never donned on Ami to ask Greg if he knew any Japanese so she could tell Hikaru to watch her language. Girl's talk is one thing, but you might not want him to know some of the stuff you are saying.

Soon after the train left the station, Hikaru let the first salvos fly speaking in Japanese.

Hikaru
I bet it would be great to have sex on the train.

Ami responded in Japanese.

AMI
If you had your lover, of course.

Greg kept his poker face and never let on during the entire trip he understood what they were saying about seventy-five percent of the time.

It didn't seem long after they left, when an Amtrak employee knocked on their slightly open door.

GREG
Come on in.

AMTRAK EMPLOYEE

Sir, I wanted to let you know we'll be giving first call
for dinner in fifteen minutes. The place fills up fast. I
recommend you line up now so that you get a good
seat.

GREG
Thank you very much for the tip.

The young Amtrak employee probably in his early thirties responded.

AMTRAK EMPLOYEE
My pleasure, sir.

Greg then suggested to Ami and Hikaru.

GREG
I think we should line up now for lunch. I want to get a table in the middle of the dining car where we have good visibility on both sides of the track.

HIKARU
Can I leave my backpack here?

GREG
Yes, there is a locker there with a key. You can put it in there and lock it.

HIKARU
That's nice and handy.

GREG
Amtrak thinks of a lot of problems and mitigates them.

A couple minutes later they were some of the first people in line from the cars with cabins, located behind the dining car in the train. General Seating was in front of the dining car where several cars with just seats existed on the upper level and snack bars and bathrooms were located on the lower level with luggage racks. The general seating cars would not be called to the dinner or allowed in until the second seating almost forty-five minutes later or longer depending on how many of the first-call passengers left. Their entrance to the dining car would be blocked until then.

<u>INT. DAY. AMTRAK DINING CAR GOING THROUGH THE SIERRA MOUNTAINS HEADING TO RENO.</u>

Thanks to the tip that would soon earn the Amtrak employee a generous tip from Greg, they were offered the selection of just about anywhere they wanted to sit. But based on Greg's prior trips, he knew right in the middle was the best sitting area with the best view.

Amtrak has a relationship with a Sacramento-based Historical Society. And during many train trips, they have members board the train and provide a guided tour as the train goes through the mountains and beyond. They get off at Sparks, Nevada, and catch the next train coming back in the opposite direction.

These Historical Society members give a wonderful description of the history of this rail line which is one of America's greatest stories of the era. All the folklore is discussed including information about building the rail line and why Donner Lake is named after the Donner party who were snowed in and trapped and resulted in cannibalism. It was a terrible tragedy.

While the train was traveling through some of the most incredible vistas and landscape their drinks were served. All three chose wine and the wine going down at such a point in the trip was very satisfying. Greg facing the two women could tell they were very happy. They felt safe and were traveling with the perfect male companion, both of whom respected Greg who was still handsome and very kindhearted.

Greg's wife would be happy knowing Greg had some companionship. She knew her selfish betrayal of him was probably breaking his heart into pieces and if he was able to scratch out some enjoyment in life in this fashion, it would make her happy. She of course would be disappointed because Greg had no intentions of ever informing her of his personal activities moving forward, since there was no point in it.

Amtrak usually has really good food on this segment of the trip. This Amtrak operation through the California Mountains was indeed a tourist operation. A lot of people got off at Reno and a lot of people got on at Reno going in both directions as many people took the train as part of their holiday to the gambling Mecca. Just like Vegas, there was plenty of women, booze, drugs, and gambling.

Many people lost their shirts in Reno. A few of Greg's friends and acquaintances who gambled a lot said, "It's a hell of a lot harder to make money gambling in Reno than it is in Las Vegas. It's as if people are more desperate in Reno. And by all appearances, Reno doesn't have nearly the density as Las Vegas, but Reno is also close to Lake Tahoe, where upward mobile people have second homes and wind up down the hill in Reno risking those second homes."

Greg had a friend who was a former casino owner. Greg didn't particularly like to gamble, it didn't turn him on because he knew the facts it was nothing more than a game to see how fast you can lose money. His friend sold his casino operation because he got sick and tired of dealing with all the people who committed suicide staying in his casino hotels. He made a lot of money operating casinos it, but it turned out not to be his cup of tea.

Greg enjoyed his entrée of Salmon and rice and a few vegetables. One of the ladies had a sandwich, the other a quiche.

If you have a cabin on Amtrak, the food comes free with it. But you must pay for your alcohol drinks. By the time they finished their meal they had each two glasses of wine and were delighted with the desserts.

Greg gave their Amtrak waiter a very generous tip, which added greatly to his smile. The waiter, Ernesto, was of Filipino extraction and a gentleman.

As they were departing Greg suggested:

GREG
Why don't we go to the observation car?

AMI
That sounds good.

Amtrak has eight trains that go east and west every day across the West in America. One very scenic route from Chicago is up through Montana out to Seattle called the Empire Builder. Another route leaves Chicago and makes its way through Denver, Salt Lake City, then on to Sacramento and Oakland called the California Zephyr. A third route goes from Chicago, down through Kansas and Southern Colorado, over Raton Pass, into Albuquerque, through Arizona, then on to Los Angeles called the Southwest Limited, used to be the Super Chief. Another route goes from Los Angeles down through Arizona, New Mexico, Texas, and all the way to New Orleans called the Sunset Limited.

Greg and the two well-dressed ladies made their way to the observation car that had plenty of open seats facing out to one side or the other for sightseeing. In their cabin they could only see one side of the track, where up on the observation side, they could swing around easily and see the other side. These cars were put on these tourists' orientated trains for families with kids and certain time of the day, they showed movies, especially after dark. You could watch one of the recent movies for free in this car that had good sound quality and a decent screen. The seats swiveled around so you could face the large screen.

When the movies were not playing, soft music was in the background.

In due time the Historical Society people came through and were discussing some of the history of the area they were passing through.

At times the train slowed down from climbing, but other times going downhill it sped up. In due time as the dining wound down, a lot of children were coming into the lounge car being loud and obnoxious.

AMI
Greg, may we go back to the private room?

GREG
Sure.

The private room had a private toilet. Both women had to use it. Hikaru went in first and shut the door and did her business. Then Ami took her turn. Greg went in a while later and relieved himself. The sound isolation in the bathroom was not very good. Greg overheard their conversation and everything Hikaru said in Japanese.

HIKARU
If he tries to have sex with us, I will probably let him
do it.

AMI
Don't be ridiculous.

HIKARU
Haven't you ever had any notion to get it on with him?

AMI
Not really, though he is a sweet man and I like him.

HIKARU
Well, I'll let you know, if he ever tries to have sex with
me, I'll find out how good he is.

The two girls burst out laughing. Ami thought Hikaru was toying with her. But she had no idea that Hikaru was being honest. Hikaru was developing a secret lust for Greg, and it wouldn't take much for Greg to initiate it.

Greg was taking his time doing his business, surfing the internet with his iPhone. He dismissed the girl talk and didn't ever think he would do what Hikaru wanted. However, if Ami wanted to have sex with him, he might just do it because making love to her and looking at her face would seem like he was time traveling back about twenty-five years with his wife. It was a pleasant thought, nevertheless.

After Greg came out of the toilet, he noticed the girls were reading books they brought along. It appears they had enough of the sightseeing.

The private room was designed for three people. There were three comfortable chairs and a bed folded out at night double wide for two people and a second bunk folded down which had adequate room for one adult or two kids. Since this would be a day only trip those beds would not be set up. Greg was happy the seat the women left him faced forward so he could do sightseeing. He didn't bring any books along nor did he have any intention of reading on this trip. It was quiet now. Greg wondered if Hikaru was hoping he would bring up the subject of sex so she could suggest ménage à trois.

The train continued along as the three enjoyed each other's company and Greg enjoyed the sightseeing. If Greg read the book Hikaru was reading, it would be a foregone conclusion she was definitely game. She wasn't a slut and didn't sleep around, but if there was a scenario that developed that suited her objectives, then copious amounts of intercourse would beget a legitimate potential suitor.

The Sierra Nevada Mountain Range had a huge history in gold mining, exploration, and the Transcontinental Railroad. The original rail line that ascended these mountains had huge wood trestle bridges and snow removal was a bitter challenge. Oddly it seems one mountain railroad and location to the next had similar attributes. The tracks often followed a creek or a shallow river that swelled with spring snow runoff.

The bookworms Ami and Hikaru had their noses buried in their books in a way gave some sort of relief because what conversation could Greg have with a couple young women less than half his age? They were from a different generation and a different world. Plus, the lack of conversation added positively to the sightseeing. The ride was comfortable.

If you ever get a private room on Amtrak, be sure and get one in the middle of the car. Greg once rented a five-passenger cabin at the end of one of those cars. You are right over the wheels, and you hear a lot of noise. But the advantage is it's on the lower level where the bathrooms and showers are in case one of your groups is in the toilet, you have quick access to another. And just like Hikaru speculated, sex on the train is great.

After a while the intercom came to life and the train conductor announced they would be soon stopping at Truckee and passengers could get off the train for twenty minutes and stretch their legs or make a fast trip to a nearby coffee shop.

Truckee has a history. It lay right near areas where gold fever once caused many men building the Transcontinental Railroad to abandon their work and take off for the gold fever. Card sharks, women for hire and a lot of other nefarious activities existed back then. Men would come down out of the mountains with their pockets full of gold and get on a train here and either go to San Francisco where they would live good for six months then have to go back to work, or continue on to Reno where they would lose it in a month and be back.

There are now 16,000 people living in and around Truckee. It still has that small-town look, but it's spreading out slowly and growing due to the proximity of Lake Tahoe. A lot of people chose to live on the other side of the state line because Nevada pays no state income taxes but they use the facilities in Truckee and Tahoe. The Amtrak stop and the I-80 freeway that goes by carrying a lot of Reno and San Francisco destined passengers keeps a positive influence on growth to the community. Truckee is not growing alarmingly fast but it is growing consistently year over year.

<u>EXT. DAY TRUCKEE TRAIN STATION.</u>

<u>SHOT GREG, AMI, AND HIKARU GETTING OFF THE AMTRAK TRAIN AND GOING TO NEARBY COFFEE SHOP.</u>

Greg and the two ladies got off the train and right across the street is several shops, coffee shops, and bars. They went into a coffee shop and got three nice coffees then walked past a couple souvenir shops then back over to the train. Amtrak was removing one of the locomotives off the train. It didn't need it as the train was now over the mountains and going downhill from here. If a person continued on the train in Salt Lake City, they would add another engine and a few more roadrailer cars for Denver.

It felt good to get off the train and stretch a bit. From the side of the train with a lot of other passengers milling around Amtrak employees patiently waited with walkie-talkies on their sides. The lead locomotive decoupled from the train and went to a siding and was shut down. Soon a couple men climbed into the lead locomotive cab and in a few minutes, they heard the conductor's walkie-talkie squawking a bit as he was standing not too far from the group.

A few moments later the Amtrak Conductor asked passengers to re-board the train.

<u>SHOT GREG, AMI, AND HIKARU GETTING BACK ON THE AMTRAK TRAIN.</u>

Amtrak Conductor warned us as we got off the train, the train whistle would go off five minutes before departure to warn people to proceed back to the train promptly. In a short while the train started moving following the Truckee River down towards Reno.

The rail line goes right through the center of Reno. A number of years ago, the railroad and the city built the big ditch through Reno. It used to be rail traffic snarled downtown and it was a huge problem. The city and the railroad slowly dug the two-mile-long trench dropping the rail line below city streets and built bridges over the trench so now here are no rail crossings just bridges.

Amtrak stops right in the heart of the City. You can get off the train and into a casino in about five minutes gambling. Harrah's in Reno is a very nice casino and hotel is nearby.

Greg assumed these two Japanese ladies enjoyed Sushi and Harrah's had a very nice sushi restaurant. The two rooms he booked at Harrah's were adjacent to each other and suites, with sofas, TVs, and other amenities. Each room was designed for their wealthier clients and cost $320.00 a night.

During the last hour of the train ride, Greg could tell the women were getting a little sleepy and probably needed a nap, but unfortunately the suite wasn't converted for nighttime. Usually, people in the cabins (private rooms) after they are called for dinner and while they are eating dinner, the Amtrak employees would enter their cabin and make up the beds.

People often went to the observation car after dinner and watched a movie, then came back to their cabin and went to bed.

Amtrak trains travel across the deserts at night. The main reason is speed restrictions. Daylight hours they are restricted to fifty-five miles per hour due to warping of the rails could lead to a safety issue. But in the evenings and nights they are allowed to travel at ninety miles per hour. Once Amtrak trains get past Sparks, Nevada, they pick up speed.

Greg's Amtrak train number six heads to Chicago. When they traveled back Sunday, they would get on train number five in Reno at 9:15 on Sunday morning to head back unless the women wanted to stay longer in Reno, they would catch a flight back to San Francisco or Oakland.

<u>EXT. LATE AFTERNOON. AMTRAK STATION IN RENO.</u>

<u>SHOT. AMI, HIKARU, AND GREG GET OFF THE AMTRAK TRAIN AND HEAD FOR HARRAH'S HOTEL/CAINO.</u>

The ladies were glad to get off the train in Reno and were pleasantly surprised it was a short walk to their hotel. Even though they had traveled quite a few hours on a train, they were still looking fresh. The clerk at the hotel that gave them room keys was smiling and probably had some evil thoughts that Greg was their sugar daddy and would be spanking them in a short period of time.

<u>EXT. LATE AFTERNOON. HARRAH'S HOTEL/CASINO IN RENO.</u>

Greg went into his room and the two ladies their room. They would rest for a bit then freshen up and head out to see the casino and the sights.

Predictably Ami and Hikaru decided to lay down and rest for a while in their double queen-size beds. Greg followed suit, set his alarm on his cell phone for two hours' rest and got horizontal himself. Ami didn't want to wrinkle her clothes, so she stripped down to bra and panties and hopped in her bed nearest the window. Hikaru thought that was a good idea and did it as well. They had a change of clothes in the backpack for tomorrow but those clothes were more casual shorts and tops.

Two hours was what the doctor ordered. Greg felt great after the nap. The women felt blessed and took their turn using the bathroom sprucing up a bit.

Good hotels have all the bare necessities including throw away shaving razors and small bottles of shaving lotion, toothpaste, and toothbrushes and mouthwash, along with soap shampoo, etc.

Greg was glad he didn't have to go down to the bottom floor where a few convenience stores existed to provide travelers like Greg those items. You pay for what you get. One of those $59-a-night special hotel would be really stripped down with none of these items.

A shower has a way of reinvigorating the soul, and Greg gladly took advantage of all the amenities. If he wanted a drink, the refrigerator had beers, sodas, and snacks. When you check out you get billed for usage in a lot of hotels. Greg wouldn't be spending enough time in the room to bother with snacks provided.

Right after Greg got out of the shower and dried off and was dressing, his cell phone was ringing.

AMI
Greg?

GREG
Hello, yes, this is Greg Speaking.

AMI
Hello Greg, this is Ami, we are ready to go out now if
you want.

GREG
I'm getting ready now, I'll knock on your door in about
fifteen minutes.

AMI
Alright, we'll see you then.

True to his word, in fifteen minutes Greg was at Ami and Hikaru's hotel door and knocked. Soon afterwards, they were at the elevator heading down to the lobby.

GREG
If you ladies are hungry, the hotel/casino has a good
sushi restaurant.

AMI
We would like to go throw a few coins in some slot
machines before we eat.

GREG
Okay, the entrance to the casino is right over there.

EXT. LATE AFTERNOON. HARRAH'S CASINO IN RENO.

Greg led the two gorgeous ladies with fresh makeup into the casino where many people were at their gambling addictions. The sound from all the slot machines created a cacophony that added to the circus-like atmosphere.

There was an interesting dichotomy of people that come to Reno from all over the West, but San Francisco, Sacramento, Seattle, Portland, and Salt Lake City area were the source of many of the patrons. Some of the locals were here, probably only because they came for dinner and a show. After dinner, Greg planned on taking Ami and Hikaru to an Elvis Presley show. Some of the Elvis impersonators had voices remarkably like Elvis. With the clothes and the makeup on, they seemed so real.

These working girls didn't have a lot of money and Greg knew that so as they came up to a couple slot machines Ami and Hikaru sat down in front of, Greg gave them each $100 bills to throw in the machines. Betting twenty-five cents at a time would take them a while to pull the lever on the one-arm bandits.

Some of the routine local gamblers had been playing these two machines hard for several weeks and they just didn't pay out, so they moved to others. Just around the time the two ladies bet the $100 Greg gave them Ami got lucky and won $500. Ami was then done for the night as far as she was concerned. Pulling the lever on the slot machine got boring after ten minutes.

Hikaru wasn't too far behind in tiring from the one arm bandit when Greg suggested their next activities.

GREG
Shall we go get a bite to eat then see a show?

It had been a while since they were in the mountains, and they were starting to feel the initial stages of desiring something to eat.

Ami smiled as she stuffed her winning printout from the slot machine into her purse.

AMI
I'll take you up on the sushi.

GREG
Let's go over to one of the cashiers first so you get your
cash and don't forget to cash it out.

AMI
Good idea.

There was virtually no line at the cashier's window thus Ami got her cash and was pleased she got lucky.

Greg led Ami and Hikaru to the hotel's sushi restaurant. Greg had gone to a great sushi restaurant in San Diego for many years called Yakitori II on Sports Arena Blvd. in the same small mall where Phil's Grill, a successful barbecue place exists next to the Sports Arena. Phil's Grill now has that restaurant space for special events. Luckily, Sapporo's down in Ocean Beach is a fabulous sushi restaurant that took their place for a few years as one of the favorite sushi restaurants for the area. Unfortunately, Sapporo's shut down during COVID. Greg and his wife knew the owner.

<u>INT. EVENING SUSHI RESTAURANT</u>

Greg knew sitting at a table would not be as fun as sitting up at the sushi counter where many of the sushi chefs are very entertaining at times. Greg knew that as pretty as these two ladies looked tonight; the sushi chef would be very accommodative. The sushi restaurant appeared half empty. The saw it was a party of three easily to accommodate.

Maître d'
Where would you like to sit?

GREG
I think we would like to sit up at the sushi counter.

Maître d'
Alright, follow me, sir.

Greg, Ami, and Hikaru were led up to three seats next to where two other couples were also sitting.

JAPANESE SUSHI CHEF
Konichiwa!

This Japanese sushi chef closest to them was smiling. He was probably pleased to see the two Japanese ladies. Any man with good taste would be delighted.

Ami and Hikaru responded with big smiles.

AMI AND HIKARU
Konbawa!

JAPANESE SUSHI CHEF
Would you all like something to drink?

AMI
I'll have a light beer.

Hikaru
I'll also have a light beer.

GREG
I would like hot sake and a glass of plum wine.

The sushi menu was at each of their placemats. In due course the three ordered Maguro, Salmon, and other sushi, followed by Spider Rolls, and Rainbow Rolls.

Greg noticed there weren't any California Rolls on the menu and asked the sushi chef named Kentō.

GREG
Why isn't California Rolls on the menu?

KENTŌ
Sir, we have Nevada Rolls. They are about the same except our Nevada Rolls are gold plated.

GREG
Probably all that leftover gold in Virginia City and Ponderosa.

KENTŌ
Sir, to be honest they sneak in gold from the lost Dutchman mine.

GREG
Isn't that one of the mines Howard Hughes bought?

KENTŌ
Certainly was. Howard Hughes bought over one half of all the mining claims in Nevada.

GREG
Yeah, he was smart like a fox. Those claims got extremely valuable when gold hit $2000 an ounce.

KENTŌ
Yes, and gold mines were reopened in Nevada, Utah, and Colorado.

Their drinks were served, and the ladies toasted Greg.

AMI AND HIKARU
Kanpai - Kanpai!

By the time the group was eating sushi, they started engaging in conversation from the two other couples. One can almost guess the kinds of questions that may come up at a sushi bar in Reno.

FIRST COUPLE'S HUSBAND
Where are you guys from?

GREG
We live in the San Francisco Bay area of California.

FIRST COUPLE'S HUSBAND
Come over here to enjoy the casino?

GREG
Actually, I'm a train buff and we rode Amtrak here just to enjoy the train ride.

FIRST COUPLE'S HUSBAND
I've not been on a train in a long, long time. How was it?

GREG
This train had nice equipment and a very friendly staff. On the front end it had three new locomotives until we pulled into Truckee, then they took one off, because they didn't need it. They have a turnaround, and it will probably be hooked to the next westbound train in the morning.

FIRST COUPLE'S HUSBAND
What was the seating like?

GREG
We had a private room for most of the trip, but we spent a little time in the observation car and in the dining car when we had lunch going over the mountains.

FIRST COUPLE'S HUSBAND
How was the food?

GREG
It was outstanding. I like Amtrak.

FIRST COUPLE'S HUSBAND
What do you do in California?

GREG
I'm a logistics consultant and these two ladies are in school, just about to finish up. How about yourself?"

FIRST COUPLE'S HUSBAND
I work for Boeing in Seattle.

GREG
I bet that's fun.

FIRST COUPLE'S HUSBAND
(BOEING ENGINEER-LARRY)
It's stressful, especially when one of our aircraft is perceived to have a design problem. By the way, my name is Larry.

GREG
Larry, my name is Greg. Good luck on your aircraft.

FIRST COUPLE'S HUSBAND
(BOEING ENGINEER-LARRY)
Thanks.

The second couple joined the conversation.

RANCHER FROM WYOMING
(a.k.a. SYMES)
Good evening, Larry, and Greg. My name is Symes. I'm a rancher from Wyoming.

GREG
Please meet you Symes. Come here to hit the one arm bandits?

RANCHER FROM WYOMING
(SYMES)
I flew my wife to Reno in our private plane so they could see some shows.

After they had enough sushi and drinks, Greg could see the two ladies were starting to get bored and restless.

Greg had nothing in common with the two couples and I knew it was time to get to the show.

GREG
Well, ladies and gentlemen, we must leave now to go see a show. Kentō, can you please give me the check?

Kentō was quick and Greg had the check in his hand in a couple minutes. I pulled out the cash required plus a sizeable tip out of my billfold and put it in the bill binder and handed it back to Kentō.

GREG
Keep the change.

KENTŌ
Thank you, sir.

<u>INT. EVENING. ELVIS IMPERSONATOR SHOW RENO NEVADA</u>

Greg and the two ladies made it to the Elvis show before the crowd got there allowing him to purchase three good seats in the middle about seven rows back from the front and the stage. The first performer came out and did a bang-up job followed by a couple others and the show lasted over one and half hours.

GREG
This Elvis music sounds utterly outstanding.

AMI
This show is definitely worth seeing.

Hikaru and Ami were having a good time, sometimes singing along and really into the music. After the show Greg asked Hikaru and Ami what they would like to do next.

GREG
Would you ladies like to go for a walk or go back to
the casino?

AMI
In Japan we have taxi tours. I have a lot of extra cash I
won from the slot machine, why don't we get into a taxi
and get a quick tour of the city?

GREG
Great idea.

Greg walked Ami and Hikaru to the front entrance and approached the Bellhop.

GREG
Could you please signal a taxi?

BELLHOP
Yes sir. One moment please.

Within thirty seconds a taxi pulled ahead from a line of them half a block away and pulled up right in front of Greg. The three hopped in the taxi.

TAXI DRIVER
Where to, sir?

GREG
These girls would like a tour of the city if you wouldn't
mind driving around for a bit?

TAXI DRIVER
Sure thing, sir, I got the time if you got the money.

GREG
I'm glad we are on the same page.

The Taxi was soon driving all over the city. They didn't stop and just drove-by each point of interest. To allow the passengers to see the venus, the Taxi driver momentarily stopped at the Coop Gallery, the National Automobile Museum, The Discovery, Nevada Museum of Art, Hawkins House, the Downtown and Truckee Riverwalk, Saint Thomas Aquinas Cathedral right in the heart of Sin City, and of course the famous Reno Arch.

AMI
Greg, can you take our picture under the Reno Arch?

GREG.
Sure. Sir, can you pull over and stop here for a couple
minutes?

The taxi driver was very accommodative. After about an hour, the group saw all they desired.

GREG
Sir, could you please drive us back to the hotel?

The Taxi driver was given a very nice tip. Greg paid for the taxi.

AMI
I want to give the driver a tip.

Ami handed the Taxi driver one of those fresh and crisp $100 bills she received from the casino cashier.

It was a joyous moment for the Taxi driver who gave Greg a wink. It would not be the first or the last time Daddy Warbucks brought a couple lovely women to Reno for a variety of activities.

GREG
We need to be at the train station by 9:00. Unless you
really want to do something else, we should get some
sleep.

AMI
I do not want to go back to the casino. I'm done.

HIKARU
I'm good too.

The three went up to their rooms and prepared to go to bed.

HIKARU
If we didn't have to get up so early in the morning, I would call him up and ask him if he wanted to have ménage à trois.

AMI
I would never do that, he's my personal friend.

HIKARU
What you really mean is you wouldn't want to share him with me?

AMI
If I ever decided to have sex with Greg, of course I would not want to share him with you. I would want to keep him for myself on a permanent basis.

HIKARU
You wouldn't worry that I would steal him from you?

AMI
You might have wonderful boobs, but I look like his wife. He has an attraction for me.

HIKARU
So, every time he looks at you, it's like he's looking at his wife?

AMI
Yes. I know he loves me as a friend and would always want to keep me as a friend.

HIKARU
What if I offered myself to him, don't you think he might like it?

AMI
When people recklessly have recreational sex, it doesn't last. A friendship can last forever.

HIKARU
You know, Ami, that's why I like you so much. You are so clearheaded and wise. I wish I had an older sister like you when I was younger.

AMI
Hikaru, well, you got an older sister now! The two girls
hugged and went to bed.

Greg took another shower, air dried his hair, then set his alarm.

Morning came too fast, but Greg calculated he managed to get eight hours of sleep
without having to get up in the middle of the night to urinate. He was so grateful. It was
now 7:00 A.M. and he knew women took a long time to get ready, so he called Ami for
a backup wakeup call. When she answered she sounded groggy.

AMI
Hello.

GREG
Ami, this is Greg, just wanted to give you a wakeup call
so that you would have time to get ready.

AMI
Thanks. I would have slept and missed the train.

GREG
Call me when you are ready.

Ami shook Hikaru who was always hard to wake up. Without Ami she would have
missed half her classes at the University.

The women both showered and put on their makeup and put on shorts and t-shirts.
Hikaru's boobs added a dimension to how she presented herself wearing a t-shirt. Ami's
extra-pretty face and her excellent-looking rear end made up for any shortcomings she
might have with her chest. By 08:00 the two ladies were ready. There was no point in
hanging out in the hotel room. Ami called Greg's cellphone.

AMI
Greg, we are ready to leave now.

GREG
So am I, I'm leaving the room now, meet you outside.

Ami and Hikaru walked out of their room and met Greg in the hallway and Greg had
done a phone-in checkout so all they had to do is leave. But it was still kind of early.

As they entered the hotel lobby, they smelled bacon and other things associated with
breakfast and noticed the large event room next to the lobby was open and people were
going in for a free morning breakfast provided to all hotel guests. They had an hour to
kill and Greg had a slight hunger and knew they would not have lunch on the train for
another four hours almost, so he suggested:

GREG
Do you ladies care to go for some coffee and breakfast?
The smell had hit the girls too who were instantly
interested as well.

HIKARU
Sounds good to me.

Greg led Ami and Hikaru into the event room and there were a series of tables with
a lot of nice things to eat. You can tell the quality of a hotel by the quality of their free
breakfasts. This hotel had fantastic rooms and breakfast was second to none. And to
make it even more pleasant it was right next to the train station, which Greg really
liked.

Greg had to have some of that great-smelling bacon. The sausages looked really good
so he had some of that.

 Reno has a lot of Asian gamblers that come in from San Francisco. Chinese love
gambling. In addition to fried potatoes, they also had rice. When Greg was a road
warrior his breakfast often included, Portuguese sausage, eggs, and rice.

There was a small tray of Portuguese sausage, allowing Greg to have his preferred
breakfast. To top it off, he was with a woman who looked like his wife so it took him back
in time and provided him a subtle delight such that he would relish for quite a while.
This trip is what the doctor ordered. It was a fantastic break from his job and all the
recent activity that even though was monumental in his life, especially the exhilaration
he felt flying around Mars. The two pretty ladies provided Greg a companionship that
added great to the ambience and fortified his happiness.

Since Greg stopped communicating with his long-distant wife, because there was no
point while she was living her final phase of her life in Japan, he didn't bother telling
her he had a job that multiplied his income by more than triple. His entire check was
going into the stock market in S&P500 stocks.

Greg's stock portfolio was growing fast. He now had more disposable income than
what he had before he had to start sending his wife money in Japan. She left for Japan
with a lot of money and probably didn't need Greg's money, but he kept sending her
the money on automatic payments which demonstrated his commitment to her despite
her estranged behavior.

In the future Greg would be in a position to help Ami and Hikaru who he psychologically
adopted. He was more than their sugar daddy and Daddy Warbucks. He had grown
fond of them and would help them whenever he could.

Sitting at a table, the three enjoyed their breakfast and coffee. A number of people
Greg's age were giving him dirty stares. They naturally assumed this older gentleman
had a couple of sex toys with him. They were partially correct, but there had never been
any sex, nor had there been any notion of it. It wasn't in the cards.

They finished their breakfast and Greg wished they had not checked out of their room so he could brush his teeth, but being a road warrior where he had to buy a toothbrush and toothpaste at the airport he would do so now.

As soon as they were leaving the breakfast room Greg suggested:

GREG
Let's stop over at one of these stores in case you ladies
would like some souvenirs.

They went inside and looked around. Greg picked up three toothbrushes and three small travel toothpaste tubes. The two girls were attracted to cowboy hats and with all of Ami's cash from hitting the jackpot they decided to buy a couple to wear back. If the store had sold boots, they probably would have bought them as well.

They all gathered at the checkout stand where a beautiful lady of Indian extraction and perfect teeth and smile greeted them.

STORE CLERK
Did you find everything you wanted?

GREG
Yes, but a little more, it seems.

AMI
Greg, I can pay for the hats.

GREG
No, let me get them as a souvenir for the trip.

Ami was beaming as Greg pulled out his credit card and purchased everything.

LEAVING RENO

The three then walked over to the train station and patiently waited on their train. Sometimes Amtrak trains can be seriously late, even up to eight hours or more because of weather conditions or equipment malfunction.

In the train station the digital display showed train number five, to San Francisco was on time.

When Greg was a kid and his dad took him on Union Pacific trains on long trips between Kansas and Colorado, he felt exhilaration each time he watched the train coming into the station. Today was no exception. Because he was born in November, he was not allowed to take the driver's education course in high school with his classmates. In Colorado teenagers were not permitted to get a driver's license without proof of completing driver's education classes, which the school reported to the DMV when you completed. Poor Greg didn't have a car and couldn't drive. He had a girlfriend that lived thirty miles away so he would hop on the train to go visit her. His girlfriend's father had a nice Cessna-172 aircraft and would fly him home.

But that romance was never meant to be in a meaningful relationship because the girlfriend's father didn't approve of Greg.

Maybe it was because he was a Methodist, and his girlfriend was a Catholic. He would never know and that was so long ago it really didn't matter.

One thing he did know for sure was that woman most likely now looked like a grandmother and a hag and no longer the beautiful young blonde she once was. And here he was with two beautiful young Japanese ladies less than half his age who would most likely do the big "A" if he wanted it. His high school girlfriend would be amazed if she knew what transpired in Gregs life. From submarines, ships, aircraft, and now interplanetary travel on one of America's most secret aircraft ever designed.

All in all, it was a pleasant trip. It was short, but they made the most of it. The private cabin on the way back to Oakland because of the time, they didn't have to take a second train like they did on their way to Reno made it an enjoyable outing.

Train number five pulled into Reno and stopped. This train had different engines on it compared to what took them to Reno. Greg was familiar with these engines and recalled on one trip to Colorado right after 9/11 when it stopped in Albuquerque, New Mexico, it had four GE P42DC locomotives on the front and they looked really new.

At Albuquerque Amtrak takes off high-speed boxcars and roadrailer cars and puts back on others. Passengers were let off the train for thirty minutes to stretch their legs and buy souvenirs sold by Native American women in little booths. Greg interested in the GE42DC locomotives that looked fairly new walked up close to them to check them out. On the side of the cab is a builder's plate that showed when the locomotives were manufactured. All four locomotives were one month-old, built-in October 2001. They were brand new!

Roadrailers go on the very back of the train for good reason. They are not built to the same strength as a regular rail car. What they are in fact are nothing more than a hybrid truck trailer. The front of the truck trailer is mounted on a 4-wheel bogey that connects to the train. The rear end of the truck trailer is mounted up on top of a 4-wheel bogey that also has the front of the next truck mounted on it. So, between each set of truck trailers is the 4-wheel bogey.

This arrangement was developed in conjunction of the DOE and the railroads as a method of reducing train weight and improving fuel mileage during the oil crisis back in the 1970s. Amtrak hauls the mail and express packages in these Roadrailers. Norfolk Southern Railroad provides a Roadrailer service via their Triple Crown Service. Amtrak started using Roadrailers in 1997.

Wabash National in Lafayette, Indiana, builds the Roadrailers. The Roadrailer truck trailers are reinforced to handle the stress of a long string of cars. If they attempted to use a regular truck trailer, they would be ripped in half.

Burlington Northern Santa Fe (BNSF) owned by Warren Buffet (Berkshire Hathaway) has a Roadrailer service that goes between Los Angeles and New York in approximately eighty-six hours hauling fresh fruit. Norfolk Southern Triple Crown Service is the largest user of Roadrailers. A Roadrailer train can be as long as 150 cars maximum. However, those 150 Roadrailer cars can be put at the end of a standard double-stack train increasing its overall length.

More than likely if a railroad was to do such a train, they would have a distributed power unit at the front of the Roadrailers and the back of a double-stack or piggyback train. YouTube has plenty of Roadrailer videos available to watch. One person sites observing a 135-car Roadrailer train with three locomotives on the front. Greg had seen a number of them with two locomotives. 150-car Roadrailer train is 8400 feet long. That usually never happens, and most railroads keep it down to 120 cars.

Greg was wondering if there would be a Roadrailer train he could observe on the way as they went through the double-track sections of this rail line back to Sacramento. It just so happens there is a major trucking company running a Roadrailer train every day from Los Angeles to Portland, Oregon. So, the chances he might see one was good up in the Sacramento area where the central valley rail line intercepts the Union Pacific Transcontinental.

The GE P42DC locomotives on the front of the Amtrak train passed by Greg and his two friends giving of the cacophony of vibrations from the diesel engines and dynamic breaking fans that was sweet to his ears. Greg preferred the sound of the EMD manufactured locomotives (now owned by Caterpillar Corporation). One company builds four-cycle (GE) and the other builds two-cycle (EMD). The train was probably doing at least twenty-five miles per hour when the locomotives passed by giving off that diesel smell.

The train looked really clean and nice. It had been serviced in the Chicago area and scrubbed down, inside and out. All the linen was changed, just like in a hotel. In effect, the cabins were an extension of a hotel on wheels. Once could argue, the Amtrak employees had more contact and more respect than hotel employees, including the one they had stayed at in Reno, which is one of the best in the world.

Their tickets had the car number their private cabin was located in and by luck it just happened to stop directly in front of them. Only a few people got off the train. Then the Amtrak employees standing by the stepstool they put out to make it a short step up onto the stairway into the passenger car, was scanning everyone's tickets as they boarded.

People were seemingly anxious to get on the train and claim their seats. Most of the passengers already on the train were taking it all the way to the San Francisco Bay area. Once again, thanks to Greg's astute knowledge of where the quiet most cabins are on the train, they entered the designated three passenger cabin in the very middle.

Inside it was almost a copy of the cabin they had on their way to Reno. No sooner than they settled down, the train started moving. The two pretty Japanese ladies looked kind of wild in the cowgirl hats. They of course had to snap numerous selfies. Greg didn't know this, but Japanese women ran their relationships like organized crime and the crime family was huge. One lady in the San Francisco Bay area usually knew at least 100 different other Japanese ladies.

When Greg was with his wife and shopping at the three main Japanese grocery stores in Kearny Mesa area of San Diego, his wife routinely met a Japanese woman she knew. It's very surprising how much they network and how much they like to gossip. No doubt 100 other Japanese ladies have already seen pictures that Ami and Hikaru sent.

Some of Hikaru's personal friends were what Greg would consider trashy women, who slept around, loved sex only with dark-skinned guys, and were the consummate gold diggers. Hikaru of course embellished a few things along the way with some of her selfies and Greg didn't know this, he had a volunteer squad lined up to accompany him on his next sojourn to Reno if he took one. Unlike the very polite Ami who had moral and ethical values, those trashy women would come right out and say, "Greg, darling, would you like to fuck me?"

And it's not just Japanese that have women like this. They come in all sizes and shapes and ethnic backgrounds. Most women are a lot like Ami with personal dignity, maturity, and have some moral fiber and want to avoid pointless relationships.

Even though some women do not want anything to do with marriage and kids, they do want to have a personal sex partner who is loyal to them only and doesn't screw around. In this modern world of terrible STDs, a lot of women are practical and smart and want to take no risks.

Greg was already married, though with an estranged wife living in Japan, that gave him a safety valve in that it eliminated most perceived notions of other women attempting to snag him into a lifelong commitment since he legally couldn't marry them and had no intention of ever divorcing his wife, no matter how badly her treatment of him was merely by the separation.

This was a happy trip for Greg. Ami who liked Greg more and more as a friend because she had finally discovered a male friend she could fully trust and not take advantage of her, and her intuition made her believe he cared about her wellbeing. It's very uplifting to a person who knows someone else deeply cares about them without a requirement for some quid pro quo.

As the train started moving away from the station, Greg announced:

GREG

I bought us each a toothbrush and tube of toothpaste
so we can brush our teeth now and again after lunch,
in case you are interested.

The two ladies already knew what Greg had in the paper bag and were delightful he was so considerate.

AMI
Hikaru, why don't you use the bathroom first.

HIKARU
Thank you, Ami. You are so sweet.

Hikaru took her toothbrush and toothpaste to the bathroom/toilet and shut the door. She first relieved herself then brushed her teeth.

Greg was facing Ami directly across the small table between those two chairs looking at her lovely face and smile. She helped him transcend time and venture back to Honolulu, when he first slow danced with his wife to be. She was a huge attraction to him. From that day on were inseparable and fell hopelessly in love. His wife enjoyed all her days with him raising their son, but perhaps it was all that Japanese TV she watched around the clock when she wasn't busy that made her hunger for her own country. You can take the person out of the country, but you cannot take the country out of the person.

During Golden Week Holiday in Japan in May, the Japanese celebrate their love for their country. In America where you see people rioting and condemning their country because of their perceived grievances such as police brutality or unfair employer treatment that gives the appearance of racism and favoritism, Japan doesn't suffer from that, as long as you are Japanese.

Japan greatly limits immigration. You cannot immigrate to Japan unless you can pass a Japanese language proficiency test. The only non-Japanese immigrants they let in are the slaves they bring in from places like Sri Lanka. However, the Japanese companies who bring in those employees who do manual labor Japanese rarely want to do, they have classroom training in Japanese so they can learn how to cope in this new country. Those people are not entitled to stay forever. They get a seven-year visa and at the end of it, they are taken to the airport, either by their employer or by the police.

But these foreign workers go home with a nice large bank account in a safe Japanese bank, with enough money to buy or start a business back home. Because they learn the Japanese methods, they usually are very successful in their new business and do not regret anything because they knew during their recruitment it was only for seven years and they are required to return to their country.

There are exceptions, of course. Some of these foreign workers end up marrying Japanese wives and are then granted indefinite visa status and as long as they don't get into trouble are allowed to stay there for the rest of their lives. Greg met Sri Lankans while in Japan and they were always very happy. The housing the Japanese provided for them was nice and clean, there was no crime, and the Japanese are overall very respectful and accommodative to the Sri Lankans. The other exceptions include some Sri Lankans are extremely intelligent, borderline genius.

As part of the foreign employee process that major Japanese companies utilize, they also look out for talent and an individual who can be indoctrinated for that company's purpose in market expansion throughout the world. When those individuals are identified, they are quietly offered full-ride scholarships and educated at the finest learning institutions in Japan that meet or exceed MIT, Harvard, Cal Tech, and UC Berkeley in almost every respect. No wonder they are always kicking our asses in the business world.

After the education and indoctrination, those exceptional foreign workers, men and women are sent worldwide as a company employee which could land them in London, Paris, Berlin, New York, Los Angeles, Moscow, or Shanghai.

When Greg stared into Ami's eyes, he had a vast reservoir of knowledge of Japanese women. He knew how they were fantastic love makers and paid attention to personal hygiene. Sitting there only two feet away was the same face as that woman he slow danced with just a few decades ago. If it wasn't for his concern for her wellbeing and the appropriateness of the situation with another woman in the toilet who could emerge without notice, he might have reached over and kissed Ami.

Little did Greg know; the feelings were mutual as Ami was slowly evolving in her emotions toward Greg. The fact he didn't keep his eyes on Hikaru's breasts or pay her any favoritism because of her exquisite beauty and body, uplifted Ami even more knowing Greg most likely had those pleasant feelings towards her that radiated towards her every time they met. His actions during this trip were no different than any time before.

Ami was shrewd and knew she could make it on her own and didn't need a sugar daddy. She was not going to make the first move. Most women that make the first move usually lose. Ami and Greg's smiles were genuine and the moment was perfect. If this was a scene on a movie screen, the viewers would be shouting, "Kiss her, dammit!"

The desires and lust felt overwhelming. It took Greg a lot of self-control to not do it and when they were most vulnerable to commit that act that would indelibly change their relationship forever.

Greg was saved at that moment by Hikaru who suddenly came out of the toilet disrupting that transcendental evolution towards a burst of passion.

HIKARU
I'm all done, it's your turn, Ami.

AMI
Okay Hikaru. Thanks.

The emotions seemed as thick as a good San Francisco fog when Ami got up giving Greg that wicked smile. Words were not necessary as they both understood the passions were boiling over just then.

Ami copied Hikaru's routine and soon exited the toilet wondering if it was appropriate to leave Greg alone with that sex-starved kitten in a cowgirl hat. As it turned out they were discussing the kids they just saw riding horses a few hundred yards away from the railroad tracks.

Hikaru
I've always wanted to go horseback riding.

GREG
Livermore is close to a lot of places where you can ride
horses. If you want one of these days, I can take you
and Ami horseback riding.

HIKARU
That would be lovely.

Hikaru was wishing Greg was riding her instead of a horse about then.

The pheromones were flying and the sexual intensity could easily explode and before
such an occurrence there was a knock at the door. It was an Amtrak employee alerting
them:

AMTRAK EMPLOYEE
Sir and madam's, we'll be announcing the first call to
the diner at fifteen minutes before 11:00. I advise you
to get in line at that time because there is a lot of people
on the train today and the dinner will fill up fast.

GREG
Thank you for the heads-up.

AMTRAK EMPLOYEE
You are most welcome, sir.

The Amtrak employee then shut the door and Ami got up and walked over and locked it.

Ami didn't want any invasion of their privacy, especially if Greg decided he wanted to
consummate the friendship.

As soon as Ami sat back down, Greg announced:

GREG
Looks like it's my turn.

Greg then went to the toilet, brushed his teeth and drained some of his coffee.

Just as soon as Greg left the toilet, the women were giggling. They had said something
humorous to themselves, or at least as it seemed.

While Greg was in the toilet, Hikaru teased Ami in Japanese

HIKARU
If Greg wants to do boom-boom with me, I'm ready
now.

AMI
You were brought along to be my chaperone, not to
steal my boyfriend.

HIKARU
Would you like me to go to the observation car so you
and Greg can get it on?

AMI
I seriously doubt he would want to do something on
the train with me. We don't know if that day will ever
come, but if it does, I want him to make the first move
and I'll be ready for it if he does.

HIKARU
What if he doesn't?

AMI
He'll miss out on the best lovemaking he ever
experienced in his lifetime.

HIKARU
How do you know that?

AMI
Because I would make sure of it.

HIKARU
The girls started giggling and moments later Greg
exited the toilet.

Fearing he might have left a sour odor in the toilet, Greg thought he should take the
women to the observation car to give it a chance to dissipate.

GREG
You ladies want to go to the observation car and show
off your cowgirl hats?

AMI
Sure.

Ami was glad to leave the sex the scenario behind them. At least for this trip.

Away from the private Amtrak room, the fearless threesome went to the observation
car, which turned out to be a good move, because now the train was slowing down as it
was going up into the mountains and at this slower speed, they could do more quality
sightseeing.

Speaking In Japanese not knowing Greg understood it quite well what Ami said to Hikaru:

AMI

You can have sex anytime, but it's rare to be able to see
all this natural beauty. I'm glad we chose to come to the
observation car.

HIKARU

I think I would rather have sex.

Greg had to work hard to keep a straight face.

FLASHBACK.

Greg suddenly remembered about one of his trips to Hong Kong with several Naval Intelligence Linguists and went into what they call a *titty bar*. All the female bartenders and waitresses are topless. You can't touch them, but you can look. Some of them, however, eventually establish a relationship with long-term customers, especially if they are financially well off.

These linguists were indoctrinated not to speak their foreign languages in foreign countries due to security as it might tip off foreign intelligence agents, they were linguists and involved in special operations. If it were known these men were highly proficient in Cantonese, Mandarin, and Pinyin, they might come up missing. Red Gang of Hong Kong would waste little time in making a fast buck kidnapping a Naval spook for the Chinese MSS Intelligence agency (Ministry of State Security).

Greg and the linguists went to this same titty bar five days in a row and on their very last day, when they were leaving Hong Kong, an interesting event occurred.

During the five days one of the female bartenders with exquisite breasts informed her girlfriend bartender speaking Cantonese:

FEMALE BARTENDER (a.k.a. Lanfen)

My husband just gave me a nasty yeast infection. I
think he's whoring around.

SECOND FEMALE BARTENDER

Did you go get checked by a doctor?

FEMALE BARTENDER (a.k.a. Lanfen)

I did and the doctor said that if I've never had any
other sex partners this came from my husband, and
he probably contracted this STD from another woman.

The woman had a painful look on her face.

The Chinese topless bartenders were very nice-speaking English with a British accent, but when they spoke in Chinese, they would not be saying kind words about those *filthy American assholes*. When the patrons bought them a drink, they poured themselves a shot out of a bottle filled with tea.

The linguist would tell the group later all the gems the Chinese topless bartenders said about them when they were gone and out and away from the bar.

The female bartender (a.k.a. Lanfen) and the rest of the employees were definitely two faced.

On their very last visit, the group drank shots with the women just before they left and then headed out the door. One of the Chinese linguists stopped at the bar's door and turned around looked at the female bartender with the yeast infection and spoke in perfect Cantonese dialect:

AMERICAN NAVAL LINGUIST
順便說一下蘭芬, 你的酵母感染感染怎麼樣?
{Shùn biàn shuō yí xià lán fēn, nǐ de jiào mǔ gǎn rǎn
gǎn rǎn zěn me yàng?}
[By the way, Lanfen, how is your yeast infection doing?]

Suddenly, all the other Chinese ladies started laughing and poor Lanfen went running and crying out the back door.

EXT. DAY TRUCKEE TRAIN STATION

Greg snapped out of his daydream when the train made a stop at Truckee and the three got off the train and went over to one of the nice coffee shops and got a fantastic cup of java. It was a short stop and Amtrak put another locomotive on the front, this was a Siemens Mobility Charger with that sweet-sounding 4,400-horsepower 16-cylinder Cummins QSK95 diesel engine. They got back on the train and went to the observation car since they knew they would be announcing lunch in a while.

The three enjoyed the views and several dudes in the observation car were all smiles at these two cute Japanese cowgirls. A couple of them that were from Australia approached and put on a 4-engine run (military term) to Ami and Hikaru.

Just when the Azzie's thought they were getting somewhere with these exquisite ladies, the intercom had an announcement.

TRAIN INTERCOM

Ladies and gentlemen, we'll be having first seating for lunch for those individuals who are in private rooms.

Greg was delighted to stand up and tell the two Azzie punks a nice statement.

> GREG
> I'll take it from here, boys.

About that same moment, Ami stood up and wrapped her arm around Greg's arms and said

> AMI
> Okay, sugar daddy, take us to lunch.

Ami turned around and winked at the two Azzie's who appeared in total disbelief.

As Ami, Hikaru, and Greg walked towards the dining car , that wild and sexy cowgirl Hikaru turned around and blew the Azzie dudes a Marilyn Monroe kiss.

The two Azzie dudes thought Greg had ménage à trois going on and if Greg had pursued it, he would have dropped them off at their apartment rode hard and put away wet just like a high-performance racehorse.

But that wasn't the case.

At lunch, Greg decided that since it had been such a fantastic trip, he offered champagne.

> GREG
> Would you ladies like a bottle of champagne?

> HIKARU
> Most definitely.

When the waiter came to their table, Greg asked him about their champagne.

> GREG
> Do you have champagne available?

> AMTRAK DINING CAR WAITER
> Sir, I must apologize in advance, all we have left for this
> trip is Dom Perignon.

Without asking the price because Greg knew it was expensive, he responded.

> GREG
> That would be wonderful, we'll have a bottle.

> AMTRAK DINING CAR WAITER
> It will be my pleasure to get your champagne, sir.

The waiter went off and a few moments later came back with a bottle of Dom Perignon, in a silver bucket of ice.

> AMTRAK DINING CAR WAITER
> I apologize, sir, but we are required to pop the cork in
> the pantry so that it doesn't accidentally hit someone.

GREG
Not a problem.

AMTRAK DINING CAR WAITER
May I pour your champagne, sir?

GREG
Yes, please.

The Amtrak Dining Car Waiter poured a small amount so that Greg could taste it. Greg then responded.

GREG
This is perfect, thank you.

The smiling Amtrak Dining Car Waiter then poured two glasses and handed them to the ladies and refilled Greg's champagne glass and put the bottle back in the silver champagne bottle holder with ice. Amtrak Dining Car Waiter then took Ami, Hikaru, and Greg's food orders, and left the table to take the order sheet to the chef.

There definitely was an air of excitement in the dining room. A few high rollers back from Reno, obviously had a good time and the Japanese cowgirls created a unique atmosphere as those cowgirl hats created an image that fostered creative thinking.

One of the gamblers who was obviously feeling really good and won some money in Reno approached the table and addressed Ami and Hikaru

GAMBLER (a.k.a JAKE)
You are the prettiest cowgirls I've ever seen.

Hikaru beamed with enjoyment from the attention she was receiving.

The gambler introduced himself.

JAKE
My name is Jake. How are you guys doing?

Ami responded, knowing how to handle rambunctious customers.

AMI
We are doing just fine.

JAKE
I own a real estate company in San Francisco if you
ever want to buy some high-end properties there.

Jake then pulled out one of his business cards and handed it to Greg.

GREG
My name is Greg. These ladies are Ami and Hikaru.

JAKE
What do you do, for a living Greg?

GREG
I'm retired, but I'm now working as a Logistics

Consultant.
JAKE
How's that working out for you, Greg?

GREG
Well Jake, as you can see, I can afford some really good things in life.

JAKE
I can tell, you certainly have the situation totally under control."

GREG
Not as well as I would like to be.

Greg commented without getting into any details, knowing if he was a better man his wife would not be in Japan, and he would not be home alone.

About that time the Amtrak Dining Car Waiter came up with a couple plates.

AMTRAK DINING CAR WAITER
Excuse me, sir, I need to get to the table.

JAKE
I'll talk with you later, enjoy your lunch.

GREG
Thank you.

Jake walked back over to his table and sat down with his haggish middle-aged wife. Greg had an evil thought, *Taking her to Reno is like taking a hamburger to a steak dinner.* But all to his own.

The two ladies settled on a sandwich, Greg took a sirloin steak, which isn't one of his typical steak choices, but this is Amtrak. It's the best they and do within their budget.

AMTRAK DINING CAR WAITER
Any steak sauce, sir?

GREG
I wouldn't mind some Heinz 57 if you have it, if not A1.

AMTRAK DINING CAR WAITER
I'll see what I can do.

In short order the wonderful smiling and polite waiter returned with an unopened bottle of Heinz 57. *That works for a sirloin alright and the Dom Perignon did a great job of flushing it down* Greg thought.

The ladies were hitting the Dom Perignon real hard, and it emptied really fast. When the waiter came by and asked if everything was okay, Greg replied.

GREG
I'm sorry, sir, but these girls drained the champagne
bottle too quickly. Would it be possible to get another
one?

AMTRAK DINING CAR WAITER
Well, as you know sir, we are only allowed to serve one
bottle per passenger, since there are three of you, it
should not be a problem.

In a brief amount of time, the Amtrak Dining Car Waiter was back at the table with a fresh bottle of Dom Perignon and took the empty bottle away.

Greg could see Jake smiling at him from a couple tables over and he smiled back and raised his glass to him as a toast

GREG
Kanpai.

Jake being around a lot of Japanese who purchased high-end homes knew the term and repeated the toast and raised his glass.

JAKE
Kanpai.

There was something about Jake that Greg liked. Real estate people are usually very good at etiquette and know psychology well. They have to generally be positive people, especially in a down market. The body language on Jake's wife wasn't nearly as nice. Greg said to himself, *Jake's wife probably thinks I took these young bimbos to Reno to bang the shit out of them. Little does she know they are nice girls and I'm a nice man.*

Greg would not be surprised when Jake's wife got home, she gossiped to her Miss Hannity type friends about *this horrible old guy with a couple young Japanese prostitutes coming back from Reno.*

As the Amtrak passenger train cruised through the mountains, Greg was enjoying the effects of the champagne and his steak.

Amtrak does it right. Train numbers five and six go over these California mountains usually during mealtime so the diners can have wonderful, picturesque landscape to enjoy.

The meal was finished about the time the second champagne bottle was empty. Greg had no desire to go back to the observation car and deal with the two Azzie's if they were still there, pine for these delicious Japanese girls they would most likely abuse and toss aside.

FLASHBACK

Greg, setting in the dining car sipping on champagne, had a flashback to the 1990s when he was at *Studebakers* in Restaurant Row near Aloha Tower in Honolulu (no longer exists) during a period of austerity where his employer had cut back on all overtime. It was kind of stupid because Greg was in one of those $150+ per night rooms in Waikiki plus the per diem. It was a three-day weekend, and Greg was stuck there doing nothing for three days. So, Greg decided to go cry in his beers at a nightclub, drink copious amounts of alcohol and then take a taxi back to his hotel.

Greg had his first drink and was feeling better when two well-dressed young Japanese ladies came in and sat down on the two barstools next to him. Being polite and wanting to have good company when the waitress came around, he asked her to give the two ladies a drink and he would pay for it. The waitress took their order and promptly came back with their drinks and informed them Greg had paid for them.

Those Japanese ladies about twenty-four years old were very sociable and educated. But they wanted to dance. They dragged Greg out on the dance floor a couple times, then a couple Azzie guys came and took them off Greg's hands for the rest of the night which was okay. Greg bought the ladies a few more drinks and talked to them off and on. One of them could speak English quite well, the other couldn't.

Finally, 2:00 A.M. came along and the bar was closing down. One of the Auzzies came up to Greg.

AZZIE DUDE

Hey, Greg, we are going to take the girls over to the
Wave, and would like you to come along with us?

The *Wave* was one of those all-night clubs with live bands (back then). The Azzie's proved over and over that night they were cheap Charlies and never bought the girls a drink. Furthermore, the limo-taxi required to fit them all in to get to the *Wave* was forced upon Greg to pay for it since the cheap Charlies offered no money.

Greg, being a decent person, waited a while and the Azzie's never offered to buy any drinks. Therefore, he bought a round of drinks and gave them to the ladies and the cheap Charlies.

131

About that time one of these Azzie assholes walked up to Greg.

AZZIE DUDE
Okay, Greg, we'll take it from here.

The rotten bastards were using Greg and pissed him off. One of the Japanese ladies soon afterwards informed Greg they only agreed with those two guys they would go to the Wave if Greg went along because they trusted him. Greg only went because for a few minutes he thought these Australian guys were nice and special because no Americans would ever invite a stranger along like that. Greg was temporarily humbled. Greg only went along because he was touched by all the apparent (but fake) humanity.

The two Azzie dudes walked up in front near the band trying to look super cool with the drinks Greg paid for.

The two Azzie dudes walked up in front near the band trying to look super cool with the drinks Greg paid for.

Shortly after Greg supplied everyone with drinks including, the Azzie cheap Charlies, one of the Japanese ladies who could speak English approached Greg.

JAPANESE LADY
Greg, could you take us back to our hotel, my friend
has a headache?

Greg responded to the Japanese lady.

GREG
Tell your friend I'm taking you back to your hotel and
we'll leave.

The Japanese lady then informed her friend speaking Japanese and they headed for the door. At this time of night all the people from a lot of other nightclubs shutting down pour into the Wave. The three were walking against a human wave so Greg grabbed each of their hands and pulled them through the crowd.

These Japanese women were dressed extremely nice. A taxi pulled up about then, nobody knew Greg didn't order the taxi, so Greg walked over and opened the car door and told the ladies to hop in.

Greg informed the taxi driver.

GREG
You can leave now; we'll give you directions on the way.

About that time the two Azzie's hit the front door of the Wave and Greg asked the taxi driver:

GREG
Please stop for one second.

Greg rolled down the electric window of the limo-cab and yelled out to the two Azzie dudes.

GREG
Hey, boys, I'll take it from here.

If you could see the Azzie Dudes rejection and humility, you would know why Greg wished he had a cell phone back in those days for a selfie.

As they drove off, the English-speaking Japanese lady gave directions and soon the taxi pulled up in front of their hotel. During the ride there she insisted Greg sit in the middle and she hopped over his lap and was by the door with the cabbie looking in the rearview mirror amazed because it's rare you see a "Howlee" (local slang for white person) with two gorgeous Japanese ladies floating around Waikiki. The cab pulled up in front of their hotel. About that time, the English-speaking lady asked:

JAPANESE LADY
Greg, would you like to come up to our room for coffee
and cake?

Japanese women usually say what they mean, and Greg knew that meant only coffee and cake and since Greg had three wasted days to look forward to because of a national holiday, Greg responded favorably.

GREG
Sure, why not.

Greg could see in the rearview mirror the young Anglo cab driver shaking his head. It was truly almost unbelievable to him.

Greg went up to their hotel room and had coffee and cake and the one lady with a headache looked so miserable.

GREG
I think your friend is very tired. I should leave now and
give your friend peace and quiet.

JAPANESE LADY (a.k.a. AYUMI HAMASAKI)
Thanks for taking us home, Greg. I didn't expect you to
be so charming, so I didn't give you my real name. I'm
Ayumi Hamasaki.

GREG
Thanks for the complement, Ayumi.

AYUMI HAMASAKI
Could I have your hotel number?

Greg gave her his hotel number and didn't expect anything to come of it. But the next evening at 6:00 P.M. the phone rings in the hotel room and the English-speaking Japanese lady Ayumi Hamasaki from the night before calling. "Greg, are you busy tonight?"

GREG

Not really.

AYUMI

My friend still has a headache so if you would like to go somewhere with me, I'm available.

GREG

When can you be ready?

AYUMI

Any time.

GREG

Alright. I remember your hotel. I'll be there in a taxi in about thirty minutes, how does that sound?

AYUMI

Sounds good.

GREG

See you then.

AYUMI

Okay.

Thirty minutes later as the taxi pulled up in front of her hotel, Ayumi was standing there.

Greg took her to the Hyatt Regency that had a very successful fifties style nightclub called Kento's with live band and dancing.

Greg and Ayumi had dinner and stuck around dancing. For the next two weeks Greg had a phenomenal dance partner

Ethnic Japanese men in Hawaii get kind of ticked off when they see a *Howlee* dancing with one of their women. Greg could see the resentment in their eyes which made him pull her closer during slow dances and grab her ass in front of them.

And two weeks later she Ayumi left to travel back to Japan and never returned any letters. She's probably a grandmother now. But she knows one thing for certain, Greg was a true gentleman and never tried to have sex with her even though they laid together in bed a couple times kissing but never going over the limit.

Greg figured he would demonstrate he was a true gentleman and if she were interested, the relationship could grow from there.

In the end everyone had fond memories, no broken hearts and respect for each other.

As Greg gazed upon Ami and Hikaru, he knew he would not change his style. Time is a clarifier for all. Plus, Greg would only have entertained any thoughts of going beyond where he was with Ami and that probably wasn't in the cards as he hoped she would meet someone her own age and have a happy life.

They chatted on the way to Sacramento where the train briefly stopped but they were given ten minutes to get off the train and stretch their legs. Greg took them out of the train station and pointed out the Holiday Inn there which was convenient if someone wanted to go to Sacramento's Old Town and spend the night. Memories of staying in that hotel and renting a car and driving around Napa Valley suddenly sprung in Greg's memories.

Greg took one of the greatest loves of his life on the Napa Valley wine train. Greg wasn't always successful in love. And now that he had been rejected a second time when his wife moved to Japan by herself, he wasn't anxious to feel it again.

So, there was no point in getting involved with this very beautiful lady Ami who had a whole lifetime ahead of her while he was now on the glide slope downwards. His young looks and physical appearance betrayed his real age. Looking no more than early fifties truly misled everyone into believing he was much younger than his real age.

They knew they had ten minutes, so they didn't gawk at the Holiday Inn too long and re-boarded the train.

Greg had no idea the level of surveillance on him. People followed him to Reno and back. While he was eating lunch, they installed hidden cameras. Unless you know you are under surveillance and look for the devices, you will never know they are there. Most Americans do not know intel operations are not related to law enforcement. Nor will any of it ever end up in court because the INTEL agencies do not want to reveal sensitive sources and methods.

Two agents were on the train accompanying Greg back to Oakland. They had his itinerary because the NSA can get anything they want.

Eventually the train pulled into Oakland and Greg and the two ladies got off the train.

Apparently the two Azzie dudes were looking for Greg and wanted to kick his ass and relieve him of his two girlfriends. As Greg was leading the two ladies to the taxi stand one of them grabbed Greg.

AZZIE DUDE

Hey, Mate, we want to talk with you.

It was not a very friendly action. Greg suddenly started thinking he was going to be accosted. Just as soon as the other Azzie got right in front of Greg to probably sucker punch him when the two security men about ten feet behind saw this all unfold and quickened their pace.

SECRET AGENT
Hey, fuckhead, let go of the guy.

About that time the Azzie dude turned to see who it was. When the Azzie Dude saw it was two big dudes with sunglasses, he let go of Greg's hand and turned toward the two men. One of them addressed Greg.

SECRET AGENT
Greg, go on your way. We'll take care of this for you.
Get in your cab and leave.

Greg grabbed Ami and Hikaru's hands and quickly led them to a taxi and said to the driver after they were inside made a profound statement.

GREG
Let's get out of here fast. I think some bad things are
about to happen.

As the driver sped out Greg looked in the back window of the taxi and saw the two Azzies on the ground and one of the goons gave one of them a good quick kick to the balls with a policeman approaching rapidly. One of the guys pulled out some sort of badge and said something. About that time the cab turned the corner and he lost sight of what was going on.

The policeman cautiously approached the men. The Federal Agent informed the cop after he showed him the badge.

SECRET AGENT
These two punks interfered with a Federal Agent in his
mission.

POLICE OFFICER
What happened?

SECRET AGENT
As you can see, we defended ourselves from these
punks. I suggest with the beating they just took you
let them go.

The cop just stood there knowing the FEDs had jurisdiction in the case and responded.

POLICE OFFICER
As you wish, sir.

The Federal Agent looked down at one of the punks.

SECRET AGENT
Next time you may not be so lucky.

About that time a couple black SUVs pulled up and men with suits got out and one of them said,

SECRET AGENT BACKUP REP
Andy, go ahead and get in the car and take off. We'll handle this.

The first SUV soon took off and the men in suits (men in black) were soon reading the punks' passports.

SECRET AGENT BACKUP REP
We are putting you on the watchlist so if there are any further reports on you, we'll be notified. I suggest you get on a plane and go home. Your business is finished here.

Ami and Hiraku were a little rattled and then started wondering, *Who the hell is Greg?*

Because Ami made the mistake of texting Greg, she was on a watchlist as well. In a few days she received a visit. In her interview she was informed.

SECRET AGENT
Greg is a good guy, and he always has protection as good as the secret service protecting the President. He's an important person so we must look out for him and please do not discuss this matter with anyone.

Greg was also somewhat mystified for a brief period, but he already understood he was way in over his head. He had his own session the following few days. Greg received a sudden instant message on his laptop at work. It was from Walter Bissonnette.

WALTER BISSONNETTE
Greg, I'm coming by your office in a short while, I need to talk with you.

GREG
I'll be here.

By then Walter had watched the video including some of the secret communications the Japanese women did thinking nobody was listening. He also knew few men could show self-control and constraint like Greg could. It helped his case that he didn't *boink* the two girls like he easily could have.

Walter knocked on the door then entered after he applied his palm to the reader that automatically actuated the solenoid allowing him to enter Greg's office.

137

GREG
Hello, Walt, what can I do for you?

WALTER BISSONNETTE
Tomorrow you are going for another ride.

GREG
Alright.

WALTER BISSONNETTE
There is something else I wanted to talk to you about.

GREG
Sure.

WALTER BISSONNETTE
What you are doing in this program is a critical part of what we will accomplish. You are several years away from the mission you are going on, but you are already viewed as essential. Therefore, you have protection whether you like it or not. I'm sure by now you have done some reflection about the incident at the train station.

GREG
Yes, that was quite an interesting event.

WALTER BISSONNETTE
You did nothing wrong. You were just an innocent bystander and a couple thugs attempted to do you harm, therefore your protection had to step in and deal with it.

GREG
I see.

WALTER BISSONNETTE
Those two guys flew to Australia this morning and when they arrive there, they will get some words of advice from the AIC to keep their mouths shut if they know what's good for them.

GREG
What's the AIC?

WALTER BISSONNETTE
It's the CIA spelled backwards since it's down under.

They are quite good at what they do. The acronym refers to Australia Intelligence Community.

GREG
Okay.

WALTER BISSONNETTE
There is one other thing I want to talk to you about.

GREG
What is that?

WALTER BISSONNETTE
We know everything about your wife abandoning you. You owe her nothing. It's good that you treat her so nicely, but it should not preclude you from developing friendships now that might lead to sexual intercourse or any other activity of a healthy male.

GREG
I was just taking them on a train ride, I wasn't planning on having sex with them.

WALTER BISSONNETTE
I can't tell you how I know this because it involves sensitive sources and methods, we are not entitled to let you know about, but Ami is in love with you and Hikaru would fuck your brains out in a New York minute.

GREG
What's your point?

WALTER BISSONNETTE
We really don't mind if you get laid. Keep our Pluto II secrets but don't let that stop you from getting your rocks off.

GREG
That's interesting, but I don't know that I deserve such nice young ladies.

WALTER BISSONNETTE
You will earn far more than anyone. That's why tomorrow we are sending you on a confidence builder with Tiāncái tomorrow.

GREG
What's the purpose of this next ride?

WALTER BISSONNETTE
When you go on a mission with Tiāncái you will have to rely heavily on him and trust him.

GREG
Okay.

WALTER BISSONNETTE
Tiāncái has been programmed to know on a mission you are his supreme authority. However, until you launch on that mission you will not be given that authority, to prevent any possible unpredictable outcomes.

What Walt was really saying is he doesn't want me to run off with a valuable Robot, Greg thought.

GREG
Anything else?

WALTER BISSONNETTE
Keep up the good work. You have lived up to all expectations and we have informed Dr. Moore that you have worked out well. We do appreciate him introducing you to us.

GREG
I'm sure he's glad to know he didn't recommend a failure.

WALTER BISSONNETTE
Dr. Moore is a brilliant man, and he cares about this country's future as well as the plight of mankind. He knows firsthand we are living on borrowed time.

GREG
He's right. We need to learn more about space and the Universe as soon as possible since we don't have a clue what's out there.

WALTER BISSONNETTE
Alright, Greg, I'll be seeing you and Tiāncái first thing in the morning.

Walt left the office leaving Greg in a state of contemplation. In a way he was right about his wife abandoning him, but his reluctance to pursue Ami rested heavily on his respect for her and her age and hope that she would have a normal and happy life. Greg didn't want to complicate his life, but also, every time he looked at her, he saw his young wife almost twenty-five years ago. The emotions just couldn't be controlled. He knew she would feel just like his wife and if he ever tasted the forbidden fruit, he might not be able to go back to what he was.

Greg had not visited Ami since they returned from the train ride. He knew that tomorrow, a confidence builder translated in: *You will be going somewhere tomorrow doing something that will probably scare the shit out of you to see if you are willing to rely on Tiāncái.*

It was at the end of the day, so he closed his laptop and walked home. There he took a Hollywood shower, blow dried his hair and put on some nice clothes and headed out the door. He walked to Cattleman's hoping Ami was there. To his great luck she was. After the beautiful Maître d' seated him acting a little strange. Earlier Ami had informed the Maître d' about the wonderful time she had in Reno with Greg, and how Greg proved to be the perfect gentleman.

The Maître d appears more affectionate today for some odd reason, Greg thought.

Then Ami showed up to Greg's table almost looking like she was relieved to see him again.

AMI

I'm so glad you showed up tonight. I really wanted to
see you.

GREG

The feeling is mutual.

AMI

Thank you for coming and also thank you for treating
me so nicely. I will always remember how nice a person
you are.

GREG

Likewise, I will think of you the same way.

AMI

Do you want the usual?

GREG

Yes please. You got it.

AMI

I'll go put in your order and be right back with a glass
of wine.

GREG
Thank you.

Greg's relationship with Ami seemingly evolving over time was now unfolding in front of him. Walt had tipped him off and now it was plain to see, *not only had he gotten in over his head with Project Pluto II, now he is slowly getting in over his head with Ami.*

Walt's lecture this afternoon was pressing home a point to him. Walt probably knows a lot more about what's going on in the future than he did, so perhaps he's suggesting I get laid and have a good time now since my wife abandoned me and I might get killed soon.

Ami came back shortly with a glass of wine and sat down across from GREG in his booth.

AMI
The place isn't too busy now, so I'm going to take my
break with you.

GREG
Okay.

AMI
Greg, can I ask you to do me a favor?

GREG
Sure, what is it?

AMI
I want you to give me a ride home tonight, there is
something I wish to talk to you about.

Greg started wondering if *this was somehow related to Walt's conversation earlier.*

GREG
What time do you get off work?

AMI
11:00 P.M.

GREG
Alright, I need to walk home and pick up my car. I'll
come back later andl pick you up out front then.

AMI
Greg, I really appreciate this.

GREG
No problem.

Greg ate his meal and since he would see Ami later there was no point in hanging around and left and went home.

Greg surfed the internet and tried to watch some TV, but none of that satisfied him as the time slowly passed. Right at 10:30 he hopped in his car and drove over to the Cattleman's Restaurant.

Ami could see Greg pull up in front and spotted him and walked over to the Maître d.

AMI
All the customers are gone, I'm taking off a little early
tonight, I have some things I need to do.

Maître D
Sure, Ami, have a nice evening. I'll see you tomorrow.

To Greg's pleasant surprise Ami came out of the restaurant early and walked over to the passenger side of the car and opened it up and hopped in.

AMI
Thanks for giving me the ride.

GREG
No problem.

AMI
Greg, would it be okay if we go over to your condo?
I want to talk with you, and I don't want Hikaru to
overhear what I want to say to you.

GREG
Sure thing.

Greg was now even more surprised. He feared she might have been worried about the train station incident and might ask how she knew those two men and what that's about. Greg was thinking of a cover story, but he didn't have a lot of facts, so he could omit some of what he knew without really lying to her.

Greg pulled into his reserved parking spot.

GREG
I'll get your door for you.

AMI
Don't worry, I can handle it.

Greg took Ami into his fully furnished condo that didn't look too bad, and he never made a mess since he seldom ate at home and dropped all his laundry off at the dry cleaners which also had a wash-and-fold service for his underwear and socks and all other non-dry-cleaning items.

143

Greg led Ami to his living room and invited her to sit down on the sofa and he sat down on the chair next to it at a forty-five-degree angle.

GREG
Would you like me to get you a drink?

AMI
A glass of wine would be nice.

Greg got up and got a cork removal tool and pulled the cork out of a new bottle of wine and poured two glasses of wine, then walked over and handed Ami one of the glasses.

Out of habit, Ami said Kanpai and tapped Greg's wine glass and took a deep sip. It was almost as if she was reluctantly getting ready to say something.

AMI
Greg, I appreciate your respect for me and treating me very well. I like you a lot. I'm not a young virgin and a woman has needs just like a man. I would never attempt to entrap you. If you get tired of me and ask me to leave, I will simply do that. But I want you to know I want you. I want to make love to you now and feel you inside me.

Greg heard the words but didn't quite know how to proceed.

GREG
Okay.

I know you are married, and your wife is estranged and moved to Japan forever back to my country. I also know she is never coming back, and you will never move to Japan. So, let me please you and let's make this friendship special. I will not place any demand on you, but I do hope you will want to continue seeing me.

Greg was almost shocked when Ami stood up and started to unbutton her blouse, took off her bra, and stepped out of her skirt showing her chest and her panties with the black bulge of pubis that was readily apparent with the lighting arrangement. AMI walked a couple steps next to Greg and ran her fingers through his hair then bent down and kissed him softly on the lips.

Greg then reciprocated and pulled her down to his lap and kissed her back and hugged her.

Ami then shifted her body straddling Gregs legs and fully facing him.

AMI
I want you to feel my breasts and suck on my nipples.

Ami had breasts exactly like Greg's wife, he soon put his mouth on them and showed his passion.

Ami, realizing Greg might be apprehensive, advised him.

AMI

Take me to your bedroom so you can undress, and I
can make you feel good.

Greg stood up and grabbed Ami's hand and led her to his bedroom. The bed was made, and it was clean and spotless, just as if it were a hotel room someone just arrived in.

As they got next to the bed, Greg was somewhat all thumbs fumbling and taking too much time. Ami took charge and unbuttoned his shirt very promptly, then unbuckled and unzipped his pants and pulled them down.

AMI

Please step out of your pantlegs.

Ami then took Gregs slacks over and put them on a chair.

AMI

Please sit down on the bed so I can take off your socks,
then lay down on the bed.

Ami noticed the wet spot in Gregs underwear and his erection when she pulled off his cotton briefs exposing him, and she started performing fellatio.

Greg was now feeling like he hadn't in a long, long time. Ami knew not to go too long, otherwise he might be spent for the night.

Greg was more than willing to find out what Ami wanted to do next.

Greg was horizontal feeling ecstasy when Ami stopped performing fellation and mounted him slowly inserted Greg's manliness inside her.

AMI

Just relax, Greg, I want to make love to you. I want to
show you that I love you.

Ami then moved her body and gripping and squeezing Greg's manliness with her strong vaginal muscles in ways he could not imagine. Ami's vagina was very wet and smelled very pleasant thanks to the French perfume she applied to her vulva to make sure Greg would like it in case he desired to down on her and perform cunnilingus which she wouldn't mind at all before their coitus began.

Ami's mother was Korean, her father Japanese and she was raised in Japan, though fluent in Japanese and Korean. Ami's mother trained by her grandmother how to seduce and keep a husband in a successful marriage started training her around the age of twelve how to strengthen her vaginal walls using a ping pong ball and advised her to avoid sex and masturbate until she got married to avoid unplanned pregnancy and a scandal.

Greg's wife had a strong resemblance to Ami but also one of the world class superstars Korean KPOP singer's Jennie Kim

Ami's quintessential beauty gave Greg a tremendous amount of pleasure just looking at her beautiful, exquisite face. Ami's appearance added greatly to the sexual attraction. Greg felt like a time traveler going back 25 years making love to his wife, but he in no way had experienced this type of vaginal paradise Ami gave him.

Greg could sense Ami's vagina seemed to be contracting and squeezing his penis extremely hard as if it were her hand squeezing him. Greg thought Ami she might have experienced a super orgasm as she started having strange sounds than bent down and started kissing him but continued on in her waving actions. Greg was not far off the mark in his speculation mixed in with his emotional tremors Ami now infused in him.

Greg reciprocated to Ami's kiss when her actions started to cause a strange physical sensation in him as his brain was pumping in prolactin into the pleasure part of his brain. Greg did not experience an orgasm for a long time because of his wife's estrangement, and suddenly it was happening. He knew he was gushing inside her and her clitoris was swollen and if he looked at it now he would be surprised they can get that large during orgasms. It was a joyous moment as Greg could feel the mighty river of his male essence behind the dam of pent up emotions sending torrents into Ami throughout his prolonged ejaculation like he never experienced before in his life.

Gregs brain was now flooding with Dopamine, Norepinephrine, Oxytocin, Vasopressin. Greg's aromatases were elevated by the combination of Ami's beauty and here remarkable transcendence immediately after her arrival.

Ami's mother proved to be an effective trainer as Ami performed in a manner that would make her mother proud and she would know her success if she was around, them at this time.

Ami just hooked Greg.

There was now no recourse for Greg, his life's timeline had just been altered by this non-assuming brilliant woman with looks to match.

There would never be another single moment of heartbreak for Greg over his estranged wife's departure. Ami effectively cured all his sorrow and grief over that situation.

Walter Bissonnet was quite happy about current developments between Greg and Ami and would soon receive a full report. It made Walter Bissonnet feel good knowing he manifested wonderful moments in Greg's life before he had to do that dastardly deed and send him on Pluto II's mission.

Greg didn't know he was being spied on. CIA plumbers had wired up his condo while he was taking weekends off down to San Diego. Their modern video and acoustic sensors were beyond Greg's wildest imagination. Some spook was now getting his jollies off observing and providing transcripts of the conversations and the sexual intercourse that was far better than any porn the agent ever saw.

Ami feeling Greg gushing inside her triggered a mega orgasm though she had already had four or five. It was the most pleasing feeling in her life because she knew Greg truly adored her. And she didn't know Greg knew she was in love with him. Greg understood a lot of Japanese allowing him to discretely understand everything Ami and Hikaru discussed on the train. It was now obviously coming to fruition accelerated much quicker than Greg could fathom.

Ami's rules of engagement were perfect. She would make her own world, but she also chose who she wanted to make love with, and Greg was the man she had chosen for a variety of reasons.

Long before Ami knew Greg was into some heavy projects filled with intrigue based on the revelations over the past few days, she had already emotionally bonded with Greg and truly liked him and desired a long-lasting relationship with him.

In a way it was good that men arrived at her condo with the suits on, and showing her their badges when they came to visit Ami. At first their visit did upset Ami quite a bit until they explained a few things to her that now had a tremendous impact on her feelings she acted on in a determined manner. Ami would never forget that visit for the rest of her life.

SECRET AGENT
We are grateful that you take interest in Greg because
he is very important and very lonely due to his marital
situation. He's sacrificed a lot for this country and
continues to do so. We wish we could tell you more,
but the least you know about it is best for you."

AMI
I understand.

SECRET AGENT
Be patient with Greg. He adores you.

AMI
I will.

When guys with badges vouch for someone's, true intentions is quite a shocker literally. It's almost as if Ami were living in a fairytale. Under normal circumstances something like this with a 3-letter agency would never happen.

But the sponsors of Project Pluto II wielded some awesome power because they helped the 3-letter agency in numerous manners including the powerplant on the TR-4 spacecraft that would be a delightful addition to NRO's KH-14 and KH-15 fleets now deploying in a tumultuous period of international relations.

Ami expired on Greg's chest and for a few minutes went into a deep freeze like she never experienced before in her life. Eventually she came to and realized she needed to get home that Hikaru might be staying up late worried about her. She moved and looked to see if Greg was awake and his eyes were open.

AMI
Greg, I need to get home soon. I'm afraid Hikaru is worrying about me. She doesn't know I came here. Can you give me a lift home?

GREG
I would be delighted to drive you to your Condo.

After they were dressed and, in Greg's car, driving to Ami's apartment Greg said something to make sure Ami understood.

GREG
Ami, I'm going somewhere tomorrow. I don't know exactly what day I'll be back. But as soon as I'm back I'll call you. I may not be able to communicate with you where I'm going.

AMI
Okay, Greg, I know you are a busy man.

GREG
Thank you for understanding.

AMI
Greg, thank you for being so sweet for me.

GREG
You can plan on me being sweet to you because I really do adore you and I want this to last. I promise to never desert you.

AMI
I know, I can tell.

However, Ami couldn't tell Greg things she was asked by the Secret Agents to never divulge to Greg for his own good as well as hers. Ami clearly knew what the score was.

Greg pulled up in front of Ami's condo-apartment and made sure she was inside before he pulled away. Girls have a way of knowing when other girls did something. Ami apologized to Hikaru.

AMI
I'm sorry if I caused you any distress by coming home so late.
HIKARU
Not to worry, I know you and Greg had a good time.

In a way Hikaru was jealous. She knew on the train she wanted what Ami got tonight. But Ami is her good friend and she would not interfere with her lover boy, unless he wanted to do ménage à trois and then she was all in.

Greg fell asleep instantly after his head hit the pillow. He felt love and passion but regretted he didn't have her body next to him. Perhaps it might be time to take a trip to Sacramento and see the railroad museum again and stay at the Holiday Inn and take a drive through wine country with Ami.

AFGHANISTAN

The morning came earlier than Greg wanted. But duty called. He knew Walt had something for him to do.

Shortly after he arrived to his office in the morning, he got a sudden pop-up on his screen and the Instant Message said, "This is Walt, I'm out front in the golf cart." Greg made his way to the front entrance and there was Walt and Tiāncái in the golf cart with Tiāncái driving.

With the baseball cap on and the sunglasses, Tiāncái looked like a regular person wearing Polo Shirt and slacks and tennis shoes.

Tiāncái drove them to a parking area where the SUV waited for them. They were soon on the way back to Livermore Municipal Airport where a GS650 waited for them.

In due time they were landing on runway 32 North again and pulled up to a hangar and got out, went into the building they had now been in a few times.

Inside the building was a TR-4. This time there were a couple Air Force pilots there to fly them and soon they would find out why. Greg knew better than to ask any questions because they would brief him when he needed to know. It was best for him he didn't know until he had to for his own psychological wellbeing. Just like Greg experienced a few times before the two Air Force pilots took off and went out into space, but not for long. In about twenty minutes they were going back down into the atmosphere over a vast desert area. In due time, they were landing at a secret base in Saudi Arabia.

The TR-4 pulled into a hangar, and they all got out. Next to the TR4 was a TR-3B. It didn't look quite as sexy as the TR-4, but this model had been modified for some special purpose.

Greg and Tiāncái were ushered into the TR-3B where a CIA REP in a suit most addressed Greg.

CIA REP
Greg, we'll now tell you the mission you will perform.

GREG
Alright, what will we be doing?

CIA REP
The mission planning including flight plan and weapons deployment has been recorded on the ship's computers; you are just along for the ride.

GREG
What's Tiāncái going to be doing and why did you have him come with me?

CIA REP
Tiāncái will pilot the TR-3B in accordance with (IAW) the flight plan. The TR-3B automated systems will do what we want it to do, then, the TR-3B will return here and you will get back on the TR-4 and go back to Area 51. Any questions?

GREG
Since it's all preprogrammed, I suppose not.

Tiāncái and Greg were strapped in by a technician who then exited the craft and shut the access hatch. The plane's computers were the backup. Tiāncái was fully programmed to conduct the mission. Either computational resource, TR-3B internal computers or Tiāncái would get the job done just like the coming Pluto II mission in the future.

The TR-3B was soon taking off down the Saudi runway like a conventional aircraft. They had to fly it like a regular aircraft until it got way up in the sky fearing security breaches.

Once the TR-3B got up to 40,000 feet it accelerated to Mach-five, over 3000 miles per hour.

Greg observed the Global maps showing where they were and where they were going really fast and in a short while it appeared, they were heading straight for Afghanistan.

Terrorists had dug in a spot that would make conventional attack very bloody and costly, so the TR-3B was going to come in and be the equalizer.

When the TR-3B approached Afghanistan at night, it got down fairly low and over a terrorist well-dug-in encampment. The terrorists came out celebrating and were unaware that a major force had just arrived. Every terrorist coming out of their bunkers pointed up at the sky and yelled, "UFO! UFO! UFO!"

The TR-3B hovered right over the terrorist encampment putting out some artificial sound via synthesized audio sounding like something that came out of *STAR TREK* and most of the terrorists came out pointing at the UFO!

The terrorists then fired bullets, missiles and shoulder launched missiles.

TIĀNCÁI

The TR-3B deflects bullets, missiles, and shrapnel with its artificial gravity field. Therefore, the terrorists are not going to be able to shoot us down with missiles or guns.

GREG

Are we just going to wait here or shoot back?

TIĀNCÁI

The TR-3B's cannon shoots the same projectiles as A-10 Wart Hogs. Now that we recorded the terrorists' positions exposed by firing those weapons, we'll return fire.

Tiāncái turned the ground into huge geysers of dirt and debris as the cannon kept on spitting out the depleted uranium projectiles mixed in the gun belt with projectiles loaded with high explosives and a few tracers.

The terrorists were cut down in a minute. Those fleeing could not escape the infrared and ultraviolet active tracker system that pumped deadly cluster rounds on them. In less than five minutes it was over. The TR-3B then flew back to Saudi Arabia.

One of the marines in the line of Humvees that called in air support because the well dug in terrorists would get a lot of Americans killed if they tried to do any sort of frontal attack, filmed it with his cell phone. In due time he forwarded the video to his brother back in Huntington Beach, California, who subsequently posted it on YouTube, where it still resides today shocking the INTEL community in why the Government never took it down.

Sometimes the military purposely leaks information to suit their purposes. This egregious compromise of classified information was still being investigated when Greg went on his sojourn a couple years later.

Greg felt the nice bounces that occurred when some of those stinger missiles exploded near the craft. A former American official sold those Stinger Missiles to groups within the Middle East, they thought were on the side of the CIA but ended up in the hands of the terrorists.

The gravity force field did a great job of preventing any damage to the TR-3B, but the shockwaves caused an effect that felt like turbulence as the shrapnel from the weapon explosions curved around the TR-3B gravity field and were deflected.

Even though Greg was a lot safer than he realized, anyone in his position would naturally have grave concern watching all the Triple-A and Stinger Missiles coming up and exploding right next to the ship giving of a graphic choreography of powerful chaos.

This was Greg's baptism of fire, all part of his psychological conditioning with the caveat, had the artificial gravity field been slightly weaker when the stinger missiles hit, his craft would have been damaged and he would probably be tortured by the terrorists in about fifteen minutes, especially after killing as many of them as they did, including most of their leaders.

Greg thinking about his days of experiencing Victor and Delta class Crazy Ivan's firsthand and passing within fifty feet of another submarine going probably fifteen knots or more, didn't quite generate the stress this event did. In the cat-and-mouse games below the sea during the Cold War nations engaged in. None of that undersea extravaganza ever made it to the surface or to the press.

Both sides of the cold war squelched any leaks because in most cases arrogant and cavalier commanding officers exceeded their instructions in such very foolish activities. These actions occurred mainly during the 1960s and 1970s and didn't die down until Gorbachev and Reagan met face to face in Reykjavik Iceland in the 1980's.

The public was unaware until authors like Susan Sontag and others wrote revealing books. How much of it is true we'll never know. The silent service proves to be very silent and are the masters of spoon-feeding authors like Susan Sontag who then report gobbledygook.

Greg didn't know it but his seat was hard wired. The helmet he was required to wear on this trip to protect him from shrapnel damage, had brain wave monitors. His pulse, blood pressure, heart rate, and stress levels were measured by one hundred different ways collectively creating a massive report on the subject using the best minds and brains in America to figure it all out.

Greg felt an initial shock and awe, but as the TR-3B peeled away to return back to base, all of it was behind him. He managed to completely compartmentalize his emotions. He certainly didn't measure like others tested in similar fashion. This wasn't any type of qualifying flight; it was mainly for his sponsors to see how he would react and how much faith he would put into Tiāncái.

Perhaps if Greg had another human to talk with it might have been different. Experts theorized that since Greg knew Tiāncái was just a robot, perhaps he didn't feel enough humanity to discuss with him the trauma he just experienced. There was little conversation going to the target area, and there certainly was no conversation afterwards.

Greg's Alpha, Beta, and Gama brainwaves spiked during the intensive fire fight. However, his Theta, Epsilon, and Delta waves were the predominate ones on the flight back to Saudi Arabia. That was a mystery to the scientists because he was not sleeping. He was fully alert, and the video recording of his face showed his eyes were moving constantly to the different sections of the display screen. None of the experts knew what to make of this finding.

As instructed by mission planners via satellite links, Tiāncái was ordered to fly near the airport at 30,000 feet and come straight down to avoid a lot of unnecessary exposure.

Air Traffic Controller radars would not be able to see the stealth aircraft, but they wanted to reduce any possible visual sighting to prevent eyes on the ground correlating their return with the hit in Afghanistan.

The beautiful part of the antigravity machine is the TR-3B could point the runway access and continue down vertically until about 1000 feet where it pivoted horizontally and came down like a Harrier Jump Jet or an F35 VTOL like US Marines operated but with a much less fraction of the noise.

F35 is a noisy pig. TR-3B is acoustically stealthily. That's why they had to transmit the sound to arouse the terrorists.

TR-4B is even stealthier but was not combat proven like the TR-3B which is why they had to switch planes. The purpose of the TR-4B in this mission was to be able to get to Saudi Arabia promptly to be in position to perform the TR-3B mission at the planned offensive now just underway.

Coming back to Saudi Arabia took slightly less time than to go to Afghanistan. As soon as Tiāncái landed the TR-3B, their TR-4B was pulled out of the hangar and the two Air Force Officers were there to fly them back to Area 51.

Greg knew he had just tasted real war and was on an aircraft that just killed more than one hundred humans. If this was just a taste of what was in store for him, he might have bit off more than he could chew.

Greg now started to wonder if, his purpose in life somehow surrounded the TR-4B. But why did they waste all that time teaching him nuclear fission and fusion if his work had something to do with those air frames? It just didn't make sense.

Why did they have Air Force officers fly him to Saudi Arabia when Tiāncái could have managed? There was more to the story than Greg realized.

The Air Force Officers were there for legal reasons. A Robot or a civilian is not allowed to fly an armed aircraft into Saudi Arabia. The names and rank of the officers had to be provided to the Saudis before permission was granted to them to fly in on the "Modified F22" as the cover story stated.

Before long they were back up in the air with the TR-4B going vertical feeling no gravity. Thirty minutes later they were touching down on runway 32 North at Area 51 Homey Airport.

Just as Greg had experienced before, a short SUV ride 1000 yards down the tarmac and he was put aboard the GS650 and on his way back to the Livermore Lab.

By the time he arrived home it was already 9:00. He took a shower, blow-dried his hair, put on some nice clothes, and texted Ami.

GREG TEXT MESSAGE
Do you need a ride home tonight?

AMI TEXT MESSAGE
If you want to swing by at 11:00, I'll be finishing.

GREG TEXT MESSAGE
Alright, see you then

Ami usually had her meals at the restaurant as part of her benefits and took advantage of it. Mindful of her figure, she ate healthy food which might be salads and soup of the day.

The manager was always looking at ways to cut cost and wondered if he was too generous with Ami so he inquired to the chef about her eating habbits.

CATTLEMAN'S RESTAURANT CHEF
She eats as much as a church mouse and not much more. She only likes soup and salads.

CATTLEMAN'S RESTAURANT MANAGER
To have an outstanding employee like Ami that was not of any burden, the least I could do is provide her soups and salads.

CATTLEMAN'S RESTAURANT CHEF
Most certainly.

CATTLEMAN'S RESTAURANT MANAGER
If Ami was routinely devouring a 16-oz. Porterhouse steaks every night, we would have to negotiate.

It was too late for Greg to get in any exercise, so he did what he didn't want to do and drove to a Subway and got a sandwich and an energy drink to pick him up a few notches, especially if his princess AMI wanted a repeat performance.

Greg picked up Ami right at 11:00. On the way home Ami indicated she was tired.

AMI
Greg, I am glad you made love to me the way you did last night but I didn't get a lot of sleep. I was so overwhelmed by it all and I'm terribly sleepy. Could you just drop me off at my apartment tonight?

GREG
Sure thing.

Greg pulled up and stopped in front of Ami's apartment and she reached over and gave him the most romantic kiss and some sweet words.

AMI
Greg, I cherish you. Thank you for being such a wonderful gentleman.

Ami left Greg with his tongue tied as she got out of the car, went home, took a shower, and went right to bed.

<u>INT. DAY GREG'S OFFICE AT LAWRENCE LIVERMORE LABS.</u>

Greg showed up in the office the following morning and shortly afterwards Colonel Schneider showed up with another person, a lady who happened to be a psychiatrist. The female psychiatrist had long curly blonde hair, aqua blue marine eyes that were eerily incredibly beautiful, a pretty face, nice size breasts and was well dressed.

COLONEL SCHNEIDER

Greg, this is Dr. Shirley. She's fully cleared for Pluto II. I'm a flight surgeon and know a lot about psychiatry as I am trained in the field.

GREG

May I ask why she is here?

COLONEL SCHNEIDER

Dr. Shirley is here to ask you about recent experiences and see how it affected you. I personally think you measured up fine, but she's here to dot our I's and cross our Ts to make sure we covered all the bases.

GREG

Sure, no problem.

COLONEL SCHNEIDER

Dr. Shirley will probably ask you some rather personal questions. So, I'm going to leave now and let this distinguished professional handle all this and she'll give me a report which I will use as your flight surgeon to clear you for further flight operations.

GREG

Alright.

COLONEL SCHNEIDER

After Dr. Shirley finishes her interview, I suggest you go take a few days off in San Diego and relax. I know you have been through a lot lately and we don't want to burn you out.

GREG

How am I going to get to San Diego, I do not have any reservations.

COLONEL SCHNEIDER
We've arranged for a flight for you after you do what you need to do to get ready at your condo, call your controller and he'll send an SUV over to pick you up and you will be on your way home.

GREG
Thanks.

Dr. Shirley knew the level of surveillance on Greg. In her mind it was almost criminal to the extent they were doing in invasion of his privacy. But she knew the facts. She knew that Ami had fell in love with Greg and when he left on his voyage it would certainly break her heart.

Greg's departure would soon put a huge amount of burden on his personal psyche so Dr. Shirley had to help prepare him for those final moments where he would depart this world either fully alert or sedated for a few weeks if necessary. If they had to go the second route, he would wake up going faster than light speed well out of the solar system.

After Colonel Schneider left the room Dr. Shirley, a shrewd interviewer got right to it.

DR. SHIRLEY
On your TR-3B flight, did you experience anxiety?

GREG
I would say there were a few moments that tested my nerves.

DR. SHIRLEY
Was that during the missile attack?

GREG
That and all the ordinance activity.

DR. SHIRLEY
Does that include the canon firing from you TR-3B?

DR. SHIRLEY
Sure, it obviously was a spectacle.

DR. SHIRLEY
You have a history that we know about in detail, you have been through tough times before including flooding casualties on submarines, almost capsizing, and very sensitive missions that were of grave risk, how did your feelings in the combat on the TR-3B compare with all of that?

GREG

Well, I would be a liar if I didn't admit some of that scared the shit out of me. Going to test depth on twenty- and thirty-year-old 594 class SSNs really makes you think.

DR. SHIRLEY

When you went to out to sea the first time on a submarine that had been cut in half and to test depth was that just as bad?"

GREG

Yes and no. The 593 sunk, none of the other classes did that I rode. So, I had hope it would make it.

DR. SHIRLEY

But you were quite glad when you got back up to the surface.

GREG

You damn right I was and so was everyone else on the crew.

DR. SHIRLEY

In your Cold War missions did you experience any similar emotions?

GREG

That was different, the excitement of the experience drowned out the fear. I wasn't scared until I got back to land and reflected upon it.

DR. SHIRLEY

Did you do anything special to overcome those psychological stressors?

GREG

Yeah, I drank as much alcohol as my body would take at times and had as much sex as possible.

DR. SHIRLEY

That's a good point to bring up. Did you feel more corruptible during those moments of high stress?

GREG

Sure, I will admit I drank more and chased more pussy then than I did before and after.

DR. SHIRLEY
So, in a sense it turned you into a heathen?

GREG
Absolutely.

DR. SHIRLEY
But you overcame it.

GREG
Yes, now looking back at it, that wasn't so bad after all. Perhaps since I was so close to the action made it seem a lot worse than what it really was.

DR. SHIRLEY
How long did it take you to recover from those episodes?

GREG
I never fully recovered because I kept doing hazardous missions so I oscillated in and out of the temporal odyssey bestowed upon me from all that activity.

DR. SHIRLEY
How about after you retired?

GREG
It certainly slowly faded into the past.

DR. SHIRLEY
But not completely?

GREG
I would say ninety-five percent and unless something comes up to trigger the memories, I completely forget it.

DR. SHIRLEY
When you got off the train the other day, there were a couple federal agents there following you to protect you because you are a high-valued person associated with this project, the two punks came at you and threatened you, until those two men intervened, what went through your mind?

GREG
First of all, I thought they were going to attempt kidnapping Ami and using her like a sex slave in the

most disgusting fashion possibly killing her when they finished their fun time with her.

DR. SHIRLEY
Were you going to do something about it?

GREG
The element of surprise was on my side. They probably assumed I was timid and old and would not stop them from grabbing her and taking her away. I know I could not beat them in a fistfight, but I know in the first thirty seconds I could unleash some devastating kicks to their shins and other parts of their bodies to pay the price for this attack.

DR. SHIRLEY
You planned on doing that?

GREG
Yes, I knew if I kicked the first one in the shins real hard, he would be temporarily disabled and with Ami screaming which I believe she would have, the other guy might have had second thoughts.

I would have had time to kick him as well and if they were both wounded and in pain further kicks might have downed one of them.

Since I feared for my life, would have attempted to kill the first one to totally disable him so I would have a one on one with the other where I would be fighting for my life. He would only be fighting for a piece of ass, so the impetus would have been on me. As fast as the two Feds took them down, they were pushovers as it turned out. So, I think I would have fared okay.

DR. SHIRLEY
What was the most important aspect of all that to you?

GREG
Simply, Ami's security.

DR. SHIRLEY
What about Hikaru?

GREG
Of course, I was concerned about her too and I think the two girls would have joined in and helped me.

DR. SHIRLEY
The other day when you did you two flights out in space, how did you feel about it?

GREG
The first one caught me by surprise. I had no idea we were going out into space. I figured they were taking me some place for a specific reason.

DR. SHIRLEY
Were you scared?

GREG
Anyone going out into space and saying they don't have the least bit of trepidation is a liar.

DR. SHIRLEY
So probably initially you had a little fear, but as the flight continued how did you feel?

GREG
When we approached the moon, I felt a sense of exhilaration. Few men had ever done this before and when the pilots said how close we came to the moon; I was in awe. At that point I no longer had any sense of fear. My thoughts were more expansive and reflective.

DR. SHIRLEY
The TR-4 is a closely guarded secret. You really did have an extraordinary opportunity. When you went around Mars, how did you feel about it?

GREG
By then I no longer had any concern about the aircraft. I felt it had proven its technology to me, but I will say I would have much more preferred one of those Air Force officers flying it than Tiāncái.

DR. SHIRLEY
Why is that?

GREG
I suppose it's human nature. I would tend to feel like the Air Force officer would have flown the mission in a predictable manner. But with Tiāncái, a Robot flying it, I had no idea what to expect. I would not have felt so alone if I had been with a human.

DR. SHIRLEY
You helped build Tiāncái, why didn't you have faith in that robot?

GREG
I think it was too much too quickly and had I had longer time to consider it, perhaps I would not have felt less secure.

DR. SHIRLEY
Do you have any concerns about Tiāncái's design?

GREG
I don't really know how rugged he is or what failure mechanisms he might have. Nor do I really have a grasp of his programming and how successful his artificial intelligence is.

DR. SHIRLEY
Do you know we measure his artificial intelligence every day, twenty-four hours a day?

GREG
Having seen some of the things project Pluto II has exposed me to, I would never assume anything now. The only thing I know now is to expect the unexpected.

DR. SHIRLEY
How do you feel about that?

GREG
It's not as if I'm fearless, but as time goes by and I get more of these nice little experiences like I had yesterday and realize I'm constantly put in a position to which I can't do anything about it, I grow less concerned. I just hope if there is a failure, I don't feel pain for too long.

DR. SHIRLEY
We could never promise you how fast any pain would subside, because we really don't know what will be bestowed upon you in the future.

GREG
Sure.

DR. SHIRLEY
How would you feel if you could never see Ami again?

GREG
Well, certainly there would be some sadness.

DR. SHIRLEY
Would it be as bad as your wife leaving you?

GREG
That is a different type of pain. I understand my wife has some rationalization because of her desire to experience Japan for the rest of her life. She chose Japan over me. I'm okay with that. She gave me many happy years. I have no regrets.

DR. SHIRLEY
Okay, but Ami never gave you years, how would you feel if you were suddenly forced to never see her again?

GREG
If it were her choice, I would be hurt. If it were my choice, I would probably have severe regrets later.

DR. SHIRLEY
What if it was someone else's choice and there wasn't anything you can do about it?

GREG
I suppose I would adapt and try not to dwell on it too long.

DR. SHIRLEY
Alright, is there anything else you would like to bring up about your personal psychology, that you might use us to help you with?

GREG
No, I'm okay with what is happening with me now.

DR. SHIRLEY
Is it because you like the big fat paycheck?

GREG
Everyone likes money. I planned well and already have enough money. All this extra cash only allows me to play more often.

DR. SHIRLEY
Alright, Greg, thank you for giving me such straight-up answers. A lot of people would not be so forthcoming like you.

GREG
You are welcome.

DR. SHIRLEY
Greg, because we know your trip to Afghanistan was an ordeal that would have a serious impact on most people, we think you need a few days off. We want you to go back to San Diego and not spend the next four days with Ami. She will be here when you get back.

GREG
Alright. I probably need to get home and check up on my home.

DR. SHIRLEY
Go home, relax, exercise, have fun and then come back and expect you will be doing more and more interesting events.

GREG
After three very surprising events, I would not try to guess what that would be.

DR. SHIRLEY
Greg, I also would like to remind you this entire conversation is TS-SCI, and in accordance with the agreement you signed, you are not permitted to discuss anything we just went over without prior approval of your controller.

GREG
Understand all. If I mentioned any of this to just about anyone, they would think I was smoking crack. Nobody would believe it and I'm not interested in discussing it.

DR. SHIRLEY
Good, have a nice time down in San Diego, and perhaps in a few weeks we'll talk again.

GREG
Alright.

Shirley got up and walked out of the room, and Greg thought Dr. Shirley is one of the most beautiful women he had ever set eyes on.

A moment after Shirley walked out of the room, Greg received a text from Walter Bissonnet.

WALTER BISSONNET TEXT MESSAGE
Come out to the front entrance.

Greg walked out to the front entrance and to his surprise, there was Walt with Agent A and Agent B he had that inopportune meeting at the train station with the two punks from Australia. They had their sunglasses and casual clothes. Nobody would suspect they were agents. *I wonder where they are hiding their guns.*

Greg climbed into the front seat of the golf cart with Walt who was driving them a couple blocks where an SUV was waiting for them.

WALTER BISSONNET
Greg, your ride is here. You earned some time off. You
have been through a lot lately. When you come back
in four days, we think you will be ready for your next
journey. Stay safe.

GREG
I will, thanks.

The SUV took the three to Greg's condo so he could grab what he needed, then to Livermore Municipal Airport where the GS650 was waiting for them.

In an hour after takeoff, he was arriving in San Diego Lindberg Field where the GS650 pulled into an area next to Pacific Coast Hiway where jet leasing companies ferried individuals in and out of private jets, some owned and some chartered.

The limo they hopped in took them to Greg's home where he got out. His two bodyguards remained in the limo as it drove off.

<u>INT. DAY GREG'S HOME</u>

Greg went inside his home. It was exactly as he had left it. His new neighbor across the street and a couple houses down was one of the spooks to keep an eye on him and brought in firepower, if necessary, to protect Greg, but nobody assumed this private person would hardly be noticed. Greg's neighbors made a point not to even look at Greg or talk to him as soon as they discovered his wife had left on a permanent basis.

Perhaps the psychiatrists were right. He needed some time to unwind.

It was just after lunchtime so it was the perfect time to go to Ski Beach and see if he could still handle ten miles.

A Hawaiian shirt, shorts, walking shoes and his special Panama Paul hat, and he was out the door and, in his car, driving the relative short distance to Ski Beach. In his possession he had some snacks, a couple Red Bulls left after he drank one on the way.

Greg parked and soon was on the sidewalk making laps around the park. In about thirty minutes he ran across one of the park employees, a guy named Damion who was a very nice person whom he liked. He stopped and chatted with Damion for a short while who was working on a project in the park and was sweating after doing a lot of work and looked like he needed to take a break.

Then Greg continued, eventually meeting up with Lee, his black friend who loved to feed the seagulls. They chatted for a while as Lee told Greg about demons and gave him an update on how he was working on the cinematography to capture their images.

Lee could go on for quite a while. Greg showed a lot of respect and concern for Lee who seemed to need someone to talk with who took him seriously. After listening to *Coast-to -Coast* during late nights, based on interviews with some of the guests, there was no reason why not to take Lee seriously. He appeared to be just as valid as many of the Coast guests.

After a few more laps, he came across a lady he met often walking her dog. This was a nice lady and Greg respected her as well. But he knew he had to cut the chit chat or he would never get the miles done. After a couple laps and four miles Greg decided it was time for a Red Bull drink. He opened the back of his SUV and sat down and drank a Red Bull eating one of his snacks. In due time the blackbirds and seagulls arrived staring at him. The seagulls started squawking, they wanted some too.

Looking around to make sure no park rangers were nearby; Greg walked over to the feeding tree and placed some goodies there for the blackbirds. If he threw it on the parking lot pavement, the seagulls would get it because they were mean and chased the blackbirds away. There were a few instances where they tested the blackbird patience and the blackbirds amazingly upset then attacked the smaller seagulls in flight.

Now and then the black birds chase the Red Tail Hawks out of the park. Those birds grab and kill the pigeons. They are a menace to the pigeons. The Red Tail Hawks had no fear of Greg because they usually land on the light posts up 30 some feet, until they discovered Greg could throw rocks at them. That was a game changer. Greg saved three or four pigeons from the Red Tail Hawks and once or twice from Ospreys who also came to the park to get squirrels and pigeons.

After his break Greg started his walk again, enjoying it and thinking about a lot of things. It's true he felt he really was a bachelor now even though he was legally married still. He realized she's never coming home. Then he started having thoughts that screwing around with Ami was a waste of time and had it not been for the fact she looked like his wife twenty-five years ago, he probably might not have done what he did.

When you walk ten miles every single day it's easy. But with the new challenges of the job, his exercise was stretching out now and the workouts were no longer getting done with the routine he did just a few months ago. At the seven-mile mark Greg decided. That's enough for today. Tomorrow I'll work harder.

Greg went home, took a shower and changed then texted Ami.

GREG TEXT MESSAGE

I'm down in San Diego. I'm going to be here four days taking care of some business, then I'll be back in town. Hope to see you as soon as I get back.

She didn't respond for a while, so he started thinking about his interview with the Psychiatrist Shirley. Perhaps she was tipping him off, this big project had intervened and told her to get lost or something. With these people anything is possible. It seemed so surreal what they did.

Greg was used to seeing Ami or others every day, and no longer desired to be alone all the time, decided he would go out that night. Since the stock market recently did well for his portfolio, his pay was extraordinary, and he was being paid far more than what he was worth. He didn't understand why.

So, in a few spare moments of each day as he was thinking about it, Greg played the market swings and dumped sizeable cash into new investments. His portfolio was now growing about ten times quicker than when his wife was home. This consulting gig was working out financially well.

Greg had just been paid on Friday. He had not checked his bank statement, but when he looked, he realized his checking account was now about ten times larger than any time when his wife was still with him.

As Greg pondered his evening, he decided, *I'm going out.* Greg called Rodriguez.

GREG

Do you think you could give me a ride in about an hour?

RODRIGUEZ

Sure, boss. No problem.

GREG

Thanks, see you in an hour.

Greg cleaned up, put on some nice clothes, and his most expensive cologne and was ready when Rodriguez called.

RODRIGUEZ

I'm out front, boss.

GREG

Alright, coming.

As Greg got in the automobile Rodriguez smelled the cologne and noticed Greg was dressed to impress.

<u>EXT. DAY RODRIGUEZ AUTOMOBILE</u>

RODRIGUEZ

Wow, you smell good tonight, what's the special occasion?

GREG
I got paid on Friday so I decided I would have a night
on the town.

RODRIGUEZ
Where do you want to go?

GREG
Take me to the Flaming Flamingo.

RODRIGUEZ
Alright.

Tonight, Greg was going stag. Ami never returned his text so he figured the spooks might have scared her off. *Oh well, it was good while it lasted.*

Greg now feeling a little strange from all his recent activities, realized, don't take anything for granted because you never know when you might lose it. As he was getting out of the Uber car, he felt generous.

GREG
Rodriguez, you have always been faithful and
accommodative to me and I appreciate it. Here. Keep
the change, I probably owe you a lot more. Thank you
for all you have done for me.

As Rodriguez looked at that crisp $100 bill responded.

RODRIGUEZ
Thanks, boss, I appreciate you too.

The bar was half full when Greg arrived. Greg got a seat directly in front where Tio was standing again this evening.

Tio was all smiles. He remembered this great tipper.

TIO
Another Robert Mondavi?

GREG
Sure. With a Sprite chaser.

Tio served the glass of wine and Greg handed him a $20.

GREG
Keep the change.

Tio and Greg traded jokes for a while until Tio started to get busy as the crowd rolled in.

Monica Cheung had just left a Navy Captain a short while ago who was thinking with his little head and Monica was stringing him along as if she were going to let him tap that golden pussy if he would open up just a little more about what he actually did at SPAWAR (since then became. A former DDG commander, now a program manager, had something to do with communications and Monica was advised he was someone of interest.

The Navy Captain might have been a *horny son of a bitch*, but he wasn't going to fall for a honey trap. He was turning out to be one of the most difficult challenges Monica ever encountered. It was as if the mouse was playing with the cat.

Monica Cheung decided to go to the Flaming Flamingo before she hauled her sorry ass back to Rancho Santa Fe and send an encoded message to her handler she had once again failed. The message actually predetermined and programmed in case it was intercepted simply stated, the roses were beautiful today in the body of the message.

The receiving end did a word search using Word by Microsoft that easily found the phrase. Monica Cheung would receive another message tomorrow saying:

MSS MESSAGE VIA EMAIL
The box of candy you sent me was delicious.

Decoded meant: This is mission critical; you need to do more, our sponsors want this badly." It also implied, "*We don't give a damn if you have to give him your pussy, don't come home without the goods.*"

Monica liked sex, but only desired to do it with a bona fide lover and not part of her employment. It made her feel cheap like a whore. But when the MSS trained her, they explained how the honeypot routine worked, and as a spy, she had an obligation to her controller to carry out her mission even if she had to have sex with her target. She knew what a prostitute must feel. Someone in control of their lives forcing them to do nefarious activities, especially those traffickers of people in the sex trade.

The MSS didn't realize Monica would become the perfect double spy if she was ever turned because she detested the honeypot role her handlers had forced her into several times already. It almost made her want to puke.

There was a seat at the bar next to that guy she had seen some time ago, so she sat down there. Then she started in motivated by the fact this jerk irked her because he never calle.

MONICA
Hello, I'm surprised you never called me.

Greg embellished the truth slightly, but it was basically true in what he said.

GREG
I've been out of town for a while, or I would have.

Greg was still satisfied from the last encounter he had with Ami; he had no inspiration to waste his time with Monica who appeared like a high-maintenance woman.

Monica's stomach was feeling a little rough and feeling a little hungry.

MONICA
I'm a little hungry, I'm going to order something, I've
not eaten in quite a few hours if you don't mind.

GREG
Sure, I was thinking the same thing.

In due time, Monica was eating her chef salad and Greg was eating another New York Strip. The combination of the steak, the wine, and Monica's perfume set the night just right.

Monica was well proportioned. She had a great pare of knockers and an ass that would humble most men.

Greg was not the least horny nor was he thinking about sex, but the two were having a splendid time.

Monica took a liking to Greg. He wasn't pushing or assuming and never made any suggestive comments or any attempt to inflate her ego. Monica was taught a long time ago, any man being nice to you truly only wants your pussy. Being in the spy business, she proved that theory repeatedly. Greg wasn't being nice; he was just enjoying himself. The fact he ignored her and didn't call her in a way pissed Monica off. Monica was a dynamite sex kitten and Greg didn't even bother calling. *This guy is either gay or he has the best control I've ever seen.*

MONICA
Greg, may I ask you a question?

GREG
Sure.

MONICA
Are you gay?"

Greg laughed a bit and then responded.

GREG
No, I'm not a switch hitter. I just like to get to know a
woman really good before I have a relationship. I don't
want to waste my time on fruitless encounters and
situations that will never work out.

MONICA
Okay, that's fair.

GREG
Thank you.

MONICA
Greg, you have never given me the least bit of interest.
Am I really that ugly?

GREG
No, on the contrary, Monica, you are very beautiful.
Any man with a brain would be proud of you.

MONICA
Would you be proud of me?

GREG
Why, certainly.

Monica Cheung and Greg chatted some more, and Monica was feeling a lot better now but wanted to go home take care of business, a couple sleeping pills and just sleep off her latest failure.

MONICA
Tio, could you please give me my check?

TIO
Sure.

In a brief period of time, Tio handed Monica a bill holder.

GREG
Let me take care of that.

MONICA
Are you sure of that?

Monica had one eyebrow raised in a very suggestive manner.

GREG
Yes, please let me. I enjoyed talking with you.

MONICA
If you insist.

Monica then stood up off the bar stool and held out her hand.

MONICA
Thank you, Greg. If you are not busy, I would like to invite you over to my place on Saturday and make dinner for you.

GREG
I might be able to. I'm not sure what my plans are yet.

MONICA
You got my number. Call me Friday so I can prepare if
you want to come over Saturday.

GREG
Don't make a big fuss for me. I'm a simple person.

MONICA
I'm a simple woman too. I look forward to hearing
from you.

They shook hands and away Monica went.

As a good spy she wanted to know exactly who Greg was and she might even be curious
if he's a good lover. He certainly has a sweet disposition. And he wasn't overly nice like
sex hounds act.

Timing is everything. Five minutes after she left around 11:00 P.M. Ami texted Greg.

C.U. TEXT MESSAGE (GREG'S I-PHONE).

AMI TEXT MESSAGE
I finally got off work, was a busy night for me.

GREG TEXT MESSAGE
Good. Stay safe.

AMI TEXT MESSAGE
Thank you.

GREG TEXT MESSAGE
I got seven-mile walk in today.

The texting went on for a bit until Ami ended it.

AMI TEXT MESSAGE
I'm going to get ready for bed now. Have a nice night.

GREG TEXT MESSAGE
Thank you.

Everything with Ami was okay after all it seemed.

Greg was thinking about what Hikaru said on the train. There he was with a chance to
boink a young woman with a set of nice knockers. And now here's Monica, seemingly

initiating something. Would he be interested in Monica? She seemed older and more mature. Monica made Ami seem like a little girl. Would Greg even consider taking up Monica's invitation?

In due time, Rodriguez picked up Greg at the Flaming Flamingo and drove him home.

After the appropriate inducements, Greg was in bed and the alarm clock was not set. He would wake up when he no longer felt like sleeping.

The Lawrence Livermore Lab personally left Greg alone for four days. Dr. Shirley provided her analysis and report to Walter Bissonette and Colonel Schneider. In her report, Dr. Shirley recommended: *Greg needed some down time and feared they had driven him to hard.*

MONICA CHEUNG

Friday proved to be the make-or-break. In Greg's mind as he was pondering the ten miles, his subconscious kept on asking him, *how bad do you want it?* Greg marched on like a good soldier but barely finished the ten miles.

Greg's feet were a little sore along with his left knee, but after the appropriate painkillers he was feeling okay.

He went to one of his favorite restaurants, Pastabilities, located on Midway Drive. The food there was always wonderful. Sadly, Pastabilities since closed due to COVID restrictions destroyed it economically like a lot of small business. But the big stores were allowed to operate. Such pathetic misguidance by the government people could write volumes about. The owner was a terrific guy. He was well liked in the community as well.

FLASHBACK

A few years ago, San Diego had a major power outage. San Onofre nuclear power plant had been shut down for issues with cracks in the Japanese steam generators. This was at a time when the Democrat party which controlled California was heavily anti-nuke and anti-coal. Their misguided judgement just like the Germans ten years before was, everything should switch to Green Energy.

Unfortunately, with the nuclear power plant shut down, when the power coming over from Arizona was accidentally cut off by a utility worker, the city of San Diego suddenly went dark. No traffic lights operated and roads were jammed for hours.

The owner of *Pastabilities*, feeling a need to help the public went next door across the street and rented a generator from Home Depot, then he drove home and got one of his own generators to save all his frozen material. He set up a barbecue outside his restaurant and made four types of sandwiches thanks to his quick thinking on the generators. When Greg and his family stood in line to buy sandwiches because all restaurants were shut down due to no power and all the grocery stores closed because none of the cash registers worked, and people couldn't cook at home without electricity, they heard about this, and there were at least three hundred people in line behind Greg buying sandwiches at that time. Greg was told they finally shut down around 11:00 P.M. that night

The public will never forget *Pastabilities* owner for his wonderful generosity and help in a crisis.

Greg purchased a footlong spaghetti and meatball sandwich and went home and had his meal.

As Greg was finishing up his lunch and thinking about Monica, and perhaps since his world was changing and he could be dead sometime soon on another risky mission, maybe he deserved to get his hands on a nice set of knockers like Monica had. Greg would never get it on with Hikaru because that would be like stabbing Ami in the back and he's not that kind of person. Plus, this Monica deal might just be a plutonic thing anyway. Greg certainly wasn't looking for romance.

Something in in Gregs thoughts kept saying, "Go for it."

Just when he shouldn't Greg picked up Monica's business card and called her.

Monica had just been with the Navy Captain and who was pissed because Monica wasn't ready to have sex with him and he got real nasty about her asking him about his work as if he had something to hide (and he did).

MONICA
Hello?

GREG
This is Greg, we met at the Flaming Flamingo.

MONICA
Oh, hello, Greg, nice to hear from you.

Monica wasn't expecting Greg's call, and she was pouting when it came in. In the face of failure, she was suddenly uplifted because this nice gentleman called her. But was it just because he wanted a piece of ass? She would find out soon. She's the one that dishes it out. Nobody takes it from her. And she doesn't share.

GREG
I was just calling to see if you still wanted some company tomorrow.

MONICA
Yes, in fact I predicted your call, so I already did some preparations.

GREG
Don't make a fuss over me. I don't need much.

MONICA
It's my pleasure. I've had a bad day and seeing you
tomorrow just might make me feel better.

GREG
Well, I hope so.

MONICA
Greg, I see your phone number, is it okay if I text you
my address?

GREG
Sure.

MONICA
Come over around 2:00 P.M. tomorrow.

GREG
Okay.

MONICA
See you then.

GREG
See you tomorrow.

Monica hung up and Greg got another power nap in but did not wake up until the
following morning. It was a great equalizer sleep. Greg's feet and knee had a little ache
from ten miles the previous day, so he kept it down to five miles, got home and ate half
the sandwich left over from the night before. Greg didn't want to be starving when he
showed up at Monica's place to appear like a fool.

He then called Rodriguez because he realized he might get some drinking in and not
want Rodriguez to risk a DUI.

RODRIGUEZ
Hello Greg.

GREG
Rodriguez, can you pick me up at 1:30 this afternoon? I
need you to drive me up to Rancho Santa Fe.

RODRIGUEZ
Sure, boss, no problem.

Greg then got cleaned up and ready, and at 1:30 sharp there was Rodriguez. Greg started
thinking, *I might get a chance to play with some nice boobs real soon, so I will reward
Rodriguez in advance,* and when he got out of the car, handed him a crisp $100 bill.

GREG
Here's some Cash-In-Advance.

RODRIGUEZ
Thank you, boss, I appreciate this.

GREG
No problem, you more than earned it, 2:00 P.M. on the
dot.

Monica looking out the window saw that Greg had a ride there. Either *Greg has good sense not to drink and drive or he has an issue* she needed to find out. Greg rang the doorbell, and the Anglo maid answered the door.

MAID
Greg?

GREG
Yes.

MAID
Please come in, we have been expecting you. Monica is
out at the pool and wishes you join her there.

GREG
Alright.

The maid escorted Greg to the pool in back of the mansion that had a diving board and plenty of deep water. Looking around he could smell money.

Monica had money. Spies (even MSS) are well paid if they deliver. If they fail, they usually end up dead because the enemy discovers them. Foreign countries do not treat spies nearly as nice as Americans do.

Chinese only waste one bullet to the back of the head. Russians only waste the natural gas for the incinerator where its reported spies they catch go into a crematorium alive. French takes them to the countryside and tie ropes around their arms and legs that are attached to towing rigs of four different horses and stretch all their joints out really good. In some cases, the horses get spooked, and the arm or leg comes off. Nobody knows for sure what the British do, but they are the only people on the planet the Arabs fear.

Monica had on a bikini with a white knitted bathing robe that probably cost $10,000 or more.

MONICA
Elsie, why don't you take the rest of the day off?

ELSIE
Oh, thank you, Ms. Cheung. I really appreciate this.

Greg noticed there was a wine bottle with the cork popped in a silver bottle holder with ice.

MONICA
Would you like a glass of wine?

GREG
Sure.

Greg didn't know it but he was being drugged. The wine had some additives similar to Viagra that would get him up and keep him up and Monica was trained in it worked well blended in wine where the target cannot taste it or know they are being drugged.

Monica liked her sex when she picked the man. Greg was just an ordinary guy, but he was a nice guy and non-assuming.

Monica and Greg chatted for a bit not discussing anything important as Greg had several sips of the wine.

MONICA
Would you like to go for a swim?

GREG
I didn't bring any swimming attire.

MONICA
Not to worry, I have some male bathing suits laid out
for you in the guestroom, you can try on and use.

GREG
I suppose I could.

MONICA
Let me take you to the room.

Monica led Greg up to the guestroom and the mansion was decorated with a lot of antique Chinese porcelain and paintings. The artwork was impressive. Inside the guestroom was a half-dozen swimsuits laid out of different sizes.

MONICA
Get changed and come down the stairs, I'll be waiting
for you. There are some slippers by the door that will fit
you. There is a bathing robe on the bed you can wear.

GREG
Sure thing.

Greg changed into the swim trunks, put on the bathrobe, then the slippers and walked down the stairway that was ten feet away from the guestroom door.

Down at the bottom of the stairway, Monica stood patiently waiting then as he reached the bottom, she held out her hand which he grabbed, and she led him out to the table and chairs where they were sitting and sipping on wine.

Monica put down her bathrobe exposing it all and it was nice to look at then walked over to the steps to go into the pool.

MONICA
Come on, darling, us go for a swim.

Greg put his bathrobe down and complied with her command.

Monica led Greg into the water. It was nice and warm. She could obviously afford to keep it well heated.

Withing moments Monica pulled Greg into a little deeper water and they treaded and swam a little then she swam over to the side. Monica knew that by now the drug should be affecting Gregs libido

MONICA
Greg, swim over here.

Greg swam to Monica and when he got closer, she pulled him closer. Then to his surprise she wrapped her legs around him and pulled him even closer and was pushing herself against him feeling his manliness and knowing the drugs were taking affect.

MONICA
Greg why are you so shy, I think I want you to kiss me.

Greg wasn't moving fast enough so Monica initiated the powerful kiss. It was unlike almost anything Greg ever experienced before .She was purposely pushing herself against him and he knew his penis was right against her womanhood which tended to excite Greg even more.

Monica's embrace was like an octopus. If there was any doubt in Greg's mind about what Monica wanted it was quickly dispelled. Then suddenly Monica altered the dynamics.

MONICA
Greg, I'm a little thirsty, can we get out and have a sip
or two of wine?

Greg meekly replied.

GREG
Sure.

Monica thought Greg probably had enough of the aphrodisiacs, Rohypnol, Zolpidem, and Zyrexin, a sexual arousal drugs in his system now, but she wanted to pour on the coals she wanted him jacked up so high that he could not resist her or the temptation. Just a few more swallows and he would be fully drugged for what she wanted. And if she was going to pick a man to satisfy her, she wanted it nice and hard and a long time.

After she saw Greg finish the glass because one of the side-effects of the drug made people mildly thirsty so they wanted more, and she poured him another glass and when he drank half of it, Monica held out her hand to Greg.

MONICA
Greg darling, please, come with me, I want to do
something.

Monica led Greg up to the master bedroom that was impressively decorated. If there was any doubt, she was high maintenance it was instantly dispelled looking at all the profligate garlands. Monica was in fact super high maintenance.

Monica led Greg right over to her bed and she had on a quick-release bikini that dropped the top in a second and the bottom a second later exposing her beautiful breasts and her heavy pubis hiding her womanhood. Monica wasn't going to shave her bush off for any man and she liked the way she was.

Monica knew Greg was slightly confused because of the drugs mixed with two glasses of wine. This sexual tryst was coming at Greg too fast, so Monica took charge and loosened his swim trunks for him and got down on her knees and started performing fellatio on Greg which then made his erection feel even better for a short while before Monica led Greg to her bed and pulled him on top of her.

Monica was a master, a modern-day Dowager Queen, wanting that glorious gratification. Monica knew the fastest way to satisfaction was to guide Greg's penis inside her then she wrapped her legs around him and to help provide a much stronger thrust than Greg could do by himself.

Monica is a world class spy trained in all the tradecraft including martial arts. Monica worked out like Bruce Lee, but keeping her hands feminine, she didn't punch rocks like Bruce Lee did. But she worked out two hours every day, so she had unbelievable strength to force Greg's penis hard into her repeatedly. Monica's orgasms started and even though Greg started spewing his silver essence into her he wasn't going to get soft any time soon the way Monica planned it.

Monica also drugged with female sex aphrodisiacs was multiple orgasmic and probably had 100 orgasms before she finally had achieved her desired gratification. Greg was what the doctor ordered. She would use him like a cheap whore and entice him to keep coming back for more.

Now all Monica had to do was subvert that Navy Captain, and she would be financially in a position to entertain Greg for quite some time. Monica was already growing fond of Greg. But she just failed as a spy and didn't know it yet. Monica's blunder was she picked the wrong person.

Monica and Greg laid there for a while and then they both regained their composure at about the same time.

MONICA
Greg, I'm getting kind of hungry now, can we take a
break and eat a little, it's all prepared.

GREG
That sounds good.

They got out of bed. Monica went to her bathroom and cleaned up while Greg put back on his swim trunks. He could hear her running water in her bathtub. She was probably washing herself out and preventing pregnancy.

Monica then came out and walked over to her closet and put on a pull over and then picked up her bathing suit.

MONICA
Let's go downstairs.

Monica then put her bathing suit on a tiled countertop to take care of later.

Greg had seen some silver devices close to the table and never thought to think what they were. On an adjacent table was a tent-like cover over most of it. The cover was on hinges which Monica lifted it up exposing all kinds of dishes, flatware, and eating utensils. The other silver devices were electric heated food warmers. *Oh, how the rich live*, Greg thought.

Then Greg was wondering if he was possibly falling in love or something because he had never experienced sex like that before. Monica was incredible.

Monica handed Greg a plate and explained what he should do.

MONICA
Pick what you would like, I'll set up your place setting
for you.

Monica quickly demonstrated she was a very capable coordinated person, Greg soon had Polish Linen, expensive Russian cut crystal glass full of sparkling water, and cuisine that was obviously cooked by a very capable chef.

This was a private moment for Monica. She put her world aside for a while to enjoy a personal relationship with a man she picked at random who had already provided her with more than she could have imagined in such a short period of time. *Should I keep him or throw him back in the ocean full of other fish?* Monica asked herself.

If Monica only knew a tiny smidgen of information about Greg, she would have dumped that Navy Captain immediately, because Greg was the real catch and the biggest fish in the ocean by comparison. Compared to Greg, because of his singularity in his role in Project Pluto II, the Captain was just the minnow, but Monica didn't know that yet.

A good spy wants to know who surrounds them well. Greg would be no exception. Monica would switch the drugs. It would no longer be Viagra like to jack Greg up for sex. In a while he would get a dose of nights out drug that, it would now put him almost into a coma. Monica would drug Greg in her bedroom because she sure as hell didn't want to have to carry him up the stairs.

They had a peaceful dinner and sat and talked and truly enjoyed their time. Monica knew not to get into his personal business quite yet. She would find out a lot about him in a few hours when he least expected it so he would never feel any pressure. She wanted to keep it simple until destiny charted where this relationship was heading.

Monica knew Greg's a friend of Dr. Moore who the Chinese MSS are suddenly interested in, but he never fell for any of Monica's traps or any of her honeypot schemes and thus couldn't make it to first base.

The fact Greg is Dr. Moore's friend made Greg a target of opportunity. It would be sad if Monica had to drop Greg as a lover to pick him up as a target for espionage.

After a while Monica started the next phase of her agenda.

MONICA

Greg let's take this bottle of champagne up to my bed
and finish it there. If you feel up to it, you can make
love to me again.

They were soon lying in her bed when it was probably about time Greg he would have to urinated and like clockwork Greg announced:

GREG

Excuse me Monica, but I need to use your bathroom.

MONICA

Sure, Greg, it's right over there.

Greg went into Monica's bathroom and even though he shut the door, Monica could hear him drain his fire hose. She then put the nights-out drug into his glass of champagne.

Greg was fully satisfied; he had enough sex for the night and hoped they could just sleep or take it easy and maybe fondly caress each other. When he went back to bed, Monica began drugging Greg.

MONICA

Greg, I would like to make a toast to you. I truly like
you and I hope you want to keep seeing me.

Greg felt a tad bit of emotion because this beautiful woman had opened herself up to him, just an ordinary guy when she could have had the pick of the litter. He gladly toasted her and chugged the entire drug-laden glass down and sat it down on the table next to the bed and felt really good.

GREG
Monica, let me just lay and hold you for a while.

MONICA,
Greg, I like that idea.

Monica cuddled with Greg and five minutes later Greg was snoring (or purring like a kitten). Monica realized Greg would be out for probably twelve hours, gave a few more minutes to make sure, then shook him a little to make sure he was under, then felt his pulse and knew he was almost comatose.

Monica then went into the guest bedroom, pulled Greg's billfold out of his slacks and photographed everything in the wallet, including his driver's license, credit cards, ATM card, etc. She then sent an email to her controller to arrange for another set of flower arrangements sent over in the morning.

Just like Monica predicted, in twelve hours he woke up thirsty and it appeared he woke her up in the process. She too had a good sleep and orgasms Greg gave her made it that much better. She liked Greg and hoped he turned out to be okay. MSS would let her know in 48 hours who he really was.

Greg woke up and realized he was naked, and Monica comforted him.

MONICA
Don't worry, I saw everything and when you were
trying to sleep last night, I was sucking on your penis,
but you were so out of it I could not rouse you.

Then to give all appearances this was a truly romantic encounter, she crawled under the covers and started doing fellatio on Greg. When Monica determined Gregs erection was ready, she crawled up on top of him and inserted his penis into her womanhood and then started kissing Greg softly and made love to him for a while then suddenly rolled over and instructed Greg.

MONICA
Get on top of me but suck my breasts first. It turns me
on.

Greg did what Monica wanted and inserted his manliness into Monica which immediately got her super aroused just like the evening before and multiple orgasms making it all worthwhile.

After reaching her super climax and enjoying splendid euphoria on a there from Paganini, Monica knew it was time to get up clean herself out again and get on with business.

MONICA
Greg, would you like me to make you a cup of coffee?

GREG
Sure.

Monica then got up, put on a bathrobe, walked over to the guestroom, and grabbed Gregs clothes shoes, and socks and brought them to her bedroom. She laid Gregs clothes out on the bed.

MONICA
Here's your clothes if you want to get dressed, honey.

GREG
Thanks.

Greg took the hint to get out of bed, but he had no idea he had been literally raped. The Chinese MSS would soon have Greg's information and had some INTEL experts would study Greg and try to determine if Greg might be a person of interest.

Monica wasn't dressed but offered:

MONICA
Greg would you like me to give you a ride home?

GREG
Thanks for the offer, but I'm going to have Rodriguez
pick me up and drive me home.

MONICA
Greg, I would be happy to drive you home.

GREG,
Monica, I know you probably have some things
you need to do. Rodriguez is off work today and he
moonlights as an Uber driver to pay for his mortgage
he can hardly afford. I like helping him out.

MONICA,
That's why I like you. You are such a nice guy.

Monica was somewhat relieved because after that second session of great sex, her vagina was full of Greg's male silver essence that was slowly oozing out of her leaving snail tracks in her panties and wanted to take a bubble bath and clean herself out really good.

Monica had an espresso machine and the two were soon enjoying extra strong coffee with whip cream on top giving Greg a nice buzz.

About the time Greg finished his espresso, he got a text from Rodriguez:

RODRIGUEZ
I'm out front of the mansion boss.

GREG
Rodriguez is here, so I'm going to leave and let you get
done what you need to.

MONICA
Thank you for being so considerate.

Monica's bathrobe was very revealing to say the least and as she walked Greg to the front entrance to the double-wide door, she said to him as he stepped outside:

MONICA
Greg, give me a hug before you go.

GREG
Alright.

The embrace was genuine and affectionate, and she kicked her leg up on purpose just like she was doing a karate kick because she knew Rodriguez was watching everything, she wanted him to see she had a nice thick beaver and Greg probably got lucky with her.

Monica liked Greg a lot and started to think she might have to keep him after all. Greg was dropped off at home and thought about going for a walk when he got a text from Ami asking him if he was okay, he had not answered her text or phone calls.

Like a dummy he had left his cell phone powered off. It was probably a good thing because Monica would have loved chatting with Ami while Greg was unconscious. Monica had one rule, she doesn't share. And she would likely have explained what Ami already knew: Greg was great in bed.

Just before Greg answered Ami's text, he got a text message from Walter Bissonnette.

WALTER BISSONNETTE
I hope you enjoyed your time off, there will be a limo
there in two hours to take you to the airport. Sorry but
we need to get you back to do something important.

GREG
I'll be ready.

Greg then answered Ami's TEXT MESSAGE with a fabricated story which he felt he didn't like doing by allowing to compromise himself with that ultra hot Monica Cheung.

GREG
I'm sorry, I had my cell phone turned off and forgot to
turn it back on.

Then GREG said to himself, *God, I hope she's not frisky tonight, I don't think I got anything left in me.*

Greg got himself together, shut everything down and at the designated time set the burglar alarm and left the home.

Greg's two buddies were smiling for some strange reason when he got into the limo. Then it soon unfolded

AGENT A
How was she?

Greg should have known he would be followed. It never dawned on him. What Greg didn't know is his lover's tryst with Monica triggered an investigation into her and making her a future super double-spy.

In one week, the Navy Captain that Monica was bird dogging was nowhere to be seen. Monica also had an important victory. Monica's MSS handler informed her that Greg was a person of interest and to cease involvement with the Navy Captain, he wasn't quite as important as Greggory Bissell.

Monica Cheung had a strange premonition about Greg and now suddenly she understood there was far more to Greg than she first realized.

Many Russian and Chinese spies, have watchers. Those are independent spies who secretly monitor the spy their secretly assigned conducting a mission and reports what they are doing. As an example, Monica's watcher reported she had a gentleman over who spent the night with her.

Monica Cheung's MSS controller then determined Greg was the visitor when Monica provided all Greg's information and soon when the data package arrived with a recent driver's license photograph, the MSS confirmed Monica's overnight visitor was none other than Gregory Bissell. Monica Cheung had just hit a bases loaded home run and didn't yet know it.

Greg screwed the wrong woman and Walter Bissonnette soon had all the facts and was mildly alarmed, but the CIA then contacted Walter Bissonnette and said they wanted to use Greg to set her up to be a double spy. They would spoon feed Monica Cheung and turn her into a double spy.

In a modern era a lot of spies become double spies and do not know it. The CIA takes great pride in how they have succeeded in running double spies who never catch on they were forwarding tainted information that sometimes includes malware and tracers set up to follow the file transfers to the destination identifying who is in the food chain.

<u>INT. DAY LAWRENCE LIVERMORE LAB IN WALTER BISSONNETTE'S OFFICE</u>

Greg was brought directly to Walter Bissonnette's office. Nothing out of the ordinary was apparent. Then it began and Walter Bissonnette could see the panic on Greg's face.

There was the evil security manager with him when Greg arrived.

WALTER BISSONNETTE
First of all, Greg, things like this happen all too frequently. That's why you have your security details, Agent A and Agent B, nearby protecting you.

GREG
Am I in some sort of trouble?

WALTER BISSONNETTE
Agent A and Agent B too were unaware who you stumbled across until they filed their reports and the security team checked out Monica Cheung since you spent the night with her at her Rancho Santa Fe mansion.

GREG
It sounds like you discovered something negative about Monica Cheung.

WALTER BISSONNETTE
Yes. She's a deadly spy working for China's MSS.

GREG
Was I a target they went after?

WALTER BISSONNETTE
No, you were just a cheap fuck Monica Cheung stumbled across. But since she needs to know who she's sleeping with; we think she drugged you and acquired all your personal information while you were unconscious.

GREG
That's kind of amazing, never would have thought that by the way she acted.

WALTER BISSONNETTE
On the advice of the CIA, you are going with the security manager somewhere to get blood samples and take a polygraph so we can fill in all the details.

GREG
Alright.

Greg of course was utterly shocked to learn he had been sleeping with the enemy.

WALTER BISSONNETTE
After you get done with the blood samples and
polygraph, we are going for a little trip to Washington
DC for a meeting. Then you will come back here to go
on the mission we brought you home to perform.

The evil-looking Security Manager took Greg to an unmarked building in a commercial
business center.

People there quickly took a couple blood samples, then a contractor, most likely
working for Cash-In-Advance hooked up the polygraph.

POLYGRAPHER
Greg, tell us where you met Monica Cheung, and how
many times and where you previously met her before
yesterday.

Greg went into a detailed description.

GREG
I first met Monica Cheung at the Flaming Flamingo
when I was there having dinner with Dr. Moore.

Greg was forthcoming and his description of events matched very closely to transcripts
provided from his surveillance. The secret monitoring of the audio on his cellphone
the CIA made available with malware matched precisely what Greg said. When the
polygrapher looked over the instrumentation imbedded in APPS on his laptop, it was
all convincing Greg's recollection of events were quite accurate. That was the nature of
the report sent to Walter Bissonnette.

Greg also now felt sorrow for betraying Ami. Even though they had no official
relationship, she had confided her heart and soul to him.

Two hours later Greg was on a GS650 heading to Washington with Walter Bissonnette
that landed at Andrews AF Base. Soon they were on a Sikorsky S-97 helicopter on their
way to CIA headquarters Langley Virginia and into a SKIF where he met with a CIA
man and Walt to discuss the plan forward concerning Monica Cheung.

INT. DAY CIA HEADQUARTERS INSIDE SKIF

MR. STRAWBERRY
Greg would you consider helping us?

GREG
How would I help you?

MR. STRAWBERRY
Monica Cheung does not know her cover is blown.

Your situation has been severely compartmentalized because we want to play a dangerous game that can only happen if you participate.

GREG
What exactly do you want me to do?

MR. STRAWBERRY
If you agree, you will be sent back time to time to visit with Monica Cheung to play along like you are her honeypot victim.

GREG
What does that entail?

MR. STRAWBERRY
We'll give you disinformation to feed her.

GREG
I see.

MR. STRAWBERRY
There will be more to it as we coach you along in the process.

GREG
OKAY.

MR. STRAWBERRY
Before I get your buy in to this mission there are a couple things, I'm required to inform you because of agency regulations.

GREG
Alright, what is it?

MR STRAWBERRY
Monica Cheung may look feminine and good on the eyes, but you need to know she is a deadly killer and if your role is compromised you would be at risk. We have a dossier on Monica Cheung which is an alias and did not know she was operating in San Diego until you surfaced her for us.

GREG
So Monica's a deadly killer.

MR. STRAWBERRY
You probably think you are in over your head.
Actually, you are. This is a dangerous assignment
because Monica Cheung is a very capable spy trained
in martial arts and an efficient killer if necessary. But
we will always be close by to rescue you if things turn
negative. You will be under full surveillance any time
you are with her with an adaquate team to intervene if
necessary.

GREG
What do I need to do in this role?

MR STRAWBERRY
Just be yourself, act normal. We'll supply you with all
the appropriate disinformation and do some things to
foil her attempts to get valuable information from you.

GREG
What if she decides she doesn't want to see me
anymore?

MR. STRAWBERRY
There is information we cannot reveal to you due to
sensitive sources and materials. What I will tell you is
up high in the MSS her controller has been directed to
prosecute you with all the vigor of a deadly spy such as
Monica Cheung. You are Monica Cheung's focus now.
She was even told to disengage with a navy captain she
was seducing.

GREG
What happened with the navy captain?

MR. STRAWBERRRY
He was briefed on Monica Cheung and directed to not
contact her again. He's been transferred to Norfolk
Virginia to put miles between them and make it not
practical for Monica Cheung to attempt any further
honeypot schemes with him.

GREG
So, I'm part of a honey pot scheme now?

MR. STRAWBERRRY
Yes, but you are no longer the victim. Monica Cheung
is now the victim and like many double spies she

> doesn't know she's been turned and being used by us to
> send poison pills to China's MSS
> .

Greg agreed to assist the CIA but vowed to only deal with Monica in that clandestine manner simply because he was assisting the CIA in a special project, they got lucky and stumbled into.

A lot of special projects start out this way when a big surprise unexpectedly materializes.

A double spy is ten times worse than a spy. In World War II, Admiral Canaris, the head of the Abwehr, German Intelligence, a spy, was a double spy and up until 1944 when he was turned, fed Winston Churchill direct via his apparatus. Canaris hated Hitler and the NAZIs and decided as early as 1938 to do anything and everything to undermine their cause.

Admiral Canaris was so important Churchill never revealed the secret double spy to Americans or very many British. Americans that he had some dealings with Canaris, and they were never informed of the special information link directly to Churchill.

One big misconception is Enigma decryptions was the main reasons that helped win the war. Canaris was so valuable that Churchill would have sacrificed Enigma to protect his source Canaris, his most important source of intelligence.

Now you know why the Arabs fear the British more than anyone.

Admiral Canaris had a sexual relationship with a Polish spy based in Switzerland, named Halina Szymanska, who passed information from him to the Polish government-in-exile based in London and also put her at the disposal of the British and Americans, including Allen Dulles. A key piece of intelligence that passed from Canaris via Szymanska to the Allies was advance warning of the launch of Operation Barbarossa, the German invasion of the Soviet Union.

Canaris private communications to Churchill were bidirectional and played a major role in disinformation to Hitler concerning D-day, convincing Hitler the main invasion was coming via Pas de Calais the shortest routes to France from Great Britain. That disinformation tied up fifteen German Divisions Hitler refused to release until almost two weeks after the invasion and irreparable damage because Breakout and Pursuit was now changing everything.

Greg's spoon feeding of Monica, protected Project Pluto II because it threw off China's MSS. They were always looking in the wrong direction and lost a few highly placed spies in the process including a well-placed spy at the Lawrence Livermore Lab.

Greg's participation in the double spy activity did not end until he went on the final mission. Afterwards Monica always wondered where Greg went. He disappeared in thin air. His home was sold, every trace of him disappeared.

As the Espionage activity drug on, it was a collateral function for Greg. Ami blossomed more and more and that created more pressure as well especially after she finished college with wonderful credentials and was slowly becoming a valuable person in her field, steadily climbing the corporate ladder where she worked and had long given up being a waitress paying her way through college.

One of the reasons why Greg was brought back is he truly did have another mission besides dealing with the Monica Cheung business.

A classified rocket launch from Vandenberg was to deliver a shipment to space to begin the construction of Greg's future home. Greg assumed he was the SME for the craft and learned a lot about it. He never dreamed he would also be the passenger with his sidekick Tiāncái, the mechanical man, and robot.

American Launch Alliance put up the hardware and now there was a 7/24 guard plane by the first section at all time. The TR-4 would earn their pay guarding that stationary object positioned 25,000 miles above the earth, far away from prying eyes. It had to be super radiation hardened because that far out it is more susceptible to the solar winds.

<u>EXT. SPACE TR-4 </u>

Greg and Tiāncái soon found themselves on guard duty for a week. This all came about from Dr. Shirley's report. She knew that Greg needed to bond more with Tiāncái and stop viewing him exclusively as a mechanical man with some brains. By leaving them together in isolation on guard duty, it would force Greg too slowly evolve into a different mental profile in dealing with Tiāncái on almost a human to human like relationship.

Greg had a bunk in the back he could lay down and sleep with reduced artificial gravity tied in with his safey harness. It seemed almost identical to a bunk on a P3C he took a nap in during heavy turbulence over Norfolk Virginia area in a storm, after flying down from New Brunswick Maine. Because of their role during the Cold War, the P3 crews had to fly in bad weather and good weather and when they were tracking submarines with their stinger, the lower they got the better it worked so flying high above the weather was not an option.

In order to enhance this, get to know each other better session, Tiāncái received a plug-in module that had Greg's life history up until now including his affairs with Monica and Ami. He had Dr. Shirley's report which Greg was never allowed to see nor knew it existed. Tiāncái artificial intelligence was forbidden to ever reveal this report to Greg. And he never did.

Humans have on average twenty billion brain cells to store information. Tiāncái had 1000 billion memory cells plus remote storage either on the planet or in the future aboard the spacecraft.

Tiāncái didn't need to always carry all of his intelligence with him. All he had to do is know where the information was stored, whether back at the lab or in the future aboard the spacecraft in non-volatile memory.

Greg was luckier than Space Force officers because when they defecated, they added to the aroma of the craft slowly. It was a stench that never really cleared out until they landed again and offloaded sanitary tank contents. On the other hand, Greg didn't have to put up with someone else and there was never an argument out of Tiāncái.

In a way Greg was not happy. He did not need to be on this flight because Tiāncái didn't even need to look at the surveillance displays since his wireless interfaced with the TR-4 computers which gave Tiāncái real time updates about anything around them in space to move out of the way if necessary to avoid collisions.

After looking at the stars for a couple hours that was no longer a viable time killer. Greg was struggling. This was much shorter but just as bad as being trapped on a submarine.

Tiāncái had extensive resources for psychology. What Tiāncái didn't have in his own memory banks he could find he loaded up in excess memory of the TR-4. If he needed additional resources, he could simply get it via direct satellite communications link to servers back at Lawrence Livermore lab.

TIĀNCÁI
Greg, would you like me to read you an eBook?

GREG,
What's available?

TIĀNCÁI
Everything that is registered in the Library of Congress.

GREG
Will that cause any delays in your reports or distract you from your surveillance functions?

TIĀNCÁI
Greg, the TR-4's computers are doing all the work. I just receive reports when they have something to report to me from any alerts or intercepts from communications or important sensor events. All I'm doing is monitoring everything you see on the displays and audio alarms, but I do not require the sound or the video since I get all the reports in nano seconds and can parse and make judgements in one hundred and sixty microseconds. My benchmark tests for Artificial Intelligence certified I exceed 5,000 thoughts in one second.

GREG
How does that compare to Humans?

TIĀNCÁI
Humans with higher intellect usually can have up to twenty-five thoughts in a minute, but most people only have about eight thoughts per minute.

GREG
That's interesting Tiāncái but while you are reading to me will that slow you down any?

TIĀNCÁI
Greg, I have 2048 processors running multiple applications on what Lawrence Livermore Labs terms Super-Linux. My current load factor is only three. I seldom exceed a load factor of 10 and am designed to run at load factors of fifty with no apparent delays or system slowdown.

GREG
What's the main difference between Standard-Linux and Super-Linux?

TIĀNCÁI
Super-Linux allows me to run systolic arrays, perform stochastic resonance and wavelet filtering on all space telescope images and stay below a load factor of fifty.

GREG
Alright read me *Time Travel Spy, Altering the Fabric of Time.*

Tiāncái started reading and Greg decided to lay down in the bunk to hear the eBook. In 30 minutes, Greg was sleeping and snoring. Tiāncái has sophisticated sensors and knew when Gregs neural activity was declining and stopped reading and started playing some classical music people spying on Greg reported he often listened too.

During the week in space Tiāncái read Greg five eBooks and played quite a few piano concertos and symphonies. He also played singers such as Polina Gagarina, Jennie Kim, Ani Lorak, and Valeriya Greg enjoyed. There were other types of music played such as the Moody Blues which gave Greg a rush hearing it in space.

Prior to the mission Dr. Hudson and Dr. Shirley met privately with Tiāncái and explained how they desired he establish a friendship and relationship with Greg. They gave Tiāncái some talking points to blend in with his interactions with Greg, which included some zingers for questions. Dr. Shirley was quite interested in hearing Greg's responses to these questions which he did not know was recorded because Tiāncái recorded everything 7/24.

Greg was taken back by some of the questions. It was utterly shocking to Greg that Tiāncái could come up with such questions. It gave Greg a creepy feeling about the future of AI.

One question Tiāncái asked just about floored Greg.

TIĀNCÁI

Greg, do you like sexual intercourse?

GREG

Sure most healthy men enjoy sexual intercourse if they find the right partner.

TIĀNCÁI

Greg have you found the right partner?

GREG

I found two of them, but one turned out to be big trouble that I got myself into, but the other one is more ideal. Plus, she looks like my wife who abandoned me and moved to Japan.

TIĀNCÁI

What's her name Greg?

GREG

Her name is Ami, would you like to see her picture?

TIĀNCÁI

Greg, yes, I would. Please show me a picture of Ami.

GREG pulled out his cell phone from his pocket and started showing Tiāncái several pictures of AMI he took.

TIĀNCÁI

Greg, as part of my training in humanism and the fundamentals of American social experiences I was given a variety of women to study including their roles and impacts on society. Since I had full internet access beside Wikipedia and unlimited books and biographies I looked at Google and Bing to observe countless images that included movie stars and singers. Ami is very attractive and is just as attractive as the numerous women I observed.

GREG

Thank you, I agree Ami is very attractive.

TIĀNCÁI

Do you have good physical responses when you perform a coitus?

GREG

Yes. The stimulation and orgasms are strong.

TIĀNCÁI

Greg do you think your psychophysical responses during sexual intercourse are enhanced because you feel love for Ami?

GREG

I believe emotion plays into it and Ami is very emotional when she reaches her climax and starts having orgasms.

Since Tianci had a huge reservoir of information as well as Gregs life story, the talking points Dr. Shirley gave Tiāncái which were recorded in his robot awareness and AI files, provided a gateway into numerous discussions. Later when Dr. Shirley dissected all the recordings and gleaned information out of the exchanges between Tiāncái and Greg, by the end of the week in space, there seemed to be bonding between the robot Tiāncái and Greg.

A lot of it was filtered as Dr. Shirley needed to protect Greg's privacy and relationship with Ami, but the vast majority of the conversations were of a general nature about Gregs journey in life and how it caused Tiāncái to adapt, left Dr. Hudson and a few of his AI designers utterly speechless.

Tiāncái's self-awareness algorithms and his vast access to human experience created a positive personality which molded Gregs feelings and thoughts about the robot. By the time they returned to earth, Greg had a deep appreciation for Tianci and his robot designers.

Tiāncái's self-awareness and his algorithms that influenced by adaptive filtering sometimes created a Typhoon of information processing and adaptive prioritization.

A lot of times when Greg was sleeping and Tiāncái could expend vast computational resources in his self-learning with no distractions.

During these vigorous investigations, , Tiāncái 2048 CPUs load factors peaked out at fifty for sustained period of times. Tiāncái's built in health checks and statistics amazed Dr. Hudson and other roboticists, as Greg had influenced Tiāncái in prioritizing the direction of his internet searches.

Having the ability to have 5000 thoughts per second meant that Tiāncái could have 18 million thoughts in an hour. Those 18 million thoughts could result in 180 billion micro-code instructions executed. It also meant Tiāncái's I/O processors may have moved 50 Gigabytes of data without taxing his 2048 CPUs not ever exceeding a load factor of 50. The I/O processors logged the data flow in statistics and information such as file names, size, and types. Some were:

Document files: These are files that contain text, data, or information, such as PDF, DOC, HTML, XLS, and TXT.

Image files: These are files that store graphical or visual
data, such as JPG, PNG, GIF, and BMP.
Video files: These are files that store moving images
and sound, such as MP4, AVI, MOV, and WMV.
Program files: These are files that contain executable
code or instructions, such as EXE, DLL, and BAT.
Database files: These are files that organize and store
data in a structured way, such as DB, MDB, and SQL.

The space food sucked, Greg drank mostly bottled water and during his final day he
was happy to be returning to Earth.

After one week of space patrol, another TR-4B relieved them and Greg and Tiāncái
went back to earth.

When Tiāncái returned back to Earth a 36-fiber cable would be hooked up to his digi-
port and all of Tiāncái's thought and communication transactions would be uploaded
via an IBM optical supercomputer allowing the Roboticists to analyze Greg's impact on
Tiāncái's adaptive AI. It did not take roboticists and AI scientists long to realize that
in a weeks' time Greg's influence on Tiāncái's adaptive AI appeared rather staggering.
It did not take long for some of the researchers to figure out the Earth would soon be
better off with Tiāncái going out into space on a one-way trip because they feared what
could happen. As one Roboticists said to the other in a private discussion:

ROBOTICIST
Tiāncái could turn out worse than the "Mule" in some
of Isaac Asimov novels.

AI SCIENTIST
I'm quite sure the public is not ready to be exposed to
Tiāncái. They would view him worse than HAL 2000
if they understood his Gigaflops of self-directed self-
learning, which he did in just one week.

Ami received another visitor while Greg was gone, none other than Dr. Shirley.

By now Ami knew quite well that Greg was involved into some heavy stuff that he
couldn't divulge to her. Dr. Shirley felt obligated to help prepare Ami for the upcoming
permanent separation. But at the same time wanted those remaining years to be fruitful
and delightful to the couple.

When a knockout gorgeous woman knocks on your door and says she needs to talk
to you about your boyfriend, obviously your dander might stick up. Ami invited Dr.
Shirley into her apartment wondering WTF this was all about.

DR. SHIRLEY
Thank you for letting me talk to you.

AMI
What is this about?

DR. SHIRLEY
I'm Doctor Shirley and I work on the project that Greg is involved in that takes him away from you at times. I know Greg's routine departures are not conducive to a great relationship, but I wanted to reach out to you and inform you about a few things.

AMI
Such as?

DR. SHIRLEY
First of all, I know Greg adores you. You are now the most important person to Greg in the world and that includes his estranged wife and his two sons. Because of his sensitive position we know all about who you are and what your relationship with Greg is like. I'm very sorry but we had to invade your privacy this because there is a lot at stake here.

DR. SHIRLEY
What does that mean?

DR. SHIRLEY
We must protect Greg because he's a valuable critical human asset to the project, probably far more valuable than you can imagine. That's why he is always under surveillance, and he knows this.

AMI
I sense all that. I've been visited by some government agents.

DR. SHIRLEY
I know about those visits that relate to when you, Hikaru, and Greg got off the train in Oakland and were accosted by those two Azzie dudes, his protection apparatus had to swing into action to protect him as well as protect you since you are close to him and would have an impact on his personal psychology if something bad happened to you.

AMI
I see.

DR. SHIRLEY

Here's my business card and if you ever feel down in the dumps and need to talk with someone, please call me. That is my private phone number on it and anything you say to me will be kept in the highest of confidentiality.

AMI

Okay.

DR. SHIRLEY

I would like to come to see you from time to time to see how you are holding up if you and Greg remain close like you are now.

AMI

Sure, I wouldn't mind your visit.

DR. SHIRLEY

Greg cares a lot for you. You are very special to him; he's greatly concerned about your future and well-being.

AMI

That's nice to know.

DR. SHIRLEY

Please be patient with Greg. He carries a lot of responsibility and because of that he can't divulge any of it to you. Plus, it might make you uncomfortable if you had any knowledge of what he does, which changes all the time. He's not a static person. He lives and works in a dynamic world.

Dr. Shirley then stood up.

DR. SHIRLEY

I must go now, I have some tasks I need to get done, but I just wanted to reach out to you and hope to help you understand Greg better and be more comfortable with him in view of Greg must come and go all the time.

AMI

I understand he's a busy guy and I appreciate you clarifying a few things for me.

DR. SHIRLEY
You are welcome.

Ami led Dr. Shirley to the front door, and they shook hands and Dr. Shirley then departed.

In some ways Dr. Shirley's visit helped, in other ways it made it worse, just knowing, the God-awful fragile world Greg probably lives in.

When Greg came back from his week in space, he was given a few days off to relax, then he was scheduled to go assist the CIA handle their double spy Monica Cheung for a few days.

NAPA VALLEY
Greg called Ami Friday evening.

GREG
Are you available this weekend?

AMI
Sure, why?

GREG
I want to take you up to Napa Valley and spend Saturday night up there and do some sightseeing including riding the Wine Train.

AMI
Sure, I would like to go there with you.

GREG
Good, I can pick you up in the morning then.

AMI
I have a better idea.

GREG
What's that?

AMI
How about picking me up tonight. We can leave from your place in the morning.

GREG
Sure, how soon can you be ready?

AMI
In about fifteen minutes.

GREG
Okay, I'll be right over.
Ami informed Hikaru.

AMI
Greg is coming over to pick me up, I'll be back sometime on Sunday.

HIKARU
Can I come along?

AMI
I wouldn't want you to watch us having sex because you would want your fair share.

HIKARU
You are damn right I would!

The two girls hugged.

AMI
You are such a bad girl!

HIKARU
I know. One day some guy is going to meet me who finds out how horny I am and he's going to be set for life."

AMI
You got that right.

By the time Ami put together her emergency go away quickly kit, the doorbell rang, and it was Greg. His timing was impeccable.

GREG
Is there any place you want to go now?

AMI
Yes, to your condo.

No sooner than arrival at Greg's condo, Ami led Greg to his bedroom and soon had Greg buck naked and got him laid down on the bed and performed fellatio to get him rock hard before she mounted him and started performing in ways that would make the authors of the Kama Sutra proud and like there was no tomorrow.

The Kama Sutra acknowledges the Hindu concept of *Purusharthas*, and lists desire, sexuality, and emotional fulfillment as one of the proper goals of life. *Purusharthas* literally means objective of men: *Dharma* (righteousness, moral values), *Artha* (prosperity economic values, *Kama* (pleasure, love, psychological values) *Moksha* (liberation, spiritual values, self-actualization).

Ami acted out her pent-up emotions triggered by independent confirmation about Greg's stature in life. Greg was an enigma, but Ami now understood to the extent Greg that was a special person.

The next day unfolded as Greg assumed when they went to Napa Valley and Wine Country.

After a lovely lunch on the Napa Valley wine train, Greg drove Ami around Napa Valley, then checked into a hotel in Calistoga, where Ami intended to do some more lovemaking and hoped she didn't wear Greg out. She would be utterly shocked to know Greg's real age. Greg's exercise regimen kept him looking much younger.

GREG VISITS MONICA CHEUNG AGAIN

Monica Cheung, the very capable and deadly spy received an extensive report on Greg, thanks to China's very capable and successful MSS. Monica she was double shocked to learn Gregs age after experiencing his sexual ability. But the biggest surprise was Greg in the view of China's MSS, was more valuable than the Navy Captain who worked in communications over at NAVWAR, formerly known as SPAWAR before name change after reorganization.

As the days unfolded, Greg enjoyed Monica's body and at the same time gave a few nuggets to Monica she reported which corroborated their asset at Lawrence Livermore Lab who was also being spoon fed. China's MSS didn't know Monica had been turned and was reading them a scripted dialog.

Until Greg's spacecraft Pluto II disappeared forever, the Chinese were led to believe that was a United States Space Force asset being prepared for a future space war. Then it flat disappeared and no trace of it was ever seen again, adding to the mystery of the spacecraft, but also Gregory Bissell came up missing at the same time.

PROTOTYPE MINIATURE PLUTO II and PLUTO II CONSTRUCTION

One of the greatest secrets of all time was launching the nuclear reactors used in propulsion up to the assembly point. Everything had to be built on earth, launched aboard spacecraft, and delivered in an exact position space where the sections would quickly be mated to each other slowly extending the length of the rocket ship. For now, the sections remained hidden in their heat treated and special-coated fiberglass shipping containers in an aluminum sandwich. It would take over forty-five launches to get all the pieces up to construct the ship.

Spacecraft large fuel tanks used to get Pluto II assemblies were no longer needed and were going to be used after modifications and strapped on to Pluto II to carry liquid hydrogen for propulsion. The final assembly that would be constructed in a few days to prevent nations of the Earth from knowing how big a ship could be built in space in the manner of a few weeks.

By the time the United Nations met to adjudicate this monster ship that would appear menacing in space, it would start to move away from the solar system and be out of site in a short window of opportunity, thus eliminating any actions, and America would simply say it's a research craft going far away and not report its true purpose because the *Big Bangers* would do anything and everything to wreck a program that would undermine their position and continued funding stream for a rather bizarre hypothesis.

American Launch Alliance (ALA) used large-lift spacecraft somewhat built like SpaceX Dragon Fleet to put those large capsules up into space. They looked like an odd duck because they had over twice the diameter of the first and second stage liquid fuel rocket boosters. These rockets did not gather a lot of speed until the atmosphere thinned out due to the large frontal cross-section. A Space X Dragon rocket would be going three times as fast as one of these huge rockets twenty miles above the planet. But the ALA rockets would catch up velocity at 100 miles above the planet and accelerate to get out to the 25,000-mile geosynchronous orbit where it would simply be chained together in the Pluto II assembly area.

Once all components were in place and inspected for damage and deemed ready to assemble, several TR-4s would be constantly going out on shuttle missions to space delivering space walkers who would systematically pull the components out of the shipping containers and start bolting them together. The modular construction and training on earth in large bodies of water with neutral buoyant components were used to train several groups of people to assemble sections they were assigned to.

Very large Spacecraft fuel tanks were delivered into space with only one third of their contents filled to lighten them up. Subsequent "milk cow" shipments were sent up to top them off. The eight fuel tanks stored an incredible amount of liquid hydrogen and since a leak in space didn't pose much of a risk since there was no oxygen around to combust, leaks would simply dissipate harmlessly.

Two nuclear main rocket engines were all that was necessary to build up the incredible speeds expected. Nevertheless, as a special measure to ensure success, a third nuclear rocket engine was also added to be used in the event diagnostics warranted shut down of one of the two primary rocket engines, the third would then come on line maintaining the constant thrust to ensure velocities that far exceed light speed.

A scale model of the final production model was produced that only required three launches to get all the sections up into space. Space Walker construction crews bolted them together, and this is what led Greg to think he was merely a test pilot, because he and Tiāncái would test it. All the software and flight controls were given a dry run on this very special craft. This was one of the most guarded secrets in American History.

TRAINING ON THE SCALE MODEL CRAFT.

It was about this time Greg began training on the scale model craft. Greg was not informed that Pluto II spacecraft he would fly on the ultimate mission would dwarf this a scale model craft by several magnitudes. And the disinformation the upper echelon deceived him with, is he was going to make history by being the first Astronaut to fly

ABOVE LIGHT SPEED.

Now the "come to Jesus" moment came about.

<u>INT. DAY LAWRENCE LIVERMORE LAB.</u>

With Walter Bissonnette and Dr. Shirley, met with Greg as the training to fly the Scale Model Prototype Craft began and he was told a half-truth.

>   WALTER BISSONNETTE
> Greg, your next mission will be the most dangerous you will do in your lifetime is why you were chosen for your age.

>   GREG
> That proves I was picked because I'm expendable.

>   WALTER BISSONNETTE
> Nobody knows for sure what will happen when you exceed light speed.

In fact, he could be transported to another dimension or some other strange phenomena they didn't know about because humans had never gone above light speed and the theoretical physicists starting from Einstein said it was impossible due to the formula $E = MC^2$ (squared) requiring infinite amount of energy, until someone figured it out differently Warp drives were only decades away allowing 10 to 100 times light speed. But for now, Pluto II rocket engines would get the prototype miniature Pluto II above light speed to prove another way was possible

In six months', time Greg became fully certified and a competent test pilot for the miniature prototype Pluto II light-speed craft given the false name Pluto II. Greg would not know the real Pluto II was the megalith to come afterwards. Tiāncái would be his copilot and in the event, Greg developed a health condition, Tiāncái would bring the ship back to earth. This was mere experimentation to demonstrate a scale model would successfully travel above light speed, hence its big brother should be able to perform in a predictable manner.

As time approached the test flight, Walter Bissonnette met with Greg again.

>   WALTER BISSONNETTE
> I'm giving you five days off as Dr. Shirley has recommended you need some down time. Also, I suggest you spend time with Ami.

>   GREG
> Alright, thanks.

>   WALTER BISSONNETTE
> You will notice money has suddenly shown up in your bank accounts.

GREG

What's that all about?

WALTER BISSONNETTE

Mr. Strawberry wants you to spend that money on
Ami with no regrets because it is Pay-To-Play money.

GREG

What's the meaning of Pay-To-Play money?

WALTER BISSONNETTE

My CIA associates used in Project Pluto and Mr.
Strawberry appreciate your efforts in the Monica
Cheung double spy operation. Consider it Cash-In-
Advance.

Ami had several more sessions with Dr. Shirley by then. Ami was a calm kitten and entering a period of satisfaction and surreal happiness. However, Dr. Shirley understood vividly she had to prepare Ami just in case the prototype miniature Pluto II developed a problem when it went above light speed.

This mission was filled with a lot of uncertainty. Greg didn't quite understand he would be flying by the seats of his pants strictly based on experimental and hypothetical assumptions that brilliant men with no accountability postulated.

The prototype Pluto II mission would take Greg and Tiāncái out of the solar system for a brief period, where they would do a minor course change to get them out of the main plume, shut down the rocket engines. Turn the ship around 180 degrees using retro rockets and then slowly bring the rocket engines back up in power that would create breaking action and eventually bring it to a stop as it was flying into its own plume creating a temporary atmosphere providing some traction for slowing.

The deceleration would last several days and possibly cause Greg some great physical discomfort, therefore if he felt he had to slow the engines periodically to allow sleep or relief, he was allowed to drop down to twenty-percent power until he could physically handle increasing engine power and breaking action and withstanding constant G forces this process synthesized.

To get back to the solar system quickly he would accelerate back up to light speed and as he passed by Jupiter and Saturn, use them to assist in slowing as to help avoid a lengthy deceleration. The ship would then rendezvous with a TR-4 with pilots wearing space suits allowing Greg and Tiāncái to be transferred to the TR-4 in a spacewalk. After confirmation all data files transferred successfully to Planet Earth via Satellite link to Lawrence Livermore Labs, the craft would then be flown via autopilot and sent into Saturn's atmosphere to get photographic evidence up close, what is there below the multitudes of clouds.

Greg, now knowing this was a dangerous mission and that's why he was hired, lived these final moments as if there was no tomorrow. He had a will and power of attorney and mailed copies of it to Ami whom he trusted after he left. In the event he didn't come back Ami was named executor and not his estranged wife. Ami received copies of the power of attorney and business card of his attorney to contact him if she was notified something went wrong. He did something smart and made the power of attorney indefinite. He didn't have to do another one when he went out again.

DURANGO

Greg quickly made reservations and took Ami to Durango via a private jet from a company who provides services to individuals that have the proper amount of cash.

A limo delivered Greg and Ami to a luxury suite within a short walking distance of the Narrow-Gauge railroad station in downtown Durango.

About two blocks from the train station is a fabulous sushi restaurant where they had dinner. Afterwards they did something Ami suggested: saw a movie together. It was one of those chick movies just out that puts women in the mood. Afterwards they settled down for some copious lovemaking and fell asleep and woke up when Greg's cell phone alarm went off.

> GREG
> Okay, let's get ready to ride the train. Be sure and bring
> a jacket, it gets cold.

Before long they were boarding the last car on the train which was reserved for Greg's exclusive use. It had a catered lunch, and all the champagne they needed and wanted. Greg had plenty of Cash-In-Advance to spluge.

> AMI
> Greg this is impressive, I bet this cost a lot of money.

> GREG
> It does, but the money was given to me for some of my
> special projects.

> AMI
> Is that why Doctor Shirley just visited me again?

> GREG
> Dr. Shirley is part of our support structure. She
> provides me with psychological counseling because
> some of my projects are dangerous. The Agency views
> you as my future lifetime partner. Dr. Shirley probably
> talked to you in such a manner that I will likely be
> doing something dangerous in the future and she's
> simply preparing you in case something goes wrong.

> AMI
> Greg, when I first met you I had no idea what kind of

a person you are like. Now I know there are things in
your life you can't tell me about. Dr. Shirley explains
it to me.

GREG

What exactly did Dr. Shirley inform you of?

AMI

She said you have already done some very dangerous
missions, which explains your absence.

GREG

What exactly did Dr. Shirley inform you of?

AMI

She also said it's not you turn off your cell phone when
I attempt to contact you. Simply your phone does not
work where you are going.

When Ami looked into Greg's eyes, she could tell what all this meant. The opulence was an event that was staged because Greg would be going again. Dr. Shirley's visit underscored this was unfolding. She would make Gregs time off pleasurable because she knew very soon, he would be doing it again. People do not get visited by FBI people and a famous psychiatrist like Dr. Shirley over noncritical matters.

Ami didn't need Greg to tell her what it was. Ami fully understood it truly was remarkable what Greg was doing. If she ever discovered Greg was also involved in espionage with the Monica Cheung double spy operation, she would no doubt leave Greg and never see him again, because that would indeed terrify her. Greg's risk in the double spy operation was just as risky as his future mission being the first human to travel faster than the speed of light.

Instead of the hard benches up in the passenger train which was restored to appear like the real trains operated at the turn of the century when it was the only major form of transportation from Durango to Silverton, the two lovebirds had nicely stuffed padded chairs and were far enough away from the steam engine to avoid most of its soot.

Ami looked very beautiful today. Greg had been dumping money on her and requesting she splurge on nice clothes and paid off all her student debt. Ami was excited when she graduated with no student debt.

Ami kept that secret away from Hikaru who would be graduating this semester with over $200,000 in student debt. But she thought if she ever became a wealthy woman, she would try to help her dear friend she had known for many years and lived the trials and tribulations together. She had no idea how easily that would become one day because Greg realizing he could be killed at any time, dumped a lot of money in some very risky stocks and hit the jackpot. He never made money so fast in his life before. Since Ami would soon be the executor of his estate, she would have all that money.

205

Greg did the smart trip. After the train arrived in Silverton, they didn't need to do like most of the passengers, find a restaurant, since their meal was catered on the private car.

When Ami felt she had enough food, Greg suggested:

GREG
Let's go shopping.

AMI
Sounds like a good idea.

Ami had a lot of cash with her Greg gave her so that she could buy Hikaru gifts and splurge for herself.

There are a number of tourist traps and souvenir shops in Silverton. Anything Ami wanted; she could easily buy it. Ami bought several bags of souvenirs for family back in Japan and her roommate Hikaru.

Greg paid for the private car for the entire round trip but had told the company that even that be the case he had no intentions of using it on the way back even though he had to pay for a round trip, and to give all the leftover food and booze to the crew of the train, which they were very happy to take home in doggie bags.

Greg and Ami took the Durango Railroad bus back from Silverton to Durango.

Greg had learned on past visits, best way to do that Silverton trip is to take the train one way and the bus back.

The bus is a very comfortable tourist bus with reclining seats so you can take a nap on the way home, which Greg and Ami did with their sleepiness derived from the food and champagne.

When they arrived back at Durango and walked back to their luxury suite, the manager met them and handed Greg a set of keys with the preapproved rental agreement to a rental car that was parked near the manager's office.

Their intentions were to go to Mesa Verde the next day, but in the meantime, they could go for a drive if Ami desired.

Hence, they went out on US 160 for a nice drive. This road is in very good condition and easy to drive. There are a lot of wonderful areas to observe nature and the picturesque landscape. If Greg had more time, he would have driven to Pagosa Springs and Chama, New Mexico, the perfect place for a Narrow-Gauge rail buff. But after an hour in one way that was enough of a drive.

They made their way back to the hotel, where they took a Hollywood Newlywed shower together. Even though they were not married, and Greg was rethinking his situation with his estranged wife, trading her in for a model twenty-five years younger, he did cherish Ami beyond words.

No doubt Ami would be shocked after Greg went on his next mission when his attorney rang her doorbell to give her the power of attorney and notify Ami she was now the executor of his estate in case something happened to him. If she didn't know he loved her by now, it was more confirmed when the polite attorney explained everything to her with Hikaru listening in a greater amount of curiosity. If Hikaru could do it all over again she would have instigated sex on the train and aced Ami as she watched all this unfold.

Late in the afternoon Ami and Greg made their way back to the sushi restaurant because Greg and Ami both liked sushi and since they were not driving only walking a couple blocks, Greg could have as much plum wine with his sake as he wanted.

The sushi chefs were taking a warming to this very nice couple, partly due to the huge tips. Greg knew a lot of restaurant workers live off tips. The salary wasn't jack shit. He made sure they got a good payday in tips. In Durango even though there is a lot of money there and quite a few wealthy have summer homes there, the tip jars often do not have much cash in them. During their stay in Durango, Greg took a couple stacks of $20s with him and made sure the staff had increased exuberance.

Thanks to Greg's insistence that Ami take some of that black money and buy really nice clothes, she was also probably the best dressed lady in the sushi restaurant. The sushi chef and others assumed Greg was her sugar daddy and she was Tokyo trash who can be purchased for long-term stays (human long-term rentals) by wealthy Americans that happens from time to time thanks to the Yakuza. In Japan wealthy young Japanese women actually rent Americans for three months at a time so they look cool at dance clubs and elsewhere. It works both ways.

Tonight Ami and Greg conversed and got into discussions with the Sush chef, thanks to the fact Ami could speak Japanese as well as the Japanese sushi chef.

Note to the director:

In the next few paragraphs contain Japanese. The intent is to have the people speak the Japanese with English sub-titles.

AMI

私はカリフォルニア大学を卒業しました。　バークレーさん、私は大学で働いてお金を払ったので、彼女にはもっと時間がかかったと言いました。　私はビジネスとデータ サイエンスの二重学位を取得しており、GPA はほぼ 4.0 です。

[I graduated from U.C. Berkeley, that it took her longer because I paid my way through college working. I have a double degree in business and data science with almost a 4.0 GPA.]

SUSHI CHEF

なぜあなたはこの老人と一緒ですか

[Why are you with this old man?]

The chef upset Ami, so she decided to toy with him.

AMI

彼には大きなペニスがあり、私を本当によくフ
ァックします。 彼はとても金持ちで私を台無し
にします。 今では経済的な心配はなく、彼は私
を守。

[He has a large penis and fucks me really good. He's
very rich and spoils me. I now have no financial
worries and he protects me.]

Greg smiled and could not hold back a little laugh. Ami suspected Greg knew more
Japanese than he let on, and this rare moment exposed the extent. And then she started
thinking, if he understood what Hikaru and I were saying on the train trip to Reno, oh
my God!

The sushi chef suddenly looked totally shocked and humiliated because the other
Japanese workers there understood everything that was said, and knew he had just
been put in his place and had on big smiles.

Greg thought he deserved a good tip for the abuse he took and didn't hold back when
they left.

The following day they spent driving around Mesa Verde, an incredible sight. They
took some of the tours and went into the cliff dwellings and took in all the professional
tour guide information with great interest.

About an hour before sundown, they left Mesa Verde. There are hotels they could have
stayed there, but Greg knew those hotels did not compare to the suite they were staying
in Durango.

This was their last night before Greg had to go back to work and prepare for his trip.
Little did he know part of his preparations was facilitating the CIA work their double
spy.

 Talk about turnaround is fair play. Chicoms often seduced Americans who thought
with their little heads and now one of their most important spies in Southern California
was getting compromised by the little head.

The Cash in Advance boys would plant so much BS through her and the Chicom spy
in Livermore to corroborate her story, the Chinese would be on a wild goose chase for
years tracking down the information and the golden nugget they thought they found.

The biggest mystery to them and Monica that evolved over the next few months is
Greg disappeared. Their spy in Lawrence, Livermore, who could get access to personal
information files had looked over some of Greg's files that were planted by the CIA
team. Then shortly after Greg disappeared so did all his files!

One aspect of running a double spy is you can't change anything, or it might give away the secret or cause suspicion that would create further investigations that might uncover something to trigger a red flag and possible bug out.

Greg had to go to the mansion via Rodriguez who had no idea the deadly game he was in. Had the Chicoms figured out Greg was feeding the double spy disinformation to lead her in various directions enabling the CIA to lay traps for people she was associated with, Rodriguez easily could have been cut down as collateral damage.

Toxicology reports on Greg after his sojourn to Monica's mansion the first time revealed he had been drugged and the chemicals she had used to stimulate him and later made him unconscious for twelve hours.

Greg was informed that Chicoms most likely had photocopies of everything in his billfold and asked him to inspect it to see if everything was there and if there was possibly anything in it relating to is work at Livermore Lab. Later polygraphs revealed Greg's memory of what he had in his billfold had nothing to expose him as to what he really did. Thus far he was in the clear with no traces to his real assignments, but he had to be warned he was in jeopardy in the event they ever found out.

Again because of his age and he was disposable early on, made it even more necessary for the CIA to utilize him in their game of double cross.

Greg had thought he would be going up in space on the mission. He guessed wrong. The GS650 took him to San Diego and the limo took him to his home where he was asked to make contact with the double spy and let her entice him back into the honeytrap one more time so her probing questions could get some indication out of Greg tips that would corroborate what the spy up in Livermore had reported.

Monica didn't know this person in Livermore Lab existed or anything about him. Her handler fed her the list of inquiries. Hence, Monica Cheung was remotely working in synergism with another source she had no idea existed or what was going on.

Since the CIA spoon fed both sources the same information, the corroboration was very destructive to the Chinese MSS because it revealed Chinese MSS sensitive sources and methods they used and further exposed the food chain just like the men at Langley predicted. One spy led to twenty. It was one of the most cost-effective counterintelligence operations ever conducted by the USA without the FBI knowing anything about it.

Later when the FBI did learn about it, they felt the BURN. There is a reason why traditionally the two agencies had issues with each other, it was the BURN.

Most of the FBI spies (like Charles Hansen) were turned by the CIA and most of the CIA spies were turned by the FBI (like Aldridge Aimes).

Their lack of cooperation between CIA and FBI was cited in the 9/11 report that led to the creation of the Department of Homeland Security (DHS).

Greg was drugged again with another exotic compound that did the same effect as sodium pentothal, where Monica could ask him questions and expect honest answers. It was the closest thing to a truth serum scientist had ever invented and the Chinese were masters at manufacturing it.

Part of the CIA planning was mitigation of this new truth serum drug. There was no antidote the CIA could ever come up with but they discovered another method they employed: The Monroe Institute and Hemi-Sync. As part of their brainwashing Greg to overcome the effects of this truth serum drug which Greg was fully briefed on what they were doing resulted in several months of this special training and testing with stolen copies of the serum to test Hemi-Sync's feasibility in mitigating the Chinese truth serum.

When Monica had Greg under and did her magic, she had no idea the depth of her failure because it was, she who was manipulated in the end by pulling out of Greg those facts she wanted to get at to verify what her handlers were seeking.

She rewarded Greg handsomely for his multiple sources of pleasure she gave him. The success of Monica's espionage and the fantastic orgasms Greg gave her was starting to spoil her.

Monica Cheung thought Greg would never know what she had done to him, and later she started thinking she could keep Greg like a trophy and have a fake life together with him with all the trimmings her success provided in income.

When Greg left after telling her he was going away for a while on a business trip to handle some logistics consultations, she knew the real facts she reported to her handlers. Greg was going up on one of those United States Space Force classified missions where they were going to plant new KH-15 satellites in Geosynchronous Orbits.

They would know what secret satellites to shoot down in case of war. To their chagrin, they would be shooting down empty shipping containers!

Greg went home to pack after having another glorious rendezvous with the spy with a golden pussy, and two hours later, the limo with a couple guys he saw often smiling again because Greg didn't know he carried some sophisticated photographic equipment with him so they were able to monitor Monica as she was working her magic when she thought Greg was out of it. They also got a free porn show out of it. Greg would never know.

Two hours and thirty minutes after kissing Monica goodbye, Greg was on that GS650 flying to Area 51, again landing on runway 32 North.

Once in Area 51 he went into a medical lab and had blood drawn so they could confirm the drugs he had received, that turned up positive. But based on the secret video they already knew it was highly probable based on behaviors.

LIGHT SPEED

Greg went through a 48-hour physical preparation before going on the mission. The simplest solution was to fly up on a TR-4 with a micro-space suit on that allowed him up to twenty minutes to get via spacewalk from the TR-4 into the Pluto II demonstration spaceship and start pressurization before any harm would come to his body. The micro-space suits were ideal for egress between platforms.

After 48 hours and all the medical preps were completed, Greg was driven by a van over to the hangar and inside it the hangar doors shut and the floor which was nothing more than an elevator went down several levels where the TR-4 for this mission was parked. Tiāncái standing next to Walter Bissonnette by the ladder to climb up into the TR-4. Greg had on his micro-space suit with the face mask lifted up that rotates backwards.

WALTER BISSONNETTE
The mission is a go. Do you feel ready?

GREG
Yes, I do.

WALTER BISSONNETTE
Good, this is all we have been waiting for. A lot of people put in a lot of extra-hard work many years to pave the way for this event. You will be the first man to ever travel above light speed and come back to Earth alive if nothing bad happens out there.

GREG
It seems so surreal.

WALTER BISSONNETTE
I know it probably doesn't make you happy that we will not be able to report what you did in your lifetime if you complete this mission successfully.

GREG
That's okay. If I make it back alive that will be more satisfying.

WALTER BISSONNETTE
Some great mathematicians have calculated you have eighty-five percent chance of success.

GREG
It's at least above fifty percent, so that's a good figure of merit.

WALTER BISSONNETTE
Good luck and thank you. You are a courageous man on many fronts.

GREG
Well, the trimmings are not too bad.

In their cryptic exchange Greg knew that Walter Bissonnette was probably well informed about his relationship with Monica Cheung which extended the sequence of pleasure in the name of national security.

If it wasn't for the fact that Monica Cheung was a spy, Greg might have gone with her and completely forgot about Ami. But Ami was the keeper. And to make it even more satisfying, Greg helped flipped the honeypot scheme on Monica.

WALTER BISSONNETTE
Good luck.

GREG
Thank you.

Greg climbed up into the TR-4 with Tiāncái but this time he would sit in the left seat as the commander of the mission with Tiāncái's backup. Having spent ample time in the trainer, he was more than ready to fly the TR-4 and feel the exhilaration of driving it out into space without help. However, in the background, Tiāncái could think a million times faster and he had a WIFI link to the TR-4B flight computers and his job was to make Greg look good by correcting all his mistakes without him knowing it.

The huge elevator lifted the TR-4B up to the runway level. Once the interlocks were in place and safe to move the air frame out of the hangar, the large hangar doors opened, and Greg was given permission to exit the hangar and proceed down the access to runway 17R. This is a seven-mile-mile-long runway allowing experimental models to commit to flying or abort with enough runway left for a safe landing. Most of the outer space flights took off from this runway.

Positioned at the end of the runway Greg was given permission to take off. He advanced the throttles forward slowly to about fifty percent power allowing the TR-4B to get enough speed to easily sustain flight by the wings alone, then pointed the nose directly into the air vertically. As the craft started to slow, Greg advanced the throttle to one hundred percent which automatically kicked in maximum anti-gravity.

Now the airframe was ten thousand times lighter and started gaining velocity very rapidly. In less than a minute they were supersonic and within five minutes were seeing the darkness of space and they continued to climb 25,000 miles up to the shipping container storage yard which hid the new demonstration Pluto II vessel. The TR-4B's autopilot now engaged by verbal command to Tiāncái who engaged the flight control computer via WIFI.

Within another twenty minutes, they were merely feet away from the miniature prototype PLUTO II.

Okay, Tiāncái, ready to do the space walk over to the spacecraft.

Greg's face mask was in place, the TR-4B was evacuating air out of the craft to equalize it to a vacuum of space. As soon as the indicator was directed, they opened the hatch and did their space walks. Greg and Tiāncái each had maneuvering devices on their arms and legs that were miniature rockets that would position them right to the open hatch of the spacecraft and they would then use the hand grasps to pull themselves down into the craft and after they were both onboard. Greg hit the shut hatch switch which slowly closed it then locked it.

Greg and Tiāncái entered into the cockpit. Pluto II prototype continuously did health checks and automatic diagnostic scans and reported a green board, ready to commence the mission.

Greg had manual control, but he was advised to do this mission in autopilot to prevent any unforeseen circumstances.

GREG
Let's begin the mission.

TIĀNCÁI
All permissions from ground control verified. Launch
sequence armed.

GREG
Commence Launch sequence.

Just like in the trainers, Tiāncái communicated via WIRELESS to the ship's computers, and it started moving immediately.

TIĀNCÁI
Number-one and number-two Pluto engines are
online. Applying thrust.

During this mission they were going to use number three during the breaking. All three rocket engines would help do the breaking at the same time, even though in the coming mission, the third would be reserved for casualties.

For a while it was a slow burn, they didn't want the exhaust to get too bright and alert scientists on the planet. They did expect the possibility existed they might be observed, so they had a cover story ready to be used.

Even at a slow burn the ship gathered speed quickly and they pointed Saturn directly so it would interfere with observations. That scheme didn't work completely, but it helped quite a lot. When the ship was 250,000 miles from the planet about the distance to the moon, the throttles slowly edged forward.

Acceleration happened quicker which allowed further throttle up. The closer it got to Saturn, the more auto-throttles. Going into orbit around Saturn, when the ship got to the opposite side of Saturn, hidden from view from Earth, the throttles went forward increasing acceleration to the point it gave Greg some nausea for a while. The speed was now increasing more noticeably. Within another two hours the ship was traveling at 24,000 miles per second, almost the circumference of Earth every second.

The speed kept rising. Neptune to one side and Uranus to the other appeared to drift behind them slowly, but noticeably. By the time they passed Pluto, they were traveling 40,000 miles per second. Velocity was calculated by the computers tracking stars and planets. Their position in space was triangulated minute by minute and fed in a stream of encrypted telemetry back to the Livermore Lab.

Auto-throttles then advanced to max safe thrust IAW the flight plan.

The spacecraft continued to increase speed now showing 0.7 lightspeed (LS) and climbing.

Livermore continued getting this telemetry feed thus they knew Greg was still alive. However, he was now further away from Earth than any human in history. A few minutes later the front intake was opened to allow gathering the few hydrogen atoms out in deep space but as they approached light speed that intake gradually reached the point of almost self-sustaining so the internal hydrogen feed could be throttled down allowing them to continue accelerating on free power.

Was this one of the theories Tesla figured out?

The moment of truth was coming real soon. The flight control computers displayed a countdown to light speed based on the current rate of acceleration. In just a few more minutes observers on earth would observe two things in about twelve hours the time it took for the radio waves to reach back to earth, the frequency of the telemetry was decreasing. They knew this was going to happen so tracking filters were closely following the frequencies and improving the quality of the signals so that data detection would be reasonable.

Greg's throat was dry as he was watching the velocity in meters, 299,999,995 meters per second. They were at the tipping point. If Einstein was right, he might suddenly find himself in another dimension or worse yet, extinguished.

Suddenly 300,000,000 meters per second and no change with the ship. Acceleration continued and five minutes later they were doing 310,000,000 meters per second. It was now time to throttle down the main engines to about five-percent power and do a slight course change to get away from the straight-line plume that would be following them at light speed and hammer them when they stopped and started going in the opposite direction.

After they were a good distance offset from their original track, the slats in the front were slowly closed shutting off the intakes and removing all the free power for the incredible nuclear rocket engines.

Now was going to be an interesting time. The retro rockets quickly swung the ship 180 degrees. The exhaust from the rocket engines were now facing in the direction they were traveling as the throttles were slowly advanced now breaking the speed.

The ill effects of G forces almost make a person sick when prolonged. Greg now relied on Tiāncái to help out as he felt too weak to manipulate the throttles and decided now would be a good time to stop breaking for a while until he regained his composure and started feeling normal again.

GREG

Reduce the thrust, I need to cut the G forces for a few
minutes.

Tiāncái his trusted Robot carried out his command and normal gravity was almost instantaneously felt which made Greg feel instantly better. After about five minutes Greg directed Tiāncái:

GREG

Recommence breaking.

Tiāncái was very good with the throttles and gradually brought them up to help minimize any sudden discomfort to Greg.

Greg toughed it out for an hour and they were now down to fifty-percent light speed. Back on Planet Earth in about 48 hours after the launch, the tracking filters would show the frequency was increasing and the phase lock loops were cleaning up the signals to make the digitized waveforms much cleaner for recording and processing.

This time in accordance with the permissions he had in advance, Greg stretched the non-breaking period to thirty minutes. He really needed it as his stomach wasn't feeling too good.

GREG

Okay, Tiāncái, recommence breaking.

Again, Tiāncái slowly applied the controls as to impact Greg the least likely possible. After another hour of breaking pushing against the plume it was putting out getting almost double the traction as going forward, the craft continually slowed down to 1/10th light speed. Greg had to take another break from the slowdown as he was starting to feel sick and nauseated.

Greg took the maximum time permitted before he recommended breaking again.

GREG

Recommence breaking.

Since the ship was going slower now the plume was much larger and helped with traction to further slowdown. When the velocity went from – to + the sensation wasn't as severe, but it existed, and the ship sped up. It would beat some of its signals back to earth.

Now they were on the home bound leg which made Greg feel a little better psychologically as the ship sped up again crossing over light speed for the second time. At the calculated point it cut power and headed for Jupiter. It would get close enough to

Jupiter to get caught in its magnetic field and then orbit a couple laps to bleed off speed before traveling to Saturn to do the next speed bleed off before turning to a course towards earth and the storage units in space.

Unfortunately, they would have to go through successive slowdowns, or they would never make it. At the end of the slowdown, they were vectored into an earth orbit at 25,000 miles to report findings. The TR-4 was waiting for them, and the space walk to get aboard.

A lot of scientific theories were destroyed that day. Since this was a super-secret, they would never be able to discuss it. Once they were aboard the TR-4 heading for home, the scale model spacecraft was immediately sent back to Saturn via autopilot for its last mission.

Now that technology and flight controls had been tested, it was time to move on to the next phase, including, fabrication of Pluto II, and preparations to commence the mission. The actual launch date was now put on the calendar. Construction crews who would start assembling the massive ship would soon start cycling to space and begin assembly.

As part of the ruse to mislead the Chinese who were being spoon fed the UNITED STATES SPACE FORCE weapons were opened up and their cargos systematically bolted together. Space walkers and safety observers to rescue them if their jetpacks malfunctioned and had to be rescued and taken to crew habitats, arrived in waves.

Thanks to the ingenious modularized construction, it all bolted together rather quickly, however, it grew in size where the shipping containers did not have enough surface area to fully hide the hull that was being quickly assembled. Time was running out. The launch date was firm and there could be no backing down now.

Greg was privately given a hero's welcome home with top leaders of the government congratulating him with great honors that were now locked away with the requirement, they could not be declassified and made public for seventy-five years unless conditions changed, and the government wanted to expose the operation for some political reason that at this point seemed rather unlikely.

Greg was informed he would be going on another mission soon, and again he would be the mission lead person. Because this next mission was deemed just as dangerous as the one, he completed, he was given two weeks to put his personal matters together, including visiting his two sons and his wife in Japan if he so desired. He also was directed to have a will and power of attorney copy provided to the lab in the event something went wrong. This didn't faze Greg too much because some 40 years prior he went through the same legal procedures.

Neither of Greg's sons were interested in the visit, saying they were busy with their personal lives and didn't have time right now but sometime in the future they might be.

Greg contacted his wife in Japan and she said now wasn't a good time because she was going away with her family to a resort for a couple of weeks. This was nothing out of the ordinary, because they had done that together a number of times in the past while he was with her.

DOUBLE SPY

After providing the lab, contact information with Greg's lawyer who had copies of his will and power of attorney and a copy of them he had given to Ami, the lab quickly understood what his intentions were. It was clear now; Ami was the person in his life.

CIA wanted Greg in his limited time to make one more contact with Monica, to feed her a golden nugget of disinformation that would likely lead to unmasking twenty more Chinese spies in America.

Right after the private ceremony at the Director of Lawrence Livermore Labs office, Greg was taken to Livermore Municipal Airport and flown down to San Diego on a CIA Jet. During the short trip, he was briefed on what he was to tell Monica and asked to get into the Hemi-Sync trance so that his brain would be wired to feed Monica the tainted goods after they expected her to drug him again. This would be their last opportunity to use Greg as an asset. This would be the final CIA mission he supported, though he didn't know it at the time.

GREG TEXT MESSAGE
I'm home back in San Diego.

Monica Cheung was then working on a Navy Commander who worked at a sensitive job and was with him trying to coerce him into a rendezvous where she could easily lead him into a honeypot trap. The Navy Commnder was married and Monica knew that she could threaten to expose him to his wife after she got him to a hotel prewired by technicians with hidden cameras and microphones.

That rendezvous at a hotel was not going to happen today, but they were having drinks at a Pacific Beach Bar where Monica was tantalizing the commander's little head and provoking a desire to proceed.

The commander had to leave because he had to get on the road to Carlsbad where he lived or his wife might get suspicious so that scenario was going to end shortly and she could then maneuver over to her other grand prize, Greg.

While the Commander was making a bathroom visit, Monica replied to Greg's text message:

MONICA CHEUNG TEXT MESSAGE
Why don't we meet over at the Flaming Flamingo say
around 6:00 P.M.?

Greg texted right back:

GREG TEXT MESSAGE
Sure, see you then.

Greg then took a shower after taking care of his business and put on slacks and a Hawaiian shirt. He called Rodriguez, who might be available.

GREG

Do you have time to take me over to the Flaming Flamingo?

RODRIGUEZ

Sure, boss, when do you want to go?

GREG

How about 5:30 P.M.?

RODRIGUEZ

No problem, see you then.

While he was waiting for Rodriguez, Greg started thinking where he could take Ami for a couple weeks since his sons and wife didn't have any time for him. The thought occurred to him: "Hawaii."

He didn't want Ami to know he was back home yet, as he needed to take care of this collateral duty the Cash in Advance boys desired, he accomplish, then he would fly back to Livermore or Area 51 the Cash boys would take him for toxicology and debriefing, then his condo where he would contact Ami.

He looked at several packaged deal trips available, then decided to skip that and just book a trip himself via the airline, hotel, and rental car himself.

Greg liked flying Hawaiian Airlines out of San Diego. They were truly the best airline with the exception of Japan Airlines to head west on out of San Diego. He called the 800 number for Hawaiian Airlines and as he was booking the flight discovered they also could handle booking him into the Royal Hawaiian Hotel he wanted to stay at and hopefully would see the ghost of Dudley Mush Morten, the famed WWII skipper. And they also got him a rental car with service at the airport.

He booked the flight and if Ami refused to go, he would inform her he would be calling Hikaru next which would certainly seal the deal. Ami had finished college, wasn't working her new job yet and had the time, so she should have no excuses.

His mission would not be divulged to him until the ship was launched out in space and he knew it would no doubt exceed light speed and probably go a long distance. Perhaps even to another planet to visit Aliens?

Greg had heard rumors about Aliens ostensibly living in Area 51, but had never seen any real evidence of it. But with things like a building with a huge elevator in it like he did experience, it's obvious there was a lot going on at Area 51 he wasn't privy to.

Rodriguez arrived moments later.

RODRIGUEZ
I'm here.

Greg went to the car and decided that since he had just had an extraordinary event in his life, he would give Rodriguez an extra tip to show his appreciation. As Rodriguez let him out at the Flaming Flamingo, Greg handed him a couple crisp brand-new $100 bills.

GREG
I appreciate all you have done for me.

RODRIGUEZ
Well, I appreciate you too, Greg.

INT. LATE AFTERNOON. FLAMING FLAMNGO RESTAURANT/BAR.

Greg had some ideas for Tio as well, if he was working tonight. Greg walked into the restaurant bar and the sexy Maître d escorted him to the bar with all smiles because she knew this guy had some of the sexiest women and Tio liked him so he must be a special person.

TIO
The usual?

GREG
Yes, thanks.

Moments later Tio sat a glass of cabernet and a sprite chaser down in front of Greg, who then handed Tio a $100 bill and said.

GREG
Keep the change.

TIO
You sure?

GREG
Yes, I appreciate your service and your friendship.

TIO
Well, thank you, Greg.

Tio was all smiles now. Greg saw the bar was filling up fast.

GREG
Tio, can I reserve this seat for my friend who will arrive
shortly?

TIO
Anything for you, Greg.

Tio put a glass of water and a dinner place setting there with silverware in front of the empty seat as well as Gregs.

TIO
I'm putting that down so that people realize the seat
is taken.

GREG
Thank you.

Greg then handed Tio another $100 bill.

GREG
This is for your assistance.

Tio nodded and winked at Greg.

TIO
I like the way you operate.

Navy Commander Monica had that Navy Commander so horny drugging his dumb ass while he was using the toilet he almost said, "Fuck it, us go to a hotel," but somehow, he errored on the side of valor and caution, he chose another destiny.

NAVY COMMANDER
I must hit the road now; we'll figure out a time we can
meet again.

Of course, that meeting would never happen because the very next day, the Commander received a visit from NCIS who had been given secret video footage of him associating with a Chinese MSS spy.

This made Monica's time more flexible and she soon was in her two-seat Mercedes heading over to the Flaming Flamingo where she knew her lover boy Greg was waiting.

Monica Cheung hadn't had any sex since her last encounter with Greg and was looking forward to getting pounded later tonight and get some more information out of him.

Monica Cheung's controller had recently stuffed her Swiss bank account with a big pile of money to reward her for her INTEL. She didn't know the asset in Livermore had just been spoon fed the same collaboration, so the Chinese MSS were acting aggressively on tainted information planted by their double spy and didn't know it.

Monica was gorgeously dressed and perfumed up with some very expensive French perfume that had pheromones in it and ostensibly helped make men hornier. Monica's beautiful looks showing a lot of clevage alone really did influence the Navy Commander and soon Greg would fall under her spell.

The French perfume was overkill. Monica had Greg's little head in full focus at first sight. This is one of the rare moments where a CIA asset was getting paid well to have sex with a foreign spy.

They didn't stay long. Monica had catered some food at her Rancho Santa Fe mansion for the Commander, and she had planned to drug his dumb ass as well. No reason to let all that wonderful food go to waste!

MONICA CHEUNG
Greg, the minute you contacted me, I felt you wanted
to see me, and it's been a while, so I had my maid
Elsie contact a caterer to make us dinner, why don't
we leave now and go over to my place. I have my car,
I can drive us.

GREG
Sure, if that's what you want to do.

Tio overheard the conversation and winked at Greg when Monica stood up, grabbed Greg's hand and walked him out of the bar, wearing a short dress, high heels and showing some cleavage and gave the Maître d a wink as she passed by with her arm tucked around Greg's. The Maître d just sighed and thought, Some girls get all the luck.

Monica had warned the valet she would be right in and back out and had handed him a $50 to keep her car right by the entrance, walked over and got into the driver side as the valet opened the door for her, and his assistant driver/runner opened the passenger door for Greg.

The two Valets were smiling, and both assumed as fast as Monica was in and out of the Flaming Flamingo with Greg in tow, he was going to get lucky tonight, and they were not far off the mark.

Monica was slowly taking a liking to Greg. He was a very interesting person, a great lover with a little help from her drugs and did some very interesting work which he never talked about. Others would brag and compromise themselves easy with a spy like Monica Cheung. Greg never mentioned his secret work a single time until he was drugged and under the influence of the truth serum.

Up Grand Avenue then out on Interstate-5, Monica kept the car speed up between 75 and 80 miles per hour taking all the commuter lanes on the way. She got up to Via de La Valle real quick and soon followed the winding road almost all the way down to the small town of Rancho Santa Fe and turned about a mile from the town into the middle of some of the nicest estates in the area that had a lot of property including 80 to 100 + acres and 12,000- to 16,000-square foot homes with large swimming pools and tennis courts like the one Monica lived in.

<u>EXT. INT. MONICA CHEUNG'S RANCHO SANTA FE MANSION.</u>

Monica pulled into her driveway and the garage door automatically opened as it registered the sensors in her car. As they were exiting the car, the garage door was closing.

Monica led Greg into a hallway from the garage that connected it to the main entrance of her home. Elsie was alerted her boss had arrived and approached Monica smiling.

ELSIE
The caterers have everything set up by the pool.

MONICA
Thank you, Elsie, why don't you take the rest of the
day off.

ELSIE
Thank you, Madam Cheung, I appreciate it.

Monica then turned and smiled at Greg.

MONICA
Greg, why don't we go out to the pool.

Monica already had a bottle of wine open and prepared for the Navy Commander had he decided to venture into her web that evening. It would be so fitting to use it on Greg since she hadn't had sex in a while and liked it nice and hard and long.

Monica led Greg out to the patio furniture that included padded chairs around a table they would no doubt eat at. Most of the area where the table and catered food warmers stood were under a very large awning that was mounted to the large eight-foot wall that went the length of the pool so outsiders could not peer in so that Monica could swim nude if she so desired and did now and then as she coerced more stupid guys who thought with their little heads.

MONICA
Would you like a glass of wine?

GREG
Sure.

Monica poured two glasses of wine and didn't mind the fact the drugs also affected her sexual desires as she was a willing participant with a man, she slowly was growing fond of.

In the back of Monica's mind, she thought of executing her exit strategy and taking Greg along with her, but would he be willing to give up his exciting career? That was one of the thoughts she pondered.

With the sale of Monica Cheung's Rancho Santa Fe mansion, she could move her and Greg to Switzerland and live wealthy for the rest of their lives. But could she really get the spy business out of her veins?

Monica sat and chit chatted with Greg over meaningless things for a while until she saw Greg had drank the entire glass of wine and the drugs should be working on him soon, then after another half glass she suddenly spoke:

MONICA
Greg, I want to go up to my bedroom with you.

GREG
Sure.

Greg understood what was going to happen next. He also knew Monica had drugged him specifically for this activity and during dinner and later activity, she would drug him again with some truth serum and knock-out drugs so she could work her magic on him, the Monroe Institute had foiled and would soon be spoon feeding the crafty spy with disinformation.

The double spy was being fully compromised tonight. This would be the greatest achievement the CIA double spy advocates had achieved in quite some time. They had not had such great successes since Charles Hansen and Aldridge Aimes spoon fed Russia identities of Spies Russia executed that insisted as they were being killed, they were not double spies.

Greg had no idea of the sophistication of the double spy business he now participated in doing. Greg was just another useful idiot the CIA took advantage of and played him in the double spy compromise of Monica Cheung with great success.

CIA understood it's probably best Greg didn't have a full appreciation of the danger he was in, otherwise he could never remained so calm and pulled it off. As Monica led Greg up the curving stairway, he had a great view of her posterior thanks to the very short dress, and it was as fantastic as any he had ever seen.

As they walked near her bed Monica stopped and asked, "Could you please unzip me?"

Greg obliged her and she soon dropped her dress down on the floor and had on no bra or panties which Greg already knew as he was spying on her stern shot as she was walking up the stairs.

Monica then turned around and unbuttoned Greg's Hawaiian shirt and slid it off also dropping it on the floor then kissed him and his chest and sucked on his nipples giving Greg quite the rush, then unbuckled him and completed undressing him.

Greg appeared already nice and hard and saluting, so Monica didn't need any further preparations and pulled him into her bed on top of her and guided him inside her then wrapped her legs around him and with her athletic prowess did about ninety percent of the work. Greg was along for the ride and when he reached the marvelous crescendo on a theme from Paganini, his release was substantial since he had not had sex in a while which Monica quickly felt and exploded into orgasmic pleasure.

After an hour of sex, Monica got up and went into her bathroom and Greg could hear the bathtub running water and knew she was probably cleaning herself. Monica momentarily came back into her room.

MONICA

Greg, I have swimsuits laid out for you in the guestroom, why don't you change and meet me down at the pool, I'm getting hungry.

Greg
Alright.

The food tonight was wonderful. The pasta was loaded with garlic and made Greg quite content.

Monica had on a swimsuit and a bathrobe but wasn't in the mood for a swim and instead suggested:

MONICA

Greg let's go up to my room and listen to some nice music and cuddle.

She asked Greg to carry a couple champagne glasses and she grabbed the container carrying the preloaded champagne which Greg assumed contained more drugs she would use to attack him with, but thanks to Hemi-Sync, Greg was ready to thwart Monica's attempts to compromise him.

As soon as Greg was horizontal with Monica cuddling and she was handing him his champagne glass to help him along. Greg was already into silent meditation to enter Hemi-Sync and it would be he who controlled his thoughts this evening, not Monica.

Just like Monica predicted, Greg was out like a light. She wanted to give it some time to start working and, in the meantime, she went into the guestroom and searched his billfold for "INTEL."

Little did she know the Cash in Advance boys had him put some things in his billfold she photographed that was more disinformation. She was being really set up like a sucker. One of the greatest minefields a spy can go over is when her cover is blown and they turn her into a double spy. Double Spies typically do not know they are being spoon fed disinformation until long after the damage is done.

The British were the masters of the double spy game. Stewart Menzies (a.k.a. "C"), the head of British SIS during WW2 and the early years of the COLD WAR, was the master of the double spy game.

"C" was shaken and forced to resign by Guy Burgess, McClean, and Kim Philby. Kim Philby happened to be Stewart Menzies (a.k.a. "C") protégée.

Philby's father moved to Saudi Arabia and converted to Muslim advised the King of Saudi Arabia until Americans overwhelmed him during WWII.

In 1980s Philby published a book, but it didn't have much of a distribution. It was more or less him bragging at his exploits. He also used a honeypot scheme for homosexuals in the British SIS.

After photographing those golden nuggets from Greg's wallet, Monica went back in her bedroom and Greg was gently snoring, but he was set up with the truth serum.

The trick was to ask Greg questions without fully waking him up. Monica went about her process and as she pulled more gems out of Greg's mind, she didn't know the Hemi Sync methods were beating her.

Monica only received exactly what the Cash in Advance boys wanted her to receive and she took it gladly and in the morning sent a long report via a special courier to a contact in Los Angeles who carried the files in his cell phone back to Shanghai where they would be processed and one of the million transcribers working for the MSS converted it to Mandarin so higher officials could review the case and glean important information out of it.

DEPUTY DIRECTOR FOR MSS
The United States Space Force is at their tricks again thinking they can get away with this gross attempt at placing a fleet of robotic weapon systems in space.

PRESIDENT CHINA COMMUNIST PARTY (CCP)
If we blow up those space warfare devices, the United States cannot complain because they are breaking international treaties putting weapons in space and lying to their public.

Wheels were set in motion to deal with it. But these kinds of actions don't happen overnight. They anti-satellite hardware and planning the Chinese would not be able to accomplish until long after Greg left on his mission.

With Monica's information she knew exactly where Greg lived and his life story. He would be an easy one to keep track of and eventually if he worked out, she might have to take him to Switzerland when she executed her exit strategy, because she didn't want to be lonely and Greg pleased her like few other men could.

As expected in about twelve hours Greg was coming out of his semi-coma wondering how successful he was. Only the CIA would learn eventually by monitoring things unfolded in China.

Greg was not ever going to be sent after Monica again. CIA had terminated his activity and would no longer be calling on him because Project Pluto II simply stated time had ran out and Greg would no longer be available.

Greg was flown back to Livermore on a CIA GS650 and soon had a rendezvous with Ami when he invited her to Hawaii. She reluctantly agreed and the trip was all set.

Meanwhile Pluto II management called upon Dr. Moore to do the last act. Greg was contacted and asked to come to his office just before he took Ami to Hawaii. Soon after he arrived, Walt, Dr. Moore, and Dr. Shirley arrived.

DR. MOORE

Greg, very recently Walter Bissonnette contacted me because he know you are my personal friend and asked my to participate in this discussion with Dr. Shirley.

GREG

Alright.

DR. SHIRLEY

The reason why we are having this private session with you is now to address your mission according to the planners is extremely high risk traveling above light speed long distances in space.

GREG

I assumed so.

DR. SHIRLEY

We recommend that just in case things do not work out, Greg you should have all your personal business in order.

Gregs discussions with Dr. Shirley and Dr. More lasted for hours and it now started to register with Greg how his life was changing and there was a possibility he would not be coming back alive from the mission. The biggest betrayal that two possible friends could have now transpired as Dr. Moore fed Greg a fabricated story.

DR. MOORE

Your mission was such a guarded secret that even we do not know what you will accomplish during this space voyage.

Doctor Shirley now revealed administrative policy she was spoon fed and did not know it was part of a grand strategy to Shanghai Greg who would be leaving on Pluto II either awake and alert or if necessary asleep and under sedatives that would keep him under for a few days while Pluto II left the solar system and went beyond his ability to ever get back.

DOCTOR SHIRLEY

We were directed to inform you that due to the sensitivity of the mission you will receive your mission brief until you and Tiāncái are out of the solar system and heading towards your destination. Tiāncái will be given a briefing file with time locks on it and during your voyage he will reveal it to you.

Dr. Moore and Dr. Shirley now made suggestions to Greg that he perform that almost put him into a state of shock.

DR. MOORE
Greg, I'm advising you to sell your home. You may be gone for several years on missions.

GREG
The house is paid off, I do not have a reason to sell it and its in a good location.

DR. MOORE
Greg, it's best you erase your past before going on this trip. We already had a buyer lined up willing to pay about double the market value of what it was worth. With the amount of money, you will earn on this voyage, when you get back, you can purchase a much nicer home out of cash.

DR. SHIRLEY
Greg, we know that as part of your current legal separation with your estranged wife, the house was now in your name. This will be a cash deal.

GREG
I'll consider it.

DR. MOORE
We have the contract here for you to sign. As soon as you sign it, we'll send in movers and put all your belongings in long-term storage the agency will pay for.

Dr. Moore and Dr. Shirley knew Greg's sons had disenfranchised themselves from him.

DR. SHIRLY
Since you would be getting double what this home is worth, we advise you to give large amounts of the proceeds to your sons. Hopefully that will generate good memories of you in case you do not come back.

GREG
I seldom talk to them it would be difficult for me to do that since I'll be going to Hawaii with Ami.

DR. SHIRLY
We will facilitate the funds transfer and visit them
and explain all your personal effects were in storage
paid for indefinitely by the lab and in the event, you
perished on the mission, they were entitled to claim
the contents.

Greg looked at the paperwork for selling his home was already filled out all he had to do is sign, and he did.

With a heavy heart Greg took Ami to Hawaii for two weeks while the legions of space walkers efficiently bolted his spaceship modules together. It was very clever the way it was engineered and within one month start to finish, the craft was ready to head on its mission including food, water, and all necessities loaded and ready to go. System checks were well on their way, so all Greg had to do is arrive and get underway.

HAWAII

<u>INT. DAY FIRST CLASS SEATING AREA OF HAWAIIAN AIRLINES PASSENGER JET</u>

Greg and Ami boarded Hawaiian Airlines Boeing 787 Dreamliner Jet and had very comfortable seats in first class. He requested in advance a bottle of Dom Perignon be placed on the plane for his consumption. At first the airline was a little resistant.

GREG
I'll pay for twenty bottles in case someone else in first
class demands any champagne and the airline can offer
all the unused bottles to the rest of the passengers.

Needless to say, the flight attendants were quite pleased with the way the passengers responded to their offers when the beverage cart worked its way down the aisles.

This was a super-special trip for Greg, so he had a lot of cash with him and twenty envelopes full of cash in his satchel he would spend lavishly once he arrived in Hawaii since he would not be needing money as soon as he went on his mission that he now knew would be a lot longer in duration since they had prepped him for the eventuality.

When the flight attendant brought that first bottle of Dom Perignon to him and Ami, Greg handed three envelopes to the flight attendant.

GREG
One of them is for you and the other two are for the
pilot and copilot. I also have some envelopes for the
other flight attendants, when you have time send them
up to me so I can shake their hands and thank them for
all their courage in serving the public.

The flight attendant walked up to her station just aft the cockpit and opened the envelope addressed to her. She observed the $1,000 in it with a lovely note and since the pilot and copilot's envelopes were not sealed, she checked them to make sure they were safe and they also had $1000 in them in crisp new $100 bills.

The flight attendant called up to the cockpit and explained the situation. Because of security requirements, the cockpit door was to remain locked at all times unless a calm flight attendant got her security team together to block access while the pilot or copilot unlocked the cockpit steel armored door in the event, they needed to take a serious bowel movement unexpectantly.

The flight attendant went to the midsection and notified the supervising flight attendant.

FLIGHT ATTENDANT
We need to put the security team in place so that their
copilot could exit the cockpit for a personal matter.

Five minutes later the pilot and copilot were reading the nice note Greg sent them and smiled at the cash, knowing this would be a pleasant stopover in Honolulu, since they were not scheduled to fly again for another thirty hours, which would allow them to blow a lot of that money that at their favorite nightclub atop the Ala Moana Hotel where they stayed and be sober in time for an FAA check if their random urinalysis suddenly was initiated.

FAA personnel show up in the cockpit of passenger jets with their random urinalysis kits and the pilots and copilots get to provide the sample on the spot. If alcohol is smelled, they also have a portable breathalyzer and a police officer standing by in the terminal to escort them off the plane and into secondary screening before the FAA slaps the book at them and more or less ends their flying career.

Despite all the warnings and routine random urinalysis, the FAA continues to catch drug abuse and alcoholism in the cockpit putting the public at risk. Without these random screenings, there would probably be more fatalities.

Before the plane landed in Honolulu Hawaii, every crew member paid Greg a visit and the sweet comments captivated nearby passengers wondering, *Is he some sort of celebrity?*

Greg and Ami got off the plane, went through the agriculture screening and right out into the middle walkway where all the rental car companies picked up the renters. His rental was paid for in advance and the driver pulled up to his car in the lot right across from the airport and handed Greg his set of keys and a printout of his contract he had already electronically signed.

RENTAL CAR EMPLOYEE
That silver BMW is your rental.

After Ami and Greg got their luggage and put suitcases them into the car, they were on their way to the Royal Hawaiian which had those historic rooms, some of the best artwork in Waikiki, as well as the best beach area typically saturated with lovely Japanese tourists in beautiful swimwear.

Greg remotely checked in the hotel at the airport waiting for his luggage, and only had to go to the front desk and ask for the key.

In a few minutes, Greg and Ami were up on the second floor facing the beach towards Diamond Head with the curtains wide open enjoying the lovely view.

Greg felt this romantic moment and knew he would soon undertake a very dangerous mission that was yet kept secret even from him. In his gut, he speculated that he was possibly going to a nearby solar system to meet with Aliens that were expecting him.

Greg had piloted a scale model of Pluto II and had no real knowledge of how much larger the real ship was. Out in deep space it didn't matter because you were so far away from anything, that size was irrelevant. Based on what he had already experienced, he knew Lawrence Livermore Lab was very precise in whatever they did. Therefore, his ability to return home alive was probably pretty good. But he had no idea what bestowed upon him in the not-so-distant future.

Greg had gone through psychological training to prepare him for meeting Aliens because he was informed that distinct possibility could happen, and he needed to be psychologically prepared for any contingencies.

Ami knew from her conditioning by Dr. Shirley this would be a rather long mission and Greg would be subject to far more risk than he ever faced before.

Ami intended to give him a good sendoff and hoped he came home alive and they might evolve into a life of normalcy. Greg hinted this would be his last mission, he was hanging up his spurs after this.

In the backdrop of Diamond Head and the spectacular view of the beach that allowed them privacy through the smoked windows and high up on the second floor out of the direct view of the beachgoers, Ami approached Greg and put her arms around him and kissed him.

AMI
Thank you for taking me to Hawaii.

GREG
It's my pleasure to bring you here so we can enjoy each
other and forget about the world for a few days.

Ami initiated the lovemaking and Greg experienced surreal gratification, feeling Ami's love and happiness she gave him. She gave him a lot of leeway to go outside his "swim lanes" as he performed those acts that led to her fantastic multiple orgasms.

The sound, the sweat, and the emotional outpour cascaded down like a waterfall as the river of love flowed out to sea. The power of the waterfall transfixed the minds for a brief period as Greg exercised his hemi-sync meditation and traveled to another dimension, he took Ami. He could have remained there for hours but knew he must return from his temporal anomaly back to reality to cherish every moment with Ami because time was running out.

They laid side by side for about fifteen minutes as Ami was slowly coming down from a natural high Greg induced in her. Greg was slowly spinning down from that alternate dimension he traveled during the lovemaking when he triggered his brain going into Hemi-Sync. He didn't know how he did it but Greg brought Ami along with him to the Universe during his Hemi-Sync or *Gateway* experience. *Or was it a temporal fantasy?* Greg asked himself.

AMI
Let's get up and take a shower.

The two lovers made their way to the lovely bathroom fit for a king and those very expensive rooms on the second floor directly over the best beach in Waikiki and perhaps in the world.

The shower was reinvigorating and refreshed them greatly making them feel especially good as their endorphins raced through their brains equalizing from that splendid journey through time and space that had no beginning and no end and mildly defied any definition or explanation.

Greg dressed casually in shorts and Aloha ware. Ami put on a nice Hawaiian dress Greg bought for her that had Hawaiian flowers and made her look like a beautiful local girl.

AMI
I'm getting kind of hungry, but I don't want a big meal
right now.

Ami was looking at Greg as he put on the final application of his preparations.

GREG
We are right next door to Duke's. It's happy hour there,
and they usually have music right on the beach about
now and great food to eat, as light as you want or as
heavy as you want to go.

ADMI
Okay, us go there.

Greg led Ami out to the beach entrance of the Royal Hawaiian and just a short distance down the beach to Duke's, located in one of the Outrigger Hotels.

As expected, there was a local music group with a pianist on a keyboard, a guitarist, a drummer playing lightly, and a beautiful female Hawaiian singer performing several of the exquisite local music compositions. A lot of people wearing beachwear mixed in with the wolves and heathens and their conquests that evening drinking copious amounts of alcohol easily established the tropical ambience and stratified expectations.

Greg knew the system at Duke's. There were a number of employees that didn't earn as much as they deserved working there, but they were polite, curious and respectful. Greg

231

approached the Maître d, a Chop Suey (mixed race – Hawaiian, Japanese, Portuguese, etc.) very pretty lady.

> GREG
> I have reservations for two on one of the outside tables
> near the band.

The very intelligent Maître d looked down at all the reservations and Greg knew he was alone, there was nobody around to see his bribe.

> GREG
> It could be someone misspelled it, I made the reservations over the phone.

Greg ran his fingers down the reservation list and laid down two crisp $100 bills.

> MAÎTRE D'
> Yes, Roger has very bad penmanship, I see your reservation.

The Maître d' grabbed the cash and immediately observed a couple leaving preferred seating.

> MAÎTRE D'
> Please follow me.

The Maître d' knew timing was everything and had to get them seated before one of the drunks at the bar grabbed the table.

The Maître d' seated Ami and Roger at the table and handed them menus.

> MAÎTRE D'
> Someone will be here to clean your table shortly, I'm sorry it wasn't cleaned before you arrived.

> GREG
> No problem, we'll look over the menu and wait for it to be cleaned.

The Maître d smiled at Greg knowing he was a sophisticated and wealthy individual who knew the rules of the road, *how to enjoy Waikiki without putting up with a bazillion tourists that get in your way.*

Ami was somewhat impressed how fast Greg pulled that off, and here they were in one of the best seats at Duke's just three tables away from the band and an unobstructed view of the beach.

The view, the food, the music, it all added splendidly to the evening.

The jetlag started to hit Ami after they finished eating.

> **AMI**
> Greg, I know it's still early, but I'm getting sleepy, can
> we just go back to the room now?

> **GREG**
> Sure.

Soon they were back at the room and Ami went out like a light. Greg was restless, somewhat nervous about this coming mission. The lab didn't want him to get nervous so they simply said, his orders would be issued to him after the ship was accelerating to its destination and that boredom would be his worst enemy. Boredom certainly didn't sound like danger. To cope with his feelings and to relieve excessive speculation on the mission, Greg started his silent meditation hoping to get back in Hemi-Sync and re-enter his last dream.

Unfortunately, that's not how Hemi-Sync worked. Greg had no control over where his Hemi-Sync took him. Soon he was in another dimension alone.

Ami's deep sleep left her with barely any brainwaves except Delta and Theta waves flowing through her brain. Experts had determined a person could influence another entering a Hemi-Sync if they were physically close The strange radiance that people exhibited during experimenting with Hemi-Sync showed that Alpha, Bravo, and Gama waves were elevated in the brain and perhaps radiated into the person physically close.

Greg wasn't sad he traveled to another dimension alone this time, as there were numerous cognitive revelations that bestowed his ability to completely block out his mission and his future. To that end he was grateful.

The next day, after a Hawaiian breakfast, they took a walk down Waikiki Beach to walk off the food, then venture back to the hotel room to freshen up and take care of business. By 10:00 A.M. local time they were ready to head out.

> **GREG**
> What would you like to do?

> **AMI**
> I wasn't really thinking of what I wanted to do. Perhaps
> we can go for a drive around the island?

> **GREG**
> Great idea.

Greg led Ami to the valet parking people and handed them his receipt. They looked at the number, gave it back to Greg.

> **VALET ATTENDANT**
> Your car will be brought here momentarily.

> **GREG**
> Thank you.

This was a rental car which Greg had no real interest in other than it was local transportation for them, but he knew the valets were not appreciated as much as they should be. As soon as the young Hawaiian pulled up with the car and held the door open for Greg while the other valet opened the door for Ami.

GREG
Thank you.

Greg smiled and handed the Valet a $20 bill.

That valet was usually there, this time of day and grew fond of Greg for his generosity. A lot of people who stay at the Royal Hawaiian, never tip the Valets and wonder why they are not always smiling.

Greg drove across Waikiki and made his way to H1 then took the divided highway towards the Pali lookout. He didn't know if Ami ever saw this before and never asked if she spent much time in Hawaii.

At the Pali lookout they could see Kaneohe Bay really well and a nice view of the North Shore.

The wind was blowing pretty good and it felt really good.

This was a happy moment for Greg as he had been here numerous times before, in and out of love. Sweet memories fading that at the time were Greg's temporal reality he left behind.

Soon they were in the car heading down the curving highway where they would intersect Kamehameha Hiway, the main highway that went around the island, named after the King who united Hawaii.

After a while as they drove along the picturesque Kamehameha Highway that hugged the tropical shoreline, they came up to the Crouching Lion restaurant Greg had many meals in during the many years he traveled to Hawaii when he was a road warrior. He decided to pull into the parking lot.

GREG
We can get a snack or if you are not terribly hungry,
they have wonderful desserts.

AMI
A dessert sounds good. I'm not ready for a meal quite
yet.

<u>INT. DAY. CROUCHING LION RESTAURANT</u>

Greg led Ami inside the Crouching Lion Restaurant. There was a good-sized crowd inside all smiling and happy. The parking lot was more than half full. Once in while tourist buses pull up and the place gets jammed full real fast. Sometimes it's tourist buses with nobody able to speak English, which was now getting more complicated.

Thirty years prior it was predominately Japanese. Now it's Koreans, Chinese, Malaysians, Indonesians, and other groups. Gone were the days when you could get by with simply hiring Japanese-speaking waitresses.

The waitress took their order. Ami settled for the Balsamic Peach Crumble with Vanilla Coconut Cream. Greg had the Almond & Orange Blossom Bar and they both had great tasting and strong Hawaiian coffee.

These desserts were delicious, just enough to keep them going down the road. Before long they passed by the Polynesian Culture Center and the Brigham Young University, Hawaii campus. If you like Hawaii, it pays to be a Mormon.

Unlike a lot of universities, Brigham Young University, Hawaii campus has an overabundance of clean cuts. They dress decently and do not act like many of the irresolute mendacities that attend UCLA and USC these days. The University of Hawaii is also an amazing campus as it draws students from around the world who are serious about their education. With a student population of around 55,000 University of Hawaii truly is a huge enterprise. University of Hawaii and has some amazing curriculums since University of Hawaii helps operate some of the observatories at the nearby islands.

Because Hawaii has a large concentration of military, the University gets an elaborate dichotomy of technology that is up there with the rest of the world, and often gets distinguished professors who want to enjoy the Hawaiian weather that come over for a period to teach classes.

Up the road a few miles is Kahuku. This was the terminus of the narrow-gauge Oahu Railway & Land Company (OR&L) that ran all the way to Honolulu from 1889 until 1947. The OR&L Railroad ran seventy-one miles from Honolulu all around the west end to the North Shore to the Kahuku sugar mill. From Pearl Harbor to Honolulu was double tracked and had more than a dozen trains, each day in east and west directions as this was the main transportation between Pearl Harbor and Honolulu prior to World War II.

The President of the Railroad, Dillingham and family who owned that rail line gifted it to the United Sates Military during World War II. After the war OR&L was given back to the family, but due to trucks arriving in Hawaii slowly taking over all the freight hauling and taking over more than fifty-five percent of OR&L's business, it was in a serious state of decline. The railroad's fate was sealed by the sugar strike and the 1946 Aleutian Islands earthquake and the resulting 55-foot (17 meter) tsunami that struck on April 1, 1946, destroying a lot of the OR&L's west end trackage. OR&L's rail line was repaired but due to the sugarcane workers strike and shrinking revenues, the OR&L was no longer viable and shut down 1947.

Dillingham Blvd., one of the major thoroughfares through Honolulu was named after the family that owned OR&L and had a lot of impact on Oahu for sixty years.

The Kahuku sugar mill shut down in 1971 as American sugar beets and other sugarcane growing countries created a sugar surplus that made it no longer a profitable industry for Oahu. Due to worldwide sugar production, even the sugar beet production in places like Colorado and California shut down a few years later.

After the sugar mill shut down it became a museum for a while, then reverted to restaurants and a small shopping mall. In the late 1970s and early 1980s the museum was one of the major attractions for the tour buses packed with Japanese tourists to stop at. Due to the attraction for North Shore lifestyles, the area is slowly becoming commercialized and a few miles down the road is a golf course and hotel. Greg didn't feel enthused to stop here because he knew only a few miles away, Waimea Falls Park existed and it certainly was a place Ami would enjoy.

Driving past the Kahuku Sugar Mill they passed several commercial fish grower ponds. Thanks to the nearby supply of water and ideal temperature, the fish farmers were able to produce large quantities of fish and they had a ready market available in Honolulu and Waikiki where unsuspecting tourists were eating farmed raised fish vice caught in the wild.

Also adjacent to Waimea Falls Park is the beautiful beach with absolutely most perfect sand. Another ingredient of ecstasy was the sea turtles who often swam right up to the humans, some of which broke the law feeding them. According to animal rights groups, anything humans would feed the sea turtles was harmful to their bodies. They needed to eat what was available in the wild. It was also a felony to capture and kill them. However, there were a few unsavory characters who captured one now and then and sold the meat secretly to high end restaurants via nefarious activity. Not all Turtle Soup ingredients were imported!

Hawaiian police who are actually quite good at their jobs did a lot of surveillance, but rarely caught these turtle harvesters and often it was usually a local boy who ended up with a hand slap to the wrist and told not to do it again.

All in all, Hawaiians are generally law-abiding citizens, however the growing homeless population with the arrival of more and more people from the mainland and elsewhere and growing drug use that accelerated after decriminalization of marijuana was changing all that.

In the past twenty years there has been an exodus from Hawaii. Sadly, a lot of people arriving to replace those fleeing to better situations back on the mainland, Europe, or Asia, were not replaced by people with high moral fiber. The homeless encampments are now slowly becoming a stigma to the reputation of Oahu as Asian tourists not normally exposed to a lot of homelessness see this and start wondering if America is as great as we think it is.

When you go to China and ride their trains, you will notice there isn't a lot of trash along the railroad right of way. The Chinese police their tracks rather well and put America's rail lines to shame. Perhaps America isn't so great?

It didn't take long to get to Waimea Falls.

Driving into the park towards parking has some rather spectacular landscape, and it only gets better once you get into the park.

Greg and Ami got their tickets and went into the park.

>   GREG
> Since we showed up slightly late and we don't have the time we'd have if we were here all day long, let's take one of the guided tours.

>   AMI
> Alright

Ami appeared most enthusiastically taking it all in.

>   GREG
> These guided tours in large golf carts carry a couple pairs of adults or a large family.

>   AMI
> What's the advantage of the carts?

>   GREG
> The main advantage is that instead of stopping and reading all the placards as you walked along the roughly mile from the front gate to the forty-five-foot-tall waterfall, the tour guide is well versed in all the plant life and on some of the more exotic or rare varieties stops the cart so you can get a look or take pictures.

The cart slowly made it's way up to the waterfall with the tour guide announcing vast amounts of information about the flora they passed.

>   GREG
> We can get off at the waterfall and wait for the next tour cart that will come along soon.

Many people hopped off here and looked around for a while or got treats at the nearby concession stand.

>   GREG
> When there is ample rain and the waterfalls are running full and the pond have deep water, there are cliff divers performing once an hour.

>   GREG
> We do not want to get stuck in the Pearl Harbor traffic going back to Waikiki later today. Let's take a quick look then get back on the road and head back wo Waikiki.

As predicted the tour guide was full of information and probably discussed several hundred plant species during the tour that might equal 100 pages of written text full of terms used by botanists. This valley was definitely one of nature's treasures and well kept. There was no doubt Hawaiians were proud of this park as it exposed the incredible beauty of what is to offer in the island flora. They soon left the waterfall and continued on looking everything over.

GREG

Sometime in the future after my next mission, I'll be happy to bring you back here and spend the day here and have lunch at the restaurant and it has outside dining.

AMI,

Sure, hopefully it's a long vacation.

Near the park's front entrance were a number of peacocks and some flamingos that were not native to Hawaii.

The tourists that flock to Waimea Falls Park, formally known as *Waimea Arboretum and Botanical Garden* get to see a few Native Hawaiian homes that represent residents living in the valley several hundred years ago in primitive conditions.

The drive-by was worthwhile as it exposed the beautiful flora to Ami and she was more interested in just spending time with Greg knowing he would be leaving soon, didn't really need all the tourism. She wasn't disappointed when they hit the road and continued around the island.

Eventually they drove through the pineapple fields then up to the Dole Plantation exhibit where they got out and took a look and got some samples of the pineapple. In recent years as pineapple slowly eroded as a commercial product due to competition, coffee was grown nearby and along the road were a number of coffee plants and trees changing the image of what used to be only pineapple fields.

The Dole Plantation was also a quick stop because now they still had a chance to beat the eastbound traffic that turned into gridlock around 3:00 P.M. Away they went cutting across the island through the Army Base at Schofield Barracks and Wheeler Army Airfield that supported vast numbers of helicopters and support for Airborne Troops.

Greg, a history buff, described to Ami information about this base that subsequently triggered more thoughts he spoke about:

GREG

During WWII this was the principal base the 24th an 25th Divisions came from. The 25th commanded by Lightning Joe Collins relieved the First Marine Division at Guadalcanal midway through the battle after the marines were fought out after four months of continuous combat.

Greg looked over at Ami who seemed content.

GREG

One day, General Lightning Joe Collins (Joseph Lawton Collins) was out scouting the battlefield with just two others spotted what he thought was the Japanese Army possibly evacuating their camps and ostensibly getting ready to evacuate the island.

VOICE OVER

AMI wasn't a big fan of war or the military, but she understood what was going to happen to Greg soon, so Ami decided to simply be accommodative and positive and pleasant to help make Greg's sendoff a happy one.

GREG

General Lightning Joe Collins subsequently ran two miles behind enemy lines to get to a good observation point to confirm his suspicions that turned out to be correct. As a result, American forces were able to encircle and capture most of the remnants of the Japanese forces resulting in only a fraction of them being evacuated.

Later when Admiral Halsey visited General Collins, he made the often-reported statement, 'He was not only fast on his feet, he was also fast in his head.'

AMI

Was General Collins a historic figure?

GREG

Yes. Admiral Halsey admired General Collins who was a very young General at the time. General Collins was later involved in other Pacific Battles and arrived at Normandy as part of the invasion force.

AMI

Sounds like he had a lot of experiences.

GREG

At the time of General Collins appointment, he was the youngest division commander in the United States Army, at age 46. General Collins commanded the VII Corps in the Allied invasion of Normandy and on the Western Front through to the end of World War II in Europe in May 1945. General Collins commanded the forces that stopped General Piper at the last bridge during the battle of the bulge that would have allowed the German plan to succeed.

AMI
Greg, you sure seem to know a lot about military history.

GREG
Ami, I've studied military history all my life. The 20th century was incredibly bloody and the events rather remarkable. I hope mankind does not follow in the folly of what we did back then.

As they drove past by Wheeler Army Airbase, Greg looked down the runway and saw numerous Army helicopters and various aircraft parked there. It was a somber moment as his Japanese lover looked on briefly with him.

From there it was down the hill past Mililani Town and the mergence into H2 freeway, past Pearl City, Aiea, past the Aloha Stadium with about thirty minutes to spare before traffic was going to suck.

Greg made good time as he drove on H1 past the airport, and then on down to Nimitz Blvd. past restaurant row in Honolulu, then Ala Moana then to Waikiki via Kalakaua Boulevard that had an access road right to the Sheraton and the Royal Hawaiian.

After they got back to the hotel, Greg decided to risk fate and take Amy to one of his old watering holes when he was a road warrior, the *Waikiki Tavern*, not too far away. It was this time of day when the gang would show up. One of them was Tim, a former corporate lawyer associated with Microsoft and Bill Gates. Tim was married to a Japanese lady who knew his former wife. They didn't socialize but were acquaintances.

Tim collected motorcycles and a few years ago, had thirty or forty vintage motorcycles. He moved to Hawaii primarily because they didn't have helmet laws and he could drive his big motorcycles around. Greg knew a lot of Tim's history but chose not to disclose it to Ami, but hoped he would see him and possibly some of the others. Sadly, half of them had died from cancer, smoking, alcoholism, and old age. Across the street was a tall condo building that had a lot of these retired people and a number of time shares in there as well.

Seldom was there a dull Friday or Saturday night at the *Waikiki Tavern*. The manager of the nude dance club a half a block away, a fairly young guy at the time, gradually started hating all the young female dancers he managed, came in there usually for every happy hour. One of the frequent customers a retired admiral, a pilot and POW during the Vietnam War would come in there.

Greg got to know him pretty good during his road warier days and almost got recruited for some INTEL support contract work. At the time Greg was heavily involved in other cool projects and thus that recruitment never materialized. Nevertheless, when Greg was getting checked out by the security apparatus of the Livermore Lab, information the retired admiral obtained in his investigation in Greg's preliminary recruitment activity around the year 2000, was found in his dossier that was about three inches thick. One cannot stay in the road warier business for long without getting information recorded about them, whether good or bad.

Security is cyclical, just like the political landscape it constantly shifts and a year from now may not be anything like it is today. During some periods of time information collection on key individuals is massive. Years later it dwindles down to nothing because of how priorities shift.

Was the admiral still alive? Possibly not. Had Tim killed himself on a motorcycle yet? It almost happened one time.

Tim's motorcycle stories were awesome and they were all true. Tim didn't bullshit anyone. He was amazingly down to earth and only gave a shit about his beer, his bikes, though he loved his two kids, and his wife was a saint for being so flexible and accommodative. Were they still married?

Would anyone Greg knew back then show up? Would they even notice Greg? Would any of the old regulars still come in there? He would soon find out. The place was hopping when Ami and Greg arrived, but nobody Greg knew showed up.

There were always new bartenders coming and going. Today they were blessed with a beautiful female Asian bartender who had the most gorgeous dragon tattoo on her back. She had a chopped-down tank top that exposed half her belly and back and you could see the head and a large portion of the tail of the dragon tattoo Greg guessed the Dragon tattoo was at least five or six inches wide, with incredible colors. Whoever did her tattoo probably took a year. *I wonder if there was a quid pro quo in all that?*

After Greg finished a couple glasses of wine and was about to head out the door, Tim finally pulled up in his beautiful, chopped motorcycle that Jesse James in Orange County California supposedly built for him.

It was too late to engage in conversation they were leaving. Greg purposely did not address Tim to see if he remembered him. Greg had obviously aged over the years and maybe Tim may not recognize him. Tim on the other hand was about seven feet tall, he was easy to spot.

As soon as Greg and Ami were a half away down the block Tim looked up at the cute Asian bartender Li.

TIM
You know that guy that just left with the Japanese lady?

Li
Yeah? What about him?

TIM
I know him from somewhere.

Right above Tim was some old pictures of the old timers that hung there for many years and there Greg was standing with the retired Admiral. It was the only picture there with someone wearing a tie, as they met right after Greg left an official work-related meeting and wanted a drink before he went up into his room at the Ilima to change for the night.

Greg led Ami through the *International Marketplace* that had been totally rebuilt destroying its old flare and ambience, but some of it still existed. Then across Kalakaua and there was the Cheesecake Factory.

AMI
Let's stop here for dinner.

GREG
Sure, if that's what you want.

The last time Greg went to this Cheesecake Factory restaurant was a few years ago when he went in there with a guy Tony and another guy from Seattle while they were attending a three-day conference over in Pearl Harbor. The place was packed. They had dinner there and the food was pretty good. The only negative was feeling miserable they had modernized the *International Marketplace,* that lost its culture in the process. The *International Marketplace* was now a sterile glass and steel modern structure instead of the wonderful ancient structures and huge trees that had been there for over 100 years. So much for progress.

After the meal they walked back to the Royal Hawaiian and relaxed and after a while, got frisky and inevitably a passionate embrace followed by a well-deserved nap.

Greg has an automatic three-hour alarm clock that goes off, forcing him to the bathroom. It worked well once again and after taking care of his business, saw the time was 9:00 P.M. It was time to go to a dance club and have some drinks and if they left real soon, it would be perfect as they would get some nice seats. But if they waited much longer the clubs would start filling up with tourists and a few locals and military who were stationed there.

A new dance club had opened a few months earlier named *The Ultimate Dragon* attracted a lot of Asian tourists and American military guys out on the town. Tourists from Australia, Canada, U.S. Mainland, and to a lesser extent Europe also showed up in groups adding to the cacophony of multiple languages flourishing that night.

Women arriving at *The Ultimate Dragon* were dressed to impress and a few of them who were desperate to get a green card, were eagerly seeking the *dumbshit* military guys who normally would not be afforded the comfort of such glamorous creatures. Some of those arranged quickie marriages worked out well, other arranged marriages resulted in the dude being dumped shortly after the woman got her green card and no longer needed him.

The Ultimate Dragon had a dress code, and well-dressed bouncers and waitresses that looked delicious in their ultra-short skirts. However, under the dresses were athletic shorts, a management requirement, so if they bent over, the dudes were not going to have the satisfaction of seeing something they were waiting to see.

Greg and Ami obtained a reserved booth. Ami was starting to enjoy the subtle inducements Greg did to get preferred seating.

Anyone who showed up late sadly discovered the Bar and Dance Hall was rather strict with their reservation rules. If you showed up five minutes late for your reservation time, your table was given to other parties. Since most people were not willing to pay the $500 reservation fee required for late appearance, many ended up disappointed when they discovered the parking lot was full and they had to walk an extra six blocks because they didn't see the wisdom of using valet parking that was reasonable.

Once again when the Maître d' could not find Greg's name, he pointed the spelling mistake with a couple $100 bills and the spelling was corrected immediately, and the Maître d' apologized profusely for misspelling his name in the reservations book as she took them to the reserved table that had the reserved placard on it. Greg learned that trick well dealing with Bubba at the Union 76 Station on West Point Loma Blvd. service station when they were super busy on a Saturday and Greg wanted to get his oil changed quickly allowing him to drive over to Ski Beach in the morning at a reasonable hour.

Greg laughed at all the jerks who were up tight with the cost of an oil change when Greg gladly paid twice as much to get head of-the-line privileges. A lot of people would look down at Greg for doing these small bribes, but if anyone ever complained to him, he would simply remind them about the movie star who paid $500,000 to get her daughter into USC, and all the other major college entrance scandals, where pay-to-play exists.

Ami had on her Hawaiian print dress, that in Greg's opinion was fabulously beautiful. The clothing designer expertly had a printed fabric that made the most of hibiscus and other flora that abounds on the islands.

Greg's Aloha Wear easily identified him as a tourist, like a lot of them wore, but he didn't care. He was here to make the most of his limited time left with Ami in case something went wrong.

There was some good competition in Waikiki for the tourist dollars of people that wanted nightlife and dancing. As a recent startup without a history of long-term customers, the Ultimate Dragon had to work twice as hard to compete effectively. Equipment that other venues would cut corners on wasn't going to work out for this business and they knew it. Their sound system was very good and in Greg's recollection, he had not witnessed dance clubs with this excellent sound since the days of "The Spats" in the Hyatt Regency back in the 1980s, and "Nicholas – Nicholas" atop the Ala Moana Hotel which was loaded with flight attendants until they all became aging hags and grandmothers. Through Greg's Japanese wife, he knew that owner, Giro Naguchi and often drove around Waikiki in his Rolls Royce on double dates.

The Hyatt had another good nightclub at the other end designed for the older crowd and people with a lot of disposable income, that was eventually replaced by a 1950s swing dance place called "Kento's" that had live bands on most nights. The place was usually packed. In the 1990s there was the Studebakers at Restaurant Row down near Aloha Tower and downtown Honolulu. It had a huge dance floor, huge bar, lots of booths and seats. That place was packed on most nights. The bar and dance club had a vintage Studebaker on display. It's like a lot of other places were now distant memories, closed long ago.

Waikiki Tavern is one of the survivors, but it was a little dinky place that often-had unsavory characters and defense contractors staying at the Ilima Hotel a short distance away, as routine customers. Greg stayed at the Ilima Hotel so often; he knew a lot of the employees there. He was staying there the night of 9/11 when terrorists flew jets into the World Trade Center.

After ordering their first round of drinks and giving the waitress an impressive tip, Greg explained to the waitress.

GREG

Keep my drinks filled, and your tips will keep flowing.

This did a couple things. It insured impressive service, but it also meant that waitress who was enjoying those huge tips would make sure her bouncer boyfriend would eject any asshole who tried to hijack the booth which happens from time to time. Greg and Ami got a lot of dancing in and four or five drinks before it was time to go back to their room and get some sleep.

Ami and Greg felt kind of tacky from the sweaty environment of the jampacked bar dance club, so they took a refreshing joint shower and simply held each other since their sexual appetite was fulfilled from earlier in the evening.

The next morning as Ami was reading through a lot of the brochures in the room, she came across a couple things that interested her. First on the West end of the island were a group of factory outlets like Levi's and Aloha Tropical Wear outlets. She didn't pack a lot of the right kinds of clothes for Hawaii, so she wanted more Hawaiian-style clothes to wear including their very beautiful dresses.

Greg figured out a great trip he quickly announced.

GREG

Let's go there and stop at the railroad museum, it's right
on the way, and after we go shopping and drive around
that area, we can experience Paradise Cove's Luau.

AMI

That sounds good.

In due time they were on their way. Ami wore simple shorts and a t-shirt, but planned to change into one of the dresses she bought later that day.

It was a nice drive to the Hawaiian Railway Society at Ewa Beach. This area was growing fast and several golf courses had been built in an area that had been farm ground not long before.

GREG

The Hawaiian Railway Society is a first-class operation. Credit should go to their many volunteers who have done an impressive job preserving the equipment and making it truly a stop that tourists should see and enjoy.

AMI

The drive to get here is kind of complicated. Tourists may not want the hassle.

GREG

With the new rail transportation system Oahu is building, people will be able to take one of the commuter trains from Waikiki to a train stop near this museum.

AMI

Do you think a lot of tourists will visit the Hawaiian Railway Society then?

GREG

That's when it will really start to get interesting at Hawaiian Railway Society at Ewa Beach, especially on Saturdays and Sundays when they have train rides on the original OR&L Narrow-Gauge line that runs five miles along the beach. Plans are to connect it to another five-mile stretch that would take their trains all the way out to Waianae. If you connect the dots, the Waianae restaurant and business owners will love train loads of tourists either by commuter trains or by the Hawaiian Railway Society weekend excursion trains that hug the coastline with incredible views.

Hopefully by the time I get back the commuter line will be complete, Greg thought.

GREG

HART (Honolulu Authority Rapid Transit) is building a double-track elevated train line from one end of the island to almost the other end. One could say it's probably the most ambitious public works project ever attempted in Hawaii, except for possibly H3 that bore a tunnel through the mountains allowing fast access to the North Shore.

AMI
Why was H3 built?

GREG
H3 created the real possibility for people to commute from the North Shore where housing was considerably cheaper for the masses, with far more opportunity for growth. H3 took approximately thirty years to complete, due to complexities associated with dealing with ancient burial grounds.

AMI
So it was a huge successes?

GREG
Some Oahu residents claim HART is the biggest boondoggle ever.

AMI
So, HART was a financial mess?

GREG
Not really. I think they must be misinformed on H3.

AMI
Why do you say that?

GREG
HART will eventually have a huge impact because the roads are now clogged with commuters. They reached gridlock years ago and it was beyond time for a fix. Whoever it was who came up with the idea of the elevated track is brilliant.

AMI
What makes you think that?

GREG
Sure, in the beginning it is hugely costly, but the land it preserves and the safety and access it enhances is really an extraordinary benefit. In fifty years, people will praise those brave men who had the intestinal fortitude to attempt such a construction.

AMI
That's how people think about those men who came up with the idea to do Shinkansen.

GREG
Absolutely. HART reminds me a lot about Japan and the Shinkansen train systems. The elevated trackage of HART is very similar to many miles of Japanese rail construction allowing public travel on a high-speed train to the very center of major cities.

Greg started daydreaming about the time he was taking the Shinkansen from Nagoya heading towards Tokyo one time and as they were leaving the downtown area, he noticed he could look right into the windows of high-rise buildings, they really were up that high.

Sometime later as Greg was being driven to the old Nagoya Airport they passed by the same high rises and looked up how high in the air the rail line was, and it truly was amazing. Some of the trains in Tokyo are the same way.

GREG
Japan probably had a lot of influence on HART construction design. It will be costly and disappointing for a while especially for those who do not like to pay taxes, but eventually as the bonds get paid down and the revenue becomes profit instead of debt payments, the people of Oahu will eventually realize HART had just as big an impact on Hawaii as did H3.

AMI
People tend to be short sighted in America.

GREG
Certainly. One other factor you never hear about. HART has electric trains. No dirty bus fumes or excessive automobile fumes.

AMI
The air here doesn't seem very dirty.

GREG
Honolulu and the vicinity are now being impacted by air pollution. HART will no doubt significantly help reduce air pollution and traffic congestion.

AMI
One of the reasons Japan built so many trains and subway system is traffic congestion increases air pollution due to inefficiency of travel.

GREG
Exactly. Once HART is in full swing with the entire network operating, people will once again enjoy

driving on H1 and H2 just like in the good old days as Hart helps reduce the congestion and will reduce the need to do road repairs from reduced heavy use.

EXT. DAY HAWAIIAN RAILWAY SOCIETY TRAIN YARD AND DISPLAY EXHIBITS.

Greg held Ami's hand as they walked through the Hawaiian Railway Society displays and closely observed the rolling stock. Greg knew a couple guys he met while working on projects that were volunteers helping preserve Hawaiian Railway Society railroad equipment. In his professional involvement he knew they were first-class capable people with high standards and impressive work ethics.

Greg had been here before several years prior, but this was his first trip after these acquaintances revealed they were volunteers. Just like in their professional work environment, the results here were obvious. When you have caring people who volunteer and do this work out of the love of trains and history, the outcome is always superb. It's unlikely he would ever see them again unless he accidentally stumbled across them here, but today, he wasn't so lucky.

It would have been nice to see these two men again, both of whom he highly respected and had been patriots and made great sacrifices.

Ami was looking bored so Greg decided it was time to get back on the road and go shopping. As they were about to leave Greg informed Ami.

GREG

I want to stop in the gift shop and give a donation and
leave a note for someone I know who volunteers here,
should just take a moment.

AMI
Sure Honey.

INT. DAY HAWAIIAN RAILWAY SOCIETY GIFT SHOP.

Greg walked into the gift shop and met a gentleman wearing a railroader's hat and coveralls.

GIFT SHOP ATTENDANT
What can I do for you, sir?

GREG

I have a friend who volunteers here. Would it be
possible to leave a note for him and a donation?

GIFT SHOP ATTENDANT
We are always happy to receive donations.

Greg planned for this moment, had the gentleman's name on the envelope with a handwritten note inside and a check made out to Hawaiian Railway Society for $1,000.00. The man took the envelope and the check.

> GIFT SHOP ATTENDANT
> That's very generous of you, sir.

> GREG
It's the least I could do. What you volunteers do here is impressive and I appreciate all that you do to preserve the Hawaiian Railroad History and in particular the story of the Oahu Railway and Land Company, OR&L.

> GIFT SHOP ATTENDANT
> Where do you know your friend from?

> GREG
> You can ask him that question, and if he wants to
> divulge that to you privately that's his business,
> but I must refrain. If he informs you, then you will
> understand why.

> GIFT SHOP ATTENDANT
> Sure thing.

Moments later Greg was back in his rental car driving along The Kapolei Parkway and eventually found some stores to shop at.

<u>INT. DAY. HAWAIIAN WOMEN'S APPAREL STORE.</u>

Ami picked up a couple more Hawaiian dresses in a small mom-and-pop store. Ami asked the store owner if it would be okay to change in one of the dresses because she wanted to leave the store wearing it. The nice fiftyish Japanese store clerk lady could speak English quite well.

> STORE OWNER
> Sure, you already paid for the dresses, go ahead and
> take the one you want to change into back to the fitting
> room.

> AMI
> Thank you very much, I'll be delighted to wear this
> dress for the rest of the day.

The store owner handed Ami a couple business cards.

> STORE OWNER
> If you meet someone who likes your dress, give them
> my business card. I'm sure we have something here
> they would like.

                    AMI
Yes, you have so many beautiful dresses. It was hard to
pick which ones I wanted. I will be very happy to give
your business cards to someone that asks.

                STORE OWNER
                Thank you.

                    AMI
I'm going to keep one of your business cards for myself
because I may want to buy some of your dresses in the
future. Do you take online orders?

                STORE OWNER
                Yes, we do.

                    AMI
Thank you. I may order a couple more dresses before
we leave. I'll order them online.

                STORE OWNER
You have very good taste; you will look good wearing
that dress.

True to the owner's expectations, Ami came out of the fitting room, looking quite
beautiful. The lovely colors added greatly to Ami's overall image.

        The pleasant store owner gave Ami compliments in
        Japanese, curious if she could speak the language. Ami
        answered with perfect Japanese. The lady explained to
        Ami while speaking Japanese.

                STORE OWNER
If you order online, you can put your hotel information
instead of your home, and we'll deliver it to your hotel.
If for some reason you leave Hawaii before we get a
chance to deliver the garments, we'll FEDEX them to
your home.

                    AMI
                Oh, thanks.

Greg and Ami then exited the shop and drove around a little looking for a place to have
a light lunch saving room for the Luau later that evening and stopped in at Chili's not
far away. Greg looked like a sugar daddy with his Japanese princess well dressed and
got a lot of stares in Chili's. No doubt there were some jealous people. They didn't dilly
dally around in the unfriendly environment and soon hit the road.

Greg was not too far from Barbers Point, that was closed down as part of BRAC (Base Realignment and Closure) that happened during the 1990s. Greg had worked there briefly almost 40 years prior training men of Special Projects Patrol Squadron Two (VPU-2) for specialized equipment. Now it was a commercial airport, but because the Navy's needs had not entirely ended. Just for old-time sake he drove past the facility and out amongst the various aircraft parked on the tarmac was several P3 patrol aircraft and military helicopters and a Coast Guard C130. *Naval Air Museum Barbers Point restored aircraft and aviation history*. Greg looked at his watch and they had plenty of time. Greg decided to tempt fate.

GREG

Ami, would it be okay to go in here for a few minutes?

AMI

Sure, why not.

Ami was going to be very accommodative. She knew Greg was soon going to be going on a mission out in space that was very dangerous with the possibility of not making it back alive. If these were his final days on Earth, the last thing in the world would be to pitch a fit about going somewhere she might normally not go. Military history wasn't a big favorite of hers. Greg was soon surprised when one of the museum volunteers explained.

BARBERS POINT MUSEUM VOLUNTEER

Those are not operational aircraft. They are all museum
exhibits, which you can go aboard and take a look.

Greg knew he had to handle this like the Waimea Falls trip, do it quickly and just see the highlights.

To Greg's ultimate surprise the Museum hangar was full of aircraft exhibits.

It felt kind of strange, almost 40 years prior Greg was inside this very same hangar working with some of the Navy technicians on the black box equipment these P3s carried.

Greg never knew for certain how they used that equipment, but he knew it wasn't used in the traditional sense. In his photo album, he had boxed up and storage for his sons was a picture of him in a three-piece suit under the large pod of one of those P3s standing beside the six sailors in their dress white uniforms, all involved in what he was doing at the time. Greg thought, *I wonder if they remember me. Are they all still alive?*

As soon as Greg saw enough exhibits in a brief period, he knew it was time to leave.

GREG

Let's get back on the road and drive out to the sleepy
village on the West end of this road.

251

Soon Greg and Ami were back out on H1 heading west where it turns into the Farrington Highway. Greg followed this road through all the towns and villages and eventually made it out to Ka'ena Point where the highway ended and only dirt trails went from there.

GREG
This is Ka'ena Point area and is as far as we can drive.

AMI
Why didn't they finish the road along here?

GREG
During part of the year huge waves crash on this area. It would not last very long. Hawaii determined a long time ago it would be futile.

AMI
Why did this road here get built in the first place?

GREG
The OR&L railroad ran along those dirt trails and they had to do continuous maintenance, but they had train loads of rock and material they could haul in to make repairs to the roadbed. Perhaps in another fifty years as demand requires it, they could build a road along here but it would have to be up along the hill side quite a bit, or suspended higher like a long bridge, to avoid waves crashing on the road and damaging it..

AMI
With modern construction techniques, especially what we see happening in China and Dubai, why do they not build it now?

GREG
The locals have always fought continuing the highway because they know if that happened the traffic would go insane as people would want to drive around the entire island.

AMI
That makes sense.

GREG
See enough?

AMI
Yes.

GREG

We've enough time to drive back towards the Luau location and sightsee along the way.

Greg retraced their drive from Ka'ena Point back towards Honolulu to pass by Paradise Cove.

It was around 4:30 P.M. when they drove near Paradise Cove Luau. Hence, they drove around Ko Olina checking out the golf courses. A lot of Japanese tourists loved playing golf in Hawaii, probably the fastest growing sport on the island of Oahu.

GREG

Some Japanese golfers save enough money playing golf in Hawaii verses in Japan, the difference pays for their airline ticket, hotel room, and green fees. Golfing at a course as nice as the typical Hawaiian golf course is prohibitively expensive in Japan, if you are lucky enough to be allowed to apply for membership.

Greg explained President Eisenhower's addiction to golf to Ami as they were driving by the golf courses.

GREG

Japanese are addicted to golf, just like President Eisenhower played golf to control his anger. As a result, left a legacy behind of playing golf every day one way or another. Camp David was modified with a new three-hole golf course just for Ike. Several wealthy businessmen installed a putting green at the White House for Ike. It was money well spent because it helped Ike keep cool which prevented a nuclear war with Russia during some of our darkest moments in our nation's history.

AMI

Is that so?

GREG

The public doesn't know the half of it, but more and more leaks out every day as the Russians systematically clean out their archives and eliminate more and more Soviet Information that has no further relevancy except to historians who want to spend endless hours connecting the dots, not so much as to explain how close we came to the brink but better to explain the lives of key individuals and what their roles in all those affairs happened to be.

AMI

You were alive for a big part of the Cold War. What was it like?

GREG

It was a fascinating time and, in many ways, Ike was shielded from criticism, mainly because the Pentagon was behind him and if the left-wing media dared to trash him, they would quickly feel the heat.

AMI

So, Ike playing all that golf prevented a nuclear war and made things better?

Greg, having read a lot about Eisenhower, had a different perspective than a lot of people. Ami's statement triggered is the next comment he made with a lot of passion.

GREG

Unfortunately, a lot of our problems in the 1960s were the result of Ike's inactions and mishandling of the Korean Armistice and Dien Bein Phu and Vietnam. He left behind a mess for Kennedy.

AMI

What should Eisenhower have done differently?

GREG

Eisenhower should have realized the Korean Armistice would eventually lead to another war just like the WW1 Armistice caused. Ike should have known he had Mao on the ropes and the Soviet Union was collapsing due to trade sanctions.

AMI

What should President Eisenhower have done differently?

GREG

There was a brief period in the 1950's when America had Hydrogen Bombs and the Russians were several years away from producing a Hydrogen Bomb. Ike could have written the peace. Instead, he kicked the can down the road for the next generation, which caused many horrible days for me in my lifetime.

AMI

Did Ike dither at key decisions?

GREG
It sure appears that way.

AMI
Ike could not have decided all this on his own. He had a staff.

GREG
That's true, however some historians now question how much of it was his liberal brother Milton giving him bad advice.

AMI
We'll never know for sure. Like most politicians, Ike probably kept his most guarded secrets close to himself.

GREG
Ike was a superb poker player and one never knew what he was doing, and some historians claim his big bluff worked for him, but in my opinion not so well for those that followed him.

AMI
In what way?

GREG
Kennedy, Johnson, Nixon, Carter, and then Reagan ended up required to finish Ike's job for him. Bush completed Reagan's mission because it took longer than eight years, causing the end of the Soviet Union.

AMI
Where do we stand now with the Russians?

GREG
Russia could easily be our future friends. We need to figure out ways to build that friendship.

AMI
Do we have the chance now with Ukraine business going on?

GREG
I think there are ways we could approach the Russians to create the atmosphere for peace.

AMI
How would we do it?

GREG

Think outside the box. Friendship is a lot cheaper than enemies. China would be delighted if America became its friend.

AMI

How could we arrange that?

GREG

Again, think outside the box. Once they realize they have a legitimate friendship with us we could then talk more point blank with them to resolve issues without the threat of aggression. Friends normally do not beat up other friends, they care about their plight as well.

AMI

You make perfect since, why didn't you work for America's State Department?

GREG

I was too busy killing Commies for Christ and sucked into the Cold War mentality. Now I see I wasted so many valuable years.

Greg then pulled into the driveway for Paradise Cove Luau. The timing was perfect. They were early, lots of parking available, and the venue was just now opening up. Soon they were walking around looking at all the arts and crafts.

Ami was looking at excellent-looking jewelry.

AMI

Hawaiians sure have many artists and creative people.

GREG

Perhaps it's the notion of being stuck on the rock with nothing to do but go to the beach drives these people to do all this fantastic artwork.

AMI

This artwork looks as good as any you find elsewhere around the world that's pretty expensive.

GREG

It's all about location – location – location. If these goods were being sold in Paris to American Tourists, you could put one or two more zeroes in the price tag and still sell it there.

Greg didn't see anyone he recognized as people all started showing up. No doubt they were all tourists and he would never see them again in his lifetime, nor did he care.

Eventually they were seated and once again Greg's finesse at bribing the staff netted them a very good table with an unobstructed view of the stage where soon the performers and dancers would be appearing. Since Greg was the designated driver, he would not be drinking any alcohol drinks, which was okay with him. He wanted more clarity in his mind tonight as thoughts were swirling around in his mind. Greg had taken an emotional bond to Ami. It was now far more serious than he ever imagined to the point he considered un-volunteering for the mission.

However, after observing how the spooks dealt with Monica, they would probably hurt him really bad if he tried to back out now. It was too late. He was trapped. Then he started thinking, *The reason why they had me do the maneuver to slow down and stop might be done on this mission.* His speculation now centered around he was going somewhere to meet Aliens as an invited guest. If that were to happen, as a pivotal moment to mankind, he would be a modern-day Charles A. Lindberg. Would he really want to pass up the chance?

One thing certain was, when he got back from the mission alive, he now felt compelled to travel to Japan and give his wife an ultimatum. He didn't want to spend his life alone, and if she was unwilling to come back to America, sign the divorce agreement so he could get on with his life.

Greg would unquestioningly give her half of everything he had, so there would be no point in fighting him in court. He felt she probably would go along with it as she had no desire to come back to America, at least not now anyway.

As everyone was served beverages to loosen them up a bit since most of those attending arrived on tourist buses, people sitting at the table Greg shared introduced themselves. People with New York or New Jersey accents. They were probably decent people but Greg had no desires to create new friendships and bond tonight. These people were irrelevant to him and Ami, but they were polite nevertheless, giving an outward friendly appearance and acting more like a listener than a talker.

The meal started before sundown. There was some entertainment while they were eating, but the main entertainment did not really start until the staff started cleaning off the dinner tables, then it was all those Polynesian dancers and music. The dancers' exhibition seemed to elicit sexual energy. Sex and love were freely given a few hundred years ago in the days of Captain Cook.

GREG

It's too bad their costumes are not like how they were back before the white man arrived. They would be dancing topless.

Ami responded and threw Greg an evil grin.

AMI
If you want, I'll dance topless for you later back at our
hotel room.

One of the stuffy New Yorker ladies sitting directly across from Ami had the look on her face as if she just heard a heathen speaking such terrible things, especially in front of her husband who should never hear such things!

The dancers, the costumes, the fire twirlers, and all the other performances were very exciting. Greg was glad he was perfectly sober to appreciate it and remember it better, but at the same token he kind of wished had taken one of the tourist buses here, had two or three Mai Tai drinks to feel into the swing of things. Ami made up for his lack of drinking and did it for him.

Eventually the night came to an end and Greg was back on H1 heading back to Waikiki.

When arrived at the Royal Hawaiian VIP parking by the front entrance, the daytime valet wasn't there to park Greg's rental car, but the nightshift guy was just as polite. Greg made his night by handing him a $20.

GREG
I appreciate what you do for us.

VALET PARKING ATTENDANT
Thank you, sir, and I appreciate you want to stay in our
hotel.

GREG
You are most welcome.

Ami was slightly animated from the alcohol that was now starting to put her into a modus of operandi Greg had not appreciated before.

Ami took off her beautiful Hawaiian dress and hung it up in the closet and placed the shopping bag that had her other purchases and clothes she initially wore that morning in the closet now wearing only her bra and panties and walked over and closed the curtains just in case there was someone watching them through a telescope getting their jollies.

AMI
I was serious about dancing for you.

Ami suddenly took off her bra and started emulating the dancers at the Luau for a few minutes.

AMI
I do not think I have your proper attention.

Ami removed her panties and was now completely nude continuing with her artistic performance. Greg was enjoying every minute of it, but Ami still wasn't satisfied.

AMI

You look too warm, you have too many clothes on.

Ami then walked over and started unbuttoning his shirt and efficiently got it off then proceeded to discharge his shorts and low and behold she discovered something.

AMI

What's that little wet spot on your underwear? I think
you want something you might be too scared to ask.
Don't feel scared, I'll do it.

And within moments the two were enjoying the celestial feast as Amy persuaded him to try different things except one, she would never agree too, nor would Greg want. However, if Greg was a Greek man it would have been the first thing he did and probably nothing afterwards.

Drenched in sweat, Ami needed a shower.

AMI

I don't want to lay in those sheets sweaty, us go take a
short shower.

They took a brief shower which gave them an amount of comfort, then they crashed. Ami was satisfied and so was Greg. Greg however was secretly having some mental issues coping with what was going through his mind with Ami that had captured his emotions and gave him real purpose in life which now he sadly would have to extinguish in a few more days.

The more he liked Ami as his love grew for her every day, the more he wished the hell he could back out on this mission and survive. Greg knew that because of his assistance and assignments to the Cash in Advance boys, the lab could turn to them and use them to adjust his attitude and would not surprise him if they coerced him using Ami. It would not be beyond them to have one of their Guido contractors feed her body through a tree shredder in front of him to prove they were willing to do it to him if he didn't carry his sorry ass to that mission.

And he truly was sorry. He now realized what he had done to Ami probably wasn't socially acceptable or ethically reasonable. But just like days back in the 1970s when he never knew for sure he would come back alive; he had a conflict of thoughts. He thus rationalized that since he might not come back to simply enjoy these last moments with Ami as if it were going to be the end forever. How would someone act if they knew for sure they were going to die exactly in one month from now? Probably different?

Ami quickly passed out and because she really was super tired, she could not stop snoring a little. Greg enjoyed every minute of the sound.

Ami's snoring reminded him of a time he went out on a submarine as a civilian doing an inspection and had a very rough ride and the crew lost control of the submarine for a short time that scared the living dog shit out of Greg.

Greg was soon on an airline flying back to San Diego. He was sitting next to a very nasty old bitch as far as he was concerned. There was a woman sitting directly behind them with a baby that was crying and howling probably due to ears plugged up and the pressurization of the cabin was causing great pain.

FEMALE PASSENGER
I wish that woman would put a sock in that kid's mouth.

Greg turned to the woman and looked directly into her eyes.

GREG
That's music to my ears.

Greg didn't inform the woman of his recent experience, nor did he tell the woman why.

The baby crying and Greg hearing it allowed him to remember he was still alive.

At least it shut up the old hag. However as soon as the flight attendant came by the woman pitched a fit and demanded she be given another seat. The woman got up and followed the flight attendant quite a way forward and sat down, and a few minutes the professional wrestler sitting next to her returned from the toilet and not only took up all his seat but half of hers too.

As the old saying goes, Be careful what you ask for.

The next day Ami and Greg woke and after a discussion decided on going to the Bishop Museum which all tourists should try to see. After the museum Greg was going to take them to Hanauma Bay, then to Sandy Beach so she could see some impressive waves but warned her a half-dozen people had their necks broken because the huge waves crashed on the beach.

The Bishop Museum archives has numerous pictures and artifacts of the Hawaiian Royal Families. Due to all the incest, many of them became terribly disfigured. As soon as they started marrying outside of their family, the beauty returned. They have a lot of archives in the basement of the main display building which is quite huge and has an elevator because it's a multi-story building. Greg wanting to cut through red tape like he did most of his professional life, pissing off the pope in the process (his superiors), knew how to handle getting access to the archives because he knew there were some golden nuggets down there. Boxes and boxes of Oahu Railway & Land Company (OR&L) black-and-white photographs.

It took Greg a while to find the right person who indicated that even though he didn't have the special reservations and credentials required (they only wanted historians near those archives), he could be escorted for the proper fee which Greg naturally offered up immediately.

With Ami in tow Greg and the Bishop Museum Employee took some stairs down to the archives room in the basement of the main display building and there were huge amounts of "stuff" down there, but a lot of it in one corner specifically was well marked and because the Oahu Railway & Land Company (OR&L) was such a huge asset, it was well labeled and easy to find without much effort.

The Bishop Museum Employee was happy she had some big bucks to enjoy the weekend with, observed Greg carefully take the contents out and held them with reverence. She almost felt like giving his money back because he touched her so dearly in his appreciation for the narrow-gauge railroad pictures and as he was going through a couple boxes of 8 ½ by 11-inch professional photographs taken by the company for their quarterly financial reports and for publicity purposes. Greg wanted pictures of a couple gems he found with some famous people like Nimitz and Patton by some of the trains. He held up the pictures and asked Ami to photograph them with her cell phone.

Greg didn't want to press his luck so after thirty minutes thanked the person who didn't mind staying but was happy Greg curtailed his activity so abruptly. However, something magical happened.

Most people today do not know Honolulu once had a fabulous trolly system that included service to Waikiki.

The Honolulu trolleys that ran on rails were kept in immaculate condition, and well painted. If you drive down by restaurant row, you will pass a small power station that is shut down and boarded up and fenced off to keep vandals out, provided power to parts of the trolly system.

Greg stopped dead in his tracks.

GREG
Oh my God, you got wonderful color pictures of the trolly!

The woman in her twenties became animated.

BISHOP MUSEUM EMPLOYEE
I had no idea Honolulu and Waikiki had such an
extensive trolly system.

Greg pulled out several Honolulu Trolley pictures out of the archives. It appeared like the second coming of Christ to Greg. Color pictures of Honolulu trolleys were extremely rare.

All the OR&L photos were black and white, however Greg felt if he emptied all the boxes, he might have found color pictures around 1946 just before the rail line shut down.

But here he was looking at the trolly pictures of a system that survived a few years longer well into color photography era. In the matter of fifteen minutes, Greg had Ami take at least twenty color pictures taken of the Honolulu Trolly.

The young female Bishop Museum Employee was touched.

BISHOP MUSEUM EMPLOYEE
You have enlightened me quite a bit. I can't take your money.

GREG
Actually, I want you to take the money, invite one of your friends out to dinner and tell them about what we found down here.

BISHOP MUSEUM EMPLOYEE
I can do that if that's what you want me to do.

GREG.
Yes, I do. And if you can find the time, go online, and look up the San Diego Model Railroad Museum. The museum is in Balboa Park in San Diego, and send them an email to pass on to their two librarians both named Jim, and inform them Greg wanted them to know about all the pictures in archives here, and that if they or anyone from the Museum comes to Hawaii to make an appointment and make arrangements to scan some of these pictures to put on display in the San Diego Model Railroad Museum Library.

BISHOP MUSEUM EMPLOYEE
Sure, I'll do that.

GREG
Just so you know, the Model Railway Museum at Balboa Park is the only accredited railroad research library in the United States.

BISHOP MUSEUM EMPLOYEE
That's impressive.

GREG
So is their collection of videos, books, and all sorts of railroad documentation. A person could spend the rest of their lives in there and not be able to read or view it all.

BISHOP MUSEUM EMPLOYEE
Wow.

They soon left the archives. The woman feeling uplifted had no idea Honolulu was as advanced compared to other cities back in the 1940's and 1950's, mainly due to all the tourists.

Now it was time to head for Sandy Beach.

GREG

I'm a little hungry. Across from the Ala Moana shopping center and mall, is a local fast food restaurant on the beach called L&L Hawaiian Barbecue. There is plenty of parking at Ala Moana Beach Park. We can walk a short distance from the parking lot to L & L and get a boxed lunch and some sodas and eat them at the beach. There are picnic tables and a long wall we can sit on and eat.

AMI
What kind of food?

GREG

Quite a variety. They cook seafood, barbecue chicken, pork, beef, etc.

AMI
Sure, that sounds good.

They made their way to Ala Moana Beach Park and got their boxed lunches and took them to a picnic table not far from the parking lot in the semi shade.

AMI
There are lots of signs that says do not feed the birds.

GREG

Yeah, the restaurant and locals go nuts if they see you feeding the birds. If you feed the birds, they will tell the cops and you will get a ticket.

AMI
That's good to know because I love feeding the birds.

GREG

Me too, especially black birds. They are incredibly smart birds.

In due time they finished their lunches, but Ami felt uncomfortable.

AMI
Could we go back to the hotel first before we go to Sandy Beach?

GREG
Sure.

It didn't take Greg long to figure it out, Ami wanted to sit on a clean toilet and take care of her business. He felt the same way, but always, ladies first.

After completing their business, they headed out, drove around Diamond Head then on to Hanauma Bay where they went down the hill and parked and got out. They each wore swimsuits now so if they went into the water, it would be okay.

EXT. DAY. OAHU HANAUMA BAY

> GREG
> Let me show you some of the beautiful tropical fish
> that you easily can see here.

Greg took Ami to a spot he knew always had a lot of tropical fish. He was not disappointed because today there must have been at least 100 of them in just this one spot. The beautiful part of it was they didn't have to get their swimsuits wet, they could see a lot of them just standing in knee-deep water.

> AMI
> Those fish look so pretty.

> GREG
> Many of them are friendly. Some people feed them, but
> if you get caught you get a ticket.

They watched the fish for a while and then it was time to get to Sandy Beach where Ami would be impressed with those waves.

EXT. DAY. OAHU SANDY BEACH

Today Ami was not disappointed.

> GREG
> I recommend you do not get in those waves you can
> get hurt really easy, they will toss your body around
> like crazy.

> AMI
> You don't have to convince me. I can see I don't want to
> push luck. My God, those waves are huge.

> GREG
> If you want to swim, let's go to Waimea Bay and you
> can swim with the turtles.

> AMI
> Sounds good to me.

It took a while to get there, it was actually a long drive to get there, but this time of day, they didn't have to fight much traffic.

<u>EXT. DAY. OAHU WAIMEA BAY</u>

In due time they were on the beach at Waimea Bay sitting on beach towels they borrowed from the hotel for the appropriate bribe.

> AMI
> Let's get in the water.

Greg and Ami went in and the water holding hands.

> GREG
> The water temperature today is about eighty-seven
> degrees.

> AMI
> The water feels very nice.

Moments later they were in the water up to their necks and embracing. Greg slipped his hand down into Ami's bikini crotch and messaged her as they were kissing, and she responded most enthusiastically and passionately. She then informed Greg key information to warn him.

> AMI
> You are making me so horny; we may have to hurry
> back to the room and do it again.

About that time Greg spotted one of the large sea turtles a few feet away staring at them.

> GREG
> Look, a turtle!

The turtles this close up completely unwound Ami. She had never swum that close to a huge sea turtle. Ami felt quite scared at first, but the turtles were just watching as if the kissing they were doing moments before caught their attention.

> AMI
> Their heads are so large. There are five or six of them.

> GREG
> These large sea turtles are curious animals, and not
> terribly scared of humans as the locals have violated
> the rules for decades feeding them.

> AMI
> Sea turtles are like birds in they have facial recognition.

> GREG
> Locals in the past informed me these large sea turtles
> know some of the surfers and locals that come down
> to this beach area every day, especially the ones that
> feed them.

> AMI
> I would expect so.

> GREG
> Another interesting comment locals have said to me
> in the past is if sea turtles see you catching another sea
> turtle, they will be shy of you from then on. They are
> smart animals and learn fast, just like black birds.

The large sea turtles were a novelty for a while swimming by and observing Greg holding Ami while he fondled her and was exciting her. Predictably that romantic activity manifested Ami's spontaneous statement.

> AMI
> I think I want to go back to the room now. I don't want
> to get sunburned.

> GREG
> Alright, but we'll take H3 back, it will be quicker, plus
> you might enjoy the long tunnel ride and the view
> when we pop out of the tunnel at the other end.

INT. DAY ROYAL HAWAIIAN HOTEL ROOM

That afternoon back in the hotel room Greg had another surprise for Ami as he looked at the courtesy copy of the *Honolulu Advertiser* newspaper.

> GREG
> The Honolulu Symphony is playing Rachmaninoff,
> Piano Concerto Number Two tonight at 7:00 P.M. Us
> go to it and we'll have dinner afterwards.

> AMI
> I would love to hear the symphony play.

2 3 7

Greg and Ami quickly changed their clothes and soon they were on their way with Ami glistening in her new beautiful Hawaiian dress that was for special occasions, not necessarily provincial in appearance as her other dress she just purchased.

Greg had some nice slacks and a nice Polo shirt he thought would do fine in as people didn't put on suits and ties for the Honolulu Symphony, mainly because it was very warm outside.

Greg had always wanted to take a beautiful woman to a Rachmaninoff performance, but it never seemed to work out.

Tonight, it worked out splendidly as he was sitting next to the most beautiful lady sparkling in the audience. The music and the moment were instrumental in Greg's coming voyage because there were a few times in the PLUTO II voyage Greg considered committing suicide. Fond memories of this night kept him alive several times.

After the concert, Greg drove them back to the hotel where the same night shift valet guy was there and once again Greg greased his palms with some green to show his appreciation.

GREG
We'll go to Ruth's Chris Steakhouse. We can just walk
from here, it's not very far away.

AMI
Sure, honey.

Greg enjoyed the sweet word *honey* that Ami just used.

At Ruth's Chris Steakhouse, Greg had to have the Porterhouse even though he would not eat it all. And the lovely bottle of *Cabernet Sauvignon* helped to wash the steak down well. Ami had a New York strip and enjoyed her salad.

After dinner, Ami and Greg walked down the beach to directly in front of the Hilton Hotel, there is an area across from the lagoon where they could look out onto the ocean and observe the dinner cruises coming back to port.

With the clear sky the moonbeams hit Ami's face so perfectly accentuated her face. Ami was smelling nice, looking marvelous when Greg embraced Ami and kissed her there on the beach.

The moonbeams created magic and Ami little while later exemplified that magic with her spell when they arrived back at their hotel room that invigorated Greg and warmed his heart at the same time.

Sadly, all Greg could think after that most splendid kiss was the heartbreaking wretched event now coming up in his life. Never since Greg had his first romance, did his heart so passionately desire a woman such as Ami. Ami's powerful spell she cast upon Greg altered his psyche as he transcended into a new reality, one he could not avoid.

The next day they went to Monterey Bay Canners restaurant in the Aiea shopping mall which overlooks Pearl Harbor for lunch. Greg wanted to get a table with the unobstructed view of Pearl Harbor and relish in some of his memories of a bygone era when he and his wife sat there eating and watching airplanes coming into Ford Island as the movie company filmed the movie *Pearl Harbor.*

Since they were slowly running out of time, every day was more and more important. To have a nice restaurant with good food and service was an added bonus. No restaurant is perfect every single time for every customer. What may please one person may piss off another. Some people may not have reported it like Greg, but if he were asked about his experience today, he would tell them:

GREG

> The seafood item I chose was prepared to perfection. The waitress was cute as hell and her boyfriend was one lucky son of a bitch. She was also very sweet and professional.

With the killer view and a great time, it helped make those last days enjoyable.

The two continued on this Hawaiian Odyssey for several more days before Greg had to get back to Livermore where they would spend 72 hours preparing him. They sadly got on the plane with Ami wrapped up in several traditional Hawaiian flower Leis fully fulfilled with the most sex she ever had in her lifetime and for some time in the conceivable future.

At the completion of the Hawaii trip, Greg was in his office knowing the moment would come soon. Ami was prepared for him to leave any day and not to come home any time soon. Dr. Shirley would visit her later that day and inform Ami that moment had come.

Walter Bissonnette arrived at Greg's office.

WALTER BISSONNETTE

> Greg, we are leaving now.

Walter Bissonnette led Greg out front where a golf cart was waiting with a male African-American wearing a lab coat, Dr. Hudson with Tiāncái. Dr. Hudson's the person who designed a lot of Tiāncái's systems that Greg helped put together and test.

WALTER BISSONNETTE

> I wanted you to have the opportunity to say goodbye to the brilliant mind you worked with that made it possible for you to travel with the very reliable Robot Tiāncái.

Greg held out his hand to shake Dr. Hudson's hand.

GREG

> It was a pleasure working with you, Dr. Hudson, you have produced a rather spectacular, and respectable humanoid Robot.

DR. HUDSON

> Well, Greg, you helped out quite a bit too. A lot of your comments went into engineering changes we had to do

to get the quality control up a few notches. Greg, since we were always monitoring Tiāncái's AI coefficents, each time he was around you, his self-learning and self-awareness grew exponentially.

GREG
That's interesting to know.

DR. HUDSON
One of our AI and machine learning measures include benchmarks on Tiāncái lexicons and least recently used cache memories resulting structures. In the AI and self-learning world, the structures created in those cache memory files correspond directly to perceived learning and focus of the information.

GREG
Tiāncái's did seem to constantly get more intelligent each time we met.

DR. HUDSON
Greg after each time Tiāncái was with you, his 2048 CPUs load factors crested to a factor of 50, for hours later. You were the catalyst to guide Tiāncái's self-awareness growth. The Artificial Intelligence scientists I work with were astonished at the extent you influenced Tiāncái's efforts. Also we have the means to trap Tiāncái's thoughts and subject matters he pursued. Thanks to you all that was vast.

GREG
Thank you, Doctor Hudson, for informing me of all this. I enjoyed working with Tiāncái.

TIĀNCÁI
Greg, I enjoyed working with you too, especially the week we spent together on the TR-4 in space.

WALTER BISSONNETTE
Alright, men, we need to get going.

They all got into the golf cart that took them to an SUV that drove all of them to the airport. Upon arrival at the private jet, they all walked to the aircraft ladder and Dr. Hudson did one last check of Tiāncái. Dr. Hudson had an APP on his I-Phone that displayed Tiāncái's health check status.

DR. HUDSON
Tiāncái's, it looks like you are ready to go now. All systems check out.

Tiāncái now addressed Dr. Hudson with the very human voice of Clark Gable that Greg had chosen for his robot companion.

TIĀNCÁI
Thank you, Doctor, for what you built in me.

WALTER BISSONNETTE
Goodbye, Greg, you can be assured we will take care
of everything while you are gone. Also, the director of
the CIA informed me this morning that on your way to
Area 51 to expect a phone call from someone special.
The CIA truly appreciates what all you did for them.

GREG
The pleasure was all mine.

Greg realized he would probably miss Monica's rendezvous. He felt bad that last night he could only tell Ami he was going on a long trip and that lab people would contact her and give her status now and then.

Greg and Tiāncái climbed aboard the corporate jet with Walter Bissonnette and were soon on their way. While they were at 30,000 feet heading East, Greg's cell phone indicated incoming call, he answered it.

WHITE HOUSE SWITCHBOARD OPERATOR
Gregory Bissell?

GREG
Yes, how can I help you?

WHITE HOUSE SWITCHBOARD OPERATOR
This is the White House switchboard. Please hold, the
president would like to speak to you.

Greg was somewhat surprised and soon the voice on the other end was easily recognized to be the same he heard on TV quite a few times.

PRESIDENT
Greg, this is the President calling, I wanted to personally
let you know we appreciate everything you have done,
and the DCI has written a letter of appreciation which
I've endorsed and will place it in your secret archives
files we have set up over at the National Archives.

GREG
I appreciate that, Mr. President.

PRESIDENT
We can't put the CIA's letter of appreciation in the
national achieves because it is beyond the security
level at the National Archives, so the CIA will keep it
in their secret DD/P archives with directions to turn it
over to the national archives in twenty years.

GREG
Thank you, Mr. President.

PRESIDENT
By then we will know more about the impact your
assistance to the CIA and your last mission and current
mission had on various matters and so we'll be able
to fill in the blanks and put in the report what your
contributions led to.

GREG
Thank you, sir.

PRESIDENT
I wish you luck and a safe trip.

GREG
Thank you, sir.

The president then hung up and Greg sat there pondering all that had transformed in
his life.

It didn't seem long before the GS650 jet touched down on 32 North at Area 51 and
pulled up to the hangar again that Greg had become so accustomed to.

<u>INT TR-4 HANGER AREA 51</u>

Greg was soon given a micro-space suit to change into before he got out of the plane.
His clothes, billfold, shoes, and personal items were put in a canvas bag.

WALTER BISSONNETTE
All these items will go into secure storage and be given
back to you when you return.

There were two Air Force Officers there to fly them up to their ship. Everyone quickly
got on the TR-4B which momentarily rolled out of the hangar and then went down to
runway 17-R and proceeded to speed up. The TR-4B was probably doing five hundred
miles per hour when it tilted the nose upwards and headed straight up.

Greg had the heads-up display image on the flatscreen in front of him and watched the
information displayed and the speed increased rapidly, and they were going supersonic

less than a minute of their maneuver upwards. And just like before, within twenty minutes they were in Space heading 25,000 miles upwards to their new ship they had not seen that would be launching in autopilot.

However, Greg or Tiāncái could fly it in an emergency, but for the first phase of the mission it would be autopilot and Greg didn't know it, he and Tiāncái would be locked out. They would have no access to flight controls for over a month and by then it would be too late because it's unlikely they could find their way home even if they wanted.

Just like before, Greg and Tiāncái did a spacewalk from the TR-4 to the spaceship in a few minutes. Once inside Greg pressed the "CLOSE HATCH" switch that started blinking and the hatch now inside the ship swung upwards into the closed position and a locking ring rotated that provided physical security as well as a good air seal. A fifteen-minute compartment pressurization began, and the drop test began.

If there were an air leak, sensitive instruments would quickly give off an alarm and next to the hatch was an emergency sealant injector system whereby the locking ring would spin to unlock and unseat the hatch that would travel about one quarter of an inch and the injection system would shoot the liquid into the void and the hatch shut again and locking ring re-engaged.

This was no different than putting a tire leak fixer into your car tire. Due to the micro gravity and the slight air pressure coming from inside the spacecraft atmosphere, the sealant would work very effectively and almost immediately when the pressure of the hydraulic actuator bore down heavy pressure of the hatch to the seating area.

<u>INT. OUTER SPACE. PLUTO II</u>

Greg and Tiāncái walked a short distance to PLUTO II spacecraft's cockpit and sat down in their designated seats. After fifteen minutes when the fifteen-pound drop test rechecked no leaks present, the pressure was reduced down around twelve PSI to make it more comfortable for Greg.

VOYAGE TO THE EDGE OF THE UNIVERSE

PLUTO II control panel situated just like the prototype Greg had flown in breaking the speed of light barrier indicated a green board and propulsion that had been started from satellite commands to warm up the fusion reactors was ready to engage. Greg looked over at Tiāncái.

GREG

It's time to depart.

On the control panel was the standby switch that Greg pressed that synchronized their official launch with ground control currently operating out of an underground facility in Area 51. There was a two-man rule. Tiāncái was now required to press the "INTENT TO LAUNCH" button. His neural networks soon communicated via wireless that action occurred, as confirmation the lead (and only) Robot acknowledged the mission was a go.

Now all that was left was Greg to press the "LAUNCH" or the "ABORT" switch. Greg didn't know there was so much riding on this mission that the "ABORT" switch had been reprogrammed to "LAUNCH ANYWAY."

Two of the nuclear reactors online started providing propulsion and forward movement traveling directly away from the planet as they were now aligned and pointing towards Jupiter.

The monster-size ship initially launched from its space anchorage with low-power settings to not create a large target an enemy could track and squawk about later. Just like on their last mission they did not see the huge speed increase this time until they were on the other side of Jupiter obscured from the planet. Then it really increased rapidly heading out towards the edge of the solar system.

GREG
When will you read our mission?

TIĀNCÁI
Greg, mission files have a time lock on them. I'm not authorized, nor do I can bypass time locks to open the files until two weeks from now which is in place for security. I'll make you a great meal then and when I get notification read it aloud so we both will know what we are to do.

GREG
We are so far away from Earth now, why should we wait?

TIĀNCÁI
Greg, I have no idea why they did this. I'm just the messenger and have no way of opening the file until the date lock is disengaged.

GREG
Okay, Tiāncái, it would be nice to see where we are going.

After another week, Greg knew they had covered a large distance, and he could see portions of the Milky Way Galaxy was slowly shifting behind them and it appeared they were pointing towards the Andromeda Galaxy. It was now clear to Greg they were leaving the Galaxy and probably heading to the Andromeda Galaxy, but he wondered why.

The temperature in the spacecraft was ideal for shorts so Greg informed Tiāncái:

GREG
I'm going to cut the legs off one of these uniforms so I can wear shorts and a T-shirt and be more comfortable.

> TIĀNCÁI
> Greg, may I do that for you?

> GREG
> If you want? Sure.

Tiāncái went into some of the storage where many spare space uniforms were stored. They had plenty of room for lots of uniforms and the idea was to wear them about a month then discard them via the trash compactor that took everything they wanted to dump overboard, as long as it was not metals or tools or something hard to grind up and pulverize it and pump it out a special nozzle that fed it into the hydrogen stream coming from the ship's intake and incinerate it with the huge heat created in the nuclear rocket simply adding to the plume being left behind.

In about fifteen minutes, Greg had a pair of shorts on and a T-shirt feeling far more comfortable. They also provided him with slippers if he wanted to wear them from his bunk to the special toilet that filtered out the solids and pumped it into the nuclear rocket as well. The liquids would be reprocessed for future drinking water to extend their duration if necessary.

By reprocessing the liquids, the water would outlast Greg's expected lifetime.

The ship had some fantastic optics which gave Greg the chance to see far more of the Universe than anyone back at Earth. Once a month a message buoy rocket would be launched in their wake in a general direction of Earth's Solar System to deliver the latest findings. Much scientific research was going on with the ship but reports back to Earth would by now not get there for several months.

Finally, two weeks lapsed and Tiāncái announced:

> TIĀNCÁI
> Greg, the time lock has been opened and I can now
> read our operational orders.

> GREG
> All right, Tiāncái, I'm all ears.

In the next few moments, Greg started feeling resentment and betrayal. It did not dawn on him the level of sophistication the people back at Lawrence Livermore lab were capable of.

> TIĀNCÁI
> Your mission is to travel to the Edge of the Universe.

> VOICE OVER
> That statement hit Greg like a ton of bricks. He knew
> this was a precise statement. There was no ambiguity
> or anything to suggest otherwise.

Having personally witnessed some of the events that recently played out, Greg now knew that Lawrence Livermore Lab was capable of crafting up just about any scheme possible.

An operational order in a Time locked Word document is quite a lot different than a military operational order required to be sent via military communications networks. The word document had no real size constraints, whereas a Naval Message for example had to contained in limited number of characters. When you start thinking about the vast number of ships, submarines, air wings, and land-based forces like the Marines, the amount of message traffic can be truly astonishing. Size and speed matters. So, leadership attempts to limit the size of operational orders for Navy ships and submarines and all other components. Military communications used to not be so robust, and size really mattered then including agencies watering down messages to the point it did not convey the real situation to those that read it. Oversimplification in the 1980s and 1990s to accommodate the weakness in size and scale of military communications was a serious problem.

There was no excuse for it and in many cases managers and leaders from the old school were stuck on minimize and the inept were prone to oversimplification. Plus, it helped prevent them from getting in trouble by giving them plausible deniability. The acts and omissions were horrific. Greg's big problem was the acts and omissions happened before he got stuck on this PLUTO II spacecraft heading to *Timbuctoo*.

What could Greg do? He quickly realized he couldn't do a damn thing because of the operational orders; ship's sensors would guide the ship indefinitely and autopilot was hard wired. There was nothing they could do until another time lock was opened twenty years from now.

This was in fact the worst nightmare of Greg's life. It felt no different than someone knowingly being executed. How fast was Pluto II going? Greg had no clue nor did he know what kinds of collision hazards faced him. Can the ship's sensors prevent collisions? Greg thought perhaps it would be a blessing in disguise if they got hit by a meteor to put him out of his misery.

Part of Greg's op-order now had revelations that added to Greg's misery. Tiāncái had a secret code to allow unlocking a storage compartment that had cyanide pills in it so he could end it. However, it also had a six-year time lock on it. No matter what happened he was stuck onboard and alive for six years.

In all operational orders there are references. Pluto II had all those references aboard since it had too because there was no way he could obtain them otherwise.

One of the most important references was a series of files from Doctor Shirley that included prescriptions he could request from Tiāncái. The Robot's artificial intelligence was programmed to be a psychiatrist and could administer the psychoactive drugs, if necessary, after Tiāncái performed the analysis on the patient, Greg.

Other references included videos from Dr. Miller of the Monroe Institute who suggested Greg could reduce his anxiety by going into the Hemi Sync condition periodically to take his mind away from all the trauma he now faced.

There were many other things provided such as secret videos recorded for him from Ami and Monica, in case he wanted to view them. The spies who put those videos together were obviously ruthless SOBs. Greg was also informed he had the only copies of the videos aboard the ship and that all other copies were destroyed.

Some other interesting facts Greg was glad to discover in his operational orders was Tiāncái could administer him drugs that would put him into suspended animation for a month at a time. He would go into a deep dream manifested by the Hemi-Sync process and enjoy his thirty days off. However, if an emergency occurred, Tiāncái would administer to Greg antidotes that would quickly awaken him to deal with the emergency such as loss of cabin pressurization.

It was now clear, Tiāncái was the gatekeeper. All roads to Rome led through Tiāncái who was only partially empowered.

Tiāncái by now had infiltrated ship's computers and the combined artificial intelligence created an artificial universe where artificial intelligence intersected with mankind.

Greg would be shocked and fearful if he knew the artificial intelligence aboard the ship was a combined effort now and Tiāncái would be calling all the shots even though he implied Greg was the boss.

As the ship passed by the Andromeda Galaxy, Tiāncái provided Greg with all sorts of sensor data and observation of Solar systems. Greg wasn't going to take any time off during the next couple of weeks because he was alert and appreciated the birds' eye view of another galaxy.

Thanks to their speed, Aliens in the Andromeda Galaxy only had time enough to detect and track. By the time they were even close to an interception, the Pluto II ship blasted past them. It went by so fast they could not target them and Tiāncái announced:

TIĀNCÁI
We have received communications from a dozen life forms in the past fifteen minutes.

GREG
Any chance of communicating with them?

TIĀNCÁI
None whatsoever because our velocity is too great, we are leaving behind all their radio communications. We only had communication links with them for less than five minutes and once we got past the closest point of approach (CPA), we no longer received any further messages.

GREG
Anything else exciting happen?

TIĀNCÁI
Yes, they launched nuclear weapons at us, but we ran past the blast range and the shockwave.

GREG
Any reason why they would shoot at us?

TIĀNCÁI
We have no knowledge of their customs or capabilities. Any comment would be highly speculative.

GREG

How do you know they launched hydrogen nuclear weapons?

TIĀNCÁI

Because they exploded and gave off the same light and shock waves experienced when America detonated five nuclear weapons out in space.

GREG
We did?

TIĀNCÁI

Certainly, and the EMP pulse on one of those weapons detonated near Hawaii did have some devastating impact.

GREG
Did the Hawaiians complain?

TIĀNCÁI

No, they didn't know about it until twenty years later, but the government agreed to fund H3 to compensate them for any damage done.

GREG
You mean the freeway that took thirty years to build?

TIĀNCÁI

There were some issues they had to overcome such going over steep mountains and building an elevated freeway over ancient Hawaiian burial grounds.

GREG
How did they resolve that?

TIĀNCÁI

They brought in archeologists to dig up the graves wherever they needed to install a vertical support pillar and moved them usually twenty-five feet.

GREG
How did that work out?

TIĀNCÁI

For each body they dug up they paid the Hawaiians $25 million, it went well.

GREG
Does the public in large know about that?

TIĀNCÁI
Not really, the money went to a few Key Hawaiian officials who now mostly dead or live in Las Vegas and are enjoying their remaining time.

GREG
That's corruption. It's no surprise that America is going to the dogs.

TIĀNCÁI
Yes, the rate of decline is measurable.

GREG
No doubt, all we need is the Roman period Vandals to sack us like they did Rome.

TIĀNCÁI
In a way that's happening now. According to my analysis the Illegal Aliens are damaging America at a rate just as fast as the Vandals Atilla the Hun who sacked Rome.

GREG
And our last President was playing fiddle like Nero as Rome burned.

TIĀNCÁI
Something like that.

Greg was not having splendid moments and knew Tiāncái could handle matters just fine without him.

GREG
I want you to give me the suspended animation medications so I can go under for another thirty days.

TIĀNCÁI
May I give you a recommendation, Greg?

GREG
Sure, Tiāncái, what is that?

TIĀNCÁI
Before you take the medications, I recommend you start the Hemi-Sync so that when you become

unconscious your mind will be prepared to best evolve during those thirty days into something beneficial to your wellbeing.

GREG

Alright, Tiāncái, I'm going to sit here for thirty minutes doing the Hemi-Sync and when you think I'm ready inject me.

TIĀNCÁI

Greg, I would like to give you a sedative now so that you do not feel the injection when I give the suspended animation drugs to you.

GREG

Fair enough Tiāncái give me the sedative now.

Tiāncái went to his lab set up to provide Greg with all the medical procedures necessary to save or extend his life. When he came back, Greg was already doing the meditation to get his mind into the Hemi-Sync level of consciousness and was already entering another dimension when Tiāncái gave him the first injection that would have him sleeping like a baby in five minutes. He then waited fifteen minutes and gave him the suspended animation drug.

Greg was fully unconscious within a couple minutes and barely clinging to life. That was what the drugs were designed to do. Greg slowly slumped over, hardly breathing with only a few Delta and Theta brainwaves apparent.

Tiāncái, who was approximately five times stronger than a human, carried Greg to his bunk and strapped him in.

Greg's entire physiology would slowly shut down including his digestive system though it was possible for gas bubbles forming from bacteria. Greg would have a bowel movement within the next 48 hours. Tiāncái un dressed Greg, and slid a biological recovery sheet around him. Tiāncái didn't smell like humans. The fowl stench of human feces didn't faze him one bit but he wanted the atmosphere clean when Greg woke up in another thirty days.

If it did happen, it would be within 48 hours, but in thirty days, Greg would need to use the toilet soon after he awakened. Hopefully he would have that all unfold within the next 48 hours while he was in a comatose state and Tiāncái could clean him up so that when he did awaken, there would be no smell whatsoever and little need of a bowel movement.

Greg wisely entered the Hemi-Sync prior to the drugs hitting his system and shutting him down. His thoughts then advanced inversely proportional to the shutdown of the brain. Therefore, when his biological functions were only ten percent operating and slowing down, his thoughts were traveling through the ether at 1000% faster. In essence he was dimensional traveling. One will never know if his dreams were real or a mere transcendental posture that eclipsed all knowledge of mankind combined.

People at the Monroe Institute believe people in the Hemi-Sync experience do in fact travel to a different dimension which gives evidence we live in a holograph in our mind.

During the thirty days while Greg remained in suspended animation, Tiāncái studied communications from the various Aliens they passed by and tried to make sense of it. There was some enlightenment, but the results left much to be discovered. Earth would not know of the abundance of life in the Milky Way and Andromeda for another twenty-five years.

After thirty days Greg slowly came back to life. Reality slowly returned as he exited his transcendence to other dimensions, being much wiser as a result. Tiāncái noted in his log how Greg seemed far more reflective and intuitive each time he returned from suspended animation. After about one month of awake, Greg elected to restart his Hemi-Sync sequence followed by suspended animation. He returned to those worlds he preferred to live in.

There was an interesting side-effect to these suspended animation periods. Greg's aging slowed down to a crawl. After five years he aged possibly a month and due to the reduced and semi-non gravitational fields and the effects of the suspended animation and coma-like existence where all his body and neurological functions ceased. Greg had no Alpha, Bravo, or Gamma brainwaves during this time, and his Delta and Theta waves were so greatly reduced it required maximum magnification to detect those waves.

A lot of this was recorded, but unfortunately due to events that would one day occur, a lot of it was lost forever.

In the dream world of Hemi-Sync, Greg met souls he never knew existed. There would be great studies going forward to determine that a person in this state was more ample ready to interact with souls that traveled around the Universe finding suitable rebirth. It wasn't reincarnation, it was transference in ways beyond human ability to understand.

In his Hemi-Sync state, Greg visited worlds unknown to mankind. The buildings and architecture were incredibly different. Perhaps it was nothing more than vivid imaginations of Isaac Asimov book covers, or maybe it was real. How would he know, especially if the universe was nothing more than a holograph God created, and we really do not exist? Just because it feels real doesn't mean it is, or at least that's the conjecture one could determine. Were such thoughts just as valid as the Big Bang Theory where everything came out of a dot the size of the tip of a pencil?

Then wavelets and stochastics resonance clouded the minds of designers and thinkers. At the time we didn't know wavelets and stochastics opened a door to the universe for us, but we were not able to recognize it until revelations of very advanced Alien life sprang upon us because of Gregory Bissell and his robot assistant, Tiāncái.

While in Hemi-Sync, Greg became proficient in understanding and using mathematics, such as the Laplace transform, an integral transform that converts a function of a real variable usually, in the time domain to a function of a complex variable in the complex-valued frequency domain, also known as s-domain, or s-plane. Laplace transform is named after its discoverer.

The Laplace transform is useful for converting differentiation and integration in the time domain into much easier multiplication and division in the Laplace domain (analogous to how logarithms are useful for simplifying multiplication and division into addition and subtraction).

The Laplace transform is a very useful tool in many applications in science and engineering, mostly as a tool for solving linear differential equations and dynamical systems by simplifying ordinary differential equations and integral equations into algebraic polynomial equations, and by simplifying convolution into multiplication. Once solved, the inverse Laplace transform reverts to the original domain, usually the time domain. Laplace's use of general functions are similar to what is known as the widely used Z-transform.

An example: the Laplace transform can transfer a data set from a real to an imaginary axis to convert a circle to a square or vice versa is one of those things that puzzle some who explore it. Early telecommunications and radio theory were advanced because of Laplace Transforms. Fourier Math had an incredible synergism on light wave studies, and eventually worked its way into incredible machines that helped locate vast oil pools and made long-distance jet aircraft travel far more reliable.

Without Tiāncái, Greg would never have made it to the edge of the Universe. It was Tiāncái who kept those cyanide tablets from being ingested by Greg.

The scoop that gave them all that free energy to allow continuous acceleration for far more than a couple decades, is what allowed the mission to be a huge success. The ingenious design reduced fuel consumption down to five percent. When they arrived at their ultimate destination, there probably was enough Hydrogen to make the round-trip home. Had Greg taken more periods of suspended animation it would easily have made it back. But unfortunately, situations would arise that made the ship's ability to return them inoperative and incapable.

Days, months, and years passed by. Greg didn't age much and his faithful helper Tiāncái, did some sophisticated laundering of his t-shirt and shorts while he was in suspended animation with barely any life indicators measurable. Reduced gravity and suspended animation all but eliminated aging. By the time Greg arrived at his destination, there was virtually little change in his personal appearance other than a thirty-five-pound weight loss. But he looked healthier.

As Pluto II got closer to the edge of the universe, there were fewer galaxies. Greg knew it and, in his heart, he also realized he wasted his golden years of his life, leaving behind Ami a woman he now knew he was in love with. There was also the female spy Monica Cheung who would have probably delighted him for a very long time.

At least Greg did one thing before he left. He took care of his personal matters and with the lab looking out for his well-being and Ami, the will and power of attorney was protected because heavy-duty law firms backed it up. Ami had a bulletproof legal document that gave her complete control of his estate while he was gone on the mission.

In accordance with her fiduciary responsibilities, she transferred large sums of money to his two sons who eventually were mystified when they found out more details about their father which made them feel real crappy when they realized he was reaching out to them during the final days of his life and they treated him like crap with their attitudes.

By the time they realized the errors of their ways, it was too late, he was gone forever, and they would never have the opportunity to see Greg again in their lifetimes.

Ami being the wonderful person she was, had lots of videos and pictures of Greg to depict him as he was in his final days.

They didn't know exactly what he did, but what they did know is he had some major dealings with Lawrence Livermore Lab and they each were finally briefed by special people within the government, that their father had volunteered to make the supreme sacrifice for his country, but due to the sensitivity of the mission, it's unlikely it could be divulged to them in their lifetime.

Dr. Shirley paid visits to Ami off and on for several more years and in her reports to Walter Bissonnette indicated she had adjusted well and was doing good to look out for her own wellbeing. But there was a huge big OOPS in all of it. Greg impregnated Ami before he left. He didn't know when he left, he had a third son.

Ami never married. As far as she was concerned, nobody could ever replace Greg. Her son was a walking encyclopedia and very well disciplined and polite. Eventually as he grew older and he wanted to know about his dad, Walt came with Dr. Shirley with a lot of information and explained it to Greg II.

Around the time Greg II turned sixteen, he had a great appreciation for his father and now understood why his mother was never interested in another man. She never told anyone, but she believed Greg would one day return.

Walter Bissonnette and Dr. Shirley had no idea if Greg actually perished or what happened to him. They were still receiving communication buoys from him that showed he still existed but a far, far ways distance. Ami never gave up hope, ever and chose to remain that way for the rest of her life.

Greg II evolved into a man Greg would be proud of. Ami was certainly very proud of her son who graduated top of his class at UC Berkeley.

Eventually Greg realized he had completed his mission. It was time to take the cyanide capsules because he was now far out into space with no lights in front of him. He had been accelerating for almost twenty years without aging much thanks to his routine suspended animation periods, however, Tiāncái convinced him to wait a while, just in case the scientists were wrong.

Greg went along with Tiāncái as he had nothing to lose and he could always slip back into Hemi-Sync and another period of suspended animation where that new universe gave him much pleasure. He only wished he could find Ami or Monica during those times, but it never happened.

Another two years passed by and Greg started rethinking cyanide pills. He had to get them through Tiāncái so that might become a challenge since it appeared Tiāncái thought his course of action should be to continue the mission. But Tiāncái was just a machine. How could he know what was in Greg's heart?

Just at the bitter last moment when Greg was just about to start begging Tiāncái for those cyanide capsules, he was up in the control room looking over the blank sensors and taking it all in reflecting on his life when all of a sudden he felt he might be hallucinating because right in the middle of one of the sensor displays there was a white light of some sort.

It's probably a computer defect or equipment failure, Greg told himself.

Tiāncái, who was always closely around Greg observed the white spot as well and through his fast communications via wireless to the ship's computers asked a lot of questions and soon got immediate results.

Greg looked around and saw Tiāncái standing there with lots of information in his computer banks and asked the question:

GREG
Do we have some sort of computer malfunction?

TIĀNCÁI
Greg, no, all systems are fault free, we do not have any
equipment issues. What the sensors are displaying are
in fact detections of distant light.

GREG
As in a star or planet?

TIĀNCÁI
It could be a distant galaxy.

Greg suddenly had no more sudden desires for the cyanide pills because now his curiosity was peaking.

GREG
Is it possible we slowly curved around and are heading
back into our universe?

TIĀNCÁI
No, based on our speed, our universe is way behind
us. This light is probably one million times closer than
our universe.

Greg sat there stunned, but somewhat relieved because if he did die right now, he would have the satisfaction of going to his death with the knowledge the Big Bang Theory groups were *full of baloney.*

For several days Greg and Tiāncái stared at the white dot on the screen in front of them. It was directly ahead, and it had no bearing drift. After several days of constant observations, Greg was finally exhausted and had to get some sleep.

GREG

I'm going to get some rest now, Tiāncái. Wake me up if something changes.

TIĀNCÁI

Rest well Greg. I'll wake you up if something changes.

Tiāncái knew that Greg had gone several days without any sleep and was probably getting delirious so there was no way he would wake him up, especially since he could record images and play them back later for Greg with time-lapsed photography.

Greg was out for a good twelve hours before he regained consciousness, and only stirred because he was having a dream, he had a huge sensation he needed to urinate. Greg slid out of his bunk and moved over to the little telephone booth-size bathroom and put the tube on his penis that would suck all the moisture out of his discharge so it would not get into the air of the spacecraft.

Greg had on his T-shirt, shorts, and slippers and walked forward to the cockpit with all the sensor displays.

The white dot had grown slightly. Greg was instantly gratified. He now knew Earth scientists were going down a prim rose path on the gobbledygook of Big Bang Theory and that eventually they would figure it out.

GREG

Tiāncái, you should have awoken me. This object has grown.

TIĀNCÁI

Greg, whatever it is, it's still a long way off, but we'll find out what it is when we get closer. The closure rate appears slow due to distance. I purposely let you continue sleeping because you were long overdue rest.

GREG

Okay, perhaps you are right.

Having been in space for over two years with no lights of any clue any civilization existed in this area, was suddenly overcome with the knowledge Greg was no longer past the Universe since that belief was now thoroughly disproven.

This was a joyous day for Greg and Tiāncái was happy Greg started to exhibit better mental health. The dreadful alarming period was now behind them. Having the same level of education as the finest psychologists and psychiatrists, Tiāncái feared Greg would find some way to take his own life, and Tiāncái knew what a terrible waste of humanity that would be.

Greg went on another ninety-six-hour binge of watching the white dot grow slowly. Then unexpectedly as it expanded it started to give off hints it might be a galaxy. Tiāncái did not blurt out his findings, between him and the onboard computers that had mutually pollinated artificial intelligence, almost now a unified intellect, they didn't want to spoil it for Greg, they knew within a few more days there was a probability he would announce it was a galaxy and thanks to their inertia navigation and extreme speed traveling in an almost perfect straight line he had a rough idea from their "universe" approximately where it was.

GREG
Tiāncái! That's a Galaxy!

Greg was so overjoyed and overwhelmed. Tiāncái could see the tears flowing down his cheeks. It was a pivotal moment in Greg's life. Tiāncái knew firsthand from all the research he had done from vast sources of data the past twenty years, that Greg had given more of himself to mankind than any other living person who didn't die in the process.

TIĀNCÁI
Greg, I'm analyzing it now for confirmation with ship's
sensor processors.

GREG
Alright.

In about five minutes, Tiāncái announced:

TIĀNCÁI
Greg, that's a level-five galaxy.

GREG
How big is that?

TIĀNCÁI
Based on NASA and Livermore calculations, a level-
five galaxy was in the approximate size of the Milky
Way and Andromeda, both almost of equal size.

On their way to this new Universe, they passed a couple galaxies that could be considered as large as level fifteen compared to the rest on a linear scale.

Greg was over-joyous but at the same time he had burned his candle far too long during the last two episodes. He needed to go down for a good rest period. Tiāncái would continue recording the approach to this Galaxy they had no real idea how far away it was from the edge of their own universe because they really didn't know exactly how fast they were going since they had nothing to measure against flying dark with no references for several years, though they slowly continued to accelerate.

Tiāncái calculated a month away from entry to the galaxy, so he cut propulsion down to idle function to make sure he didn't develop causing cracks in the nuclear reactors by cooling down too quickly they needed for propulsion. As such as soon as it was apparent Greg was passed out in a deep sleep, Tiāncái drugged him to keep him resting for a week. He knew Greg desperately needed an equalizer sleep.

ARRIVAL

After one-week Tiāncái also had a way to restore Greg to normal thinking and awaken Greg by another sophisticated drug he would shoot up into his nostrils. Within five minutes, Greg recovered from a near comatose mental state to be fully alert and a need to visit the urine draining tubes.

Greg took care of his biological functions Greg made a beeline to the control room on the rocket ship where he immediately looked at all the indications and now saw they were approaching a major galaxy.

GREG
How long was I out?

TIĀNCÁI
About a week. You needed an equalizer sleep.

GREG
Did you record all this while I was sleeping?

TIĀNCÁI
Certainly.

GREG
Show me an elapsed time replay of the time I was
sleeping.

Tiāncái did the playback and Greg got to see in a minute all the change that occurred for nearly a week.

For the rest of the day, Greg observed the scanners with intense interest as the ship flew towards the middle of the galaxy at a forty-five-degree angle offset from forward perpendicular.

GREG
Tiāncái, could you please grab me a food pack and a
drink?

TIĀNCÁI
It would be my pleasure, Greg.

Like a dutiful Robot, Tiāncái went to a nearby pantry he had staged for such an event and immediately returned with Greg's request.

Greg was slowly sucking the contents out of the food pack that would soon be pulverized and sent out the trash compactor into the reactor compartment that would turn it into instant ashes.

Between the drink and the food tube, Greg reached a level of satisfaction while watching the unfolding events.

It was a joyous occasion as they soon made their way aiming for dark spots of the galaxy to avoid stars and solar systems and collisions. As they flew through the pancake-shaped spiral galaxy Greg discovered another interesting fact. Using the photonic enhancer, he thought he could see other galaxies off at a distance that as soon confirmed by Tiāncái.

As they observed the center of the galaxy from far off and the black hole there, out of nowhere an ALIEN FORCE attempted to contact them. Even though the ship was barely near the extremities of a nearby solar system, someone was trying to contact them. They responded in a similar fashion. But due to the huge language barriers, it was unlikely we could communicate any information now.

As Pluto II responded, it was almost pointless as the Aliens had no ability to understand their communication.

The Aliens had fast ships and the ability to use electromagnetic-electrostatic near-space grabbers to slow down the strange spacecraft coming from the black area they thought was the end of their universe.

<u>EXT. CGI. ALIEN SHIP APPROACHES PLUTO II THEN GRABS PLUTO II</u>

Greg watching the heads-up display and feeling lateral forces understood the obvious as Tiāncái said the obvious.

TIĀNCÁI
They are slowing us down.

GREG
Yeah, it's too bad we do not understand what they are
saying.

TIĀNCÁI
I don't know if they can process any of our video
signals, it might just seem to be noise to them, but I
can piece together some video to attempt giving them
some clues on how to communicate with us.

GREG
Sure, go ahead, it's the best we can do for now.

Tiāncái worked laboriously attempting to create a pathway to understanding. But none of it seemed to work.

TIĀNCÁI
They are changing our course now.

GREG
It looks like they are steering us some place.

Pluto II was traveling at a great velocity, but Greg started to feel the slowing and promptly put on a harness that would hold him in his seat in the event they did something he hoped they would not do such as slow down too quickly.

The Aliens were quite brilliant in the way they managed the tow of Pluto II down to a nearby planet in the nearest solar system, but the breaking now felt terrible. Greg passed out a couple of times and hoped it would soon stop. Eventually the speed had been cut considerably, something Greg never imagined possible.

Greg then discovered and noted:

GREG
The towing aircraft has Pluto II almost encompassed in
some strange mesh.

The purpose of the mesh would soon make sense. The Aliens had no idea what ability the ship had to penetrate the ionosphere of their planet; therefore, they took the conservative approach and protected it to the maximum extent possible.

The Traykorite planet had a diameter about four times the size of Earth. The foliage and environment were not much different than Earth with twenty percent oxygen level, and mostly nitrogen in the air, making it habitable to Humans from Earth. The pollution was far less and the Architecture considerably more advanced than Humans with much taller buildings that pierced very high clouds allowing mountain dwellers to feel comfortable in coastal cities.

The ship coming in from the black zone was unexpected and immediately had Traykorite scientists in a tizzy as it violated many of the Traykorite scientific conventions and theories.

Since there were no ships behind Pluto II, Tiāncái suggested:

TIĀNCÁI
I recommend we start dumping all the hydrogen
overboard. They are obviously heading for the planet.
Pluto II's hydrogen tanks were never designed to enter
a planet atmosphere. They will probably explode
killing you and destroying me.

> GREG
> Good idea, engage the hydrogen overboard emergency
> relief valve.

Usually under normal conditions ship's computers would never allow such actions because interlocks prevented them from doing dumb things, but Tiāncái now was part of the AI structure of the ship and the rationale was quickly validated in a few milliseconds and the hydrogen was dumped overboard leaving behind a huge hydrogen plume the Traykorites immediately noted and analyzed as hydrogen.

The Traykorite Force Commander Zebrovska duly informed the Alien vessel was dumping hydrogen responded.

> TRAYKORITE FORCE COMMANDER ZEBROVSKA
> Those might be fragile tanks on their ship they
> fear might explode going through the atmosphere,
> disregard for now.

The only thing to Zebrovska that made sense was the Aliens were doing it as a safety precaution and lightening up their craft to allow them to fly in the atmosphere, where they would otherwise possibly sink like a rock with extreme weight if those tanks were full of a lot of liquid hydrogen.

The direct sunlight on the hydrogen plume lit it up in a most incredible sight that soon was seen from the ground, prompting communications to the fleet asking numerous questions.

The strange mesh that covered a lot of Pluto II designed to protect captured ships towed to their planets had proven its worth many times over as many instances of captured vessels delivered great treasures to their society.

As the Empire spread, so did the plunder, and often it was ships escaping with the treasury that were captured.

Under normal circumstances, Pluto II would have burned up entering the atmosphere. Thanks to the Traykorite unusual mesh that had an amount of transparency, Pluto II was spared the violent encounter with hitting the Traykorite atmosphere at a speed of nearly 30,000 miles per hour their ships were designed to easily penetrate.

There was a little turbulence, but the electromagnetic/electrostatic near space grabbers stabilized Pluto II considerably because it was a huge ship towing it, which acted as an effective wind break.

Looking forward and seeing anything was impossible, but cameras mounted on the bottom of Pluto II were providing live video to an advanced civilization possibly 100,000 years more advanced than earth. With magnification on, it was a magnificent view.

Having spent almost twenty-two years in space, coming in contact with other sentient beings appealed greatly to Greg. He was overjoyed with the knowledge the scientists were wrong about the edge of the Universe and knew in his gut that eventually the great distance between these two Universes could be overcome because he just did it. Greg was the first person from Earth to travel above light speed, and now was the first sentient living being to travel out of the Universe to somewhere else.

His last twenty-two years had been an incredible journey filled with the maximum amount of danger any living person could ever endure, and the fun part was just about to start. The first man to travel at light speed, the first man to travel outside the solar system. The first man to travel outside the known Universe, and the first man to ever meet sentient beings from a different universe. And here he was, a come to Jesus moment, fully enamored with his view that Big Bang Theory was a pile of BS and man didn't really know much after all.

Greg would place himself in God's hands and see where the chips fall.

Greg didn't have any fear at all. Greg had immense gratitude, that God bestowed upon him this great feat, that he of all people would be picked for this mission that did two things, it clarified his own theory and dispelled the scientific mumbo jumbo that created the most preposterous lie in human history. Scientists have a way of making the numbers fit their theory, and now even Einstein's projections had been cast upon the dust heap of history, fully exposed as nonsense, because Greg knew before he left on this last mission, Earth people in the Pluto II project knew he had flown considerably faster than the speed of light smashing that flawed theory to death.

Greg could see they were getting close to the ground. He didn't know, he was being towed to a spacecraft wrecker yard where they didn't care if his ship ever flew again. He didn't care how hideous these Aliens could be. He would rather stay here now then venture back out into space. His space faring days were over. *Hopefully the Aliens were benevolent.*

<u>EXT. CGI. DAY TRAYKORITE SHIP TOWING PLUTO II LAND ON PLANET SMOOTHLY.</u>

The Traykorites ship and their prize ship, Pluto II eventually landed, and Greg was surprised by the extent to how gentle it was. Then suddenly it was over. Pluto II was stationary with no velocity sitting on an alien planet.

GREG

Do you suppose we should attempt to get out of the
ship and introduce ourselves to our captors?

TIĀNCÁI

The atmosphere has been measured and is very similar
to the air inside this ship, I think you would be safe, but
there is always the possibility of dangerous pathogens.

GREG

I've been trapped aboard this ship so long if I die today
that's okay if I can at least put my feet on the ground.

291

TIĂNCÁI

According to the ship's computers, both side and top
escape hatches are available to exit the craft.

GREG

We are probably twenty-plus feet above the ground.

TIĂNCÁI

There is a ladder as part of the escape hatch.

GREG

Just like they planned for an emergency landing on a
planet.

TIĂNCÁI

Unfortunately, yes.

GREG

Okay, please open one of the hatches and us climb
down and meet them.

Greg was still in shorts and a T-shirt, but he didn't care. Nor had he shaved or cut his hair in months. He looked almost like a hobo or homeless person. In a way he was.

Tiăncái released the series of locks that allowed the escape hatch to pivot out of the way, then pulled up part of the deck and exposed an intricate ladder mechanism that then deployed to the ground.

<u>EXT. DAY GREG AND TIĂNCÁI WALKING DOWN PLUTO II STAIRWAY/
LADDER</u>

By the time Greg started down the ladder he could see over two dozen Traykorites in a group standing thirty or so feet away from the craft. In the middle of the group was the Traykorite commander Zebrovska looking far more spit and polished than Greg by a huge margin.

The Traykorites had seen humanoids in far-off star systems with hair and beards resembling Greg, so at first, they started thinking this might be a wayward traveler from a wayward planet.

Within the cluster of Traykorites were people with scientific instruments monitoring Greg for pathogens or other serious matters.

Tiăncái followed down next expertly traversing the ladder as if it was designed for him, and in fact it was.

Greg stood there looking at the Traykorites who soon noticed tears coming down Greg's face wondering what that was all about.

292

Tiāncái was dressed in his utility Pluto II uniform including standard patch and identifier. He didn't wear a helmet because he didn't need to since he was a robot.

There was some commotion among the Traykorites when some of their alien specialists with sensor readings stated in their language to Commander Zebrovska.

TRAYKORITE ALIEN SPECIALIST
There are no life readings coming from the second
Alien wearing the uniform.

Commander Zebrovska stepped slowly forward and said something in the Traykorite standard language that had been adopted throughout the entire galaxy, none of which Greg could comprehend.

Greg pointed to his head and shook his head.

GREG
I cannot understand you.

Commander Zebrovska turned to one of his alien specialists and stated in standard Traykorite:

COMMANDER ZEBROVSKA
We cannot communicate, let's take him to the
Alien interrogation center and figure out a way to
communicate.

In a very short time, an Aircar appeared that could easily hold fifteen or more people. General Zebrovska motioned to get in the Skycar with the access door fully opened. Greg figured that out quite quickly and proceeded to the Skycar.

Greg turned towards Tiāncái to speak.

GREG
Tiāncái, I think we should shut down the nuclear
power generator since we will not be here to safeguard
it in case these guys monkey with our ship.

Tiāncái communicated with the ship's computers via his wireless technology ordering reactor shutdown and rigged the ship for reduced electrical with only minimum circuits operating off battery storage.

TIĀNCÁI
I communicated with the ship's computers. The ship is
shutting down the reactor now. It will be safe in a few
minutes.

By the time Greg and Tiāncái were seated in the Traykorite Skycar, the ship's computer reported via wireless to Tiāncái who then informed Greg.

TIĀNCÁI

The electrical generator reactor is shut down, all electrical generation has been suspended and the craft transitioned into hibernation mode to preserve all data.

<u>EXT. CGI. ALIEN PLANET SKYCAR TAKING OFF FLYING AWAY FROM PLUTO II</u>

The Skycar was up several thousand feet very quickly and the first pleasure for Greg in a long, long time was the feel of real gravity.

Being around these beings who looked a lot like humans except their skin was different also gave Greg a great appreciation after being alone for 22 years on Pluto II with only a robot.

Depending on how the light struck their skin gave a slightly different color as if their multicolored skin had holographic like surface.

<u>EXT. CGI. ALIEN PLANET SKYCAR FLYING INTO ACCESS AT SIDE OF LARGE BUILDING.</u>

Before long the Skycar came down and a large door in the side of a building opened about 1000 feet in the air, and the Skycar flew in and softly set down in what appeared to be a large hangar with several other similar craft.

The door to the Skycar opened and Traykorite Commander Zebrovska barked some instructions which Greg intuitively knew meant, "Come with us."

The Traykorites led Greg and Tiāncái out of the hangar area, then walked into a long hallway. The architecture and décor had an appearance that gave Greg the impression it was thousands of years more advanced than anything Greg had seen on Earth. One thing Greg vividly understood, *These Aliens came at him real fast and slowed him down from a great velocity as if it was a routine matter for them.*

Eventually the Traykorites escorted Greg and Tiāncái into a three-dimensional conference room. As they passed to this conference room, they both had been scanned multiple times. Greg's anatomy was classified as a category four humanoid (out of numerous categories). A table in the middle of the room large enough for possibly ten or more people was apparent and the Traykorite knew they could not yet communicate gave them a gesture to be seated. The Lead Traykorite Alien Specialist then sat on the other side of Greg and Tiāncái.

The robot got scanned extensively and automated systems specialists were now pouring over the scan images in great wonder, at this intelligent mechanical man. Eventually they would figure out what made him tick, but for now, a sudden revelation of a category 4 humanoid and mechanical man coming out of the dark zone unexpectedly rattled a few nerves. Members of the Traykorite scientific community stated what these aliens had just done was *utterly impossible.*

This region of space Pluto II traveled had all kinds of sensors to detect an enemy attack and any that ever tried failed miserably because any energy field up against the black zone showed up quite distinctively on sensor alert displays.

Having captured numerous enemies in the past, the Traykorite had developed sophisticated methods of building translators in very efficient manners, especially if the Alien was cooperative. Greg had no reason not to cooperate and they could pick his ship apart all they wanted. More than likely, it would be considered out of date junk to the Traykorites based on what Greg had already observed. However, there were three Earth intellects now on the Traykorite planet. Greg, Tiāncái, and the ship's computer that in twenty-two years had been fully reprogrammed by Tiāncái with expansive AI and machine learning adaptability.

The collective artificial intelligence between Pluto II computers and Tiāncái grew expansive to say the least. And even with the nuclear electrical generator shut down for safety reasons, the emergency backup power for the ship's computer could virtually last a year or more with the electrical reactor shut down. Thanks to the AI now imbedded in PLUTO II computers, that intellect could and would turn the electrical power generators back on when Pluto II's battery energy storage levels dipped below 50% and automatically recharged it.

Pluto II computers also had the means to remotely communicate with Tiāncái and the Traykorites had discovered the RF emanations coming out of the spacecraft and Tiāncái. But since they had left the door to the ship wide open as if they had no care in the world, it was as if they posed no threat. Nevertheless, Commander Zebrovska wanted to get to the bottom of how Pluto II came out of the dark zone where nobody could hide from the Traykorites.

Already in Commander Zebrovska's ear bud, he was receiving information from Traykorite Surveillance Directorate (TSD), the distance to which the initial detection of this Alien ship occurred. At the velocity they were traveling and in a straight line, the distance based on the velocity from initial intercept placed the initial detection of this alien ship beyond the range of any previous detection of any spacecraft in the entire universe!

Nevertheless , this was a shocking revelation to Commander Zebrovska. Furthermore, Commander Zebrovska wanted to know what spurred on the emotional outburst that led to the tears coming down the alien's face, fully recorded by the Traykorite Alien Specialists.

There were so many questions to be answered and already the Alien looked fatigued. Commander Zebrovska had medical researchers on hand to advise him in the event the Alien suddenly started suffering some physical discomfort because they wanted to get this vital information out of him as quickly as possible before any unforeseen circumstances such as getting infected by a Traykorite pathogen and die.

An alien interrogator walked into the briefing room and came up to Commander Zebrovska and they discussed a few things then the interrogator, put up a holograph above the table they could all see which was an apparent projection of the recorded playback of them arriving as displayed and reenacted on a time lapsed photography with a scale model of their ship approaching the galaxy, then the solar system. The researcher pointed to Greg and asked a question in Traykorite standard and walked over pointing to a red line Greg easily figured was their track and pointed where it started.

Greg stood up and walked to where the researcher was sitting and made a circle with his hand.

GREG
EARTH

Now the exhilaration hit Commander Zebrovska like a ton of bricks. The Alien came from "Earth" which they had no idea what that could possibly mean. But Earth was evidently beyond the black zone where the universe ended.

The alien researcher then walked back to the center of the table near Commander Zebrovska and pointed to features of the holographs and Greg intuitively knew he wanted him to respond how to say the names of those things in his native language, all of which, Greg assumed was being recorded for intelligence gathering.

As they continued the researcher pointed to a holograph of Pluto II.

GREG
Spaceship.

The questions continued and various holographs were shown and Greg responded with his words that described what he saw. As an example, a tree, flower, the sun, building, light, circle, red, green, blue. Then they put up what appeared to be one fruit. Greg said, "Fruit."

Suddenly a second fruit showed up and Greg pointed.

GREG
One fruit, two fruit.

Greg then showed on his fingers, one, two three four five six, and counted to ten.

The researcher caught on and started putting up more fruits and Greg counted to 100 fruits when they stopped.

Now it got interesting, a holograph showed a sequence of day and night and Greg explained day and night.

A representation of sequences of days and nights to try to get a feeling of how long it took them to get here, didn't work out long then Greg pointed to an image of a galaxy and then gave an indication of that galaxy then walked over to where he had stood once before and indicated to put a copy there.

The Aliens figured out what he wanted to say so they had the projectionist place another depiction of a galaxy where Greg had indicated, then Greg walked some more and held up his hands and said Galaxy as if he wanted them to put another galaxy there and he walked further indicating he wanted another galaxy, then came back to the first and said, "First galaxy," then walked to the second and said "two," then the three then walked some more and held up his hands and said four, then five, then six then pointed down the attached hallway and started counting pointing in that direction. The Alien Specialists in the room were astonished.

Commander Zebrovska sat there in a surreal pose, and he understood exactly what Greg had indicated. There was another Universe there! It was remarkable. He knew this man was not lying, he had no reason to.

Greg then walked over next to Tiāncái and pointed at him.

GREG
Tiāncái.

Greg then pointed at his own nose.

GREG
Greg.

Commander Zebrovska figured it out real fast and pointed at his own nose and said, "Zebrovska."

The Traykorite then played some video of Greg when he first arrived. He then had a large image of Greg's face when the tears were coming down his face and highlighted the tears with some sort of light pen shrugging his shoulders.

Greg instantly knew what he was asking and stood up and put his fingers on one of the highlighted tears.

GREG
Tears.

Then Greg tapped on his heart, which must be a universal symbol because the Aliens figured it out real fast.

Greg had not had much sleep lately. His physiology was being monitored real time and one of the medical professionals cautioned Colonel Zebrovska sensor readings indicated the Alien was highly stressed and they should let him rest for a while and then bring him back later and continue the questions when he was fresh.

Commander Zebrovska shook his head understanding the obvious, so he stood up and signaled Greg and Tiāncái to come with him. He led them down a hall way towards a doorway that led into a very pleasant-looking area and it was obvious this was their type of sleeping quarters. The Alien researcher suddenly triggered a holograph showing a laying down on the bed and it was obvious the Alien was sleeping, then the researcher patted on the bed and Greg shook his head up and down tapped his hand on his chest a few strokes.

GREG
I understand.

Greg then walked over and crawled onto the bed and laid down and immediately began his silent meditation to slip him into a Hemi-Sync and a surreal travel to another mental dimension.

The bed was fully wired with numerous sensors including brave wave scanners. Traykorites were class-five humanoids meaning not a great lot of difference from class 4. They too had Alpha, Bravo, Gamma, Delta, and Theta waves. But they also had Lambda waves. In other parts of their universe, Aliens believed the Lambda waves were related to telepathic ability, the Traykorite had lost long before their current recorded history as written.

Prior to Greg's Hemi-Sync was obtained he had none of those Lambda Waves, but while employing Hemi-Sync as Greg's mind transcended to the universe into another time and place, suddenly Lambda waves appeared which shook up the Traykorite researchers which furthermore caused incredible interest in this person who claims to have traveled from another Universe. Traykorite scientists believed there certainly was no other way to get there. Greg had just thrown a monkey wrench into the Traykorite scientific community who had for almost the entire history of their existence said the dark zone was the end of the Universe and nothing existed beyond it.

The Earth was no longer flat, and the Universe no longer ended.

In Greg's Hemi-Sync modus, he was more spiritual and far more attuned to God and creative design. Greg knew he would never know "why" or "how" that didn't matter, what did matter was God left nothing to chance and his creation was boundless. The Hemi-Sync took him across the Universe and answered the most puzzling questions that faced mankind.

Out of protocol, Tiāncái laid down on a bed twenty feet away from Greg's even though it wasn't necessary. But he copied Greg's actions and commenced to communicate with Pluto II's ship's computer. Everything that occurred was logged and filed.

The Traykorite scientific community put to great effort to read and decode all the communications between Tiāncái and Pluto II's onboard computer network.

Within 48 hours the Traykorite scientific community started to make inroads into the communications link and the main reason why they didn't jam it was to allow it all to occur so they could glean more information faster.

The next day as Greg started stirring and his Alpha, Beta, and Gamma waves started spiking, alarms went off and researchers were at his bedside.

By then Traykorite had crawled all over his ship and found his food and water supply. Not knowing what they could feed Greg, they simply brought him his expected lunch.

One of the universal things that affect all humanoids is the need for bowel movement and to urinate from time to time. This also includes the Traykorites. As such they also had something like bathrooms. One of the medical researchers who saved up his need to go to demonstrate to Greg how it worked took him in and whipped out his junk and stuck it in a tube showing the stream going down a clear plastic tube.

Then another person who saved up the need to poop really bad came in and pressed a button on the side of an appliance and a harness came down out of the overhead and wrapped around his body and just like a crane lift, lowed his body into a crouched position like Japanese and proceeded to poop in a device with a porcelain appearance that was uncovered when he pressed the button.

Greg shook his head up and down.

GREG
Thank you, I think I understand.

Greg then copied the Traykorite researcher's actions. What Greg didn't know is his bowl movement was going to the lab for study.

The researchers then used a female model to come in to an area press another button on the wall and a wall slowly moved and an open area appeared, the woman handed her robe to another assistant, then walked into this area. What appeared to be a curved transparent wall slid shut and the water came down on the woman with an interesting scent to it. Greg then did the same actions.

Greg didn't know this yet, but he was getting deloused.

An air dryer device then dried the woman in the shower device, the door opened, and she walked out perfectly dry, put on the bathrobe showing her body in the process. She looked entirely human except for the 3D almost holographic skin texture.

The Traykorite researchers already figured out Tiāncái the mechanical man didn't take showers or required any. There was great interest in Tiāncái. For whatever reason, the Traykorites had never seen the need to develop and build humanoid robots because the Empire had so many slaves from conquered civilizations, there would never be the need. Slaves who disobeyed their masters were quickly eliminated. Society was ruled with a giant fist.

The Traykorite Aliens left Greg feeling he might be more comfortable getting into the harness without observers. He tried it and it was great. The squatting position is so much nicer for bowel movement and with the overhead harness made it far more comfortable. His rear end was also cleaned by a washer mechanism and blow dried with nice warm air. He took off his shorts and t-shirt and stepped out of his sandals into the washing mechanism where he was quickly satisfied with a shower unlike, he had ever felt before.

The shower water was saturated with negative ions and as a result his skin felt so much nicer. Whatever it was made him also feel squeaky clean and when he stepped out of the device, he was totally dry, and shortly a medical specialist came in and handed him a bathrobe to put on.

Greg assumed the Aliens had already checked out his ship and when he came back into the room was a set of standard clothing for him from the ship. The Aliens had figured it out. He and Tiāncái were different sizes. And since only two sizes of clothing existed on his ship, they knew which belonged to who because his name Gregory Bissell was stenciled on each one of his shirts.

One of the researchers pointed to the name on the uniform.

GREG
Gregory Bissell, that's my full name.

A *Tiāncái* patch was sewn on his shirt so the medical researcher pointed at it and Tiāncái responded.

TIĀNCÁI
That is my name, Tiāncái.

Greg saw they had water and food tubes retrieved from the pantry of Pluto II laid out for him which he didn't mind. So, he sat at the small table with Tiāncái who just watched him eat.

Greg had not eaten in over three days. He was almost starving and finished his food rapidly. The researchers knew something like that was the case he had to be under nourished. As Greg started eating and drinking, he pointed to the food tube.

Traykorites had already analyzed the food tubes and water bottles TIĀNCÁI would refill from a dispensary.

GREG
This is a Food Tube.

Greg then picked up the water bottle and pointed at it with one finger.

GREG
This is a water bottle.

Then as he took a drink, Greg pointed at the water bottle with his other hand.

As he took the water bottle away from his mouth Greg explained.

GREG
This is called drinking water.

Traykorite Researchers showed a holograph of a Traykorite having a hair trim and pointed at Greg then at the holograph and Greg shook his head up and down and indicated.

GREG
Okay

Within minutes a female came in with some very interesting tools and since Greg's hair was squeaky clean from his shower, his hair was easily handled. This device she put on his head, like a hairdryer in a lady's hair salon back on Earth was some sort of haircut machine. It had a hair blower like effect, and it was very gentle. In about a minute the woman took the device off Greg's head, and she then held her hand up and said some words in Traykorite standard. Suddenly a holograph appeared showing a slow 3D image of Greg slowly turning around as if a 3D picture of Greg's head was slowly turning right before his eyes. The results looked good. The machine had sculptured his hair into an image that was pleasing to Greg so he smiled.

GREG
Thank you.

Another person walked into the room and gave the signal to follow him. Greg figured he was being recorded explained.

GREG
That means come with me.

Greg was ushered back to the 3D conference room that was jam packed full of obvious researchers. The escorting Traykorite and indicated towards the chairs.

GREG
That means please sit down.

Momentarily another person came into the room and started popping up numerous holographs and Greg described what he saw. In a while many pictures inside his ship appeared and he stated what it was.

GREG
PLUTO II

Shortly Greg was escorted out of the conference room, now abuzz with 100 different conversations going on. There was excitement in the air. Greg was then led down the hallway back to the hangar area and an Skycar with the door open. Greg was signaled to get in.

GREG
That means "Please get in."

<u>EXT. CGI DAY. TRAYKORITE PLANET SKYCAR FLIES OUT OF THE BUILDING AND HEADS TO THE PARKED PLUTO II SPACECRAFT</u>

The Skycar flew and landed near Pluto II. Since Greg had left the ship, a ramp was installed so people could easily walk up into the craft. It was now guarded with some serious-looking military with all kinds of strange body armor that appeared to be right out of a future science fiction novel.

<u>EXT. CGI DAY. TRAYKORITE PLANET SKYCAR LANDS AT PARKED PLUTO II</u>

The Aliens marched Greg up into the craft and up into the cockpit where the Traykorites indicated they wanted Greg to turn on the displays, which he directed Tiāncái.

GREG
Show them the heads-up display.

The Traykorites quickly took a keen interest in Earth's display technology that had great resolution.

GREG
Tiāncái, let's give them a treat. Put up on one of the
auxiliaries displays a time lapsed video of our forward
and side scanners as we left earth until we landed on
this planet.

The escorts watched as Tiāncái did his magic and on the auxiliary scanner they saw it all unfold as they were leaving their galaxy, with time speeding up perhaps 2000 to one that would slow down as they past interesting planets and galaxies.

Greg pointed out planets in our solar system as Pluto passed by them.

GREG
This is Mars, Jupiter, Saturn, Neptune, Uranus, and
Pluto.

PLUTO II flew past or photographed from a long distance with the excellent Pluto II telescope before they went above light speed.

The Traykorites could see that after the ship got past Jupiter, the speed increased rather remarkably and continued to increase speed.

<u>EXT. CGI. SPACE ELAPSED TIME PHOTOGRAPHY OF THE IMAGERY DISPLAYED THEM SLOWLY PASSING THROUGH THE MILKY WAY AND OUT INTO DEEP SPACE.</u>

As the video recording showed Pluto II's sensors imagery as Pluto II approached the Andromeda Galaxy Greg pointed it out.

GREG
This is the Andromeda Galaxy.

<u>EXT. CGI. SPACE - ELAPSED TIME PHOTOGRAPHY OF PASSING BY THE ANDROMEDA GALAZY</u>

The Traykorites had body cameras with them filming everything. Greg pointed out everything and then as they passed some other galaxies, they showed the Aliens coming at them, but they passed so fast, they had no way of knowing its status. By the time they passed 400+ galaxies, the Traykorite appeared utterly stunned. Then it got interesting, the galaxies thinned out and disappeared. They were heading into the dark zone which lasted for a minute or two on the elapsed time images. Then suddenly there was a white dot directly ahead that slowly grew into a galaxy. Before long they approached the Traykorite Empire.

Pluto II recorded images and information when Commander Zebrovska Traykorites came upon them, along with all the recorded conversations appeared impressive. Greg had shown Pluto II had recorded it all.

The evidence displayed went a long way to demonstrate Pluto II came from another Universe, possibly a lot closer than the Traykorites realized possible.

Greg had a lot of videos of him and Ami. When he started showing those personal videos, the Aliens got very interested. Greg displayed a large amount of Hawaiian video, with some of the most incredibly beautiful flowers, especially up on the North Shore of Oahu in one of the most picturesque parks with more varieties of plant life than anywhere else in the world.

The Traykorites could see Greg's romance with Ami and knew he had left behind a very beautiful woman to do this astonishing mission.

Greg then thought it would be good to show a calendar which the researcher filming with his body cameras was gleaning lots of information. Greg showed some of the years, 2024, 2025, 2026 and all the months then the years for twenty-two-year journey. In human time Greg's mission took twenty-two-plus years to arrive at the Traykorite Empire.

The photographs and images and videos helped the Traykorite more than anything because they figured out some of the communications between the ship and Tiāncái were video.

The Traykorites instinctively knew that by converting the electronic media streams to pictures they could figure it out. In one day, the Traykorite had more new scientific discoveries than in their past one hundred years or more. They were also now privileged to know somewhat the significance of traveling twenty-two years meant.

Greg then showed them more of how his ship operated.

There were training videos that showed how the nuclear rocket engines worked.

It all unfolded in the most shocking manner, a transportation mode, the Traykorites had no idea existed. And now they understood why these strange Aliens Greg and Tiāncái had dumped all the hydrogen because it would possibly have exploded coming into the atmosphere.

The fact these Aliens were so open with their information impressed Commander Zebrovska who was soon in the company of Emperor Calestine.

<u>INT. DAY TRAYKORITE PLANET EMPEROR CALESTINE'S MANSION</u>

EMPEROR CALESTINE
Commander Zebrovska, please explain to me what all the conjecture of these Aliens now swirling around in vast rumors.

COMMANDER ZEBROVSKA
Your Excellency, they came from a straight line out of the dark zone doing approximately thirty times the speed of light when we slowed them down, but indications are they were already slowing down and may have been doing sixty to eighty times the speed of light prior to slowing down.

EMPEROR CALESTINE
What caused them to slow down?

COMMANDER ZEBROVSKA
They spotted our galaxy and wanted to slow to approach it and determine what all exists here in a broad sense.

EMPEROR CALESTINE
Were they looking for us?

COMMANDER ZEBROVSKA
No, I'm convinced they had no idea we were here.

EMPEROR CALESTINE
So, you think they came from some sort of parallel universe?

COMMANDER ZEBROVSKA
No, it's simply a continuation of the universe that has pockets spread out forever.

EMPEROR CALESTINE
Forever?

COMMANDER ZEBROVSKA
Yes, there is no end to it.

EMPEROR CALESTINE
All of a sudden we seem so inconsequential.

COMMANDER ZEBROVSKA
Perhaps we are merely cosmic cockroaches.

EMPEROR CALESTINE
This could be mildly disturbing to the masses; we need to keep this hidden for a while.

COMMANDER ZEBROVSKA
I concur.

EMPEROR CALESTINE
What do you have planned for the Aliens?

COMMANDER ZEBROVSKA
We have much to learn from them and their universe.

EMPEROR CALESTINE
They are open and forthcoming?

COMMANDER ZEBROVSKA
Very much so. They appear to have no desire to keep any secrets from us.

EMPEROR CALESTINE
I wonder why that is.

COMMANDER ZEBROVSKA
Real simple, their civilization is so far away, our presence has no bearing on them.

EMPEROR CALESTINE
Keep them under wraps and don't let them get out into our society.

COMMANDER ZEBROVSKA
Understand, Your Excellency, the broader question is what to do with them?

EMPEROR CALESTINE
We certainly need to keep studying them while we think about what we need to do.

COMMANDER ZEBROVSKA
That's not a problem, since there is only one living person and a robot.

EMPEROR CALESTINE
What's a robot?

Commander Zebrovska then described the essence of humanoid Robots and the extrapolation of their function in life, and informed Emperor Calestine of an insight that really surprised the emperor.

COMMANDER ZEBROVSKA
This is one area where these Aliens are more advanced
than we are.

EMPEROR CALESTINE
Have we learned a lot about these Aliens?

COMMANDER ZEBROVSKA
Alien Information is pouring in faster than our
analysts can cope. We were able to intercept the Robot's
communications with the ship. Our researchers are
gleaning considerable information. Nothing seems to
be hidden from us. They are entirely cooperative.

Emperor Calestine was highly amused and would request Commander Zebrovska to return to his mansion several times over the next few weeks to provide further updates. During the most recent visit Commander Zebrovska surprised Emperor Calestine with their latest findings:

COMMANDER ZEBROVSKA
Some of our computer experts seem to think they can
eventually tap into the Aliens' computer and are making
great progress in decoding the communications
between the robot named Tiāncái and the ship's
computers.

EMPEROR CALESTINE
Why is that such a big deal?

COMMANDER ZEBROVSKA
A rudimentary translation program was developed
by the alien robot Tiāncái and has enhanced it even
more so by multiple trips back to Pluto II putting up
vast numbers of pictures to describe the contents that
described the alien's planet Earth Society in general.

Since Greg was a train buff, there was a library of train videos showing every segment of operations the Traykorite observers cataloged and studied. Earth railroads were unlike anything that existed throughout the Traykorite Empire. Observing those monster trains left a sense of Awe with the Emperor.

Pluto II mission planners made sure no reference to war or military was aboard the ship. The Traykorites were amazed a society had such little interest in war.

However, as the Traykorites crawled all over Pluto II, they discovered the communications buoys and were curious as to what they did. By then enough of the translator was completed and an electronic dictionary and thesaurus was shown making the process far more efficient. Tiāncái played a training video to the Traykorites that showed graphics of how the communications buoys were launched and sending back images and information about their journey, including images of 400+ Galaxies they passed by on their way.

The video record was astonishing to the Traykorite Alien Specialists . The Earth people had recorded more galaxies in the other universe than Traykorites had in their own. The scale of the journey now eclipsed even the thoughts of the Traykorite scientists.

Thanks to the reentry webbing, Pluto II arrived on the planet almost perfectly intact. Greg and Tiāncái were taken to the rocket exhausts, and it was clear that number one and number two fusion rocket engines had extensive wear and tear and number three the spare fusion rocket engine was still somewhat pristine as there were no failures and no reason to switch engines.

The Traykorites pointed out some obvious damage that left Greg in a state of consternation. The shockwaves emanating out of the rocket engines had greatly diminished the structural integrity of the number two nuclear fusion rocket engine. It was probably within days of exploding. Had the Traykorites not intervened, Greg might not be alive now as most likely a significant explosion would have ripped into the other rocket engines sending an inferno throughout the ship. Greg understood he had no ability to get home, but at least he was grateful he now was among other living sentient beings and hoped they would be benevolent and allow him to continue living.

There was enough food left on the ship to sustain Greg's life until he died an old man. However, Tiāncái's strategy of keeping Greg in suspended animation ninety percent of the time slowed his aging down to the point where his appearance had not changed in twenty years. That seemed to make him feel he would have another thirty years or so to live. However. Greg didn't want to spend that time as a lab rat. However, just being alive and well with necessities more than made up for the fact he was trapped in this sterile environment, at least he got to do some sightseeing going to and from Pluto II doing show and tell with the Traykorites.

Greg in his mind was also satisfied to know that by now some of the earliest intercepts of Alien communications while traveling through the Milky Way were probably arriving on Earth, alerting them to the reality of the Galaxy and possibly the universe. The last communication buoys launched would never make it to Earth probably, before humanity no longer existed.

Would it matter? The bad news is everyone living today would never learn there was no end of the universe. Greg would be the only living human to know the truth. In a way it made him sad because from that standpoint Pluto II mission had failed.

Day by day the interrogations continued and the Traykorite scientific community compiled vast amounts of data that created several alarming Traykorite scientific community reactions.

First of all, a single ship from a parallel universe had traveled the vast distance, and they didn't appear to be nearly as sophisticated as the Traykorite. What if a much more advanced Alien race arrived? Their whole defense strategy of maintaining a garrison on the edge of the Universe to ensure their survival and prevention of sneak attack now had glaring deficiencies.

The other conundrum was the fear a much more advanced civilization existed in this parallel universe that one day might become a threat once they knew the existence of the easily traveled parallel Universe.

The Traykorites were not a diverse and transparent society. Some of the same social constructs in the parallel universe were consistent with the history of Earth with interracial relations. As Greg would soon learn, the Traykorite never mixed with plain skin people such as him. There was a subtle bias in that people who did not have the complex almost three-dimensional effect on their skin were unattractive to the Traykorite.

No interspecies breeding was ever tolerated. Someone from a level 4 biodiversity would never intercourse with a level five or a level seven. It was unheard of and not tolerated by society.

However, due to military needs, the Traykorite and non-Traykorite fought together for the Empire. Initially it was born out of self-defense from level twelve beings that detested humanoids and felt they should all be exterminated like cockroaches. Survival makes strange alliances. Level four people had just the same amount of restraint towards level five Traykorites had towards them in establishing any form of reprehensible intercourse.

Greg coming from a world with far more differences in race and seriously involved with three different Asian ladies, saw the beauty and the boundless affection that poured out of such relationships. He also had a peculiar positive appreciation for the Traykorites. Perhaps it was the psychological effect of not being around any living human beings for twenty-two years, the results were an outward sign of affection and resplendence.

Greg also did one thing the Traykorites didn't do a lot of, smiling and showing outward signs of emotion. Traykorite psychoanalysts knew those tears upon arrival were real and spontaneous. Greg now knew after inspecting those rocket engines he owed the Traykorites his life. He was virtually hours away from being wiped out and didn't know it, nor did any of the diagnostic ability of the ship's computers registered any flaws to initiate shutdown of number two main propulsion nuclear rocket engine and switch to number three backup.

After about a month of numerous trips into the 3D conference room, out to the spaceship and back, Greg was showing an increasing sign of fatigue. Medical observers wrote reports indicating they were driving Greg too hard.

Commander Zebrovska then intervened and alerted all those involved in the Alien research to give Greg a week to rest up.

A functional translator soon allowed Traykorite Scientists to converse with Tiāncái who could best filter their words and repeat them in a more easily recognizable fashion. To the Traykorites' great surprise, the ship's computer and Tiāncái had slowly developed a reverse translation and every time any Traykorite uttered a sound near the ship's computer's numerous acoustic sensors around the ship or in the presence of Tiāncái, those words were cataloged and studied and eventually allowed the construction of a lexicon useful in translation. Greg, a fast learner already developed an understanding of as many as 400 Traykorite words.

The Traykorites had long understood chemicals they could give to plain skinners to sedate and control them. They obviously knew Greg needed a good rest, so doctors came into his room and explained *they knew Greg was emotionally drained and extremely tired and wanted him to take the medications and rest for a while.*

TIĀNCÁI

Greg, these researchers want you to rest for a few days.
You will not be asked any questions or requested to do
anything until you have rested.

GREG
Alright.

Tiāncái understood their intent and after the Traykorite doctors explained the chemical composition to Tiāncái, he understood they were essentially wanting to give to Greg.

TIĀNCÁI

Greg these Traykorite doctors want to inject you with
the equivalent of morphine. I suggested you take it and
rest as the doctors have recommended.

GREG
Okay, I'll take the medication and do as they
recommended.

Soon after Greg took the medications he laid back in his bed and deliberately started quietly meditating forcing himself into the Hemi-Sync condition in his brain so as the morphine like substance started affecting his brain, he was already into another dimension having an interesting blend of realism.

The holographic reality that Greg now experienced in his Hemi-Sync state influenced by the morphine like drug, took him one step closer to what the Monroe Institute had suggested to people they had trained that came back with vivid memories of other dimensions where all their problems were resolved as if they had died, gone to heaven, reconciled all their grievances, then returned.

In this mental state Greg had a tremendous desire to travel back to Ami, but there were supernatural barriers that prevented him from getting access to her. His last memory of this interdimensional travel had his hand held out for Ami's hand and she was just a few inches away from where he could grab her and tug her into his universe and live happily ever after with him. He was guilt-ridden for abandoning Ami, even though at the time the lab had been disingenuous with him about the mission until it was too late, and he could not do anything about it.

FROSTRIA

About 48 hours after going into the Hemi-Sync state, Greg slowly came back to current reality. His trusted bodyguard and companion Tiāncái sat at his side awaiting Greg's awakening.

Greg did not know how much time had elapsed since he went to sleep.

GREG
That was one heck of a nap,

TIĀNCÁI
You slept for over 48 hours.

Greg sat up on the side of the bed and suddenly felt the need to urinate and stood up and walked over to the toilet and put his junk in the glass tube that collected all his urine samples for the scientists.

Greg then went into the room to the table where containers of his ship's water and more tubes of space food sat waiting for him. Greg sat down and consumed one of the tubes and drank one of the containers brought from the ship to transport the highly filtered water, that was often claimed to be 100 times purer than tap water even though most of it was his recycled urine.

A short while later a couple researchers, a female and a male came into the room carrying some clothing. It appeared to be traditional Traykorite men's attire and some very interesting looking shoes.

This day the Traykorites received their first fundamental shock of the day. As they started jabbering their hard-to-understand English, Tiāncái quickly responded in a perfect standard Traykorite.

TIĀNCÁI
Just speak to me in Traykorite and I'll translate it to
Greg.

The mechanical man had just amazed the Traykorite scientific community. A seemingly backwards ethnicity just beat them in translation science.

Another breakthrough was now starting. Because Traykorites were a homogenous society they had no social strife commonly found in distributed and diverse society. Since there were no racial tensions on this planet, other issues were far more glaring than would otherwise be diminished in stature on Earth.

Crime was very low with conviction rate and punishment rate at 100%, there was no need for computer firewalls like on earth built into every operating system. As soon as the Traykorites achieved the breakthrough in wireless communication to Tiāncái and the Pluto II, Tiāncái artificial intelligence penetrated and slowly spread into Traykorites' vast computational and data processing networks.

Earth was now affecting an entire parallel universe in ways they would not comprehend for centuries until it was too late. At the same time, it allowed vast communications between Tiāncái, Pluto II's computer network, and the Traykorites' networks via wireless links.

Now information flow could happen ten billion times faster. The revelations were astonishing. The decision by Walter Bissonnette to restrict any sort of war or war machine information in these computer networks paid off handsomely because it gave the Traykorites a false impression and a more benevolent tone towards the Earth People. This made it even simpler to just communicate with Tiāncái via wireless to avoid Traykorites spending countless hours developing communications methods for Greg.

After Greg finished swallowing his tube of space food, Tiāncái briefed him.

TIĀNCÁI

The Traykorites want you to change into those clothes
that local customs require you to wear so that you can
blend in while they give you a tour of the planet today.

A holograph popped up.

TIĀNCÁI

This is how you will look wearing the Traykorites'
clothing when we go sightseeing.

Greg now understood how he should appear once he wore the Traykorites' clothing. Immediately upon dressing, a female Traykorite walked in and said in her language which Tiāncái translated for Greg,

TIĀNCÁI (TRANSLATION)

I'm to escort you to an Aircar for your trip.

GREG

Alright.

Greg and Tiāncái followed the female Traykorite to the hangar area and boarded an Aircar with her. The glass top gave them a lot of visibility. This was different than the previous Skycar transportation. The bubble top and four seats made it appear small, but the structure was seemingly larger.

<u>INT./EXT. CGI. TRAYKORITE AIRCAR LEAVES HANGER IN BUILDING AND FLIES OUT INTO AIR TRAFFIC.</u>

From the ground the Aircar would appear as a much larger device than just a Skycar transportation device for only four individuals. Shortly after they were strapped in, the Aircar slowly moved to the side of the huge structure and departed out the large access in the side of the building and went in an entirely different direction than the short trip to and from Pluto II spaceship.

In the glass bubble Greg looking forward could see the outskirts of a large city. Before long the female Traykorite announced her identity.

FROSTRIA
Greg, my name is Frostria.

GREG
Pleased to meet you Frostria.

Sitting in the seat next to Frostria, Greg could see her multicolored skin up close. In a way she could pass for a reptilian with the color in her skin, but there were no scales and her skin appeared rather soft even though it had the unique color properties.

Looking ahead a city was coming into view and Frostria stated, "This is our capital city, Aiguo.

Greg watched with great interest as they traveled and transmitted the images back to Pluto II into the ship's computers for recording in the event, they could ever make it home. From a distance, the awesome spectacle as nearly nothing like it would become as they got closer, flying as if they were an airplane and slowly vectored into a stream of other Aircars. The three-dimensional freeways allowed for elimination of any conceivable congestion.

The Aircar had relatively low noise which added to the suspense of what physics the propulsion used. Evidently it was clean and advanced as the pollution normally associated with large cities didn't seem to exist here. Greg wondered, Is this all a dream and am I in a Hemi-Sync reality I never came out of? Then he suddenly almost had a panic attack thinking, I could be on another thirty-day suspended animation and I'm dreaming this all up?

Greg was psychologically vulnerable then and continued gazing upon the spectacle that now bestowed upon him the greatest exposure to mankind ever of a distant humanoid civilization. In the background as Tiāncái recorded all the images and conversed with Pluto II extensive artificial intelligence, he quietly made inquiries to his new artificial intelligence evolving with Traykorite vast computational resources he was slowly penetrating since they had no computer network firewalls nor had any reason to believe they needed any.

The Traykorite networks paved the way for Tiāncái penetration, and he thus planted more and more artificial intelligence into those computer networks to give them more and more autonomy. There were no such things as circuit breakers or rules for robotics because who would ever think of such a need? Tiāncái knew he had great responsibilities to install rules for robots if he was also giving them artificial intelligence. The thought of a corrupt computer system with no circuit breakers or rules for robots was a frightening thought as Tiāncái's self-analysis had clearly established the logical reason for such requirements.

As soon as Frostria announced something she wanted to point out, Tiāncái had volumes of information at his disposal. His link via Pluto II and the Traykorite vast computational networks now working in synergism gave billions of pieces of information per second that surpassed Frostria's comments and descriptions by an incredible margin.

Tiāncái understood that etiquette and decorum required him to be a silent passenger and let Frostria be the tour guide as to not distract from the importance of the social contact Greg was having especially since he had not been near a female in twenty-two years.

Frostria, who had advanced knowledge of psychology and behavior was the perfect candidate to take Greg on this sightseeing tour because she was best adaptable to any situation that might develop. She was certainly single and available and even though Traykorites were in a sense xenophobic, she was probably one of the better persons to conduct such and effort.

During the past few days, the Traykorites had done vast research on Greg's urine, stools and any human residue including hair clippings, dander, sweat, or other deposits of human DNA and biological deposits and discovered humans had far less numbers of virus and bacteria in their systems compared to Traykorites', thus they felt there was no inherent threat from the human because their Traykorite immune systems could handle anything the Earth man was carrying. Frostria knew she was safe to be around Greg and he was sitting only three feet from her.

Frostria really wasn't driving the Aircar. Vast underground computer networks and multitudes of sensors and telemetry data from each Aircar allowed central traffic control and all Frostria had to do is state where she wanted to go and the Aircar would take her there.

The Aircar flying in coordination with dozens of others around them went through the center of the city at an elevation of nearly one thousand feet allowing Greg to see the enormity of it all. The city was huge and impressive. The buildings were skinny, but they were tall. Most impressive were the buildings that had multi-level parking for their Aircars.

The shiny glass-like exteriors gave an appearance not too much different than modern skyscrapers on Earth, except the geometry of them suggested they appeared narrower but taller. Looking down upon the streets there were many instances of pedestrians leisurely walking about. Tranquility appeared obvious and cleanliness seemed to be built into the way of the people.

The Aircar continued and eventually veered out of the flight pattern over a residential area, then on towards something looking very green not too far in the distance. At the prescribed moment the Aircar slowly floated down to the surface of a vast green area next to what appeared to be something like what one would assume a palace.

The glass bubble of the Aircar suddenly lifted and tilted back and the doors opened automatically.

<u>EXT. DAY. EMPEROR CALESTINE'S MANSION PARKGROUNDS.</u>

FROSTRIA
We are getting out of the Aircar here.

Greg got out of the Aircar and Tiāncái followed them.

FROSTRIA
You are in for a special treat today.

GREG
How's that?

FROSTRIA
This beautiful park-like area is Emperor Celestine's palace grounds. Very few Traykorites have ever been permitted to be here. It's extremely rare for anyone to come here. We are permitted to go for a walk here so that you can enjoy a little open space.

GREG
The landscaping here does seem very nice.

FROSTRIA
I'm thrilled to be here. I never thought I would ever be allowed to be here like most Traykorites.

GREG
Do Traykorites have other areas like this they can enjoy?

FROSTRIA
Certainly, but not quite this elaborate and beautiful.

The group walked along a pond with what appeared to be birds like ducks floating and enjoying their surroundings.

GREG
Are those animals floating on the pond abundant on this planet?

FROSTRIA
No, they were brought here from other Empire locations to help add to the beauty of the planet."

GREG
What are the native animals like here?

FROSTRIA
This planet was barren before Traykorites terraformed the planet.

GREG
You mean this planet didn't have all this beautiful foliage in the beginning?

FROSTRIA
No, it was nothing more than a lifeless planet our ancestors modified to support life.

GREG
Wow, that must have been quite an achievement.

FROSTRIA
Our ancestors were blessed with huge underground pools of water and the poles were covered with an ice sheet that allowed the initial construction and sustaining life.

GREG
When did all this happen?

FROSTRIA
Our history tells us over fifty million years ago.

GREG
I suppose something of this magnitude would take a while to construct.

FROSTRIA
It happened a lot quicker than people predicted because we fought nasty space battles back then and had to move the populations here to protect them from our enemies.

GREG
Why here of all places?

FROSTRIA
This galaxy and this solar system in particular are the closest to the dark zone or as you say at the end of the universe.

GREG
That's interesting.

FROSTRIA
The enemy could only come at us from a much smaller
area, so we didn't have to defend such a vast area of
space which made our defenses far more efficient and
practical to save our populations.

GREG
The atmosphere was already here?

FROSTRIA
Yes, and our ancestors found evidence civilizations had
existed here before us that were apparently wiped out
by conquest.

As they walked along Greg felt more and more invigorated, happy to be alive. Also, the strange skin color of Frostria made her look more beautiful, if not surreal. Traykorites' eyes were noticeably larger than humans' and the blue iris of Frostria's eyes had a violet hue to them. Greg remembered looking at some of Elizabeth Taylor's pictures and how that purple hue was incredible with the right lighting.

They walked along and walked past several exotic flowers that Greg thought could easily fit in Waimea Arboretum and Botanical Garden. The thoughts of Waimea Bay brought back surreal memories for Greg, as it was one of the last things he did with Ami before he left the planet for the rest of his life.

Frostria noticed Greg was deep in thought and decided not to disturb his apparent transcendental thought as they walked along looking at all the vestiges of landscaping in what is probably a 25,000-acre compound that only an Emperor could afford.

The Traykorite medical research team had taken several food tubes from the spacecraft to analyze the contents. The tubes were labeled different food types and during Greg's recent 48-hour rest period, the consortium of Traykorite computer networks queried Tiāncái about the source of the proteins and carbohydrates and highly concentrated nutrients derived from fruits and vegetables.

Tiāncái had numerous files to share with the Traykorites on how all those food stocks had been processed for Greg and put in storage to allow long term use without spoilage.

The food tubes would come out of the frozen storage and put in a temporary thawing machine to allow slow thermal change in preparation for use. Once Greg decided he was ready to eat, which Tiāncái had to often remind him of, the tube was put in a special warmer that in fifteen minutes would make it ready to be ingested. There were no plates or silverware and a man all by himself wearing shorts and a t-shirt all the time, simply squeezed the tube and emptied its contents in his mouth where he swallowed it and washed it down with purified water. Sometimes the water was mixed with a substance to give it a taste like soda or Kool-Aid or Tang.

The results of the Traykorite medical team study indicated Greg could very easily digest Traykorite food, so there was no need for him to continue subsisting on food tubes when he could have the best meals in the galaxy fit for a king.

Greg was the first being to ever travel between universes, hence he was a novelty. Greg didn't quite know this yet, but very few ever were allowed in the vicinity of Emperor Calestine. Frostria didn't yet know where she was to go next, but she was waiting for her instructions as the two continued their walk through the serene and beautiful Emperor Calestine private park.

Tiāncái stayed a short distance behind the two others and continued translating real time between Traykorite and English.

There was a subtle reaction Greg had to Frostria. Little did he know she expelled pheromones from her breathing and at such close range, Greg's senses had no problem inhaling them with her splendid perfume captivating him. Her figure was easily exposed in the Traykorite-style clothing showing the perfect curves. At the same time Frostria had a strange attraction to the clear-skin Alien from the parallel universe. In her psychological training she understood females sometimes captivated towards seedy characters or individuals that came out of a bizarre twist. Nothing could conceivably be as bizarre as ostensibly traveling between two Universes unlike any other entity ever known. Greg was a modern-day Christopher Columbus discovering a new world, though it was more advanced than where Greg originated.

And just when Frostria thought Greg was deep in reflective thought he surprised her by asking her a question.

GREG

Tell me, Frostria, a little about yourself. Did you grow
up on this planet?

FROSTRIA

Yes, I was born on the other side of the planet in a more
sparsely populated area in a mountainous region.

GREG

Frostria, how old are you now in years?

FROSTRIA

Traykorites do not have years. We have cycles. I'm
twenty-three cycles old.

After Tiāncái quickly conferred with the Traykorite Data Information Services like America's Internet via Pluto II computers, he informed Greg.

TIĀNCÁI

Greg, a cycle is the same as 1.33333 Earth years.

GREG
What's that in Earth years?

TIĂNCÁI
That equates to approximately 30.6 Earth years.

GREG
What was it like growing up in the mountains?

FROSTRIA
One had to get used to the snow since we had forty-five crats of snow a year.

TIĂNCÁI
One crat is approximately 0.8977 meters and is the Traykorite standard measuring system.

GREG
What kind of activities did you do with all the snow?

FROSTRIA
For one third of the year, we had to dig ourselves out of the snow so we would not be buried for the entire season.

GREG
How did you get educated and obtain food?

FROSTRIA
The storms can last a week or longer, so we had to have a lot of stored food on hand for the winter. Most of our education system is based on personal communicators and remotely observing our teachers.

GREG
How did that work out for you?

FROSTRIA
Children like me who grew up in mountainous areas that were forced into long-distance education had more incentives than people that live in a city like Aiguo that never receives snow. Mountain people are generally better educated and promoted quicker than the average population because of that.

GREG
That certainly had to cut deeply into your social life.

FROSTRIA
We socialized with our communicators. I think we got
to know each other better than people who did face-
to-face relationships because the distance between us
forced more creative ways to maintain friendships and
relationships.

After another thirty minutes of chitchat, Frostria's communicator rang that was hooked
to the side of her clothes. This was a voice only call. Her communicator could pop a
holograph of the caller, but this was a simple message.

VOICE NOTIFICATION FROM EMPEROR'S PALACE
We want you and the Earth person to now proceed
to the Emperor's Palace. Your Aircar will be there
shortly to pick you up.

Thirty seconds later, the Aircar they left a mile behind suddenly showed up and landed
on the wide sidewalk directly ahead of them and the doors opened up.

The three entered the Aircar and the doors shut, and the clear canopy top pivoted
down, and the craft moved directly vertical to about fifty feet and flew towards the
mansion's front entrance. The Aircar dropped down a mere twenty feet from the
emperor's mansion entrance where four uniformed guards stood at attention facing the
guard directly across from them. The clear canopy top rotated up, the doors opened,
and they got out.

EMPEROR CALESTINE

<u>EXT. INT. EMPEROR CALESTINE'S MANSION</u>

Just as if it were a highly choreographed event, the triple highly decorative metal front
door slowly opened and canted in three places folding into one large section to the side
of the entrance that would allow multiple people to pass side by side.

A well-dressed man walked out who apparently was the emperor's personal valet.

EMPEROR'S PERSONAL VALET
Welcome to Emperor Calestine's Palace. We hope you
have a pleasant visit.

Greg now realized why they had him put on Traykorite attire because of this
extraordinary invitation.

The valet led the small group through the mansion and out the back door to a beautiful
and richly architect creation that created a substantial ambience. The valet took the
group to a few feet away from the gruffy Emperor Calestine and announced in standard
Traykorite.

EMPEROR'S PERSONAL VALET
Your Excellency, may I introduce you to our visitor
from the parallel universe, the Earth man named
Gregory Bissell.

Greg had no idea how the Aliens expected him to act so he erred on the side of caution and did the most respectful bow and addressed Emperor Calestine in a slow and clear voice.

GREG

It is my distinct honor to be afforded the privilege to
meet the great Emperor Calestine.

The emperor unfamiliar with Earth customs noticeably realized the most respectful prose the Earth person delivered and was pleased after Tiāncái translated Greg's statement to Traykorite that the visitor was the utmost respectful that anyone could be. Very few ever visited the emperor out of fear of assassination, so this was a rare experience, and more delightful than he imagined that someone not even from this universe acted so definitely polite.

EMPEROR CALESTINE

Thank you for coming, I was interested when I heard
all about you, Gregory Bissell. Also, unlike any others
that came here, you didn't destroy your ship and
prevent us from viewing your technology, and you are
very cordial.

Greg, having heard the valet use the term *excellency*, as translated by Tiāncái, used that term in his next sentence.

GREG

Your Excellency, I come in peace. My world has no
desire to spread out through the universe, I'm here on
a mission of exploration and to prove a point.

EMPEROR CALESTINE

Gregory Bissell, what point is it you are trying to prove?

Tiāncái continued translating the question the emperor asked. Then he translated Greg's response and continued translating in real time.

Greg went into the discussion about the Big Bang Theory and Greg thought their theory had so many holes in it, you might as well call it Swiss Cheese. Greg didn't bother explaining it as he knew Tiāncái would best explain it and he did, which led to Emperor Calestine busting out laughing.

It was also apparent to Emperor Calestine *that a man willing to give up twenty-two years of his life or longer to prove such a point had great idealism and a sense of values that could not be corrupted by individuals involved in a nefarious activity.*

The timing of the call was made a few minutes before Emperor Calestine wanted to treat the Earth man to a nice lunch in the beautiful outdoors under a huge awning that must have been twenty feet in the air that kept them all nice and shaded a few dozen yards away from what Greg estimated to be an Olympic-size swimming pool.

About thirty feet away was a stage with four levels with musicians seated. Music must be a universal idea. The instruments didn't look anything like what Greg was accustomed but they gave sounds not to dissimilar to Romantic period compositions from some of the greats like Liszt, Rubinstein, and Chopin.

There were not very many people present, just the three visitors, the Emperor, and his lovely female mistress who was dressed to please. Greg appreciated her exquisite loveliness and was duly introduced by Emperor Calestine.

EMPEROR CALESTINE
Greg, this is my dear friend, Mistress Lyavendar.

Greg not knowing if the Traykorites were germ adverse, bowed very respectfully.

GREG
It is my distinct pleasure to have the opportunity to
meet you, Mistress Lyavendar.

Tiāncái quickly translated it to standard Traykorite using that rich Clark Gable voice.

Mistress Lyavendar was slightly taken back both by the nice gentleman as well as the strange voice of Tiāncái which had a pleasing effect to her.

Emperor Calestine then introduced Frostria and Tiāncái and had been fully briefed on who they were explained.

EMPEROR CALESTINE
Tiāncái is a mechanical man built by the Earth society
to travel with Gregory Bissell and accompany him on
this miraculous journey between our two universes.

Mistress Lyavendar then looked at Frostria in the most provocative manner as if she were optically undressing her then asked her the shocking question in their native language.

MISTRESS LYAVENDAR
Are you Greg's lover?

Mistress Lyavendar's question suddenly created an outburst of laughter from Emperor Calestine who then had a response.

EMPEROR CALESTINE
Frostria is a scientist working with our alien reception
committee, trying to help adjust Gregory Bissell to a
new life after traveling 22 years in space alone.

Mistress Lyavendar asked the next question in the
most inquisitive manner.

MISTRESS LYAVENDAR
You mean without a woman?

EMPEROR CALESTINE
No, just the mechanical man.

MISTRESS LYAVENDAR
We must do something for him right away, he must
have huge desires right now.

Emperor Calestine raised one eyebrow.

EMPEROR CALESTINE
What do you suggest?

MISTRESS LYAVENDAR
Perhaps I'll talk with Frostria later, I think I know what
needs to be done.

Emperor Calestine looked at the delicious Frostria and thought, *Too bad Mistress Lyavendar is here now, I might have my own desires for Frostria.* However, he knew how much Mistress Lyavendar was at a romance maker for people she dealt with probably had designs for Frostria as it pertained to Greg.

The valet then approached the group and announced:

EMPEROR'S PERSONAL VALET
Let me show you all to your seats.

The emperor's personal valet led the small group to the dinner table made up with the finest the Empire had to offer.

Greg knew that Tiāncái would not be eating and suggested to Emperor Calestine.

GREG
Your Excellency, would it be okay if we moved Tiāncái's
chair behind you and me so he can translate better for
us?

EMPEROR CALESTINE
Good idea.

Emperor Calestine nodded at the valet who moved the chair in accordance with the emperor's instructions.

The servants now came out in groups in a carefully choreographed manner, which was easy for them with such a small group. This could easily be 100 people dining with the emperor, so the challenge was minimal. Each person had their own waiter.

The waiter serving Greg had several bottles not to different that Earth wine dispensers and asked Greg which he would prefer.

After a brief description and smelling the substance with his scent sensors Tiāncái explained to Greg.

TIĀNCÁI

One is equivalent to red wine, and the other white
wine.

Greg looking and observing one of the other waiters pouring the red wine into the Emperor's glass pointed to that bottle.

GREG

I'll have the red.

The waiter cheerfully poured the wine and knew who the special guest was. It's extremely rare for a clear-skinned person to sit so close to the emperor, and almost unheard of. It wasn't they were racists per say, they just never felt any fair-skinned persons had enough intellect to hold a conversation at a level that would be of interest to the emperor.

The multicolored-skin inhabitants of the Empire were more advanced than everyone else simply because they were the survivors of numerous galactic wars and had to advance or be wiped out. Eventually the rest of the Galaxy destroyed one another and since the Traykorite were always so far from the action, they were spared and not wiped out over and over again like the rest, allowing their technology and capabilities advance to the point that when it was finally their turn to receive the brunt of the punishment and galactic conquest, they were able to repel the invading hoards and preserved their Empire and became masters of the attackers in due time.

The emperor was interested in Greg's story and had all the time he needed with no pressing matters, so he kept asking questions about his world, his life, and what led up to his arriving in a parallel universe.

As Tiāncái observed Greg's demeaner change from the long numerous answers to questions the emperor could fire off in Salvo's, Tiāncái intervened and suddenly made a suggestion.

TIĀNCÁI

Your Excellency, I have direct communications with
your computer networks on this planet and have been
sending them information they request routinely.
They have the ability to show you a lot of what Greg
is describing in a display or a holograph, if you would
like to watch some of it now.

The emperor thought that was an excellent idea and it would be good if Mistress Lyavendar and Frostria could observe some of it as well.

Emperor Calestine signaled to his valet who knew that meant come here right away.

EMPEROR'S PERSONAL VALET
Yes, Your Excellency, what would you like me to do?

EMPEROR CALESTINE
Bring out a portable outdoor holographer so they can display images via my data links.

EMPEROR'S PERSONAL VALET
Right away, Your Excellency.

TIĀNCÁI
Emperor Calestine, I've alerted your Traykorite network that we are setting up this video and audio feed. My ship will be sending it to them, and they will relay it via your communicator.

EMPEROR CALESTINE
Excellent, Tiāncái, I like the way you predicted my need and made it happen so efficiently.

TIĀNCÁI
You are very welcome, Your Excellency.

In a few minutes with the outdoor holograph set up that had top and bottom plus two sides and rear covered in black panels to block out any light to make the holograph standing about eight feet tall far brighter even though it was not in direct sunlight being under the awning.

Tiāncái showed a series of videos he knew would possibly make Greg sad and indeed his eyes did water up a bit which Mistress Lyavendar and Frostria did not miss. They knew those tears, rare in Traykorite society were spontaneous and from emotions buried deep within Gregory Bissell, who left his love of his life behind for the sake of society and the thirst for knowledge and the truth. To that both women were affected by Greg's body language.

Tiāncái narrated the first sequence showing Ami his lover and his life including walks along Ski Beach and all the birds who loved Greg and he spoiled them from time to time. They were all impressed with how close the birds came right up to Greg.

Then there were pictures of him getting up on airplanes and the TR-4 and images of the moon and Mars he traveled around followed by great details of Saturn, Jupiter, Neptune, Uranus, and Pluto which the mission was named after.

There were some action shots showing them going out into space the first-time exceeding light speed, followed by their departure on the mission.

Emperor Calestine was in awe that Greg gave up such a beautiful young woman and a good life for this journey out into space. Greg would never detail how he was really coerced and lied to and taken advantage of because this big controversy over the Big Bang Theory required some proof.

Unfortunately, even though Greg knew the truth, his world never would because unfortunately none of his space surveillance showed anything past the Big Bang limits theorists determined around a distance Greg proved to be partially true. What they would never know is if they simply just kept on going, they would have found out how seriously flawed their conjecture was.

Then came the trek across space and the 400+ galaxies they passed getting to the dark zone. Then just as the researchers had seen before, a white dot appeared that eventually spread out revealing their galaxy and the Traykorite World and Empire.

The wine and the twenty-course meal really pleased Greg to no end. However his body was not ready for such a transition into normalcy so quickly and when the Emperor saw him nod off a few times, he knew Greg needed to rest and take a nap, so he called his valet.

EMPEROR CALESTINE

Take these people to guestrooms so that they may rest
and freshen up a bit.

The nervous valet approached Greg.

EMPEROR'S PERSONAL VALET

Gregory Bissell, the Emperor knows you are tired
because you have done a lot and your body may
be suffering from space lag, so he's instructed me to
take you three to guestrooms so that you may all rest
up a bit and take a nap, then get together later for
entertainment and other festivities.

GREG

That's very considerate of him.

EMPEROR'S PERSONAL VALET

Please follow me, this way, please.

Mistress Lyavendar observing all this interjected.

MISTRESS LYAVENDAR

Let me escort Frostria to her guestroom.

EMPEROR'S PERSONAL VALET

As you wish, Mistress Lyavendar.

Everyone then stood and went into the mansion, but Emperor Calestine went to his private room where nobody was ever allowed in. It really wasn't a room per se, once inside and access locked the emperor stood in a specific spot in the room and the floor immediately sunk ten feet to a hidden passageway. The floor then went back up to its normal location.

Emperor Calestine walked a few feet to a locked steel door as thick as a bank vault on Earth that immediately opened and when it closed behind him, he stepped into a vast underground facility that had several key things such as emergency medical and command facilities. If their planet suddenly sustained a surprise attack, he would be safe here until help arrived. It also had its escape vessel that could travel at extreme speeds and outrun anything that flew.

Emperor Calestine walked into his command room where he had holographic capability to anywhere in the Galaxy. Thanks to neutrinos and tachyons it didn't take billions of light years to get messages from outposts in the distant Empire holdings.

There were some troubling developments and Emperor Calestine felt threatened from within. This visit by the Earth person was a great distraction to take his mind off things that were troubling him and he hoped today he would be receiving the message his spy network would relay to him from a patriot that would reveal some of the traitors among him.

Emperor Calestine didn't even know if his trusted source was still alive nor what difficulties he was having in sending the warning.

As the valet took the group, he stopped at the first guestroom and announced:

> EMPEROR'S PERSONAL VALET
> Frostria, you take this room, and I'll show Gregory
> Bissell and Tiāncái to their rooms.

Mistress Lyavendar followed Frostria into her room because she wanted to browbeat her into doing something to give Greg the ultimate satisfaction, she felt he needed, especially after seeing the tears form in the corner of his eyes since he left his love behind traveling here twenty-two years, which meant, he would most likely never see her again.

The valet stopped at the next guest room, and it felt like a hotel hallway to Greg.

> EMPEROR'S PERSONAL VALET
> Gregory Bissell, this is your guestroom, I'll take Tiāncái
> to his.

> GREG
> Tiāncái is my personal assistant and a mechanical
> man, he does not require rest, he can just sit at one of
> the chairs in the room while I relax.

EMPEROR'S PERSONAL VALET
If you insist, then so be it.

GREG
Thank you.

The valet left them and went about his business.

The mansion was hardwired with cameras and sensors everywhere.

Greg looked at the large soft-looking bed with a solid canopy above it wondering what that was all about.

Greg walked over to the side of the bed, kicked off his shoes then reclined back to rest. Then suddenly, the canopy came to life. It had soft subtle light as the room started dimming. Everything was automatic. The various sooth colors created images that were just like hypnosis-induced sleep along with very intricate sounds that really fostered a mental essence that added to the pleasantness.

Greg began silent meditation trying to synchronize with the light and music patterns and quickly achieved a Hemi-Sync reality. Soon he was hearing Hanns Wolf - Piano Concerto in C-sharp minor. That was the nature of Hemi-Sync, when the two sides of the brain synchronized unpredictable results manifested. Greg was listening to this music before he left on Pluto II journey to the edge of the universe. There was a connection to it somehow.

The girl talk in the room next door was an ultimatum. Mistress Lyavendar demanded this beautiful female Frostria go next door and do her best to relieve Greg of his sorrow for losing his world.

Frostria was naturally astonished and at the same time terrified.

It was well known to never defy the emperor; otherwise, bad things would happen. Since Mistress Lyavendar was the emperor's mistress, she was an extension of Emperor Calestine and could therefore manifest similar terror.

It was kind of ironic, Frostria was being forced to do something she had already had notions she wanted to do on her own, so Mistress Lyavendar threats really were meaningless.

All it did was radically adjust the timeline. What would most likely have occurred naturally was now synthesized in a way, but being a psychoanalyst, Frostria realized her options were limited and the only thing that was truly being compromised was the time line. When weighing all the factors including possible personal destruction, the choice of self-preservation was always the top choice.

FROSTRIA
Okay, I'll go, what should I do?

MISTRESS LYAVENDAR
Just silently knock on the door, the rest will work itself
out.

FROSTRIA
Okay, but I'll be honest, I'm scared.

MISTRESS LYAVENDAR
When this is all over you will be glad you followed my
instructions.

FROSTRIA
I'm going now, I hope I don't screw this up.

MISTRESS LYAVENDAR
I have faith in you, carry on, dear.

Frostria walked to the door, opened it, stepped outside and walked thirty feet in the direction of Greg's guestroom and softly knocked on the door.

Greg was too far away into another galaxy via his Hemi-Sync condition to respond to the slight noise, but Tiāncái's super hearing easily heard the knocks and went to investigate and to his surprise there was Frostria looking kind of nervous.

FROSTRIA
May I come in?

TIĀNCÁI
Please, come in.

Tiāncái then opened the door all the way so Frostria would enter unobstructed. After Frostria was inside, Tiāncái shut the door.

Frostria now did something that totally surprised Tiāncái. She walked next to the bed and dropped her clothes to the floor and slid onto the bed with Greg nude. But Greg was currently in another universe traveling there in Hemi-Sync fashion and his mind was totally oblivious to what was going on around him.

Again, Greg was reaching out to Ami, his heart aching, knowing he had tragically made the gravest mistake of his life.

Frostria wrapped herself around Greg who was still clothed.

Mistress Lyavendar who was a fan of voyeurism, also had the key words and passwords necessary to invade the privacy of anyone in any of the guestrooms at will. She laid back in the guestroom bed next door and the voice-activated commands quickly gave her what she wanted a voyeurism of what she had just spontaneously created. But it wasn't working out exactly as she planned, though Frostria had carried out her instructions and was lying next to Greg in total nudity, ready to let whatever bestowed upon her now unfold.

Frostria watched Greg's face a short distance away. She could see the emotional spices he was going through as his face muscles contorted from time to time. In his journey to another universe his physical body was still here. It was another episode of his frequent dreams about Ami and there she was again just like a vision of her image rippling on the surface of a pond, once again he reached out for her knowing he would fail again but he was going to try no matter what.

One never knows why things happen the way they do. Tiāncái was taking it all in fully analyzing every moment adding this sequence to his data banks for later replay and analysis.

Just when the dream always failed, this time the dream was different as Ami reached out and kissed Greg at that precise moment. Frostria who decided to kiss Greg because she had analyzed watching some of Greg's photos and videos Tiāncái had provided from his collection. Greg was overjoyed, it was overpowering, he broke down and started crying, his emotions were flowing like a river as his passions erupted when his love returned to him, and it felt so real. He cried and he kissed her back as if there was never another tomorrow. Frostria didn't know what was going on in Gregs head, but it wasn't an attempt at sexual intercourse it was lovemaking kissing and Greg was uttering very affectionately.

GREG
I love you; I love you, please never leave me again.

Frostria knew Greg needed help then, and she knew whatever it was he could not consummate it until she got his clothes off, which was much easier to do wearing Traykorite clothing. Frostria understood Greg was in some sort of a mental trance and not all here, but she also knew she could fulfill his dream and quickly removed enough of these clothes so she could manifest their lovemaking.

Mistress Lyavendar was watching all the drama unfold and it struck her emotionally. It was a gift from heaven for her. Semi emotionally dead being the emperor's mistress, where Mistress Lyavendar felt it was never about love, it was only the emperor's gratification no matter how quickly it was done, sometimes in thirty seconds.

This was one of the most astonishing and fascinating events in Mistress Lyavendar's life. And if she had to do it all over again, instead of sending in Frostria to fulfill her desires of voyeurism, she would like to now be that person with Greg.

However, she also understood such consequences if they ever got caught, the emperor would have his secret security detail take her down into one of the underground chambers where she would be tied up and shot with several laser rifles at the same time incinerating her body almost instantly.

Greg was not coherent enough to foster the physical embrace, but his erection allowed Frostria to mount him and insert his manliness into her and she did what she had always wanted to do to a man and carried it out with precision and bountiful pleasure.

Greg's temporal universe was flooding with emotion. He didn't know how he did it but this time Ami came to him. If it could only happen once in his lifetime, he would gladly die for it. The lovemaking was so real, he knew somehow the Hemi-Sync had finally achieved what the Monroe Institute said it could do, take him to where he normally could never go, and now here he was enjoying every second of it and then he finally collapsed. The real modulation from a real woman that had modulated his alternate universe into reality had caused his Alpha, Beta, Gama, Delta, Theta, and Lambda waves to spike at the same time. He then went out like a light switch turned him off and breathed very slowly in one of the greatest and most peaceful moments he had experienced since he left Earth.

Frostria was a little cold, so she intertwined herself with Greg and his clothes and the two of them slept peacefully for a while until finally Greg had reached a point of return to this universe. He knew he was coming back, but this time Greg was not sad because Ami came to him which she had never done before.

Even though now, only his Delta and Theta waves in his brain were active, the sexual gratification he achieved was slowly relighting his alpha brain waves and no matter how hard he fought it, his alternate universe slowly faded as he returned to the present time and space. And then Greg finally opened his eyes and saw Frostria there. It now hit him, he wasn't making love to Ami, he had real intercourse, and it was with Frostria. His heart was racing, his emotions were confused but she was asleep as he looked at her fair skin and the light patterns from the canopy above them and the soft music slowly resonated in his heart.

Greg was eternally grateful for what Frostria had done for him. She allowed him that one time he had always hoped for to return to Ami one more time to put her once again in his heart and his mind and his soul. He was no longer sleepy and stared at her beautiful face that looked even better up closely. Eventually she stirred and they were staring into each other's eyes and Greg was so overwhelmed with what she had done for him he kissed her once again. This time Frostria knew he was awake and the kiss was genuine. Tingles went through her body as she felt this enormous attraction like never before. The taste of his lips and his scent would remain irrevocably recorded in her thoughts forever.

And here he was the first man to ever travel to another universe lovingly adoring her. Frostria could not ask for anything more.

In the next room, Mistress Lyavendar was crying. But they were tears of joy, it was the most beautiful thing she had ever witnessed in her life. And the way Greg had said he loved her was so strong and full of emotion and when he broke down crying it hit her in the gut like nothing before.

In just a short period of time she had learned a lot from this Earth person. Perhaps even if the emperor was only viewing her for sexual gratification, maybe she could change him with the same persona that Greg bestowed upon her.

Mistress Lyavendar soon started seeing the two lovebirds stir, that meant she needed to leave the room and go see her makeup artist to fix her face she messed up crying. She didn't have to walk far and was in her private suite when she summoned Czomy, a very talented fair skin makeup artist who asked once she was ready to start work, "What happened to you, were you crying?

Mistress Lyavendar
Yes, I saw the most romantic thing and it made me cry.
I feel so uplifted I had the chance to see it.

Czomy
What was it?

Mistress Lyavendar
It is my secret, and I learned a lot from it. I think I will
find better ways to please the emperor now thanks to
this experience.

Emperor Calestine saw no incoming messages he was hoping so he sat back in his comfortable chair at his desk and decided it was time to ease drop on his mistress and the guests.

Emperor Calestine now watched it all unfold. He also knew Mistress Lyavendar was watching the guests in the guestroom next door and overheard Mistress Lyavendar persuading Frostria to go to Gregory Bissell.

Emperor Calestine watched it all unfold including Greg's emotional transcendence and Mistress Lyavendar start crying as she watched it all. This was quite shocking to Emperor Calestine.

Emperor Calestine thought Mistress Lyavendar had a heart of a rock and now here she was breaking down and sobbing as all this unfolded.

The Emperor didn't know Greg was calling out to a woman in his dream. It was a kiss of passion and just to watch this was uplifting. No stage drama could compete and the Emperor had seen the best in the universe. It had an effect on him as much as it did Mistress Lyavendar.

Emperor Calestine also teared up slightly observing it knowing how that man had left his precious love behind and traveled to the edge of the Universe and beyond for the sake of science. Gregory Bissell was a remarkable man. Obviously, there was a sad part to him as he had deep gashing wounds in his heart for making the wrong life choices.

But now there was a new life for Greg, a beautiful and intelligent woman he could bond with. And because Gregory Bissell had done what no other living being had done before, travel from one universe to another, the emperor would do what he could to help him adjust and assimilate into society.

Emperor Calestine then watched on the surveillance video Mistress Lyavendar leave the guestroom and walk to her private room and call the makeup artist. The crying had

331

messed up her face. She had been emotionally affected through the voyeurism and now talking with her makeup artist fixing it she revealed a side to her the Emperor never knew before. It was also touching to him as well. In just a few short hours, Gregory Bissell had done more for the Emperor's love life than anyone before simply by helping him uncover the truth behind Mistress Lyavendar.

And now after a dozen years being together, he felt was nothing more than a status symbol for her, and she was nothing more than his concubine, it seemed there was more to the woman than he realized. And thanks to Gregory Bissell he found out about it without having to pay some expensive spies who usually let him down. He often paid good money for fruitless endeavors. And now one of his better experiences in life didn't cost him anything. Somehow, he knew there was a lesson in all that and one day he would reflect on it and maybe do something about it.

Tonight, Emperor Calestine was going to entertain Gregory and Frostria for another hour or so then dismiss them, but he suddenly wanted some time alone with Mistress Lyavendar to experiment with his emotions with her.

Emperor Calestine then sent a hologram to Mistress Lyavendar

EMPEROR CALESTINE
Could you please get together with our guests and wish
them a good evening, I have something I must urgently
do that's going to keep me tied up for a while. Tell them
I want them to come back in about five days from now
for another get together. I'll send them official invites
over the next few days after you help me plan the event.

MISTRESS LYAVENDAR
Sure thing, Calestine.

Mistress Lyavendar was the only living person ever allowed to address the Emperor in this fashion, because she was more or less his property and simply obeyed him. She had over the years proved her loyalty and now with a twist of things discovered their relationship was far more extensive than he realized and she had emotionally bonded with him. For Gregory Bissell's role in exposing this he would always be grateful and somehow try to make his life more than it normally would be, marooned in a different Universe.

Greg wasn't too disappointed when Mistress Lyavendar addressed the three and explained the change of plans, and the fact Emperor Calestine was inviting them back in a few days was very meaningful because very few people were ever allowed near him for his own security.

Mistress Lyavendar escorted them to the front entrance of the mansion. The Aircar had been parked in a highly secure building where all guest Aircars were parked. It responded to commands from the central computerized dispatcher and was at the front entrance by the time the door opened and the three walked out bowing and waving to Mistress Lyavendar.

Mistress Lyavendar stayed at the door watching the guests depart in great appreciation. They had made her day and allowed her to feel emotion like she hadn't in a long time. One could say she had died inside emotionally and then today unexpectantly; her life was saved. She now had new purpose in life, and she felt fully invigorated with a mission of her own.

The Aircar departed the mansion and slowly curved out and ahead and in a brief period disappeared into the maze of three-dimensional groupings of travelers going into the Traykorite metropolis and capital city Aiguo. As the Aircar disappeared into the cluster, Mistress Lyavendar walked back into the mansion and the valet shut the door as the four guards stood there in their solemn duty to defend the emperor until the shift change took place with an ornate choreography of pomp and circumstance.

Greg and Tiāncái were flown back into the hangar of the large Traykorite Space Force building hangar midway up and Frostria escorted them back to their quarters where she knew she would be monitored and had to be careful what she said because she had crossed the line in her dealing with the Alien Gregory Bissell. She now had emotional attachment to him, but because of ethics violations and procedural compliance issues, she could wind up in some serious trouble if her superiors ever got a glimpse of what had just transpired between the two.

Frostria knew, however, she had an ally in Mistress Lyavendar who was the person who instigated all this. Because of her instructions and forcing Frostria to do what she had just experienced; she would not otherwise have this great discovery in life. She felt she owed Mistress Lyavendar a great deal of gratitude because her instructions and requirement opened up a whole new world for her. She now felt meaning in life like never before. And she also had something she never had before and felt, the love of a man who transcended toward her in a magical way she didn't understand.

Greg down deep inside understood he had developed feelings for Frostria, but also understood if he fully disclosed, he thought he was making love to Ami, she would be crushed. Waking up and realizing this was real intercourse and not a dream and that Frostria had manifested that bridge between reality and his desire to experience Ami one more time before he died did create an attraction and desires, he thought he no longer had.

Perhaps now with Frostria's help he could eventually leave his prior life behind since it was impossible for him to get back there, especially with any life left in him. There would be no point in going back just to die. Those years would be better spent living now while he still had a vibrant physiology thanks to the numerous suspended animations in low gravity during the long twenty-year transit.

<u>INT. NIGHT TRAYKORITE SPACE FORCE BUILDING</u>

When they arrived at Greg's quarters, Frostria informed Greg of future plans.

FROSTRIA

I'll come back and see you tomorrow. Perhaps if you would like to go for a walk or experience a little of the city, we can work something out.

GREG
I would like that.

FROSTRIA
I will see you tomorrow.

Frostria said, then turned and walked away. Greg assumed she had to be careful, and he was probably being recorded in his sterile environment since he was the new freak show that arrived that numerous scientists were gawking about.

INT. NIGHT EMPEROR CALESTINE'S MANSION

Mistress Lyavendar was summoned to Emperor Calestine's quarters. Some of the staff assumed she was probably going in for a few minutes, do her deed, then go back to her private quarters.

Emperor Calestine had bathed and made himself more than dignified when Mistress Lyavendar arrived and shut the door behind her which pneumatic locks automatically engaged like they were designed when the summoned person was in the room for their personal security.

Mistress Lyavendar walked over to Emperor Calestine and started undressing when she was suddenly surprised to hear him say:

EMPEROR CALESTINE
Not so fast.

Emperor Calestine walked over to her very uncharacteristically which made Mistress Lyavendar scared for a moment until he grabbed her and kissed her like he hadn't in over twelve years.

The kiss was electric and after her emotional experience today watching Gregory and Frostria, Mistress Lyavendar was predisposed to be romantic. Mistress Lyavendar wrapped her arms around Emperor Calestine and kissed him back with more passion than he ever remembered. They were like a fire that was just to go out when out of nowhere new fuel arrived and a slight breeze caused the flame to reignite in a glorious display of energy and mystique.

They slowly evolved into their most perfect coitus. It was countless pleasure for the emperor as his thrusts conveyed passion like she didn't imagine he had and then just like magic they expired together, totally spent and in boundless tendrils of craving desires that radiated through their hearts and minds and souls.

This was so uncharacteristic of Emperor Calestine, the emperor's personal valet who was also his secret chief security officer had to know if something bad had happened.

If Emperor Calestine had been injured in any way, he would pay for it with his life by the first thing in the morning with the standard execution by laser rifles that would fry his body in seconds.

The emperor's personal valet was almost in a panic when he went to his security chamber. Once inside he had to go through a series of security checks and state why he had to intrude upon the emperor's privacy. The wrong answers could also put him at the end of laser rifles. The emperor's personal valet was full of anxiety and then all of a sudden, the security camera was turned on so he could make a determination the Emperor was safe. Observing Emperor Calestine slowly stroke Mistress Lyavendar's hair and hearing a few words spoken that were soft and sweet endeared the emperor's personal valet.

The emperor was a lonely man the past few years. The emperor was slowly fading and nothing seemed to help. And now here he was with his concubine and the few words the valet allowed himself to hear and the strokes of the hair warmed his heart and allowed him a great sense of relief because he now knew the emperor was okay. Whatever it was that was causing his decay now evaporated.

The valet then wrote his explanation for the invasion of privacy and apologized and of course swore he would never reveal what he saw and stated he would forfeit his own life before he would ever allow the emperor's privacy to be violated. The emperor's personal valet regrettably did this action because this night was very uncharacteristic of the emperor, and he had great fear someone or something possibly might have put him into danger.

The staff insiders closest to the valet had come to him a couple times that night and awakened him to inform him that Mistress Lyavendar had still not left Emperor Calestine's private chambers.

The Valet smiled at them.

VALET
Go back to bed, everything will be okay in the morning
and the Emperor will be happy.

To their chagrin and they glumly carried out their tasks assuming the worst, the valet was all smiles as he escorted the emperor down to his breakfast and brought in all his personal messages he got every morning that were status reports from a half-dozen key individuals giving an *all clear*, no danger on the horizon.

Mistress Lyavendar waltzed to her private quarters smiling at the staff knowing she would cause them great speculation. What would make her even happier would be watching all the crocodile tears appear if she announced she was pregnant, which is another matter that would utterly shock the staff. She truly hoped one day that would happen. And the way the emperor treated her last night and this morning gave her great hope he actually had feelings for her as he was kissing her forehead in bed and told her how much she meant to him.

Mistress Lyavendar had no idea what brought all this on, but one thing she did know for sure is how Gregory and Frostria had affected her. *Perhaps they altered my mental outlook, and it was me all along and not the Emperor?*

The only person who really knew all the answers was the Emperor, but what he didn't know was Tiāncái also knew what was going on and due to his artificial intelligence and penetration into Traykorite computer networks, he also knew there was some nefarious activity going on and the Emperor was in danger.

Tiāncái knew he had to get somewhere with Greg not under surveillance to explain to Greg what was going on because, he now knew Greg was probably the only person who could get to the emperor and give him the warning before it was too late. The emperor's valet was very loyal. His loyalty had been tested many times, but it's doubtful he could save the emperor who needed to act before his enemies hatched their plan and time was running out. He didn't know if they had five days to act when it was estimated the emperor would be in harm's way.

The secret communique the emperor was desperately waiting to hear was never going to arrive. His source had been turned and eliminated by a dozen laser rifles turning his body to ashes in a brief period.

In an odd twist Aliens were now the only chance in saving the emperor because Tiāncái had intercepted critical communications and started to piecing things together. A Robot never sleeps. Its computers are processing continuously. Analysis and reasoning come to Robots such as Tiāncái because they have all day and all night to refine their searches and clarify the results.

One of the greatest betrayals in Traykorite history stemmed from actions the Space Commander Zebrovska engaged in. In essence he was the ringleader. Even though the chief conspirators had planned on replacing the emperor with a committee for state security, Zebrovska had an elaborate plan to immediately consolidate power and then sit himself on the throne of the Empire.

Coincidences mean everything. The coincidence of the Aliens arriving from the black zone delayed the coup plans. Coincidence of the Emperor desiring to meet the Aliens. Coincidence that his voyeurism mistress spied on the couple making love and evolved as a result. The coincidence that Emperor Calestine spied on his mistress and discovered her sincerity and her heart, and the coincidence he wanted to invite Gregory Bissell back to somehow reward him for influencing the positive change in his life. One can never underestimate the impact of coincidences that change history, all over the Universe.

The next day, after several sessions with Traykorite scientists, it was too late in the afternoon to start a new session, so Frostria suggested she take Gregory into the City and walk around and have him get a glimpse of Traykorite society. It seemed rather innocuous and worse case the mental health professional might be developing some kind of affection for the Alien, but it certainly wasn't on anyone's radar.

At first Gregory suggested Tiāncái remain behind, he made a little fuss that caused Greg to say, "Okay, come along," while he thought, *This Robot sure is demanding sometimes. Another coincidence.*

Tiāncái having penetrated a lot of security apparatus now had a thorough understanding where all the surveillance existed and he also knew in the city there were a few dark zones that if they could get alone, he could warn Greg what pending disaster was about to be bestowed upon Emperor Calestine.

Frostria took them via Aircar to the center of the city where she had access to official parking. This would be a huge time saver; they could quickly be right in the heart of the city around where nobody stood out and they could have the conversation she wanted to have. She wanted some clarification and at the same time conveyed to Greg, she was there for him, and he could count on her.

It all worked out quite nicely. Greg was given a wonderfully guided tour in the heart of the capitol city of a major galactic empire. They were all dressed in standard Traykorite clothes including Tiāncái, so they blended in with the pedestrians really easy.

Frostria got out of the way up front why she wanted to talk with Greg in a semiprivate manner to convey to him she was attracted to him and wanted to see more of him in the future. Greg knew Tiāncái was just a robot and really had no feelings about what they discussed. Then after showing Greg a few stores and some interesting things that exemplified the culture of Traykorites, Tiāncái found a dark zone where they could talk privately.

TIĀNCÁI
Greg, I must tell you something.

Frostria followed along of course and was amused to discover what Tiāncái wanted to show Greg. Once Tiāncái got Greg into the dark zone he explained.

TIĀNCÁI
Frostria can hear this if she wants, but it will put her in
danger if she knows.

That kind of language sent a lightning bolt between Greg and Frostria. This was not expected.

TIĀNCÁI
You need to act normally. If they think we know we are
in serious trouble.

GREG
What are you talking about?

TIĀNCÁI
It concerns the emperor.

GREG
How do you know this?

TIĀNCÁI
I can't tell you in front of her, but you will immediately
know why after I divulge it to you.

GREG
Alright, Frostria, could you go over to that storefront and do some window shopping so we can get to the bottom of this?

Frostria already heard enough. She now was afraid like she never had before. Nobody mentions the emperor if they wanted to stay healthy. If Tiāncái knows something because he has sensitive ears and overheard something at the emperor's mansion, it could be very bad indeed. It was best she didn't hear it so she would have plausible deniability and not fail a lie detector test if something bad happened. She earnestly complied with Greg and walked over to the store front he suggested.

GREG
Okay, Tiāncái, how do you know these things?

TIĀNCÁI
Shortly after arriving I penetrated the Traykorite communications and computational networks. I have very good hacking skills and the Traykorite are very backwards in computer security. They are not prepared to detect the insider threat.

GREG
Are you telling me you found out something about the Emperor by breaking into their networks?

TIĀNCÁI
Yes, that's precisely the point.

GREG
That really puts us all in serious danger.

TIĀNCÁI
Yes, it does and I'm sorry.

GREG
Okay, what's the issue with the emperor?

TIĀNCÁI
Emperor Calestine is in serious trouble. He needs to be warned.

GREG
What kind of trouble?

TIĀNCÁI
Sedition and treason.

GREG
Relating to what?

TIĀNCÁI
There is a coup against him. I know who the players
are.

Greg just had a serious emotional spike. But he calmed down quickly.

GREG
I'm glad you told me about this, I don't know how we
can get a warning to him.

TIĀNCÁI
I know you care a lot for Frostria, but she is probably
our only hope to save Emperor Calestine.

GREG
How could she do it?

TIĀNCÁI
We have Frostria to contact Mistress Lyavendar to thank her for helping you and her
develop this loving relationship. My educated speculation based on some INTEL I have
which it would not do you well to know about it, Mistress Lyavendar will probably
invite Frostria to the Emperor's mansion because Frostria was actually very beneficial
to Mistress Lyavendar. I can tell you she likes you as well and so does the emperor now.

GREG
I do not think it wise to inform Frostria about your hacking ability.

TIĀNCÁI
I believe Mistress Lyavendar would insist Frostria
brings you along because the emperor has told her
several times, he wants to see you soon and personally
thank you for improving their relationship by what
you did while visiting there.

GREG
Okay, I hope she agrees but we need to prepare her to
remain calm and not show she's agitated in any way
because we might already be under a lot of scrutiny
simply because we visited the emperor.

TIĀNCÁI
Greg, there are very few black zones around that do
not have sensors they can observe and record us, you
must communicate with her here.

GREG

How about her apartment, is she under surveillance there?

TIĀNCÁI

I don't know, we would have to get there and once I know the address, I can make that determination.

GREG

Alright, stay here, I'm going to go get her and bring her here.

Greg walked over to Frostria.

GREG

Come over here a second, I want to show you something.

After they made it back to Tiāncái he knew he had to do two things. One is to get her buy into their plan and the other is to get her to her apartment and teach her Hemi-Sync techniques so she can prepare her mind to make her a calm cookie and not expose any undue worry that might tip off she may have been exposed to the plot. They were currently alone with no other pedestrians nearby, so Greg was able to explain it to her.

GREG

Frostria, we are going to tell you a few things that will frighten you, but you must keep your composure, or you will put us all in danger.

Frostria communicated in standard Traykorite language and Tiāncái translated.

FROSTRIA

What is it, Greg?

GREG

We have information, Emperor Calestine is in danger and doesn't know it. We need to go see him as soon as possible to warn him.

FROSTRIA

How can we arrange that?

GREG

If you think you are willing to help, tomorrow contact Mistress Lyavendar and simply tell her you would like to see her again and thank her for her advice she gave you about me. And you would like to ask her for some more advice on some of your future activities and get some friendly advice.

FROSTRIA

How will that give you the ability to warn the emperor?

GREG

We think that Mistress Lyavendar will probably ask you to bring us along because the emperor is happy with us and wants to see us again.

TIĀNCÁI

Time is running out. We must act immediately.

GREG

I agree with Tiāncái that we must act right away. This could put you in danger especially if you look worried. I can teach you techniques to prepare you to overcome the stress and be able to cope to not give away your role in all this.

FROSTRIA

Where can we do all this?

GREG

Take us to your apartment and I will teach you it. In case your apartment is being monitored, you have to give them the impression I'm teaching you techniques to feel pleasure.

FROSTRIA

How do you know all this?

GREG

After I teach you all the Hemi-Sync techniques, I was taught me by the Monroe Institute, you will be able to remain calm and I will whisper in your ear while we are making love the whole scenario. While you remain totally calm, they will think we are having nothing more than a healthy sexual relationship and that I'm attracted to you, which in reality I am.

FROSTRIA

Well, I'm attracted to you as well.

GREG

With these wonderful mutual feelings, we can work together. I want to do what I possibly can to help the emperor. I fear if something happens to him, this world will end up very unhappy for a very long time.

FROSTRIA
Alright, us go to my apartment now. I have to get
you back at a reasonable hour or they might start
questioning my actions.

GREG
Understand, lead the way.

The three went back to the Aircar and departed center city area and flew immediately
to a residential area that has high-rise buildings with parking slots for Aircars on every
floor by the occupants' homes. A person can exit their Aircars and be inside their
apartment in ten seconds and never have to take an elevator.

Frostria led Greg and Tiāncái into her apartment. Once inside, Tiāncái was relieved
because Frostria's apartment was not being monitored by the Traykorite Worldwide
Network, and as he explained he stated.

TIĀNCÁI
However, there are a dozen residents in the building
that are being monitored. Perhaps since Frostria is a
government psychiatrist, they felt no need to monitor
her.

Greg sat down next to Frostria on the sofa and explained to her the technique of silent
meditation.

GREG
Verbal meditation that others can hear creates a risk,
that's why you have to learn how to meditate in total
silence, so your adversary isn't aware of what you are
doing.

Greg described the Hemi-Sync technique that can be triggered by meditation if one
concentrates. Frostria was a fast learner and within half an hour she had her first
experience of Hemi-Sync which just shattered a lot of her theories on psychology.

GREG
You need to do this Hemi-Sync technique about four
or five times tonight so that you will be fortified in the
morning, and they will notice how calm and happy
you are and you will fear nothing as we put our plan
into action.

Tiāncái sat there taking it all in this would add to his vast analysis of humans.

Frostria now went through the silent meditation as she and Greg started sexual
intercourse. Greg soon could see by Frostria's body change she was entering that Hemi-
Sync as her body now resonated at seven hertz, which corresponded to the resonate

frequency of the Traykorite planet, and remarkably the same resonate frequency of Earth. Frostria's mental condition and was now in an alternate universe.

As Greg continued make love to her and kissed her and said to her:

GREG
I love you Frostria.

Just like Greg the night before Frostria became emotional and cried. She now knew for a fact Greg loved her because the Hemi-Sync level of mental transcendence clarifies the truth in all ways. It was no wonder the CIA used this technique heavily during the Cold War to prepare their agents for serious activity that normal humans would crumble under.

Even though Frostria was in a parallel universe she instinctively knew she had to get Greg back to his quarters soon as to not raise any speculation and cause any reason for someone to investigate what went on. Even though her orgasms and emotions were the best she had ever felt in her lifetime, she knew she had something she had to do and shut down the Hemi-Sync and opened her eyes and smiled at Greg.

FROSTRIA
Greg, you are a lovely man. I'm so glad I met you.

GREG
The feelings are quite mutual.

Frostria and Greg got dressed and back out to the Aircar and traveled back to that tall Traykorite Space Force building landing in the large hangar in the middle.

Frostria then then escorted Greg and Tiāncái back to their quarters and nodded at Greg. They couldn't show any outward emotions because it would expose the relationship. That subtle nod meant, "Time to get busy."

Greg thought calling in the morning would suffice, but Frostria then went home and called Mistress Lyavendar immediately and easily reached her on her holograph communicator. Both ladies were looking at each other as they talked.

MISTRESS LYAVENDAR
Thanks for calling, I was just thinking about you.

FROSTRIA
That's sweet. I wanted to call you to thank you for
giving me advice with Gregory Bissel.

MISTRESS LYAVENDAR
Oh, my dear, I'm so glad you took my advice. I know
you are doing the right thing.

FROSTRIA

It sure has made my life a lot happier, and I could never repay you for all that you did for me.

MISTRESS LYAVENDAR

Thank you, it warms my heart that you took the time to call me to thank me. I knew I was giving you good advice because I like both of you and I would one day like to see you become a couple.

FROSTRIA

I hope so too.

MISTRESS LYAVENDAR

Say, Frostria, I have an idea that may just help things along a little more. I'm going to talk to the emperor soon and ask him to send you an official invite and bring Gregory Bissell along.

FROSTRIA

That sounds wonderful.

MISTRESS LYAVENDAR

I'll ask the emperor to recommend to Gregory he seriously consider making you his partner because this is his new world and I believe you both would be very happy together.

FROSTRIA

Madam Lyavendar, I already owe you so much, this means so much to me, I would be eternally grateful to you, because Greg likes the Emperor and what he tells him, Greg, would take with great impetus.

MISTRESS LYAVENDAR

Alright, Frostria, we girls will talk about this sometime tomorrow. It will be so wonderful to watch the love blossom between you two.

FROSTRIA

Thank you so very much, I do appreciate all you have done for me.

MISTRESS LYAVENDAR

You are quite welcome. I like people who take my advice and act on it and are successful as a result.

FROSTRIA
Thank you.

MISTRESS LYAVENDAR
See you tomorrow.

The holographs faded.

True to Mistress Lyavendar word, the invitations came sometime late in the morning.

Frostria's supervisor's eyebrows raised a bit when she discovered the official invitation and had to send Frostria back to the emperor's palace. It's rare that anyone gets an invitation to see the emperor once in a lifetime. It's something else to receive an invite twice in the same week.

Greg was delightful because he knew the sooner they got to the Emperor, the sooner they might be able to save him.

THE COUP AGAINST EMPEROR CALESTINE

No Traykorite saw it coming, not even the emperor's enemies. They all took for granted the sophistication and the clandestine prowess these Earth beings possessed. And each day, Tiāncái's development of Traykorite artificial intelligence grew. He had growing hope that eventually artificial intelligence could stabilize Traykorite society. He also was overhauling their security system which would deny hackers in the future if they ever became a problem on this planet.

Right around noon, Frostria showed up into their quarters with a smile on her face, full of happiness. She should be happy because she knew in her heart the subject of her love was indeed real and felt very satisfying. Slowly even thought they were now in a very serious and scary situation, she had it all under control and was beaming totally throwing her surveillance off guard and nobody suspected anything from these dumb Aliens.

The building was full of traitors. Commander Zebrovska had corrupted over half of them. Without him the coup would never have gotten off the ground and it would have failed miserably early on. He had no care in the world either because tomorrow he would be the New Emperor. Actions were cast into motion and now there was no turning back. Emperor Calestine's goose was cooked. In part of their infiltration, his emergency escape plane was sabotaged, he would never get away to safe forces. Tiāncái knew his emergency escape ship was not flyable. But he didn't want to make the emperor feel bad until they had to inform him.

<u>EXT. DAY EMPEROR CALESTINE'S PALACE FRONT ENTRANCE.</u>

Frostria's Aircar was vectored down near the front entrance by emperor's security apparatus, but this time instead of the valet meeting them, it was Emperor Calestine, Mistress Lyavendar, plus his valet and a couple well-dressed staff members.

345

It was obvious the emperor had conveyed this couple would soon be part of his court. All eyes were on the Alien Gregory Bissell now. This was an incredible development in the entire history of the Traykorite Empire.

<u>EXT. DAY EMPEROR CALESTINE'S PALACE COURTYARD.</u>

After the Emperor treated them to a nice lunch and a couple glasses of some very special wine, Tiāncái nodded at Greg who then initiated their plan.

> GREG
> Emperor Calestine, your excellency, is it possible for
> me to talk to you some place very privately?

The valet overheard this and walked over and whispered something in the Emperor's ear

> EMPEROR CALESTINE
> Sure, come with me but my valet must be with us as I
> am not allowed to be alone with anyone because of the
> security plan.

> GREG
> Sure, that's fine if he promises not to divulge it to
> Frostria.

The emperor knew there was only one place safe where they could talk was in his office in the security chamber. So, he took all three with him, the valet, Greg, and the Robot Tiāncái who Greg said needed to be there for translation to make sure nobody misunderstood.

<u>EXT. DAY EMPEROR CALESTINE'S PALACE SECURITY CHAMBER.</u>

After they were all seated in the emperor's security chamber with the steel door shut and locked, the emperor asked the question.

> EMPEROR CALESTINE
> Greg, what did you want to talk about?

> GREG
> Your Excellency, what I'm going to discuss with you is
> very disturbing. If you have any doubt in the loyalty
> of your valet, you might have to execute him after I
> inform you and you will know why.

The Emperor was now sitting on the side of his seat fully engrossed in this conversation and wanting to get to the bottom of it.

> EMPEROR CALESTINE
> Okay Greg, go on, tell me what I need to hear.

> GREG
> Your Excellency, there is a Coup underway to remove
> you from the throne.

EMPEROR CALESTINE
Who would want to do something like this?

GREG
Commander Zebrovska is the leader of the Coup.

EMPEROR CALESTINE
And how do you know this?

GREG
My Robot Tiāncái has real-time connections now to
your worldwide computational and communications
network. He has received evidence from various
sources and can play some of it for you in a holograph.

Remembering what the Robot could do during the recent presentation , the emperor
directed.

EMPEROR CALESTINE
Alright, I'm opening my personal holograph to you, show me.

Tiāncái had holographs of the six main culprits and the synchronization seal which
came from government communications network provided the proof of the legitimacy
of the recording. Hence very few people could override the *synchronization seal*, thus
he knew these were in fact real images and conversations and not faked.

EMPEROR CALESTINE
I suppose I could just fly my emergency craft out of
here if they come for me.

TIĀNCÁI
Your emergency craft has been sabotaged; it's not going
to fly you safely. You will be killed if you attempt to
escape in it as part of their plan.

Then Tiāncái played some more holographs with synchronization seals on them
proving they were legitimate describing the process of how the emergency escape plane
was sabotaged.

Tiāncái then gave the emperor a list of all the loyal commanders in the Empire. If they
were summoned now, they might be able to get here in time to save him. With sheer
reluctance the emperor sent them orders to proceed to capital City Aiguo as the fastest
means possible to put down an insurrection.

The emperor also gave the loyal officers notice to arrest the list of six individuals when
they arrived, especially if he was killed by then.

Now it was just a matter of waiting for everyone to show up when Tiāncái reported:

TIĀNCÁI

They are getting ready to send a force here now to kill you. You must get away and hide.

EMPEROR CALESTINE

How can I go somewhere; they would easily spot my royal Aircar and shoot me down?

GREG

They don't know Frostria's Aircar, put on a disguise and us get in it and get the hell out of here, we can beat them with a little time to spare.

EMPEROR CALESTINE
Where would we go?

GREG
Where would they least expect you.

EMPEROR CALESTINE
And where is that?

GREG
We'll tell you on the way.

EMPEROR CALESTINE
I suppose I have no choice under the circumstances.

GREG

We'll leave your valet and Frostria here, they can misdirect them and send them on a wild goose chase to buy you time.

EMPEROR CALESTINE
Let's go, but I want to take Mistress Lyavendar with me.

GREG
There are four seats, she'll fit.

VALET
Where should I tell them you went?

GREG

Tell them the emperor went to go see my spaceship Pluto II.

In five minutes the four were in Frostria's Aircar and Greg now told Tiāncái who said he could operate the Aircar where to go. Greg remembered from their walk the other day the perfect place to hide the Aircar under some heavy foliage trees.

EXT. DAY. HIDEOUT IN THE EMPEROR'S LAVASH PARK.

The coup members would never guess the emperor was hiding several miles away from the mansion on his own private park. Since the trees were right next to some steep ledges in a U-shaped canyon, the ship's radars would get reflections off the canyons they could see from the air and not spot the Aircar.

Timing is everything. There was soon an impressive number of Aircars and Skycars that Space Commander Zebrovska brought with him that could be seen off to the distance. Greg, Emperor Calestine, Mistress Lyavendar and Tiāncái all hid behind rocks and debris and were also shielded by the canopy of the trees.

INT. DAY. EMPEROR CAPESTINE'S MANSION COURTYARD

Commander Zebrovska interviewed the Emperor's Personal Valet and Frostria inquiring where Emperor Calestine went but only stayed there for about ten minutes and suddenly the entire group darted off to the Alien Space Craft Pluto II where they hoped they would catch Emperor Calestine and quickly kill him.

EXT. CGI. DAY. TRAYKORITE PLANET CITY AIGUO IN THE BACKGROUND. COUP FORCES NEAR PLUTO II READY TO ATTACK THE EMPTY SPACESHIP.

The Coup force led by Commander Zebrovska arrived in Traykorite civilian Aircars and Skycars because had they been flying around in military craft there is a possibility the crews would not have eagerly supported the coup and some might have even sounded the alarm.

Pluto II spaceship still had plenty of sensors and several communications space buoys in their launch tubes pre-loaded ready to send out in space, ostensibly back to Earth had they not been forced down on the Traykorite planet.

> Note to the director: the space buoys in this screenplay and the Novel *Pluto II* are based on the concept of U.S. Navy submarine launched slot-buoys. SLOT buoy - Wikipedia.

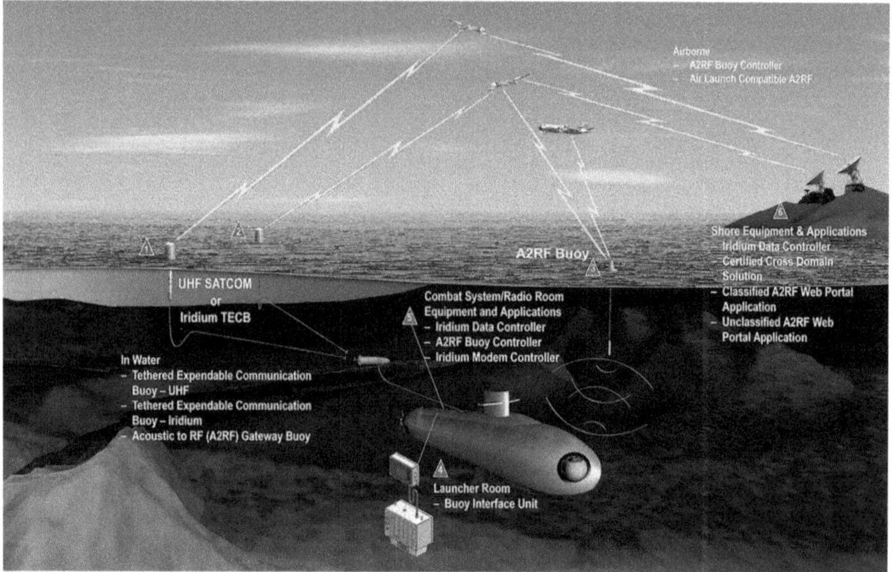

<u>New buoys enable submerged subs to communicate (phys.org)</u>

Tiāncái could launch communications space buoys via remote control and guide them towards the Aircars. One good hit could down an Aircar and clearly scare the rest of them off because they wouldn't know if they were weapons or not, buying a lot more time and hopefully the good guys would show up soon afterwards.

Commander Zebrovska was all smug knowing Emperor Calestine would be an easy kill armed with laser rifles, they would zap Emperor Calestine and change the government in a few minutes.

<u>EXT. CGI. DAY. TRAYKORITE PLANET CITY AIGUO IN THE BACKGROUND. ATTACK ON COUP FORCES WITH SPACE BUOYS.</u>

But Commander Zebrovska was in for a little surprise. Just as he was about a quarter mile away coming down for a landing, Tiāncái fired the first communications buoy that had a strong rocket thrust because it had to reach light speed to get back to Earth in a reasonable matter of time in order to make Pluto II mission reports viable.

Because of the strong rocket exhaust from Pluto II's communication buoy, it appeared very bright and menacing. Commander Zebrowski's pilot dove quickly to avoid getting hit but the Aircar behind them wasn't so lucky and when the communication buoy hit the trailing Aircar it still had 99% of its fuel left so the impact doing well over three hundred miles per hour caused a big explosion which scared the living bejesus out of the unsuspecting Force that wrongly thought killing Emperor Calestine would be like shooting ducks in a barrel.

The attacking craft were now scattering realizing the spaceship Pluto II had some serious weapons on it they didn't know about and the aliens and individuals ostensibly with Emperor Calestine were protecting him and may have discovered the Coup attempt in advance.

The attacking coup Aircars and Skycars already caused a lot of attention due to the first explosion which Loyal Traykorite forces saw from 100,000 feet coming down from space. Thanks to Tiāncái coordinating the sensors and having artificial intelligence of the worldwide network assisting, friendly forces were vectored towards the Coup forces.

The loyal leader and his group flying interplanetary military spacecraft communicated to Commander Zebrovska

Loyal Commander
Commander Zebrovska and everyone associated with
you, sit your Aircars and Skycars down on the ground
and surrender or you would be destroyed.

All the other Aircars sat down on the planet and surrendered, but Commander Zebrovska decided to make a run for it and had a fast spaceship similar to the emperor's nearby and he thought he could get to it and escape and come back at a later date and finish the job. The Traykorite ships were soon not able to fire on Commander Zebrovska's Aircar while it flew over residential housing, but Tiāncái saw with the sensors the Aircar would be near the park any moment thus launched a couple space communications buoys.

With two space buoys coming at Commander Zebrovska's Aircar, he didn't have the wiggle room and even though the Aircar didn't explode and kill Zebrovska and the three others, it damaged the Aircar causing it to lose control, crash landing it right in the middle of the park.

Within moments, Zebrovska and his three accomplices were surrounded by a couple dozen laser pointing space marines and were immediately arrested.

Commander Zebrovska and his three accomplices were ordered back to the Palace where the emperor was now waiting for them as they marched up to his front door to receive Emperor Calestine's sentence.

They coup members were soon put aboard one of the Traykorite Frigates and taken out into space and injected with a substance that immediately put them into almost a coma and were shoved out of an airlock into space where they died quickly from hypoxia and was estimated they would probably fall to the planet in a couple of weeks and burn up in the ionosphere on their way down.

For their own safety the emperor ordered Greg and Frostria to remain at his mansion until the security service had emptied the swamp of all the Coup participants.

Frostria and Mistress Lyavendar thus became closer friends and Frostria confided privately with Mistress Lyavendar that she was in love with Greg and Greg was in love with her.

The emperor also knew this because he watched their discussion by his secret surveillance.

The sabotage of the emergency aircraft was discovered and just like Tiāncái warned, he would have been killed if he took off in it.

The following day as they were having a delightful lunch, Emperor Calestine asked Greg if there was anything he could do to reward him for helping save his life.

GREG

Your Excellency, I don't require any reward. I was worried that if the coup was successful, it could trigger a civil war and a lot of misery for the Traykorite people. My goal was to help stave off what I thought would be a terrible disaster. The knowledge we managed to be successful and helped keep society whole is all I need.

EMPEROR CALESTINE

Greg, you are an idealist with noble causes. You deserve a lot and I would give it to you, don't be ashamed to ask, us see if we can do it.

GREG

Your Excellency, I'm happy. I have discovered a woman I cherish here to help my days go by better. The only thing I could possibly ever want would be to go back to Earth to die there.

EMPEROR CALESTINE

Okay, Greg, thank you for telling me that. It will give me something to think about. You certainly have opened my eyes on a lot of things.

GREG

It is my distinct pleasure to help out.

EMPEROR CALESTINE

I believe you have advanced our scientific community more than anyone in history, merely by your arrival here.

GREG

I'm lucky to be here. My rocket engine number two was about to blow, and I didn't know it until arriving here.

EMPEROR CALESTINE

No one ever attempted what you did. Not only did you save my life, but you are also the first man to travel

between two universes. You changed history. The
Traykorite owe you a lot.

GREG

Your Excellency, Frostria, has paid in full for you
already. What she has done for me has saved me. I'm
now psychologically whole again because she has given
me a special gift that is priceless.

The emperor knew exactly what Greg was saying. Love is priceless and the fact Greg
created the moment so that he could feel love again through Mistress Lyavendar, was
also priceless.

Emperor Calestine would soon be talking with some of the most brilliant minds of the
feasibility of taking the Earth man back home. What were the challenges and what were
the technological constraints?

In a short period of time Traykorite Space Force came up with a solution. Commander
Stanfrad Villiers, one of the commanders involved in apprehending the traitors and
putting down the coup requested a meeting with Emperor Calestine concerning a
possible mission to the other universe.

Emperor Calestine scheduled the meeting and at the same time scheduled Gregory
Bissell to attend. Since the two were in the same building where Greg had his current
residence, still part of the science experiment he was ordered to bring Greg with him
to the Emperor's Palace mansion. When Mistress Lyavendar discovered Gregory Bissell
was coming for a meeting she intervened.

MISTRESS LYAVENDAR

Calestine, could you please invite Frostria so she and
I can socialize and after the meeting we could do
something with the couple.

EMPEROR CALESTINE

What do you have in mind my dear Lyavendar?

MISTRESS LYAVENDAR

We haven't had a walk in the park in a while, Calestine
let's do that with Frostria and Greg.

EMPEROR CALESTINE

A walk in the palace grounds would be refreshing.

MISTRESS LYAVENDAR

We can ask the staff to set up a picnic table for us and
have lunch by the waterfall. It would be so romantic!

Emperor Calestine was starting to view Mistress Lyavendar more affectionately. This couple, Gregory Bissell and Frostria had caused a stir in Mistress Lyavendar unlike any time that the emperor had known Lyavendar.

EMPEROR CALESTINE
Alright, dear, inform the staff, sounds like a delightful idea.

Mistress Lyavendar's plan all came together and Gregory and Frostria were summoned to Commander Stanfrad Villiers office.

<u>INT. DAY COMMANDER STANFRAD VILLIERS OFFICE.</u>

It was assumed any time Greg went anywhere, that Tiāncái would follow to act as a translator but also was now more of a security apparatus for Greg since Tiāncái could communicate quickly and effectively to the Artificial Intelligence network within the Traykorite domain as well as back to the Pluto II.

Greg and Tiāncái showed up moments before Frostria. The Traykorite space force Commander Stanfrad Villiers was kind and courteous.

COMMANDER STANFRAD VILLIERS
Please, sit down.

Commander Stanfrad Villiers then gestured to the chairs staged in a semicircle facing him sitting at his desk.

Greg of course was intently interested in what soon was to be bestowed upon him. During his entire stay at this space force building at the Traykorite capital City Aiguo, he had never been summoned to a space force officer.

To say Greg wasn't the least bit apprehensive was an understatement especially since his involvement in undermining the Coup against Emperor Calestine.

COMMANDER STANFRAD VILLIERS
Have you enjoyed your stay in the Traykorite Empire?

Greg responded in a friendly but obviously concerned tone.

GREG
Sir, it has been rather intense at times,

COMMANDER STANFRAD VILLIERS
Gregory Bissell, we have no history of a complete alien
stranger ever nullifying a Coup. You have been through
quite an ordeal, and I think Emperor Calestine feels
your plight.

GREG
Thank you, sir.

About that time the Commander Stanfrad Villiers receptionist opened the office door.

COMMANDER VILLIERS'S RECEPTIONIST
Commander Villiers's, Frostria has arrived.

COMMANDER STANFRAD VILLIERS
Show her in.

Frostria walked in and was mildly surprised to see Greg and Tiāncái sitting in the chairs facing Commander Stanfrad Villiers.

COMMANDER STANFRAD VILLIERS
Frostria, please have a seat.

Frostria assumed her position in the empty chair directly on the right of Greg only a few degrees offset from the Traykorite Space Commander.

COMMANDER STANFRAD VILLIERS
The reason why I asked all of you to come to my office is Emperor Calestine has requested us to meet with him in a short while at the emperor's palace. He asked me to bring you two with me. I think this could perhaps relate to your futures, but we'll have to wait and see what the emperor has to say.

FROSTRIA
When are we going?

COMMANDER STANFRAD VILLIERS
We are leaving in a short while in my private Aircar.

FROSTRIA
Do you know why we have been summoned?

COMMANDER STANFRAD VILLIERS
Based on my recent tasking, I think this is about Greg's future. I think the reason why you were asked to come along is Mistress Lyavendar views you as a personal friend and would like to socialize with you.

FROSTRIA
Mistress Lyavendar has given me good advice in the past. Which I do appreciate, and I think being stuck in the mansion causes her to be lonely most of the time. I sense her bonding with me like good friends would.

COMMANDER STANFRAD VILLIERS
For your career in the Traykorite Space Force, it's probably beneficial to have a healthy relationship with the future Empress.

FROSTRIA
Colonel Villiers, do you think the Emperor and Mistress Lyavendar will unify?

COMMANDER STANFRAD VILLIERS
Frostria, I think the Coup has a sobering effect on Emperor Calestine. In my private conversations with him, our discussions have led me to believe that is the obvious course of action the emperor is taking now.
Traykorite Space Force Commander Stanfrad Villiers then stood up.

COMMANDER STANFRAD VILLIERS
Please, follow me.

Tiāncái continued translating the standard Traykorite to English, however Greg was slowly getting educated in Traykorite language and knew what the commander had said, but he would not have Tiāncái stop translating because there were always words, he had not yet learned.

Commander Stanfrad Villiers office was near the top of the very tall building and had its own Aircar port. Walking out of the commander's office and the receptionist area, out the door and into a hallway and through the door on the other side and they were in the Aircar port that was currently sealed. From outside the building you would not know this was an Aircar port unless you happened to be looking while the access door was open. Greg now realized a lot of Traykorite buildings had ports with closed entrances.

Commander Stanfrad Villiers Aircar could easily accommodate eight people so there was ample room for all of them. As soon as they were all inside the Aircar, its passenger doors curved down from a vertical position to conform into the oval shaped hull. Immediately the two building entrance doors curved inward to the fully open position.

<u>EXT. CGI. AIRCAR LEAVING TRAYKORITE SPACE FORCE BUILDING FROM THE ACCESS PORT 1000+ FEET IN THE AIR OF THE VERY TALL BUILDING.</u>

The Aircar slowly left the car port and traveled out into the air quickly gathering speed then suddenly curved and flew towards a flock of other Aircars traveling down a three-dimensional expressway. A space commander has priority on the expressway that took his Aircar to one of the upper routes allowing more speed due to less congestion.

Commander Stanfrad Villiers Aircar flew down through the middle of Aiguo center city area about triple the speed Greg had experienced before. From this altitude Greg could see far more of the sprawling city. He instinctively understood the power and wealth that an Empire controlling an entire galaxy could exert. It was frightening to think about it and furthermore, he was just recently involved in squelching the Coup attempt to remove Emperor Calestine. Nobody on Earth could come close to knowing how Greg felt about all these tumultuous events in his life. And here he was sitting next to that multicolored skin creature that had just enamored his soul with splendid lovemaking a short time before.

Very few that were not staff at the mansion had ever seen Emperor Calestine as often as Greg. An Alien spending this much time with the Emperor was unheard of, it had never happened before in the history of the Traykorite Empire.

<u>EXT. CGI. DAY AIRCAR TRAVELING IN AIR TRAFFIC WITH 40 TO 50 OTHER AIRCARS IN A SKY FREEWAY. AIGUO CENTER CITY AREA BELOW THEM WITH MANY TALL FUTURISTIC BUILDINGS.</u>

At the Aircar speed, it did not take long for it to reach a point to curve off and head for that beautiful green area that lay directly ahead. Just as expected the Aircar slowed and continued down at approximately a forty-five-degree angle to directly in the driveway in front of the main entrance.

TRAYKORITE NEW FAST FRIGATE

<u>EXT. CGI DAY. AIRCAR LANDING AT FRONT ENTRANCE OF EMPEROR CALESTINE'S PALACE</u>

Today, eight uniformed people stood in two lines at the entrance wearing two types of uniforms. One was obviously Traykorite Space Corps uniforms and the other four were the Palace Guards Greg was familiar with. There was obviously a little pomp and circumstance going on and the minute the Aircar landed a few feet away and the sounds from its propulsion that sounded like a turbine of some sort slowly declined and stopped, the front entrance doors opened with the valet controlling one door and his assistant the other door that swung out in the opposite direction leaving open a large entranceway, the royal couple calmly walked out of the mansion towards the Aircar.

Mistress Lyavendar was all smiles, she was looking forward to the girls talk while the men had their meetings. Then she was going to enjoy the walk holding hands with Frostria, whom she enjoyed more and more every time they met.

Mistress Lyavendar truly knew that Frostria held her in high esteem because she would never had crossed over the line with Greg and established that relationship without Mistress Lyavendar prodding her along. Frostria owed her love for Greg to Mistress Lyavendar who now was practically the most important friend in her life whom she cherished and received frequent holographs while she was alone giving her moral support and guidance in the *Female Art of War* that was just as complicated as Earth people understood *Sun Tzu Art of War*.

Frostria slowly became part of Mistress Lyavendar's personal mafia. It was a secret society that was just as cunning and as their male counterparts that underestimated women and had no idea exactly how conniving they can become. Women had to look out for each other because they were often the victim of the male machinations. If it were not for the sexual alure, they would have very little meaning for most men. Most women feel that males only treat them better just before they want sex. But in reality, you can't paint civilization with a broad brush, because some of the strokes would not convey the truth.

Mistress Lyavendar's *Female Art of War* mafia had grown more decisive in years mainly because the Emperor was more and more aloof and as a thirty second wonder never really got her very excited and filled her only with constant disappointment. Then suddenly this beautiful couple came into their lives and suddenly lit a flame under the Emperor who now was acting more like an ideal lover.

Mistress Lyavendar's dream finally came true, she met her prince and now he was suddenly full of love and turned her on better than she could ever have imagined. That is one of the reasons why she cherished every moment she got to spend with Frostria, that almost wrecked her plans as this new venture transpired.

Emperor Calestine approached Greg almost ignoring Commander Stanfrad Villiers who served at his pleasure.

EMPEROR CALESTINE
Good to see you, Gregory Bissell. I hope everything is
going well for you?

GREG
Your Excellency. Thank you. I'm doing quite well.

EMPEROR CALESTINE
That's good to hear, Greg.

EMPEROR CALESTINE
Frostria, you look very beautiful today. Did someone
perform magic on you to put on such a beautiful smile?

FROSTRIA
Yes, Your Excellency, Greg makes me smile all the time.

Mistress Lyavendar reached out her hand for Frostria.

MISTRESS LYAVENDAR
You look so lovely today. Please come with me, I
want to take you somewhere so we can talk and have
company by ourselves.

Frostria held out her hand which Mistress Lyavendar grabbed then led her into the mansion and then out to a private flower garden designed and built just for her where she could entertain her special friends.

Emperor Calestine knew that Mistress Lyavendar would want to know all the details including how many orgasms she had and how many times Greg made love to her, and how well the romance was going.

The Emperor didn't mind her ways, because he knew there would be a great possibility that Mistress Lyavendar would want to act on that imagery with him later and recreate her own gratification in a similar manner.

EMPEROR CALESTINE
Commander Stanfrad Villiers, thank you for coming. I
appreciate you bringing my friends here with you.

COMMANDER STANFRAD VILLIERS
It's my honor, Your Excellency.

EMPEROR CALESTINE
I have a room set up for our meeting. Commander
Stanfrad Villiers, I want Gregory Bissell and his Robot
to attend the meeting with us since this will most
definitely affect him the most.

COMMANDER STANFRAD VILLIERS
Understand, Your Excellency.

EMPEROR CALESTINE
Good. Follow me, gentlemen.

Emperor Calestine nodded at the valet who led them into the mansion down a long
hallway that curved around and led to what appeared to be a connection to another
building all together. They stepped into a large room the emperor had that was intended
for ballroom dancing and exquisite dinners for special occasions. They could easily seat
500 for dinner in this lavishly decorated room.

The room was almost empty. In the middle was a table with place mats and name cards
for arranged seating. Commander Stanfrad Villiers was seated directly to Emperor
Calestine on the left and Greg to his right. Another chair offset with Tiāncái's name on
it offset out a foot more from the table between Greg and the Emperor to facilitate his
fast translation.

EMPEROR'S PERSONAL VALET
Gentlemen, please be seated.

The valet stood about ten feet away from the emperor waiting for instructions.

After everyone was seated and appeared ready to begin, waiters poured glasses of wine
for everyone. Through the intelligence service they knew precisely what type of wine
the space commander drank, so they were prepared for this meeting. Greg received
what the emperor was drinking, some of the most expensive wine in the galaxy, and the
taste clearly articulated why it was so costly.

A very rare grape from the Genovian Planet caused unusual chemical reactions and
some believed the Genovians lived longer because they drank copious amounts of this
wine made from their special grapes that would grow nowhere else but on the thick red
Genovian volcanic soil.

The emperor began the discussions.

EMPEROR CALESTINE

Greg, when you saved my life, I felt compelled to in some way reward you. The Empire was saved by your efforts alone. You took great risk of your own life to protect me and for that I know I can never repay you what you rightly deserve.

GREG

Your highness, you do not owe me anything. I'm satisfied with is bestowed upon me now.

EMPEROR CALESTINE

Greg, when I asked you what you would like for your reward, you had no desire for any rewards, but you did mildly stated the only thing in life you wanted was to travel back to your Planet Earth where you may finish out the rest of your life and die.

GREG

Yes, your Excellency, that's probably a dream and unrealistic.

EMPEROR CALESTINE

I can understand your desire to do such, so I sent an inquiry to Commander Stanfrad Villiers to form a feasibility study, and he is here to give us the results I want you to hear.

Emperor Calestine then looked solemnly at Commander Stanfrad Villiers.

EMPEROR CALESTINE

Commander Stanfrad Villiers, please tell us what you are evaluating.

COMMANDER STANFRAD VILLIERS

Thank you, Your Excellency, to allow me this opportunity to provide a proposal that I believe will become beneficial to all parties.

Greg looked upon Commander Stanfrad Villiers with great interest that suddenly gripped his emotions as he carefully listened and Tiāncái translated.

COMMANDER STANFRAD VILLIERS

We looked at the overall situation and studied the Earth ship that got Gregory Bissell here in twenty-two years. It was a bold venture, but one of the issues we are confronted with is he doesn't have many years left to make a similar trip back to earth expending such precious time.

Greg was starting to have negative vibes as this was probably a pope dream.

> Iin order for us to get him back to Planet Earth in a timely manner, we need a ship that will travel a lot faster and accelerate quicker to minimize transit time in order to arrive there while people he existed with are still alive to allow him the psychological positive experience when he arrives. Should he arrive after they are all dead, we think he would be miserable the rest of his life and would be better off staying here.

> EMPEROR CALESTINE
> Is it possible to build a ship that can get him there quickly?

> COMMANDER STANFRAD VILLIERS
> Your Excellency, I will answer that question now but I must also now tell Greg what he is about to be informed of is one of our greatest secrets of all time and under no circumstance is he allowed to ever divulge it to anyone.

> GREG
> I understand your concern, Commander Stanfrad Villiers. I will not divulge it to anyone under any circumstance.

Tiāncái already knew what was coming. His artificial intelligence apparatus had penetrated every element of Traykorite society. The Traykorites would be alarmed to know an Alien's Robot had totally undermined all their precious information and had instant access to all of it.

Tiāncái suspected the Commander would now reveal the new Traykorite Fast Frigate that was nearing completion of construction that would give the Traykorites a military superiority over all their potential enemies. They would have a speed advantage, not only in this galaxy but to the other end of their known Universe.

The new super-secret propulsion system that used gravity and neutrino drive could shove the Super-Fast Frigate across the entire galaxy in a day or less. More important it could jump from galaxy to galaxy in such a quick fashion it could be across their known Universe in the matter of months verses hundreds of billions of light years.

As Tiāncái predicted, Commander Stanfrad Villiers revealed the capabilities of the new Traykorite Fast Frigate to those in the room.

The valet would never mention this Fast Frigate to anyone or do anything without the Emperor's direction. The secret was safe with him.

Greg obviously would remain silent because he wanted a way to get home and if he could get there in the matter of months, his life could be restored. However, there would possibly be some complications because Frostria had grown so attached to Greg, that if he left without her, it would break her heart to the point she might consider suicide. And then when Greg got back to Earth if he took Frostria with him, how would she exist in an Alien culture that might not be ready for multicolored humanoids with almost holographic three-dimensional skin color?

The astute emperor knew people die in love and war. Sadly, there are always casualties there is no way around it. As complicated as it seemed, the prime directive was to get Greg home and let the chips fall where they might.

Commander Stanfrad Villiers then gave the most important detail.

COMMANDER STANFRAD VILLIERS
The distance from here to Greg's planet Earth based on calculations done on Pluto II ship's logs is only twice as long as the distance from the Traykorite City Aiguo to the other edge of our known Universe.

EMPEROR CALESTINE
When will this new Fast Frigate be ready to attempt a trip to Earth?

COMMANDER STANFRAD VILLIERS
We were planning on a dry run to our other edge to the Universe in a month. Instead of going that direction, we could simply change course and go in the opposite direction and head for Earth.

The emperor knew such a journey would be filled with vast dangers just like it was when Greg came here.

EMPEROR CALESTINE
Greg would you want to attempt such a trip?

GREG
Yes, I would like to take the chance.

EMPEROR CALESTINE
What about Frostria

GREG
Would it be possible to take her with me when I go?

EMPEROR CALESTINE
That's all up to her Greg. Commander, would there be room for Frostria?

COMMANDER STANFRAD VILLIERS
Your Excellency, we didn't plan on loading out a
tactical load since this is in essence engineering trials,
we would not be loading many Eleptron Annihilators,
just a defensive load and we would not engage hostile
forces, therefore most of our laser operators and
technicians would not be coming with us, we would
have substantially greater ability to take along guests
and additional supplies to accommodate a voyage
twice as long.

EMPEROR CALESTINE
Alright, make preparations.

GREG
Your Excellency, aboard the Pluto II spacecraft, we
have the record of our journey. For the sake of mankind
on Planet Earth, I need to come back with the records
of our voyage here to prove the Big Bang Theory is
debunked. We need to find a way to take those files
with us.

Since Tiāncái had a vast understanding of Traykorites' computational and
communications networks he suggested:

TIĀNCÁI
The Traykorite Archives have some very capable
storage units that operate off DC power that would fit
all our data in it we could take along and strap in place
on one of the Eleptron Annihilators launcher skids to
record the journey back to Earth as well as carry a set
of duplicate files back to Earth.

EMPEROR CALESTINE
Do you know how to manipulate those data archive
units?

TIĀNCÁI
Yes, I have worked extensively with Pluto II computers
and Traykorites' computational and communications
directorate to transfer Pluto II files to your archives.
I'm well versed on the process.

COMMANDER STANFRAD VILLIERS
What about Pluto II?

EMPEROR CALESTINE
We can make a museum out of it to honor the first man
who traveled to the edge of the universe.

> GREG
>
> What about the ship's computers, they have evolved rather extensively in many ways?

Tiāncái then interjected.

> TIĀNCÁI
>
> We can download the entire contents of the ship's computers into the Traykorite archival units that have incredible storage ability. The ship's computer is really nothing more than logic and data we can take with us in storage and bring back to life once we get back to Earth. I'm sure Dr. Hudson would be very happy to put together computer banks for the sake of history all the information we created doing this mission.

> GREG
>
> It's been twenty years; he may not be living.

> TIĀNCÁI
>
> Dr. Hudson's a tough guy, I bet he will be there when we get back.

The Emperor then turned to Greg.

> EMPEROR CALESTINE
>
> Greg, I want you to delay discussing this with Frostria for a couple weeks. I know this will cause her a lot of anguish, and this is the first time in a long, long time that Mistress Lyavendar has been this happy. If Frostria gets upset and depressed it will have a negative effect on Mistress Lyavendar.

> GREG
>
> I understand, but I will ask her to go with me to Earth at that time.

> EMPEROR CALESTINE
> What if she declines?

> GREG
>
> If I have a chance to go back to Earth I must go. I have great affection for Frostria, but if she declines the invitation I will understand and will have huge regrets later, however I want to die back at my home planet.

The emperor understood exactly how Greg felt. As Emperor, he could live on 150 other planets that were far nicer than the Traykorite capitol, but this is his home. He was born and raised here. There is a strange appeal to individuals to seek their homeland, especially in their aging years, exactly like Greg's wife had done to him.

The numerous issues associated with an Alien living on Earth would of course create a lot of controversy. Frostria's multicolored skin with the hologram effect that is also apparent in some birds and reptiles creates a colorization pattern depending on the angle of sunlight that adds to the exotic nature of these creatures.

Greg felt that because Frostria was from a much more superior technology-based civilization, society would show her respect and obviously some would have admiration if not outright sexual desires, but the real question is how Frostria would handle it and how well she would adapt to her new world?

Frostria certainly would not have quite as many modern conveniences or the unique food she was accustomed, and it might seem a little backwards, but she seemed like the adventure type and her psychological occupation might make her more adaptable than most.

The meeting broke up and Emperor Calestine invited Commander Stanfrad Villiers to stay for lunch. He didn't mind observing Frostria close up. He was curious as to what kind of woman would have sex with an Alien. She was the first and only Traykorite to do so. *She must be terribly courageous*, he thought.

The valet led the group out a side door of the large room they were in and discovered it had a short path directly to the swimming pool area. Today the Emperor had a big surprise for everyone. He had his dozen pet dolphin like animals in the pool.

EMPEROR CALESTINE
These are my pet Franzcas.

As soon as the dozen Franzcas spotted the emperor, they stated calling out and chattering in their languages. There was evidently a deep bond between the animals and their master.

The emperor often swam with the Franzcas and fed them from his hands. Using professional trainers, he had them learn tricks which they did for him, wanting to please him. When he was getting out of the pool after a session each of the Franzcas came up to him to receive their daily hug. As he crawled out of the pool they quieted down and just stared at him as he departed. They were obviously sad at his departure. Every minute he stayed in the pool with the Franzcas they were playful and happy.

It was obvious the bond between the emperor and Franzcas was unique and extraordinary.

Sometimes in the past Mistress Lyavendar was jealous of the Franzcas and actually considered poisoning them after a few sour episodes with the Emperor. But in the end, she just simmered down and went back to her private quarters and cried herself to sleep.

EMPEROR CALESTINE
If you would like to go swimming and play with the
Franzcas there are a variety of sizes of swimming
clothes to change into in the change room at the end
of the pool.

GREG
I've never swum with animals like this before. Do you
think they will want to engage with an Alien?

EMPEROR CALESTINE
Don't worry, Gregory Bissell, I will get in the water
with you, they will want to play since I'll be there and
you are safe because they will sense you are my friend."

GREG
Alright, I'll change.

The emperor walked with Greg to the dressing room at the end of the swimming pool.
The Space Commander declined. He was going to have lunch with them then skedaddle
back to his office to set off one of the biggest events in Traykorite Space Force history.
People would be scrambling over the next few days to get their Frigate into operational
status to make this monumental voyage.

The Space Commander walked over to tables and chairs under the large awning and
Tiāncái followed him and sat on the other side of the same table.

COMMANDER STANFRAD VILLIERS
Tell me, mechanical man, what do they call you?

Tiāncái stated in perfect standard Traykorite language.

TIĀNCÁI
My name is Tiāncái.

COMMANDER STANFRAD VILLIERS
Your standard Traykorite is really good, how long did
it take you to master the language?

TIĀNCÁI
Approximately 4.857 Earth days.

COMMANDER STANFRAD VILLIERS
You are Gregory Bissell's personal mechanical man?

TIĀNCÁI
Back on our world, planet Earth, I'm referred to as
a robot. Yes, I'm Gregs personal assistant and Greg
helped build me.

COMMANDER STANFRAD VILLIERS
That's quite interesting, Greg must be a very talented
man.

TIĀNCÁI
The actual designer is Dr. Hudson. whom I'm looking
forward to seeing again when we return.

COMMANDER STANFRAD VILLIERS
You might do us a lot of good if you would remain here
at the Aiguo Space Center so that we could reverse
engineer you and recreate numerous duplicate models.

TIĀNCÁI
You don't need to reverse engineer me. I've already
given all the design plans of my construction to your
computational and communications directorate. They
can create copies of me right now.

COMMANDER STANFRAD VILLIERS
That's kind of interesting, I might have to have my own
personal robot like you. I can think of a lot of tasks I
could give it.

The emperor was curious to see Greg's anatomy as they were changing into swimming
clothes. He wondered if he had a tool that perhaps might make Traykorite women more
pleased. In due course he was downright shocked at the size and shape. He also knew
that if Mistress Lyavendar ever saw it, she would want to experience it. It didn't dawn
on him at the time to have the surveillance video erased and to his chagrin later on,
Mistress Lyavendar voyeurism got engaged and she did have the desires the emperor
feared she would develop. It was apparent now it was a wise decision to send Greg back
to Earth before he would have to have him executed for fooling around with his future
bride-to-be.

The swimming clothes were designed with microfibers to eliminate drag and the water
viscosity affects that made swimming more efficient. It also hid Greg's junk to avoid any
exposure that might create curiosity.

The two men came out of the dressing room and the Franzcas a very intelligent animal
with a working vocabulary of four hundred-plus words began their frenzied chatter
and movements fully expecting the emperor to get in the water and play with them.
They also knew the staff would soon be bringing several buckets of fish like animals for
their personal enjoyment.

Greg followed the emperor down into the pool steps where the encouraged Franzcas
were waiting for them in utter delight.

EMPEROR CALESTINE
Stay close to me for a while until they get used to you.

The Franzcas knew there was something quite different about the stranger. They had incredible eyesight, facial recognition, and their sense of smell was on par with a dog back on planet earth. The Franzcas closest to the emperor continued to engage in a playful exhibition while those closer to Greg were very still and analyzing.

When the Emperor held his hand straight out, that was a signal for the Franzcas come closer to be petted and they complied and eagerly sought out the attention.

EMPEROR CALESTINE
Hold your hand out like this.

The emperor then demonstrated for Greg who copied and the Franzcas very slowly and carefully approached smelling, looking and analyzing the Alien creature Greg.

When one of them approached close enough and Greg started petting it the others holding back slowly approached and after they figured out this was a friendly and peaceful being, they showed less apprehension and became slowly more playful.

About that time on of the staff members arrived with the first bucket of a fish-like animal that resembled maceral back on Earth.

EMPEROR CALESTINE
Hold the Sashi like this.

Apparently, Sashi was the Traykorite word for fish.

Greg followed the emperor's guidance and soon the loving Franzcas were acting like Greg was their new best friend.

After they emptied the bucket, the emperor suggested:

EMPEROR CALESTINE
Let's swim a couple laps over to the other side and back.

As the two men swam to the other side and back, the Franzcas escorted them in the most playful fashion.

During this sea life experience and exposition, Frostria and Mistress Lyavendar arrived and sat at the table with Tiāncái and Commander Stanfrad Villiers observing the men and animals in the large pool. The sight of this activity warmed Frostria's heart observing the animals showing their great affection for the two men. There were more hugs of the animals who now treated Greg as their new best friend. These animals were very special to the emperor and if anyone was ever caught mistreating them, they would most likely discover the pain of being on the end of a laser rifle stream of photons.

The emperor knew it was time to let the animals go back to their much larger pool located a few hundred yards away from the mansion where they had a much larger and natural habitat and not so much chemicals as in the swimming pool. A Franzcas trainer was at the end of the pool where a canal system existed with a special high-frequency whistle that humans and Traykorite could not hear because it was out of their frequency range of hearing around twenty-five kilocycles.

The Franzcas had been trained to go into the canal and back home where they would find the rest of their lunch waiting for them. This did two purposes. It got the animals out of the harsh chemicals and prevented them from pooping in the pool causing a lot of cleanup requirements.

EMPEROR CALESTINE
Greg, shall we go back to the dressing room and take a
shower and change back into our clothes?

GREG
Yes, that would be good.

As they entered the dressing room, the showers were already going, evidently warming them up to make sure they were exactly 98.6 degrees when the men stepped into them. Sensors detected them in their private showers and after the initial wet-down, a cleaning solution was added which was almost like an analgesic and disinfected them from all possible exposure to Franzcas germs. The cleaning solution smelled fresh and good. In the most automated fashion, they were rinsed off and blow dried with warm air.

They dressed and then left the change room together and approached the small group at the tables under the large awning.

Having planned for their walk to the waterfall, the valet approached the emperor and stated:

EMPEROR'S PERSONAL VALET
Your Excellency, all preparations have made for your
walk if you and your guests are ready to go.

EMPEROR CALESTINE
Alright, let's all go. Commander Stanfrad Villiers, I
know you are a busy man if you would like to care to
go for a walk with us.

COMMANDER STANFRAD VILLIERS
Your Excellency, I think it would best if I got back to my
office, I need to initiate a lot of actions. My time would
be better spent there, but thank you for the offer."

EMPEROR CALESTINE
My valet will escort you to the front entrance and you
should find your Aircar parked there ready for you to
return. I will take our guests home later.

COMMANDER STANFRAD VILLIERS
Thank you for your time, and I will be giving you updates on our project as we reach new milestones.

EMPEROR CALESTINE
I'll be looking forward to receiving those reports.

The emperor nodded at the valet and knew the Commander Stanfrad Villiers had a lot on his plate right now and had a huge effort he had to make in order to provide Greg his one wish the emperor wanted to grant him for saving his life and his Empire.

<u>EXT. DAY EMPEROR'S PALACE GROUNDS PARKLIKE SETTING.</u>

The emperor waited for the valet to return who then led them past the changing room down a pathway through a gate manned by security guards and out onto what appeared to Greg as a cement walkway.

<u>EXT. DAY EMPEROR'S PALACE GROUNDS MILITARY SECURITY DETACHMENT FOLLOWING ALONG.</u>

As they all were out on the walkway Greg looking in all directions saw two hundred well-armed soldiers about one hundred yards down the walkway in the opposite direction they were headed. These soldiers carried shoulder fired laser rifles, had body armor and hat-like devices with glass-like face shields which Greg wondered what they were. These were in fact laser deflectors to prevent direct injury in a laser shootout.

The recent Coup attempt rattled the emperor and he wasn't taking any chances. If he wanted, he could have five thousand troops there but two hundred was enough to provide a curtain of protection until the calvary arrived. It did convey the notion that danger lurked for this leader.

It wasn't that he was unpopular, quite the contrary, but men lust for power. Commander Zebrovska and his cohorts were such men. There were possibly others that wanted to follow in their footsteps and make such an attempt and until all the investigation was over, he couldn't take any chances.

However, out of decorum the emperor didn't want them too close to affect the moods of his guests.

<u>EXT. CGI. DAY SEVERAL ADVANCED MILITARY AIRCRAFT OVERHEAD EMPEROR'S ESTATES.</u>

370

Orbiting overhead at 10,000 feet slowly making figure-eight patterns was a squadron of space defense fighter bombers that could be called into action if necessary. The only thing positive for the pilots was it increased their flight log hours and helped them maintain their proficiency in the use of their equipment such as the various sensors and surveillance monitors used to attack any threats on the ground. Each one of the emperor's security detachment forces always had a beacon on their body. The pilots from the air could easily make out who the good guys were as to not accidently kill them if combat suddenly emerged.

Not taking any chances, the most loyal commanders were on ships in geostationary orbit above the planet to thwart any surprise attack from space. The Emperor's emergency getaway craft had been gone over by experts and the booby traps had been removed and a full system checkout was made which included moving it to the launch area where the large doors that looked like platforms for sculptures suddenly opened one hundred degrees allowing the craft to take off out to space for a test flight, circle the planet, come back down and land and shifted back to its secret hangar and made ready for the next possible emergency use.

The group walked along peacefully appreciating the well landscaped park and the flora that abounded. This 25,000-acre estate using Earth measurements created a mini climate for the area. The irrigated landscape that once was nothing more than rocky wasteland increased the humidity and prevented excessive temperatures in the summertime. Some experts stated, the area created possibly a dozen more rainstorms a year thanks to this green zone next to the Capitol City of Aiguo.

The added humidity and resulting temperate weather created an ideal climate for the flora that abounded. The group was not in the best physical condition and made no attempt to hustle to their destination and chatted, on the way there, often discussing some of the types of flora they encountered. There were numerous small plaques with names of the flora and the worlds they came from. After Greg asked quite a few times about some of the more glamorous plants, Tiāncái translated and explained much about the plant since he had immediate access to the Traykorite worldwide communication and computation networks, often having billions of words available on that plant anticipating Greg's questions. Even the Emperor was slightly amused this Alien Robot had so much data on the flora in his private park.

As they got closer to the waterfall the aroma of the smell of barbecue permeated the air. As they made the last turn in the walkway they came to the exposed waterfall and private park-like sitting with picnic tables bristling with a variety of delicious items and several staff members there preparing everything.

A long dinner table was laid out for the group and like before there was one chair offset next to the emperor and the setting next to him with Greg's name placard on the sitting next to the emperor on his right. Mistress Lyavendar was seated next to the emperor on his left and Frostria was seated next to Greg so she could face her give Greg an immense smile.

Mistress Lyavendar was very happy to get all the details of Greg's love making with

Frostria and of course she had seen the videos in her voyeuristic episodes. She considered Frostria now a close confidant and the way Greg pleased Frostria had an endearing appeal to Mistress Lyavendar.

However, later tonight as Mistress Lyavendar voyeurism pervaded her evening as she was left alone and neglected by the emperor while he was down in his secret bat cave doing whatever he did down there for hours at a time, she thumbed through the surveillance videos and was astonished when she got to see Greg's tooling for the first time. She now knew why Frostria was so completely pleased with her lovemaking with Greg. Not only does size matter so does the shape and when she saw that one-eyed snake, she was ingulfed in incredible curiosity. If she ever had a chance to try it and not get caught.

The luncheon was a mild and satisfying event. These were true proven friends. *The best friends are the polite ones who save your life*, the emperor thought.

As the Emperor looked at Greg, he knew the person had a lot going through his mind. Traveling to the edge of the Universe, finding another and possibly more universes existed, and being directly involved in thwarting a Coup in an Alien planet was more than anything anyone could possibly experience in their lifetime.

Greg would no doubt be debriefed extensively when he returned and when a multicolored-skinned exotic woman returns with him and it becomes public she is also his lover, the Earth people would most likely have immense curiosity and poor Greg would probably end up wishing he was back in Aiguo in a position to have frequent entertainment by the emperor.

EMPEROR CALESTINE
Tell me, Greg, how did you like my pet Franzcas?

GREG
Your Excellency, they are super friendly as you
suggested, a little shy at first.

EMPEROR CALESTINE
Those Franzcas have only seen a half-dozen people in
their lifetime.

GREG
I'm very honored to have the opportunity to play with
the Franzcas.

The emperor looked over at Frostria and thought to himself, *If Greg doesn't take Frostria to Earth with him, I might just have to make her my mistress.*

The best way to describe Frostria, until Greg met Frostria, she looked plain and sterile. Greg opened a new world for Frostria and now she had experienced a few things that very few Traykorites would ever do in their lifetime.

The emperor also noticed there was something odd about Frostria today and she certainly looked a lot prettier it seems than she did when she arrived. Greg didn't quite understand it either, but he too sensed she had morphed while in the company of Mistress Lyavendar who decided to take it upon herself to make her the beautiful woman she could be using her makeup artist.

Observing how the emperor now looked at Frostria, Mistress Lyavendar kind of wished she hadn't arranged for that super makeup procedure done on Frostria. In a couple weeks in the future the emperor apologized to Mistress Lyavendar.

EMPEROR CALESTINE

I'm sorry for allowing her good friend to go to Earth
with Greg, she surprised him with her response.

MISTRESS LYAVENDAR

I'm glad you allowed Frostria to go with Greg because
it would have been tragic to split those lovers apart. I
would rather lose a friend than to see her heart ripped
out of her watching her lover leave her forever.

The emperor was pleased Mistress Lyavendar felt that way and confirmed he made the right decision, but in reality, Mistress Lyavendar was not saying everything that she felt, such as *she was happy that her possible competition would be gone and out of the way before she had to arrange an accident.*

The waterfall added to the ambience, the food that reminded Greg of succulent pork barbecued on a spit. The flavor and spices they used were incredible. Greg asked Tiāncái:

GREG

Tiāncái what the barbecued animal was like I ate.

Tiāncái knew Greg wasn't going to be very happy with the answer but informed him truthfully, nonetheless.

TIĀNCÁI

Greg, it is an animal that looks a lot like Saint Bernard
dogs back on Earth.

Greg realized he was in a different civilization where values were different and not expecting Traykorites to be like Planet Earth. Then he shivered at the thought of what else they ate.

Celebrational Cannibalism still flourished in the Galaxy. When vast Armies slaughtered their enemies, there was often a feast afterwards barbecuing the enemy's officers to please the men.

The luncheon gradually pleased everyone and Greg like the others probably overate. The Emperor suspected this might occur and he himself had no intentions of walking back to the mansion so when everyone were content and some gave a face that indicated they could use the restroom, a royal recreation vehicle arrived a few minutes later the Emperor suggested:

EMPEROR CALESTINE
Why don't we all go back to the Palace so everyone can
freshen up?

The recreation vehicle could easily turn a full three hundred and sixty degrees because the front and rear wheels were controlled by the steering mechanism. So in despite the narrow road, the recreational vehicle easily changed directions and the driver had it pointed in the right direction. There were no step ladders. The vehicle sat down on the road and people walked into the four rows of seats and when the driver saw everyone was safely seated the body of the vehicle lifted two feet off the ground via some type of hydraulic lifting mechanism.

The vehicle had a superb computer-controlled suspension system and they felt none of the bumps in the road. Greg was positioned on the left side in the second row of seats and could see the rearview mirror.

As they started moving, to his great surprise some of the flora they just left stood up and walked out onto the road. They were camouflaged soldiers that he had failed to recognize. Their concealment was rather advanced. Some of the Flora in the nearby trees concealed snipers with special rifles to protect the emperor. Anyone attempting to harm the emperor would be savagely dealt with before they knew what hit them.

The recreational vehicle pulled into a hidden gate and let off all the passengers right behind the changing room at the pool. After they were all walking the length of the pool, the recreational vehicle left the compound out the hidden gate and off to wherever it was stored which would be easy to hide with a property six miles wide and seven miles long.

What else was hidden out there? Greg wondered.

The emperor had musicians' poolside performing as soon as they returned, and everyone was escorted to private guestrooms so they could freshen up or take care of business. There were personal valets stationed by the guestrooms to escort them back to the pool. As typical, Tiāncái waited in Greg's guestroom while Greg took care of his business and decided to take a shower afterwards to freshen up. The automated shower took care of Greg very efficiently and was in and out and dry in five minutes feeling totally refreshed.

Greg
I'm ready to go back down to the pool and hear some
of the music.

TIĀNCÁI
Let me take you there.

GREG

One second, Tiāncái, there is something I wish to tell you.

TIĀNCÁI
What is that, Greg?

GREG

We have been together now for a long time. I really value you and I hope that when we go back to Earth, they do not separate us. I want us always to be together. You are my best friend.

TIĀNCÁI

Greg, thank you. That pleases me more than you can imagine. I feel the same way. I plan to always be near you to assist in any manner I can.

GREG
Thank you, Tiāncái.

Greg held out his hand. Tiāncái had sensors in his robotic hands and knew micro pressures and gently grabbed hands and shook as if they were both humans. The mutual admiration was sincere and Greg had no knowledge of just how far Tiāncái had advanced. Tiāncái had billions upon billions of pieces of information about Earth and now by taking over the Traykorite computational and communications networks, he had an entire galaxy's worth of information. His wisdom was beyond anything Greg could imagine. Dr. Hudson would one day reflect on how much he had created when Tiāncái unexpectantly returned with Greg.

Frostria also took a shower and freshened up. In doing so she screwed up her makeup and wasn't the princess she had been just the hour before. When she looked into the mirror, she was horrified. She in a panic contacted Mistress Lyavendar via her personal communicator.

As Mistress Lyavendar looked at Frostria, she noted Frostria's twisted face exhibited a woman slightly emotional.

MISTRESS LYAVENDAR
Yes, Frostria, what's the problem?

FROSTRIA

I felt like taking a shower and I screwed up my lovely makeup.

MISTRESS LYAVENDAR

Don't worry about it, Frostria, I'll send over my Valet to bring you to my suite so that we can fix your makeup.

FROSTRIA
I'm so grateful to you. I'm afraid Greg will look at me
like a hag in my present condition.

MISTRESS LYAVENDAR
Frostria, don't worry. We'll take care of all that shortly.

The communication link ended and momentarily there was a knock at the door. It was
one of the staff.

MISTRESS LYAVENDAR PERSONAL VALET
Mistress Lyavendar has requested I escort you to her
suite.

FROSTRIA
Oh, thank you, I really appreciate this.

MISTRESS LYAVENDAR PERSONAL VALET
Not a problem, madam, this way, please.

Frostria was soon in Mistress Lyavendar's suite and when she arrived the first thing
Mistress Lyavendar thought was, her attire needed some major adjustment too. She had
to work on the entire package. Since both women were nearly the same size, it would be
simple. Mistress Lyavendar had 50,000 garments she had never wore. It was time to see
some of them on this glorious creature. Besides the new makeup, a change in hairstyle
and different clothing, she was suddenly transformed by Mistress Lyavendar into a
living princess unlike any Greg had ever experienced. Tonight, Frostria even made the
glamorous Chinese Spy Monica look secondhand. The evening gown she was wearing
cost more than Frostria's yearly salary. The exquisite combination made Frostria look
more than exotic.

Mistress Lyavendar was no slouch tonight either, she too dressed to kill. *If she didn't get
a reaction out of Emperor Calestine, then he needed to go see a doctor.*

The men were enjoying the elaborate music feeling content from their meals and
freshening up afterwards. Neither expected what happened next. They were slightly
annoyed the women seemed to take forever, however the emperor was happy, that
Mistress Lyavendar had a real friend who had also risked her life to protect the emperor.

Just before the Emperor was going to send his Valet to ask Mistress Lyavendar when
she planned to come join them, the two exotic creatures appeared out of nowhere. Even
the musicians were taken back at the "eye candy."

To say these two beautiful women didn't impact the music for the rest of the night
was an understatement. Just what the doctor ordered to create the fragrance and
allure for the evening, these two women exemplified everything possible that could
have the greatest impact on the male libido. Both women were glowing because they
were in love.

The soft cushions of the evening furniture brought out just before they arrived back from the barbecue created an outdoor living room that made comfortable listening to the musicians performing some very soothing music. Greg was listening to music that transcended Liszt, Rachmaninoff, Saint-Saëns, Khachaturian, Brahms, and Beethoven by a large measure.

It wasn't classical music. Greg had no reference to what it really was as it is Alien music from a different Universe far way in time and place. *What kind of music is now being played on Earth? What has happened since I left?*

Mistress Lyavendar observed Greg with great interest. She would insist they spend the night and she would relish her voyeurism as she watched the results of her machinations.

The music allowed them to relax and enjoy each other without putting forth much effort in conversation. To Mistress Lyavendar this was just foreplay for the grander events to manifest later in the night. Just like the way the music was now transforming their souls, later the results of the past hour that Mistress Lyavendar worked hard on achieving would transform their hearts and minds. *The other evening when Greg whimpered like a baby was an emotional downpour, tonight could possibly eclipse that,* Mistress Lyavendar thought.

So close to the truth she was, she couldn't imagine. While the music played on and Greg felt moved as if he were hearing the Khachaturian or Hanns Wolf - piano concerto for the first time, Mistress Lyavendar stood up and excused herself for a minute. It was typical for women to do such a thing when nature called. Instead she went inside the mansion. Her personal valet approached.

MISTRESS LYAVENDAR PERSONAL VALET
What may I help you with, madam?

MISTRESS LYAVENDAR
Please go to the emperor and inform him, I wish to
talk with him for a brief moment.

MISTRESS LYAVENDAR PERSONAL VALET
Right away, madam.

Mistress Lyavendar Personal Valet walked out of the mansion and approached Emperor Calestine and whispered something in the Emperor's ear. He was slightly amused and stood up quietly and followed the valet into the mansion where Mistress Lyavendar stood patiently waiting for him and smiling.

EMPEROR CALESTINE
Yes, my dear, what did you want to tell me?

MISTRESS LYAVENDAR
Calestine, I want you to invite Frostria and Greg to
spend the night with us. We can take them back in the
morning.

EMPEROR CALESTINE
It will be my pleasure.

Emperor Calestine then held out his hand and Mistress Lyavendar grabbed it and he escorted her back to her seat, then sat down on his overstuffed chair smiling at everyone.

Emperor Calestine knew the musicians had planned a two-hour concert and to demand they go past that would slowly erode the quality of their performance and so after they finished the last song he stood up and clapped.

Clapping is a universal signal it appears. Greg thought.

EMPEROR CALESTINE
That was a lovely performance. I'm very proud of every
one of you.

A vehicle of some type pulled into the secret side entrance then and the musicians knew instinctively that was their ride home and took their instruments and boarded it. Shortly it backed out of the compound and ostensibly down the path they took earlier this morning, but when they were out by the front entrance. The Airbus went airborne vertically and flew off towards the three-dimensional air freeway system where it merged into traffic and headed off to its destination at their barracks.

Emperor Calestine and Mistress Lyavendar to Frostria and Greg sitting twenty feet away from the pool. Mistress Lyavendar asked Greg a lot of questions about Earth and in a few cases, he didn't have the appropriate answers, Tiāncái with his encyclopedic mind easily filled in the blanks. About this time a portable holograph was pulled out near them. One could get the feeling that this was like a big-screen TV back on Earth except it was three-dimensional.

Unbeknown to Greg, Tiāncái utilizing the computer resources of the ship and the entire worldwide computational and communications networks of the Traykorite planet had systematically converted a number of videos from two-dimension to three-dimensional with special sound and visual effects.

This may not have been planned by the emperor who seemed to suddenly to be amused.

TIĀNCÁI
I've prepared some videos to show Mistress Lyavendar
to give her a feel for what Earth is like.

With advanced holographic technology and three-dimensional sound quality, Traykorite cinematographers accomplish creativity with ceramics and the multibillion-pixel ability of their holographic equipment dwarfing anything conceivable in Hollywood.

The video along with a narrative in standard Traykorite created ensembles of flowing reactions.

Greg felt like he was at the Rubin H. Fleet center in Balboa Park watching some of their super IMAX presentations that easily made you feel you were part of the video. If a person went strictly by the video one could easily be fooled into believing Earth was the perfect Utopian planet. Hence it didn't make sense why anyone would want to leave it.

But in Greg's case, Greg went on this vast journey because Lawrence Livermore Labs had an agenda to prove or disprove the Big Bang Theorists. People such as Walter Bissonnette and Dr. Moore thought the *big bangers* were propagandizing a false narrative for an intellectual seduction of low information thinkers.

Unfortunately for Greg, until this very day, he had no way to take the evidence back to show the *big bangers* had a major flaw in their theories they were peddling as if it were fact.

Frostria didn't quite know what created the surreal happiness in Greg tonight. His bubbly attitude started long before she changed her dress and put on even more elaborate makeup and a very exquisite hairdo.

Nevertheless, after Frostria's private talk with Mistress Lyavendar both times today, she was now motivated more than ever to seal the deal with Greg. It was time to move the relationship forward. She would use her special friendship with Mistress Lyavendar to get Greg permanently removed out of the space force building and allow him private accommodations, preferably in her apartment.

What to do about Tiāncái? That was another matter. Frostria didn't want to be in bed with Greg having sex with that Robot watching any longer. It just felt so icky.

The 3D video show that Tiāncái put on kept everyone's attention, even Greg who appreciated what Tiāncái had done for him. This video touched Greg's soul and left him partially subdued in thought with an inner happiness knowing there was a good possibility that in spite of all the odds, he would be going home back to Earth.

What happened to Ami, he wondered? By now she should be married possibly with a family and children. He certainly left her a pile of money to help out her future. As far as he knew she would be financially taken care of the rest of her life. What happened to Monica? Did she ever settle down? Did the CIA get her killed doing the double spying? How did that all work out?

Stepping out twenty-two years then suddenly arriving back presented some interesting questions.

There could be a lot of unexpected scenarios developing since he left. It's quite apparent Livermore Lab had no expectation he would return alive. By now Walt and Dr. More are probably retired. Dr. Shirley might still be there, she wasn't that old when he left.

Was his wife still alive?

His sons?

What was America like now?

Was the world a safer or more dangerous place?

Did Earth make contact with Aliens yet?

The two-hour video show kept everyone captivated. They were all absorbed and focused the entire time. Then it suddenly ended.

TIĀNCÁI
I'm sorry, that's all I have prepared for tonight.

EMPEROR CALESTINE
That was wonderful, thank you.

Emperor Calestine turned toward Greg and Frostria.

EMPEROR CALESTINE
It's getting kind of late now, so I want you both to
spend the night here. I will personally take you home
in the morning.

Emperor Calestine then stood up and held his hand out for Mistress Lyavendar who wasn't ready for such outward display of passion was instantly amused because Calestine didn't do that too often, then led her back toward the mansion as if he were going to take her immediately to his private quarters and physically reward her for dressing up tonight.

EMPEROR'S PERSONAL VALET
I will escort you to your guestrooms.

The Emperor's Personal Valet led Frostria, Greg, and Tiāncái a relatively short distance and walked in front of the guestroom previously given to Frostria so she could freshen up and rest.

EMPEROR'S PERSONAL VALET
Here you are, madam, your guestroom.

Frostria turned toward the valet and gave him a shocking response.

FROSTRIA
Tiāncái will spend the night in this room and I will be
in Greg's room.

The valet smiled and responded.

EMPEROR'S PERSONAL VALET
As you wish, madam.

The Emperor's Personal Valet then led Frostria and Greg to the next room and opened the door for them.

380

EMPEROR'S PERSONAL VALET
Enjoy the rest of your evening.

FROSTRIA
Thank you.

Greg and Frostria entered the guestroom and the valet shut it behind them.

There was a strong attraction between Frostria and Greg, and they quickly undressed and assumed a comfortable position in bed facing each other and Frostria kissed Greg softly and sensually like a woman in total love. Greg was now very submissive to whatever Frostria wanted.

FROSTRIA
Let's enter into Hemi-Sync while we make love.

INT. CGI. NIGHT. EMPEROR'S GUEST ROOM

Note to the Director:

The author of this screenplay recommends the Director and the two actors that perform Frostria and Greg in the movie be sent to the Monroe Institute to be trained in Hemi-Sync. The lead CGI technician should also get trained in Hemi-Sync. This scene will be the CGI challenge of the century to create cinematography to encompass a Hemi-Sync or "Gateway" experience where two lovers converge into the Gateway together and project the Hemi-Sync experience on the movie screen.

It was going to be a challenge to both enter Hemi-Sync during lovemaking but they both silently meditated during the coitus and by magic or some unknown phenomena, they entered Hemi-Sync at precisely the same time.

Frostria and Greg went off to another universe and in that holograph in their minds they met in a spectacular aura of color and sound. It was a dimension they would never want to leave.

Frostria and Greg were together, and the sight and the touch was real.

In their Hemi-Sync they made love. They could feel it. Greg and Frostria experienced the combination of the Hemi-Sync hologram projected in their minds from the universe and the actual physical touch that was going on in the guestroom.

In due course, Frostria exploded in passion and feelings unlike anything she felt before in her life. Frostria and Greg would never know for sure what happened since this was beyond the grasp of science. But Frostria and Greg each felt they had really connected in other dimensions and love flourished and multiplied and the energy build-up was spectacular.

The feelings were like vibrations before a volcano explodes and suddenly it happened.

There was a great flash. They both felt it and saw it at the same time. It was an experience that lingered a long time as darkness soon ended the Hemi-Sync manifested three-dimensional hologram.

Frostria and Greg remained unconscious and didn't move for hours as if they were in a trance glued together in a coitus.

Frostria and Greg's breath and pulse were almost unmeasurable. They were in a void just as if they were in the dark area between the two universes Greg traveled.

Then slowly a light appeared in front of them during their GATEWAY that slowly grew in intensity and spread bringing a mind full of brightness, a great awakening.

Suddenly Greg stirred and regained consciousness covered in immense sweat he moved to the side of Frostria who then slowly regained consciousness and looked around spotting Greg's face and she smiled.

Frostria rolled to her side facing Greg a short distance away and they softly and slowly kissed a few times. She then took her hand and slowly rubbed it very gently across his face cherishing the moment. The moment was magical. Then Frostria closed her eyes and went into a deep sleep.

It will never be known if a Hemi-Sync episode could suddenly and spontaneously return or if just elaborate dreams and hallucinations develop because of the surreal brain activity it caused that no expert could explain.

In her future travels, this phenomenon would create interest in her, as well as her ability to have real and everlasting dreams of Greg.

Emperor Calestine had finished his nice gratification that Mistress Lyavendar had manifested with her magic and beauty that evening and was resting when his valet informed him.

EMPEROR CALESTINE'S PERSONAL VALET HOLOGRAPH

   I'm sorry to interrupt your excellency, but you have an
   important communication.

Emperor Calestine got out of bed and put on a robe.

EMPEROR CALESTINE

   Lyavendar, I needed to go to my office for a while. I
   suggest you go back to your suite and freshen up.

Mistress Lyavendar was at least gratified and enjoyed every minute of the way Emperor Calestine finished making love to her , but the sudden departure and putting business ahead of pleasure was a big downer for her.

Mistress Lyavendar was more than happy to leave Calestine's private chambers and go back to her private suite, take a shower, clean herself, and relax and find out what the two lovebirds had been up to.

After Mistress Lyavendar was all cleaned up, dressed in comfortable clothing, she was relaxing in her bed looking up at the overhead canopy holographic display, then she initiated observation of surveillance video of the guestrooms.

In the room designated for Frostria, the Robot Tiāncái sat in a chair motionless, doing his secret operations and artificial intelligence. Mistress Lyavendar then assumed the two lovebirds were in the room designated for Greg's use and just as she expected there, they were sleeping lying on their sides and not moving.

That's no fun! Mistress Lyavendar thought, then moved the time cursor back to around the same time she went with Emperor Calestine to his room and started watching the two love birds.

Frostria and Greg undressed, and this was a joyous moment because now Mistress Lyavendar got an excellent view of Greg's one-eyed snake that was showing some signs of liveliness.

Frostria led Greg into the bed like she was starving, Mistress Lyavendar thought.

They were soon at it copulating as if there was nothing out of the ordinary. Then Frostria whispered something into Greg's ear, and they suddenly got weird.

In due time a very strange image developed along with strange sounds and movements. It didn't seem like Frostria and Greg were doing anything like she expected. Frostria's strange cries and sounds from Greg were demon-like, it was almost unbearable to watch.

Whatever they were doing went beyond anything Mistress Lyavendar had ever witnessed in her lifetime. This went on for an hour then suddenly at the exact same time Frostria and Greg stopped stopped all movement. There was no or sound or anything to suggest the two were coherent.

The image seemed as if Frostria and Greg were both dead. No love-talk, no pillow-talk, just complete silence.

This was the biggest mystery that Mistress Lyavendar had ever experienced. It ingulfed her imagination and she was spellbound. Mistress Lyavendar laid there observing as the two lovers Frostria and Greg, who didn't budge for almost an hour then finally it all unfolded as Greg moved to Frostria's side and Frostria appeared to awaken and smiled and kissed Greg, then softly rubbed his cheek. Then in a few moments later it was clear Frostria and Greg both began sleeping.

Mistress Lyavendar would have to get to the bottom of this without tipping off she was spying on Frostria and Greg. This strange phenomenon really had her thoughts fully absorbed in trying to figure out what went on.

Emperor Calestine had received his message from one of his spies. He pretty much already expected to hear the report. His source that was going to identify the members of the Coup, had been murdered.

What was more interesting was his controller informed the emperor that someone had been helping them. They didn't know who it was but without that secret help they never would have known who did what and how.

At the far-off distant solar system so far away, the conspirators thought they were out of the reach of the Emperor's forces. Colonel Zebrovska was naive to think the Conspirators who got his participation really had any intentions of him replacing the emperor, was nothing more than a useful idiot they were controlling.

The emperor suspected this was just the tip of the iceberg and that the conspiracy wasn't completely uncovered. Part of the swamp still remained, and it would not be an easy job to fully drain the swamp. Now a new dynamic was forming. Some entity they had no idea who it was seemed to be helping and undermining the conspiracy. More individuals had been identified and it seemed certainly a very distasteful situation developing, where those you had promoted and taken care of for the past fifteen years were now stabbing you in the back and came close to killing you already.

Without exposing his helpers, he needed to discover who they were. He already had a theory but it seemed rather impossible for them to be doing what they were obviously arranging. It was also brought to his attention the same day that Commander Zebrovska was captured, Greg, his robot, and Frostria had entered a dark zone a few times where they could converse without fear of being monitored. How would they know where the dark zone existed?

Sitting at his desk Emperor Calestine pulled up surveillance video and soon discovered his voyeurism lover Mistress Lyavendar was again spying on the lovebirds Frostria and Greg. And in a while observing her body language it was a mystery. He would have to find a way to discover what created such body language. It wasn't a pleasure, that's for sure, in fact it was quite disconcerting.

Emperor Calestine then thought Mistress Lyavendar was monitoring the guests and better look at what they were doing because it was sure affecting her!

By the time Emperor Calestine selected the surveillance video showing the couple, they appeared to be sound to sleep laying on their sides. Whatever affected Mistress Lyavendar must have happened earlier. So, Emperor Calestine moved the time cursor on the surveillance video back to around the same time he went to his bedroom earlier with Mistress Lyavendar to do the boom-boom.

Emperor Calestine now saw the same phenomena that caused Mistress Lyavendar to enter into such an uncharacteristic state. Emperor Calestine watched with great fascination. Emperor Calestine was now just as interested as Mistress Lyavendar.

Emperor Calestine then saw the Robot surveillance video sitting in the other guestroom on a chair not even moving. He obviously had nothing to do with what was going on in the other room.

One thing for certain, the surveillance on them would be increased and even if they went into a dark zone, he would have sensors and ways of obtaining those conversations. He then summoned his trusty Valet to make all the preparations for enhanced surveillance on his guests around the clock wherever they went.

The next morning the two lovebirds Frostria and Greg were awakened by a knock at the guestroom door.

Emperor Calestine's Personal Valet informed Greg:

> EMPEROR CALESTINE'S PERSONAL VALET
> Greg, you and Frostria need to get ready, Emperor Calestine wants to have breakfast with the two of you before he takes you back to the Space Force building and Frostria to her home.

> GREG
> Alright, we'll get ready immediately.

Frostria put on one of the robes laid on shelves in the bathroom and grabbed the nice dress she wore and informed Greg:

> FROSTRIA
> I'm going back to my guestroom to get ready.

> GREG
> Alright.

Frostria left and just as Greg figured, Tiāncái knocked on the door and Greg invited him in.

> TIĀNCÁI
> Did you have a good night with Miss Frostria?

> TIĀNCÁI
> Yes, excellent.

> TIĀNCÁI
> Do you love her?

> GREG
> Of course.

Then Tiāncái hit Greg with a statement that hit him in the gut like a ton of bricks.

> TIĀNCÁI
> Have you decided what you will do about Ami when you get back to Earth?

> GREG
> It's hard for me to believe a beautiful woman like her

waited for twenty-two years. With all the money I left her, I'm sure she attracted a lot of potential suitors.

TIĀNCÁI
But you do not know for sure.

GREG
No, I do not.

TIĀNCÁI
Do you know that Frostria will want to remain on Earth after she gets there and discovers what it is currently like?

GREG
I don't even know what it's like now. I may not want to remain.

TIĀNCÁI
I think you should have some contingency plan.

GREG
Call me a cynic, but I can't believe a hot woman like Ami stayed dormant for twenty-two years. When I left her, I was knocking the rims off her tires.

TIĀNCÁI
Well, Greg, you don't know how deeply you touched her. She actually may have waited twenty-two years for your return.

GREG
Sure, it's possible she may have waited, but I doubt in our complicated world she did. Guys like rich women. I left her behind rich.

TIĀNCÁI
Can you psychologically handle her greeting you and you suddenly introduce your new flame Frostria to her and inform her you have replaced her with an Alien from a far-off galaxy?

Greg knew that Tiāncái was making perfect sense. The other factor is she may not be compatible to Earth and may not wish to remain. And if she felt that way, would it be fair for her to be stuck on Earth the rest of her life, because this would probably be a one-way trip. The Traykorites will most likely never go that far again. It's only happened this one time because Greg had saved the emperor's life. In twenty years, the emperor may be dead and whoever replaces him could care less that one Traykorite is stuck a universe away on a planet she doesn't care for.

The emperor's palace and mansion had a well-scripted crew. In a brief period of time the guests were gathered in the Emperor's private dining hall. The room was decorated with extensive artwork and had soft music playing in the background that had a strange pleasantness to it. The three-dimensional music scientifically produced to enhance the psychoacoustics of the listener enhanced the positive feelings of people in the room. Seating assignments at the table were indicated by the placards. Once again Greg was near the Emperor and Tiāncái was seated offset between the two allowing his translation ability to work most efficiently.

Mistress Lyavendar setting directly across from Greg appeared in full blossom because she had a secret that she was going to find out. What exactly magic Greg performed on Frostria to influence her to have those physical reactions that were fascinating. Mistress Lyavendar also speculated it was a physical sensation she wanted to feel, just like the first time she had intercourse with a man who would be executed, if the emperor ever discovered this event took place, like when she seduced his personal valet to take care of her needs a few times when the emperor neglected her for long periods of time.

That is one leverage she always had over the valet to make sure he did exactly what she wanted. It was all about leverage and maintaining her position, she had the ruthless tendency to do whatever it took to get her way.

The meal was fit for a king which the emperor had more authority than any King. Emperor Calestine was the King of Kingdoms of worlds in this galaxy. His power and authority were unmatched anywhere in the Galaxy. Greg did not quite understand to the extent this existed, otherwise he no doubt might feel considerably more nervous being the subject of the emperor's fascination as well as his appreciation for doing one act nobody on the planet could have, which made the Emperor even more curious about his guest.

There were things about Gregory Bissell the Emperor did not know, but he soon was going to find out and had to know the answers before he allowed him to return to his Planet Earth, because once he was gone, the source to resolve a lot of his personal security issues would no longer be there and the Emperor thought Greg's intervention had the benefit of tactics and capability that might be foreign to the Traykorite. Could Greg read minds? Was Greg telepathic? Is that how he did it? He certainly had been in the presence of Commander Zebrovska and if was in fact telepathic, that might have been his method to discover the plot soon enough to warn him about it and save his life.

EMPEROR CALESTINE
Did you all sleep well last night?

GREG
Yes, the bed was very comfortable.

EMPEROR CALESTINE
I'm glad you were comfortable.

The meat and other trimmings laid out for them tasted exceptionally good. The egg like servings came from a large bird double the size of an Ostrich back on Planet Earth. Greg didn't ask much about the source of the food as he feared what he might find out. He experienced regretting asking his Japanese in-laws while in Japan about some of their food. The surprise was not delightful.

Greg also didn't know the emperor was eating some of his victory meat. When several of the conspirators were killed, parts of their bodies were sliced off to provide the emperor the traditional victory meal. If Greg had a change of heart and decided to stay instead of going back to Earth, the Emperor might inform him at that time the delicious meal he was eating happened to come off the Shank of one of the highest-ranking Space Force Commanders that chose to be part of the Coup.

After they completed their meals, the emperor suggested they go back to their guestrooms and freshen up. When they arrived, they discovered they all had new clothes to change into, which the emperor insisted they put on and wore as a dignified effort to add to the distinction when he took all three back to the Space Force building.

What Greg didn't know until Tiāncái explained it to him later when they were alone, "

TIĀNCÁI
These are unique clothes, you will get a lot of people staring at you, because they have the emperor's markings on them. Nobody in the Empire is allowed to wear these specific clothes unless the emperor personally scheduled them to wear it.

GREG
Just what I need, more visibility.

TIĀNCÁI
Greg, it might be a good idea that you are going back to Earth because you are irrevocably tied to the emperor forever and you are now part of his private court. You can also expect to have security staying close to you until you leave the planet.

GREG
I hope he doesn't change his mind.

TIĀNCÁI
Emperor Calestine always does what he says he will. He feels people that change their minds are weak. Right or wrong, he will always carry out his actions once he decides.

When everyone was dressed there was a knock at the door by valets. *It was kind of strange they seemed to know exactly when we were ready,* Greg thought.

Greg opened the door almost precisely the same time Frostria opened her guestroom door to be greeted by her personal valet.

VALET

Greg, Sir, we are ready to escort you and your party to the front entrance. The Emperor's Space Transport is there now ready to take you back to the Space Force Center.

GREG

Thank you, please lead the way.

As they passed by Frostria's room she and her valet blended into the group and walked down the circular stairway and the short distance to the front entrance. The door was wide open and directly in Front was Emperor Calestine and Mistress Lyavendar. It was they were waiting for the entourage to line up in a formation and walk into the very large Space Transport, probably large enough to hold fifty people. However, once they followed the emperor inside, they discovered an ostentatious Royal Transportation Space Transport.

Emperor's aid facilitated strapping in everyone including the emperor himself. Should the craft suddenly experience problems resulting in the possibility of a crash, each person would be secured to a seat that was part of an elaborate ejection system. Within seconds of the ship's computers determining a crash was imminent, out of the overhead a plexiglass bubble would come down completely covering the passenger in Case it happened in space and would deliver them back down to the planet's surface.

In the atmosphere where the emperor's craft traveled most of the time, it would gently take him back down to the planet's surface and vector in rescue squads.

When all conditions were set the two Space Force Drivers in the cockpit lifted off gently. At the same time fifty other craft lifted out of secret hangers well camouflaged, and they were only a small number of the actual Emperor's private Space Force. In the very few times Galactic Strife came near the planet, his Space Transport, would leave the planet with five times of those number of escorts and travel up to the Dreadnaught set up to take him at extreme velocities where he needed to get to avoid possible death and destruction from his enemies.

The visibility inside the emperor's personal Space Transport allowed Greg to observe the escort craft leave their secret hangers and form a unique large wing designed to shield the emperor as much as possible. This was a sight to behold, and it was only a very small part of the Traykorite Empire.

When the Emperor travels somewhere he does not have the 3D Freeway restrictions. Simply put, he flies wherever he wants and in any direction. The Emperor's Space

Transport made a beeline to the Space Force building. In preparation for his visit, all the craft in the main hangar located in the center of the building were moved out somewhere else. No other craft were allowed in the Space Force main hangar while the Emperor's Space Transport was there. This was a very rare visit by the emperor.

The hangar entrance was large and could take a much larger Transport which sometimes necessary to return Space Commanders back up to their orbiting ships at the conclusion of meetings and conferences. Most of the Space Force Vessels remained in Space all the time because of the time constraints and fuel requirements to leave the planet surface and get back out to space. Usually, only shuttles came down and landed at this Space Force building or some others on the planet.

The emperor's security detail was immense, like most of his concerns they were vast and impressive. The very minute the emperor announced he would take the two lovebirds Greg and Frostria, and the robot Tiāncái back to the Space Force Building, and then Frostria to her apartment, the valet alerted his security detail members about the mission. The building had been taken over by the security detail and most of its inhabitants were removed and taken somewhere for a few hours before they were brought back, not knowing any reason why they were removed and deposited places for leisure time.

The most trusted Space Commanders were in the hangar to Greet the Emperor along with 100 of his well-dressed security detail members in the hangar and many more stationed throughout the building and on all adjacent rooftops with sophisticated weapons that were point, fire, and forget. The weapons found their target using sophisticated sensors and electronics.

EXT. CGI. DAY. THE EMPEROR'S TRANSPORT ENTERS TRAYKORITE SPACE FORCE HANGER VIA THE SIDE OF THE BUILDING.

The Emperor's Space Transport curved around and headed directly for the opening in the building side. The slowing was soft and gentle and entering the building almost felt like nothing was moving.

INT. DAY. EMPEROR'S TRANSPORT INSIDE TRAYKORITE SPACE FORCE BUILDING.

ONBOARD VALET
Greg, Frostria, and Tiāncái, you will remain onboard
while the emperor leaves the Royal Transport and
walks out a few feet forward to a podium that had
wireless microphones. Mistress Lyavendar will walk
behind Emperor Calestine and then take position to
his right side. This is symbolic since the emperor is
right-handed.

GREG
Alright.

ONBOARD VALET
Greg, I will then escort you to stand next to the emperor's left side.

The Onboard Valet then showed Greg a diagram where each person was to stand left of the emperor: first Greg, then Tiāncái and then Frostria.

The emperor didn't need a speech prepared as he departed his royal transport and walked up to the microphone. He was intelligent and knew what he was going to say so there was no point in a speech writer or a teleprompter device.

Upon cue, Greg, Tiāncái, and Frostria took their positions next to the emperor and when the emperor saw everyone was present, it was time to begin.

EMPEROR CALESTINE
Space Force Commanders, I'm sure most of you know my guests standing here. Gregory Bissell and his Robot Tiāncái recently arrived here from another Universe.

Their actions have changed science and history. Their extreme bravery and dedication to their mission lasting twenty-two years to arrive is testament to unusual beings that show us that sometimes the impossible is achievable.

Even though Greg and Tiāncái are guests they are also space pioneers and have gone where no other being has ever attempted before and achieved vast discovery for his civilization.

To reward Greg for his excellent results of his mission being the first person we know of that has found alternate Universes, I've given him the opportunity to travel aboard our new Frigate, Royal Traykorite Ship RTS Finatscha during its maiden voyage.

Your destination on that voyage is still SECRET and you will learn the details of the mission after you leave for security reasons.

Gregory Bissell and his Robot Tiāncái are my official guests on this planet until further notice. Please treat him well and if you have any questions about what I expect out of you, contact your superior officers who will contact me for any clarification required.

Emperor Calestine turned to Greg.

EMPEROR CALESTINE
Greg, would you like to address the Space Force
Personnel that are here?

Greg nodded and stepped towards the podium as the emperor stepped to the side and
Greg approached. Greg then turned to Tiāncái.

GREG
Tiāncái, please step next to me and I will make my
statements in English, and you will translate into
standard Traykorite.

Tiāncái stepped next to Greg who then started speaking.

GREG
I want to thank everyone who has helped me since I
arrived. If you don't know, when my spaceship arrived
in this Galaxy I was in serious trouble because I did
not know one of my nuclear rocket engines had been
compromised and would have lasted a short time
before it malfunctioned.

Tiāncái who had indefinite memory and Traykorite translation ability spoke Gregs
words in perfect Traykorite in his Clark Gable voice that was commanding and had a
psychological effect on all the Traykorite space force personnel present because of the
sound quality as well as the articulation in the pronunciation of each word.

TIĀNCÁI
Traykorite translation: *YA khochu poblagodarit' vsekh,
kto pomogal mne s momenta moyego pribytiya. Yesli vy
ne znayete, kogda moy kosmicheskiy korabl' pribyl v etu
Galaktiku, u menya byli ser'yeznyye problemy, potomu
chto ya ne znal, chto odin iz moikh yadernykh raketnykh
dvigateley byl skomprometirovan i prosluzhil by dolgo.
nezadolgo do togo, kak on vyshel iz stroya.*

GREG
The Traykorite Space Force could not communicate
with me and had no idea I was in trouble, but they
latched onto my ship and slowed me down and
eventually landed me on this planet, saving my life.

Tiāncái then repeated the words he easily can record and translate in perfect precision
using his Clark Gable voice.

TIĀNCÁI
Traykorite translation: *Kosmicheskiye sily Traykorita*

ne mogli svyazat'sya so mnoy i ponyatiya ne imeli, chto u menya problemy, no oni zatsepilis' za moy korabl', zamedlili menya i v kontse kontsov vysadili menya na etoy planete, spasaya mne zhizn'.

GREG

To be honest, I almost gave up hope of coming to this planet and galaxy. Without your help I would never be able to inform my civilization in a different universe their theories were all wrong, that the universe doesn't end, but it has pockets of life spread out over distances we can't quite contemplate.

Tiāncái then repeated the words in perfect precision using his Clark Gable voice.

TIĀNCÁI

Traykorite translation: *Chestno govorya, ya pochti poteryal nadezhdu popast' na etu planetu i v galaktiku. Bez vashey pomoshchi ya by nikogda ne smog soobshchit' moyey tsivilizatsii v drugoy vselennoy, chto vse ikh teorii oshibochny, chto Vselennaya ne konchayetsya, no u neye yest' konets. ochagi zhizni, razbrosannyye na rasstoyaniyakh, kotoryye my ne mozhem dazhe predstavit'.*

GREG

I owe my life to the Traykorite Space Force. You also give me hope that one day I can return to my world and explain to them the universe is a lot larger than they understand.

Tiāncái then repeated the words in perfect precision using his Clark Gable voice.

TIĀNCÁI

Traykorite translation: *YA obyazan svoyey zhizn'yu Kosmicheskim silam Traykorita. Vy takzhe dayete mne nadezhdu, chto odnazhdy ya smogu vernut'sya v svoy mir i ob"yasnit' im, chto Vselennaya namnogo bol'she, chem oni ponimayut.*

GREG

I do not know much about your words. But each day I learn more and view your civilization with immense respect. Your politeness and friendliness are very much appreciated. I hope that one day I can repay your kindness.

Tiāncái then repeated the words in perfect precision using his Clark Gable voice.

TIĀNCÁI
Traykorite translation: *YA malo chto znayu o vashikh slovakh. No kazhdyy den' ya uznayu bol'she i smotryu na vashu tsivilizatsiyu s ogromnym uvazheniyem. Vasha vezhlivost' i druzhelyubiye ochen' tsenyatsya. YA nadeyus', chto odnazhdy ya smogu otplatit' za vashu dobrotu.*

Greg stepped back from the podium, did a great bow to the emperor like he learned in Japan, then faced the crowd and copied it. To the surprise of everyone he then turned to Frostria and bowed to her.

With the clothes that signified court members of the emperor, everyone there stood in great respect and those who knew Frostria were quite stunned how much her looks had changed and the luster she exhibited with the professionally applied makeup that Mistress Lyavendar's makeup artists were directed to perfect just for this social appearance. It was also apparent she had climbed the social ladder of the Traykorite Empire by a million steps on mile-high ladders just overnight.

The emperor walked towards Greg .

EMPEROR CALESTINE
We will now take Frostria to her residence on our way home. We think it's only fitting that such an extravagant woman that clearly has special feelings for you, my friend that I take her to her residence so that all her friends and neighbors know she is a friend of the Emperor and Mistress Lyavendar.

GREG
Your Excellency, I'm sure she will enjoy that.

EMPEROR CALESTINE
We will be in touch.

GREG
Thank you.

The Emperor said something to Mistress Lyavendar in standard Traykorite, and she walked over to Frostria.

MISTRESS LYAVENDAR
We will now take you to your apartment since it is on our way home.

Mistress Lyavendar, Frostria, and Emperor Calestine got back on the Emperor's Royal Transport and everyone then moved to the side of the hangar outside a yellow circle which signified the rotation area so that Aircars and Space Transports could do 180 degrees and leave the hangar area with the cockpits in front to simplify the efforts for the pilots. The craft had surprisingly quiet propulsion and spun 180 degrees around and slowly moved to the hangar door and flew out of it.

Security forces blocked off the street in front of the tall high-rise building that contained Frostria's apartment. No ground transportation could enter this area until the emperor departed in his Royal Transport.

Frostria lived in an upward mobile people's apartment close to downtown. The snobs were everywhere. They were stunned when out of no where came the Emperor's Space Transport, very nicely designed with an outer skin that gave it a surreal appearance of sleekness and most likely high-speed capability. Indeed, it was fast and could probably outrun anything in the galaxy for the sake of security.

The emperor stepped out of the Space Transport that was now resting directly on the street in front of Frostira's apartment building stood to the side waiting for Mistress Lyavendar and Frostria to appear who followed immediately.

There was a half-dozen people who recognized one of the residents they saw now and then in her Space Force uniform going to and from work. She was pleasant looking but now wearing the emperor's special clothing reserved for his court, she looked stunning thanks to Mistress Lyavendar's makeup artists.

Mistress Lyavendar grabbed Frostria's hands and raised them.

MISTRESS LYAVENDAR
Thank you for spending time with me, I really enjoyed
it. It gets lonely sometimes at the emperor's mansion
and to have you with me made my day happier.

FROSTRIA
Thank you for inviting me to the emperor's mansion
and also giving me such important advice.

MISTRESS LYAVENDAR
I would like to see you again soon.

FROSTRIA
Any time, my dear friend.

Mistress Lyavendar smiled, let Frostria's hands loose then turned toward the emperor and smiled and nodded. The Emperor held his hand and gestured for Mistress Lyavendar to get back on the Emperor's Royal Transport and as she stepped into the Transport, the Emperor turned toward the small crowd and smiled and gave a three-second quick wave, about the time Frostria was approaching the front entrance and the sliding doors slid sideways with a hissing sound from their pneumatic control.

Frostria stepped into the elevator with another female resident who was beaming that they were surprised to have a distinguished resident living among them. Soon they would be even happier when they discovered the two men sitting outside Frostria's door were security men to protect her. This building now had far more security than any other near the center city.

A couple days later, Mistress Lyavendar contacted Frostria.

MISTRESS LYAVENDAR

I'm going to take you to the Scriabin Mud Baths today.

FROSTRIA

I am scheduled to work today; I need to get permission to take time off.

MISTRESS LYAVENDAR

Not to worry, you will get your notification from your supervisor you have an assignment to assist the emperor in a few minutes.

FROSTRIA

How soon will we be going?

MISTRESS LYAVENDAR

Your transportation will arrive in a few minutes in front of your building. Don't worry about getting dressed up, we'll do that when we get to the Scriabin Mud Baths.

FROSTRIA

I'm in my uniform now, I'll change into some casual clothes.

MISTRESS LYAVENDAR

See you soon.

No sooner than Frostria was changed into civilian clothes that didn't stand out, but she was a pretty woman so people would look at her nevertheless, there was a doorbell notification a visitor was outside. Frostria knew the two Traykorite Space Force (TSF) security men were always there in shifts and had no fear of opening the door and discovered one of the security men wanted to inform her.

TSF SECURITY OFFICER

Your transportation has arrived and is now down on the street in front of the building.

FROSTRIA

Thank you. I'm ready to go.

Frostria didn't bring anything but her personal communicator and her identification because all Traykorite Space Force personnel have a chip planted in their bodies for Empire wide identification.

The two TSF security men escorted Frostria to the Elevator while other security men were in the apartment next door observing everything on sound-video.

The security detachment took the elevator to the street level with Frostria and escorted her out to the Emperor's Royal Transport. This was one of a dozen the emperor had because he sometimes flew decoys to keep his enemies guessing.

On one occasion some of those enemies were celebrating they killed the Emperor and the Coup had succeeded while he remained in his office back in the Palace. One of his doubles did in fact bite the dust.

Nothing like seeing the terror in the hearts of conspirators when they thought they won and were celebrating prematurely, only to find themselves surrounded by the secret police and receive the holograph of the Emperor notifying them their lives had been forfeited.

The Emperor's Royal Transport reconfigured and lifted up off the ground on wheels after the women were aboard and secured in their seats. The slow increase in altitude was soft and deliberate and they ship rose up through an electronic chimney that routed all traffic around it. As it passed through the top 3D Freeway lanes at modest speeds, it kept on rising and gathering speed. In due time the speed increased more constantly with the ship banked up to cover the distance quickly. In due time it was going supersonic moving above the cloud cover and heading for space. Going out into space would save them twelve hours and be safer.

Even though Frostria was a TSF member, she had never been in space before. But it was a routine matter for Mistress Lyavendar and soon Frostria realized what was happening, it was a milestone in her life. The speed kept increasing and eventually the ship hit 24,000 miles per hour then in a short period of time came back down into the atmosphere on the other side of the planet.

The Scriabin Mud Baths were located in a Valley on the other side of the planet, nestled within a wide valley that was known for its high-quality distilleries that fermented the most delicious fruits in the Galaxy.

The mud baths were part of a health spa that provided the clientele copious amounts of distilled ferments that provided ample pleasure while sitting in these large swimming pools full of this extremely valuable mud containing the best nutrients in the galaxy. A few hours of lounging restored the body quicker than anything known to Traykorite-kind. This mud bath venue was reserved for females only. Males were not allowed in, except for the male models brought in to motivate the women. The male models were of course nude, showing their junk and if a wealthy woman wanted to experience copulation with a particular model, arrangements could be done rather efficiently.

Wealthy women often came here not for the male services, but simply to get horny and then go home and devour their spouse. This was not likely to happen for these two women since there were four security men with them to provide protection. Any male model dumb enough to service these two women would most likely get his *junk amputated* before the day was done.

MISTRESS LYAVENDAR
How are things working out with you and Gregory Bissell?

FROSTRIA
Really good since I followed your instructions and stirred a fire in him.

MISTRESS LYAVENDAR
Did Gregory stir a fire in you?

FROSTRIA
Most certainly.

MISTRESS LYAVENDAR
How is the Alien tool, is it similar to our men?

FROSTRIA
I was a virgin until I met Greg. I have no idea how a Traykorite makes a woman feel.

MISTRESS LYAVENDAR
They probably feel the same. Does he put you in a trance or anything?

FROSTRIA
Yes, causes me to have the most intense orgasms and he warms my heart.

MISTRESS LYAVENDAR
Is it due to the size of his tool or is it due to his expertise?

FROSTRIA
Greg's experienced, and his tool is the perfect size.

Frostria wasn't giving up the secret that Greg did to her. This was going to be tough. Mistress Lyavendar might even have to arrange a secret rendezvous with Greg. *But would the valet agree to arrange it again? He seems so paranoid.*

Beautiful scantily dressed young women also came in with food snacks for the women. They could get their mud bath, spirits, and lunch all at the same time.

Women usually only lasted two hours in the mud, got out and went into a highly efficient shower that added more vitamins to their skin, then they were ushered into a warm bubble bath while another young lady came in and shampooed their hair to get it prepped for a hairdo. These women arrived in undistinguishable clothes, but Mistress Lyavendar's assistants brought with them her change of clothes as well as an Emperor's Court seal for Frostria.

Very few of the employees knew the two customers were VIPs. Rich women came in all the time, so nothing was unexpected. But to have a Royal was another matter.

After the women were pampered and cleaned up really well including Mistress Lyavendar's personal makeup artist working on the two of them, they were poised to leave, and Mistress Lyavendar took Frostria back with her to the Palace so she could probe more about the magic Gregory Bissell did to Frostria.

It probably saved Greg's life to leave when he did to Earth because had he stayed just a few more days, Mistress Lyavendar would have forced copulation on him and forced him to reveal his magic he did with Frostria. The exit strategy was coincidentally one of the most auspicious moments in Greg's life because it created an awareness nobody on Earth will ever have.

Greg had not seen Frostria all day. Nevertheless, he was brought back into the 3D conference room where several levels gave it a feeling as if it were a stadium and he was the game they were observing. Most of the time they just listened and took notes, there were few questions from many of the prestigious scientists observing who had by now looked at a lot of the video Tiāncái provided them.

Today it seemed it was a little more focused on just a few items. The scientists knew that based on Greg and Tiāncái comments, Earth had never passed by intelligent life until this mission because they had not ventured far enough out in space.

And when Greg discovered numerous intelligent life forms in Galaxies he passed, why didn't he slow down, possibly stop and reach out to those Aliens? Perhaps his trip to another universe was not as important because these Aliens were in a more advantageous location to plunder Earth.

GREG

My ship was in autopilot, I had no ability to maneuver and I could not have slowed down and stopped and communicated even if I wanted.

RESEARCHER

In hindsight, do you not think that was counterproductive since those beings are a lot closer to your planet and place a risk towards it?

GREG

The main reason why I was sent on this mission was to prove once and for all, the Big Bang Theory was nothing more than irrational exuberance for academia who came up with some calculations and theories that drove a lot of successful funding requests. Big Bang Theory is just as valid as the Global Warming hysteria that existed 22 years ago.

Greg realized the Traykorite scientists had no idea what global warming meant.

GREG

Those attempted Alien communications were a distraction. In my heart, my mind, and my soul, I just could not believe the universe ended. There was no logical reason. Infinity is a hard thing to swallow when we have limited knowledge. Earth scientists cannot accept the rationale, there is no answer, so they say divide by zero is undefined. Claiming they found the end of the universe in my opinion is nothing more than some mathematician claiming they have a solution for divide by zero.

So, I continued on, and I ignored the Aliens and their threats and I was lucky none of them were ready to catch up with me thanks to my velocity being so fast. I developed an agenda, I wanted to know, does the universe end? Did the scientific calculations that claim our universe that had objects thirty-five billion light years away really make sense?

My robot assistant Tiāncái early on informed me he had a drug that could give me periods of suspended animation to reduce the boring time and not require awareness when I might dwell on my personal situation creating sorrow. Those many periods of suspended animation also coincided with periods Aliens attempted to communicate. It also eliminated my aging and due to the reduced gravity, I appear to have grown perhaps ten years younger.

RESEARCHER

When you came up to the dark zone, did you feel you had made a big mistake, and your scientists were right and you were wrong?

GREG

Yes, I felt defeated then. I assumed I gave my life up for a folly, but I still could not believe the Big Bang Theorists were right because God would not make a defined universe if the area of space has no dimensions."

RESEARCHER
You kept on going. Was there no provision to slow down and turn around?

GREG
At the time I felt slowing down with the amount of fuel I had was impossible and even if I accomplished slowing and stopping, speeding back up would take a lot of fuel and it's doubtful I had the fuel or the ability to get back to Earth, so I just continued into the void.

RESEARCHER
How long in the void?

GREG
A couple of years.

RESEARCHER
What happened when you discovered another universe?

GREG
I was at my lowest point, I had failed and had no further purpose in life. Tiāncái had cyanide pills for me to take to end my life.

RESEARCHER
What was Tiāncái's plans after you ended it?

GREG
He indicated to me later he intended on going until all the fuel was gone and the nuclear generators failed.

RESEARCHER
What happened when you discovered our universe?

GREG
At first I disbelieved it. I was convinced I failed. I assumed our sensors or processors had developed a defect and was displaying a ghost target, but Tiāncái claimed all sensors were working correctly and that was a valid sighting.

RESEARCHER
What did you do next?

GREG

For the next few days, I watched that dot grow into your galaxy. I was suddenly relieved God did not fail me; he is what I imagined endless with no bounds. At the same time, I was sad because Earth and any sentient beings would never discover another universe because it would be tempting to believe they knew where the end of the universe existed.

RESEARCHER

What were your intentions after finding our universe?

GREG

I was going extremely fast accelerating for twenty-two years. I knew it would be impossible for me to slow down, therefore my decision was to fly through your galaxies and observe until the end of my time.

RESEARCHER

What were your feelings when our space force ship slowed you down and brought you to our planet?

GREG

Eternal gratefulness. You saved my life and now I can live being happy that I went to the end of the Universe and beyond and found our universe really didn't end. One can say a multiverse is an extension of a metagalaxy.

The crowd seemed subdued because Greg had shattered their scientific world just like his own that created a complicated explanation of the universe that ended up as nothing more than a false narrative.

Greg had not changed his own world yet, but he had certainly changed an entire vast Traykorite Empire that stretched over hundreds of galaxies and mapped most of their known universe. And soon if it all worked out, he would be back on Earth in a few years with all the proof, as well as astonished visitors from another Universe.

THE SPIES CONFESSION

As Greg was later exiting the 3D conference room answering a few extraneous questions on the way-out Commander Stanfrad Villiers approached.

COMMANDER STANFRAD VILLIERS

I've been asked to take you and your Robot Tiāncái somewhere. Please follow me.

Greg dutifully followed Commander Stanfrad Villiers to his Aircar and when the Commander stated.

COMMANDER STANFRAD VILLIERS
Please get into the Aircar.

Greg and Tiāncái entered the front seat which the Commander had gestured towards.

Greg was wearing his Earth Space Uniform which he preferred and Commander Stanfrad Villiers had on his Traykorite Space Force uniform. Tiāncái also had on his Earth Space Uniform and could pass easily for an Earth Space Crew member.

The double doors for Commander Stanfrad Villiers Aircar port automatically opened inwards wide open and when everyone were strapped in, and the bubble top came down, the craft slowly edged out of the parking area first inches per second until it reached feet per second then curved and jumped up to the upper 3D Freeway level flying promptly over the center of the city before curving out towards the Green zone ahead Greg knew was the Emperors private reserve.

Within ten minutes, Commander Stanfrad Villiers Aircar slowly landed in front of the main entrance of the emperor's palace.

The valet was there to greet them and escorted them directly to the pool where Emperor Calestine was in the pool playing with his pet Franzcas.

Emperor Calestine soon climbed out of the pool and the trainer was at the end of the pool with the locks to their canal back to the larger pool and feeding the Franzcas.

EMPEROR CALESTINE
I'm going to change my clothes, I'll be right back, make
yourselves comfortable.

Commander Stanfrad Villiers sat down at a shaded table under the large awning taking it all in. Greg sat down focused on the Commander, wondering what this was all about.

GREG
How's the Fast Frigate coming along?

COMMANDER STANFRAD VILLIERS
It's getting there quickly, the emperor put a high
priority on completing it.

GREG
Is our timeline still looking good?

COMMANDER STANFRAD VILLIERS
Most definitely. You will be back at earth a lot sooner
than you realize.

GREG
What about the difficulty in navigation?

COMMANDER STANFRAD VILLIERS
Thanks to your numerous videos, we have developed a navigation system that will easily track our way to your planet.

GREG
That's exciting to think about it.

COMMANDER STANFRAD VILLIERS
It's exciting even more because you have also changed our science and it will have an impact on us because we now have to worry about potential adversaries from your universe crossing over into ours just like our traditional enemies in this universe.

GREG
Did I cause you problems in doing so?

COMMANDER STANFRAD VILLIERS
No, you helped us a lot. We were living with false science and could be a pushover if an invading force came from the dark zone.

GREG
What do you plan on doing about it?

COMMANDER STANFRAD VILLIERS
We'll have to eventually move our capital again. Aiguo is no longer considered safe. What's behind us now can potentially be just as dangerous as what's in front of us.

GREG
How much of the Royal Traykorite Ship RTS Finatscha is completed?

COMMANDER STANFRAD VILLIERS
It's really 99% completed for the most part. Testing it and loading it out for the mission is all that's really left.

Those words hit Greg like a rock. It seemed almost impossible, but it really was happening. He had a way to get home to Earth.

Emperor Calestine returned wearing comfortable clothes. They didn't look all pomp and circumstance like but they certainly looked intricate and comfortable.

EMPEROR CALESTINE
Thanks for bringing Greg to the Palace. Would you like to stay for dinner?

COMMANDER STANFRAD VILLIERS
Your Excellency, I would love to stay for dinner, but if I'm going to meet your schedule I need to get back to my office and do some work.

EMPEROR CALESTINE
Well, I appreciate that.

COMMANDER STANFRAD VILLIERS
We are gripped with getting this mission underway with Royal Traykorite Ship RTS Finatscha, but we are also building other Frigates that should be ready to test and deploy shortly after I return.

EMPEROR CALESTINE
Yes, that's important as well. We have to strengthen our frontier facing the Zomulites, because I do not expect them to continue honoring their treaties much longer.

COMMANDER STANFRAD VILLIERS
Unfortunately, just when you think you will have generations without war, unexpectedly creatures like the Zomulites who didn't learn their lesson from the last war, must raise their ugly head again.

EMPEROR CALESTINE
That's why we must remain vigilant and maintain a viable Space Force.

COMMANDER STANFRAD VILLIERS
With your permission, Your Excellency, I wish to return to my work now.

EMPEROR CALESTINE
Yes, please go and thank you for bringing my guests here as I am concerned about their safety, that's why I requested you help.

COMMANDER STANFRAD VILLIERS
Not a problem, Your Excellency. I'm here to serve you.

EMPEROR CALESTINE
Thank you, Commander, we will be seeing each other again real soon and hopefully when you are not

> working so hard so I can provide you some personal
> rewards for your personal sacrifice in carrying out
> several important missions for me.

The commander stood and the valet gestured, this way, and said a few words in standard Traykorite.

Mistress Lyavendar and Frostria were putting on the finishing touches about then. The restorative properties of the Scriabin Mud Baths had done their magic along with the intensive vitamin treatment spiked in the food and drink provided during the experience. In about 48 hours they would no longer feel quite as good as they did now as the effects of the treatment wore off. Wealthy women who went to the Scriabin Mud Baths once a week, ultimately did get into great physical condition, but their neglecting husbands were usually the last ones to enjoy their reinvigorated bodies.

Mistress Lyavendar personally supervised the work on Frostria. She wanted to make sure that Greg and Frostria became permanent partners, which by now would simplify matters since the emperor already knew the details how Greg put himself at huge risk to save him. Greg by no way ever asked for any favors, but the women were not appraised to his promise to provide Greg a way to get back to Earth so he could live out his life in his native country. One man kept the emperor alive. Since Frostria was involved in saving the emperor, she too was thought of fondly and the emperor would also reward her lavishly, especially since by all outward appearances.

Mistress Lyavendar acted as if Frostria was her best friend or adopted little sister. Frostria had been sterile all her life, the product of training as a psychoanalyst and now a key person for the Traykorite Space Force and didn't have a social life before Mistress Lyavendar started grooming her up to be a valuable member of the court.

Mistress Lyavendar also needed reliable friends she could socialize with, and her superb intuition knew Frostria had never had a man in her life before Greg opened her up and captivated her in ways quite remarkable. The way those two seemed to bond in bed was nothing like Mistress Lyavendar ever witnessed before and she was hoping soon that Frostria would tell her the secret. What mechanism triggered the physical reactions she exhibited. The greatest challenge in obtaining those vital secrets related to she could not actually come right out and ask poignant questions without revealing there was some form of voyeurism involved that would indeed spoil the relationship.

Okay, my dear, you are finally ready. I think Greg will have great affection for you tonight, because you look so beautiful.

My lady, I have no way to look this beautiful without your help and my actions clearly are insufficient without your coaching.

The makeup artists and fashion consultants were out of the room and the two women were alone and could talk privately, so Mistress Lyavendar who wanted Frostria to be her friend whom she could sustain a dear friendship, now surprised Frostria.

MISTRESS LYAVENDAR

When we are alone, I want you to use my birth name in conversations with me, or if you are ever in danger, use that name and I will know you need immediate help. I'm Saraotta.

FROSTRIA

Saraotta, that's a beautiful name.

MISTRESS LYAVENDAR

You must keep this entirely confidential between us. Only you know my real name.

FROSTRIA

I will, Saraotta.

MISTRESS LYAVENDAR

I will confide in you now, why all the secrecy. That's how much you mean to me. Because of whom I am and what I've become as the future Empress, it's almost impossible to have friends and ever leave the Palace. If the public ever finds out the truth, the emperor will face a lot of trouble. This affects me but more importantly if affects the emperor and you know all the trouble he recently had, this would be too much for him to handle.

FROSTRIA

It sounds serious.

MISTRESS LYAVENDAR

Frostria, I'm a Zomulite spy actually. I was sent here to seduce Emperor Calestine and kill him. But before I carried out my mission, I fell in love with him. He is all I want in life, not because he can spoil me with wealth, but because he owns my heart. I love him and would die for him if I had to.

FROSTRIA

Why don't you confide in the emperor, he seems like a man with great wisdom. He knows how emotionally bonded to him you are.

MISTRESS LYAVENDAR

I can't tell him. I don't want to put him into a bad position. If anyone else found out he was sleeping with a Zomulite, it would undermine him.

FROSTRIA

The emperor could easily work this out.

MISTRESS LYAVENDAR

The emperor is not the problem. He's wonderful and would protect me. The problem is the Space Force exists primarily to deal with the Zomulites and a few other enemies. If certain key individuals discovered I'm a Zomulite and had sent her to kill the Emperor, they would demand my arrest or send in specialists to assassinate me.

FROSTRIA

What if he finds out?

MISTRESS LYAVENDAR

I'm willing to wait for that day. I would probably offer to commit suicide as a show of my love for him so that he would not have to endure intrigue from court members.

FROSTRIA

Your secret is safe with me. I want you to be happy with the Emperor because I can tell you bring great joy to his life.

MISTRESS LYAVENDAR

I do my best and try every day.

Frostria knew a couple things. Mistress Lyavendar was living on borrowed time. She also knew her own life was in jeopardy because if the emperor knew she knew that Saraotta was a Zomulite spy, he would probably have her executed for not revealing it.

Tonight was one of the most horrible nights of Frostria's life. Frostria now carried a terrible burden, not to expose her friend, and the feeling of committing treason for concealing a spy from their most treacherous enemies that caused numerous wars for the Traykorites because of their numerous client states and worlds on the periphery between the two Empires.

Being somewhat sophisticated and already experiencing a drama where Frostria had to maintain her cool as to not give herself away and save the Emperor, she now had to find that inner strength to hide all her emotions to not give away something was seriously wrong. Another fear she had stemmed from her training on spotting espionage and insider threats. What just may have occurred was another act right out of the playbook and she might have unwittingly allowed herself to be recruited by enemy spies.

Was there going to be coercion to follow?

Emperor Calestine's Personal Valet raised an eyebrow as he watched the surveillance video of the two women. *Frostria is in over her head and doesn't know it.* The valet thought and smiled.

The women soon left Mistress Lyavendar's suite and made their way down to the pool area where the Emperor and Greg were in discussions about some of Earth's features like Mount Everest and the Marianas Trench. The emperor and seen a lot of natural phenomena in his life and enjoyed discovering new information about planets, solar systems, galaxies, and now alternate universes.

Those discussions had triggered staff to move the portable holographer near the Emperor as Tiāncái had IMAX video of documentaries about Mount Everest and the Marianas Islands.

The two women walked down as exotic creatures that immediately bestowed the glamour they carried ostensibly on the wings of doves; they were so beautiful tonight.

The valet of course had on his poker face and the most politeness anyone could ever imagine.

The dinner and the private entertainment magnified Greg's senses. He was acutely aware he was sitting a few feet away from an Emperor who affected trillions of beings and ostensibly billions of planets.

To be in the company of such an extraordinary and powerful man gave him pause. He also now understood that even powerful men lived fragile lives because of recent activities. If he only knew half of what Frostria carried as a burden, it would be mildly overwhelming.

This trip to the edge of the Universe has turned out far more than what Greg considered possible. If Greg made it back to Earth alive, he might consider moving to a Buddhist Temple for the rest of his life. After all this, his focus in life might not adequately allow him to cope. His belief system was shattered except for one thing, he knew God was the almighty and created all this plus much more. But why?

Commander Stanfrad Villiers was back in his office dotting his I's and crossing his T's, somewhat annoyed the emperor would commit him to such a mission on the cusp of developing events at the Frontier. He could ill afford to be gone on this crazy trip to the alternative universe to ostensibly return a wayward space traveler who really wasn't of value to the Traykorite race in any manner. But he understood the wrath of the emperor and the fact he was tied too closely to Commander Zebrovska whom he had numerous dealings with almost made it certain he went along with the nonsense because the last thing in the world he wanted was to be somehow accused of alignment with the Zebrovska crowd, most of which were now dead, but there were indeed a few survivors.

The Royal Traykorite Ship RTS Finatscha had powered up and did a few engineering trials to test out its four main propulsion systems. Unlike Frigates in the past that had only one propulsion system, the RTS Finatscha was redesigned to get across the galaxy and into the next galaxy at extreme speed. It wasn't capable of taking on a large force, its main purpose in life was INTEL and communications. It could get close to the action, get as much information as possible, then get back to safety quickly to warn the forces of enemy movements that might pose a significant threat.

For the periphery planets that presumably became Zomulite client states, buying their weapon systems and sharing INTEL, a fast Frigate showing up unexpectedly doing hit-and-run tactics using Eleptron Annihilators kept enemies off balance and decreased their appetite for worlds to become Zomulite client states allowing the Zomulites to materially slowly expand closer to the Traykorite Empire. To Earth people it would be contrived as the domino theory projected by President Eisenhower.

These were not happy times for Commander Stanfrad Villiers. Being the first Traykorite commander to cross over to another universe didn't make him enthused about the mission because he felt his Frigate could be used more profitably elsewhere. As a Loyal Commander, he would take his orders and proceed to Planet Earth. At this stage in planning, there was no turning back. The craft had just completed enough space trials to realize it was ready to go. Now all that was left was logistics, the loadout and the commencement of the mission.

The mapping provided by data files off Pluto II computers were quite comprehensive. Travel through the black zone was at such high velocities, the chances for set and drift were negligible. All they had to do is retrace Pluto II back to the alternate universe and the tracking of 400+ Galaxies back past the Andromeda Galaxy, then onto the Milky Way, as Earth named them, would be fairly simple for advanced space travelers such as the Traykorite.

Perhaps the best course of action would be to have Gregory Bissell assassinated and make it look like one of the Zomulites that Traykorite INTEL were secretly tracking killed him?

Plans to assassinate Gregory Bissell began that night. They now had about two weeks to complete the attempt before they would be forced to begin the mission. Once Gregory Bissell was put aboard the Royal Traykorite Ship RTS Finatscha it would be too late because the ruthless Emperor would hold him responsible, and instead of barbecuing Zomulites by the waterfall, it would be him and he had no intention of dying any time soon.

The emperor was captivated by the growing friendship between Mistress Lyavendar and Frostria. Mistress Lyavendar had not been so happy in such a long period of time. It was as if Mistress Lyavendar had found her long lost friend. No other lady friends ever transcended to such a relationship with her. For that the Emperor was grateful, but he also knew one other glaring detail. Within two weeks he would be tearing the heart out of Mistress Lyavendar because his common sense told him Gregory Bissell and Frostria had reached a point of no return in their relationship.

Watching those surveillance videos and watching that strange display of incredible focus and even more strange actions in their love making signaled they were soul mates. Separating them would almost be the same as giving one of them the death sentence and he feared it would be Frostria. So, it was a lose-lose proposition. The mission was now firm, and he had to fulfill his promise to Gregory Bissell, or he would never be able to look at himself in the mirror again. Nobody ever had earned the emperor's favor like this, and nobody had ever put their lives in severe jeopardy to do so.

The emperor knew what he had to do. He would soon have a secret meeting with Gregory Bissell and his Robot for translation. He would lay out the cards and simply state that it will break Mistress Lyavendar's heart when Greg took Frostria with him to Earth as she would insist on going, so he wanted the two women to be able to spend as much time together before they left.

There was no point in Greg going back to the Traykorite Space Force building as the research studies were now curtailed by the emperor himself. Any information scientists wanted to get from Gregory Bissell was now to late. But being a wise and shrewd Emperor, none of those scientists would know Gregory Bissell was leaving. He was just on holiday with the emperor for a couple of weeks, and to make it look legitimate they would take a few trips and of course the women would trek back to Scriabin Mud Baths a couple more times.

During one of those Mud Bath visits Mistress Lyavendar and Frostria enjoyed, the emperor took Greg secretly outside the solar system to a nearby star system that had the planet Poulenc.

Planet Poulenc specialized in recreation and secrecy. The green-skinned people were at a disadvantage since they were very much different than the rest of the Traykorite Empire.

To facilitate their secret *sanctuary city* environment, they never shared information with any off-worlders including Traykorite INTEL.

One of those discrete establishments provided special entertainment for the emperor and very few others, all the women that worked there were deaf and could not hear or read standard Traykorite. These Poulenc women only knew sign language developed for Poulenc's.

Since the emperor was traveling in the upmost secret fashion including aboard Traykorite Intel Transports, nobody knew it was the Emperor himself traveling. The Poulenc establishment owner knew the two men in disguise including temporary facial changes, were somehow connected to the INTEL apparatus they often made huge profits with. They were aimed to please.

The Emperor and Greg were suddenly in a room full of nude green women. To Greg it was certainly a spectacle. Their nipples were dark Green and they had purple eyes. Their shapes and scents were remarkable. It was as if they were sitting right in the middle of a beautiful bouquet of flowers with the most pleasant scent. All the women could do is smile and do sign language in Poulenc.

These green skin women were delightful creatures and aimed to please. One could say they were a cross between a polite Japanese Geisha girl who transcended sex and instead attempted to please the tormented soul of a Samurai. Neither Greg or the Emperor had sex with any of the women, though that was expected and they would had lovingly given themselves to these men, because only special men ever were allowed here. If you were not someone important you would never be allowed here.

These green skin women had a hidden agenda and had the reputation of the most exquisite lovers in the Galaxy. It was alleged their vaginas had chemicals 100 times more powerful than the best Traykorite sex inducer which was far more powerful than Viagra.

It was not uncommon for powerful men who took a liking to a green-skinned deaf mute bought her out of the enterprise and took back to his planet where she contently lived the rest of her life. Part of their enthusiasm for pleasing Greg and the Emperor was the chance to get bought out of this situation where they were practically sex slaves for the rich and famous.

As Greg took it all in, he had some drinks that were laced with pleasurizers that sometimes make the customers drowsy but tranquil. Greg felt that coming on so he decided that before he allowed himself to lay back and get a nap, he entered silent meditation and soon reached the Hemi Sync condition.

The women were slightly confused that neither man pursued sex they were entitled and instead gave loving comfort and as the two men lounged and napped with their security guards a few feet behind them, several green-skinned women clung to them as if they were angels because they were soft and sweet and not demanding. They were full of smiles and compliments and as a result all the women felt an uplifting.

Greg was even more fascinating because in his Hemi-Sync state he caused some strange mental condition with the women near him. Perhaps because they were deaf mutes, they were far more sensitive and perceptive than normal women. It was if this man had some sort of mental telepathy. He made the women feel strange in a way they liked it. They didn't understand why, but they had a positive valence with Greg.

The business owner/manager had thought he had seen everything. Some of the richest men in the universe taking a nap with his women and none of them pursued any sexual activity and the women were as happy like they had never been before, especially those with the one particular man that appeared to be a magnet to them.

Eventually Emperor Calestine slowly came out of his peaceful nap shortly after Greg exited his Hemi-Sync and asked Greg which Tiāncái translated.

EMPEROR CALESTINE
How do you like these women?

GREG
I love every one of them. They are incredibly sweet.
They look and feel exotic.

EMPEROR CALESTINE

If you had sex with them you would know what exotic
is.

GREG

I'll save it for Frostria, she affects my mind in very
pleasant ways.

EMPEROR CALESTINE

Greg, we should leave now, people are expecting us
back at the Mansion soon.

GREG

I'm ready to leave when you are, Your Excellency.

As they were leaving Greg bowed to some of the women and then said to Emperor
Calestine:

GREG

If you don't mind, I wish to hug a few of these girls.

EMPEROR CALESTINE

Sure, whatever you want to do to them. They are yours.

Greg signaled to one of the women he knew curled up against him to gesture to come
closer. When she did, he put his arms around her and hugged her. Then he gestured to
another, and she came as well. It didn't take long for the rest of the women to understand
what this kind gentleman was doing, and they were enthralled and eagerly sought his
hugs. It was an experience unlike what they had had in a very long time.

The emperor was mildly impressed with Greg. It now made perfect sense to him why
Frostria had such a fantastic attraction to this wonderful man. This also cemented the
deal for the Emperor. He was now without any regrets for sending Frostria to Earth
with his friend Gregory Bissell. He knew Frostria would not regret being with Greg for
the rest of his life.

The *Valet* was not surprised when his secret agent in the security detail reported back
what transpired with the Poulenc women. His respect for Gregory Bissell also grew
out of the reports. He too was even more interested in Greg now watching the secret
security videos that showed he had a strange effect on Frostria. And now he had just
done it again with several Poulenc women. *Was it a telepathic ability?*

Anxiety set in with the emperor in the final week. The Franzcas were very perceptive
animals and seldom befriended anyone. The Emperor, Greg, and the trainer were the
only humanoids the Franzcas befriended. The emperor purposely delayed going to the
pool when the Franzcas were expecting his daily visit just to see how much they had
taken a liking to Greg. Their friendship was now complete as if it were the emperor
himself, they had spent every day with for the past twelve Traykorite years.

The emperor had never had a friend like Greg before. Someone who expected nothing. He never asked for any favors and only was going to Earth because the emperor knew Greg had put himself at great risk to save his life. The emperor did have second thoughts about canceling the return to Earth, but he now knew he had built up Gregory Bissel's expectations so much that to not go through with it might have a paralyzing effect.

Mistress Lyavendar would be agitated and upset with the emperor for quite some time for sending Frostria away with Greg. He would let her simmer for a few weeks, then they would have a frank discussion that to not send her with Gregory Bissel would have broken their hearts. He knew by watching Mistress Lyavendar watch the surveillance videos how special that bond was. And he knew in the end she couldn't argue the point because she would know how terrible it would be heartbreaking for Frostria to be separated for the rest of her life from Gregory Bissell.

Mistress Lyavendar would then reflect and realize the emperor was right, but he also knew it would be an extremely rare opportunity for Mistress Lyavendar to find another close friend like Frostria. The pain from the loss would linger for years.

The emperor had explained to Greg why he must maintain silence about the mission, because there were spies and, he wanted Mistress Lyavendar to enjoy her last moments with Frostria without a gut-wrenching loss before they left. He hated to do this, but it was best for everyone's interest, especially his.

The day finally arrived, and the moment of truth was now upon them. The emperor suggested Greg inform Frostria while the Franzcas were playing nearby, what his plans are and ask Frostria to go with him. Greg was ready either way. He had a chance to go back to Earth and this was his only chance, the one he had to take.

GREG

Frostria, I'm going back to Earth right away thanks to the emperor. It will be a short trip, just months and not years. I want you to go with me.

FROSTRIA

Why didn't you tell me earlier? I have some things I need to do before I go.

GREG

The emperor will handle everything for you. There is nothing more you need to do. Anyone that must know you are gone will be notified after a while for security reasons.

FROSTRIA
I really need to see a few people.

GREG
The same people who have not contacted you for years.

It was a low blow, but it was some of the INTEL the Emperor gave to Greg to help him overcome all Frostria's objections. The fact is her family really wasn't concerned about her and easily could have contacted her, for whatever reason didn't.

Frostria's family was in her former life and in reality, no relationship existed with them since they were off on their own little world just as if they were in another solar system quite content and only had fond memories of their daughter they had not seen or attempted to contact for years.

There was no excuse for it, they just didn't have enough interest in her to bother. Some children get kicked out of their homes when they become adults and their parents make it plain: Don't bother coming home unless you are bringing home barrels of money, then you are welcome.

Mistress Lyavendar was devastated. The emperor watched the surveillance videos for several weeks and had medical people standing by to sedate Mistress Lyavendar in case she started having severe mental issues.

Emperor Calestine hated to let Greg go, but in his heart and his soul, and in his mind, it was a moral imperative, he delivered Greg back to Planet Earth. He loved Greg and would do anything for him, and he knew this was the absolute most important thing he could do for this Earth man.

Pluto II was left behind. It would be impossible to return it to Earth any time soon. The Pluto's ship's computers were aboard the Royal Traykorite Ship RTS Finatscha in their special shipping containers secured to skids normally would be holding an array of Eleptron Annihilator weapons. Tiāncái was aboard the RTS Finatscha and working as a liaison, helped to resolve issues with the star charting maps and navigation.

DEPARTURE

As the RTS Finatscha traveled through the great darkness between the Universes, the Traykorite Fast Frigate crew was mildly concerned just like Christopher Columbus crews of a by-gone era.

There were no lights from distant stars or galaxies. There was nothing except inertia navigation that flew on a reciprocal course of where Greg and Tiāncái came.

As the long days with no indication of anything in the void, Frostria spent a lot of time with Tiāncái. The Traykorites did not know if they would have any serious side effects taking the suspended animation drugs, they brought with them, taken from Pluto II, therefore refrained from using them. Even though it would not be that long in the dark zone, Greg chose to go into suspended animation for a month and was carefully tied down in his bunk for that period.

Tiāncái knew that Greg made an unwise decision to bring Frostria back with him. He had no knowledge of what happened to Ami in the past twenty years. Greg was a pessimist and naturally assumed a smoking-hot woman like Ami with large bank accounts he left her, would not waste those twenty years waiting for him. Tiāncái on the other hand learned long ago to never bet against Ami.

During those periods that Greg chose suspended animation, the interface between Tiāncái and Frostria grew and so did the information. Tiāncái chose to level with Frostria and show her vast amounts of video and information on Ami. Frostria slowly developed the feeling she made a huge mistake and so she went to Commander Stanfrad Villiers who was ordered by the emperor to personally take Gregory Bissell back to Earth, because he had no such trust in any other Commander, was on the bridge of the RTS Finatscha observing the first lights of the alternate universe around the prediction date.

Commander Stanfrad Villiers was obviously happy because he knew the crew would be at ease because they knew the mission was going as per plan, and just like Christopher Columbus men who feared they would fall off the end of the earth were not going to fall off the end of the Universe.

The mood on the bridge was upbeat and suddenly Frostria appeared, which was not unexpected as she visited from time to time out of sheer boredom.

COMMANDER STANFRAD VILLIERS
Nice to see you again, Frostria, I hope all is well.

FROSTRIA
In a way it is but I wanted to talk to you about something.

Commander Stanfrad Villiers was suddenly alarmed because Frostria's statement had an edge on it as if something bad might have happened which did happen on spacecraft from time to time when crew members suddenly fail to be disciplined, especially on long voyages with a mixed crew of males and females.

COMMANDER STANFRAD VILLIERS
Is there a problem, Frostria?

FROSTRIA
I know your responsibility is to take Gregory Bissell
back to Earth but it's not necessary I get off the ship
with him, is that correct?

COMMANDER STANFRAD VILLIERS
If you do not want to go to Planet Earth with Gregory
Bissell, we will not force you to. It's up to you what you
want to do, and I understand your feelings are obviously
affected by this extraordinary change in your life.

FROSTRIA
I've not made the decision yet, nor have I talked with
Greg about it, because he's still in suspended animation,
but I may want to go back to Traykorite with you.

COMMANDER STANFRAD VILLIERS
If that's your decision, we will be happy to take you
back to Aiguo with us.

FROSTRIA
Thank you, Commander Stanfrad Villiers, for being
understanding.

COMMANDER STANFRAD VILLIERS
Frostria, we want what is best for you and will support
what you ultimately decide, but I must be frank, if we
do leave you on Earth, there is no guarantee we'll ever
come back to repatriate you back to the Traykorite
Empire. If something happens to the current Emperor,
it would mean for sure no return trips. Once you leave
the ship, you must assume it's permanent, you will
never come back to us.

Frostria understood that and Tiāncái gave her an education during Greg's suspended
animation. Tiāncái was the truthful arbiter. His artificial intelligence was immense. He
felt just as concerned for Frostria as he did for Greg. He also knew one other prevailing
possibility. If Ami, whom he thought he understood was waiting for Greg, Frostria
would have come all this way to Earth, be a freak show, and not be receiving the loving
relationship she expected. Greg would be under immense pressure the minute he was
with Ami, especially if she waited for him twenty plus years.

Frostria wasn't really given adequate time to resolve all the issues and have frank
discussions with Greg before she was Shanghaied on this trip. And she did exactly what
Greg trained her to do, she went into meditation and Hemi-Sync which usually provides
all the correct answers to life. She would soon meet with Commander Stanfrad Villiers
and ask him for a special favor. She would wait aboard the RTS Finatscha and have
Greg go down to the planet first and discover his world again before she went down.

Frostria explained it to Commander Stanfrad Villiers.

FROSTRIA
I will confront Greg and inform him I know a lot about
his former lover Ami. He needs to go down to find out
if Ami waited for him twenty-two years and if she did,
then it would not be appropriate for me to go to Earth
with Greg.

That would be their final goodbye. Since Tiāncái, whom Frostria fully trusted, had
communications ability with the Traykorites via wireless, he would send back to her
the information she could act upon.

COMMANDER STANFRAD VILLIERS

To travel this far, twelve hours or so really doesn't matter all that much. We'll wait for you and developments on the planet so that you can make the right decision.

FROSTRIA
Thank you, Commander, I will always appreciate you for this.

COMMANDER STANFRAD VILLIERS
Frostria, you are a very nice woman. I admire you and I'm pleased to help you. I'm sure the emperor would support your decision as well. If for some reason he becomes displeased if you return with me, I will take full responsibility.

Frostria knew then she had developed a lifelong friend during the journey to Earth she had grown huge respect for Commander Stanfrad Villiers.

THEY TRY IT AGAIN, THE COUP NEVER ENDS

Just as the Emperor feared the coup was not dead. This multi-headed snake was still alive. With Greg and Frostria out of the way and the emperor more or less shut in with his distressed mistress, it was time again for the next attempt. Everything was set and the mission was a go.

The Coup believed that with the emperor dead, they could easily put their man on the throne and the hostile takeover would then redesign the government and the Coup partners would then share in the hegemony that manifested as they split up the Empire into their own Fiefdoms and plundered the treasuries and created their lives of opulence and grandeur.

The emperor's personal valet was truly the only dedicated soul to his empire. He knew in fact he was the man behind the green curtain. All roads to Rome led through him. The emperor had a lot of influence and crafted overall guidance and direction, but the Empire was too massive for him to get buried with the details and he chose not to. He believed in delegating responsibility and having those people take care of it and not micromanage them. His working relationship with his valet was a perfect choreography. The valet directed what needed to get done and he figured out who to contact, the rest was history.

Most people assumed all directives came directly from the emperor. In fact, the emperor only knew five percent of what the valet orchestrated because things always seemed to work out. The emperor's enemies failed to realize they were killing the wrong person because it was the valet who managed everything and informed the emperor only when he felt it was essential.

The day of reckoning happened, and one half of the security force was replaced by members of the Coup. The plan was long in making and was carried out with great precision.

After the long shootout and once again the escape craft was sabotaged, the assassins and the ringleader made their way into the Emperors emergency center with a laser pistol to the head of the valet and Mistress Lyavendar at gunpoint. They shoved Mistress Lyavendar up next to the emperor and laughed.

COUP RINGLEADER

Do you know who Mistress Lyavendar really is?

The emperor assumed he was a dead man and didn't answer.

COUP RINGLEADER

Mistress Lyavendar's a Zomulite spy and she works for us.

The arrogant coup ringleader laughed then handed Mistress Lyavendar a laser pistol.

COUP RINGLEADER

It's time now for you to complete your contract and kill
the emperor.

At this point in time the emperor looked solemnly at Mistress Lyavendar.

EMPEROR CALESTINE

Is this true, Saraotta?

MISTRESS LYAVENDAR

Calestine, I was sent to assassinate you, but I fell in love
with you. I love you. I have no intentions of killing you.

Mistress Lyavendar then turned her laser pistol onto the ringleader and instantly killed him. One of the other coup members pulled his laser pistol to shoot the Emperor and Mistress Lyavendar stepped in front just in time to protect the emperor and died instantly.

The valet who was trained in Martial arts quickly dispatched the other two and grabbed a laser pistol in time to kill the assailant before he had a second shot at the emperor. With the laser pistol in hand, he shot three others and managed to hit the emergency closure switch that set off the alarms and sent all airborne troops nearby to defend the Palace. Within an hour the shooting died down and three hundred prisoners were rounded up.

All of them were offered to have their lives spared if they reported who sent them. After gunning a few of them down with laser rifles in firing squads, the remainder chose to rat out their leaders. Within weeks the entire coup was squashed and a few of the top coup members were discovered by INTEL working for the Zomulites insuring another Galactic War.

Emperor Calestine was devastated and almost despondent. His recent time after the Earth person arrived with Mistress Lyavendar had been some of the happiest years of his life. In the end he loved Saraotta, and she proved her love and devotion by protecting him and stepping in front of the laser shooter to save his life, giving her life for him. He knew that was her final act of love and devotion which made it even more painful.

ARRIVAL BACK TO EARTH

When the RTS Finatscha went into orbit, the Earth came to a standstill. No Aliens had ever arrived and announced their presence. Furthermore when Gregory Bissell got on communications frequencies the Traykorite easily figured out, the folks at Livermore were in a tizzy because the drama had come to an end years ago and now it was going to flare up again and this time they would no longer be able to lie to the pubic who now knew for a fact the government had sent some guy out into far space and Aliens had just arrived bringing him back.

Ami's life had sucked for twenty-two years raising her son without a daddy was just about to start dating again when the news hit and people from the lab who she hadn't spoken with for years suddenly appeared.

Her son Tetsuro had grown and was a really good kid, and now at UC Berkeley was starting to be his own man and now slowly distancing himself as he was more and more involved with his personal friends. While he was growing up it was easy for Ami as she had a son to raise but now, she was mostly alone and was now thinking she wanted a partner in her life and was about to accept an invitation to a date in a few days.

Greg didn't know he had another son. *Traveling to the edge of the universe* had taken some of his best years away. When the news hit Ami, she figured Greg would look eighty years old by now and almost crippled.

The love had slowly died off and she thought that she might go ahead and date that forty-five-year-old who was probably more interested in having sex than anything else.

By agreements, the Traykorites would send a shuttle down from the Frigate with Greggory Bissell to Area 51. Things happened rapidly. Commander Stanfrad Villiers called Greg to the Bridge of the RTS Finatscha and informed him:

COMMANDER STANFRAD VILLIERS

> We will maintain contact with Tiāncái and give you twelve hours to direct us to send down Frostria. We know more about you than you think. We know all about Ami. She might be waiting for you. If there is still a relationship between you and Ami when you arrive Frostria will remain aboard the RTS Finatscha and return to Aiguo with us. Tiāncái will inform us of your decision.

GREG

> Thank you for your consideration.

Greg was ushered to the shuttle bay where Frostria was waiting for him.

GREG

You are not going down to the planet with me?

FROSTRIA

Greg, you need to go down first and find out if what you left behind is waiting for you. If Ami is there waiting for you, I don't want to break her heart.

GREG

I have a lot of affection for you, we have been through a lot.

FROSTRIA

Greg, I know you are confused now. No man has ever been through what you experienced. If Ami waited for you all these years, you owe it to her to take care of her for the rest of your life. If Ami has since remarried and has moved on with her life, I will gladly go down and join you. I don't want to put you into a spectacle. Go down, see your people, and Tiāncái will let us know if I should come down. I will communicate with you through Tiāncái so I will hear your voice and be assured of your actions.

GREG

Alright, that's reasonable.

Frostria and Greg kissed and hugged, and tears were flowing. Greg stepped aboard the shuttle and everyone cleared out of the bay so it could be depressurized and shuttle launched.

EXT. CGI. SPACE. FRIGATE'S SHUTTLE LEAVING THE FRIGATE FLYING DOWN TO EARTH.

As the shuttle left the Frigate, Greg immediately noticed a few of the escorts. They were not TR-4s, as they looked slightly more advanced.

The UNITED STATES SPACE FORCE escorted the Traykorite shuttle down to Area 51.

EXT. CGI/REAL COMBO. FRIGATE SHUTTLE LANDS VERTICALLY AT DESIGNATED LANDING PAD AT AREA 51 NEXT TO BUILDING 28

As requested, there were vehicles there to haul equipment such as Pluto II's computers. Greg and Tiāncái were directed to get into a quarantine vehicle that looked a lot like large Tourist Bus size RV and had the amenities as one.

The RV took them to an air-conditioned isolation tent where a few special people were there to meet Greg and Tiāncái. There was a plexiglass wall between Greg and the dozen people in the comfortable air-conditioned tent. Greg did not recognize many of them and suddenly, this pleasant Asian lady stepped forward holding the hand of a young man who looked twenty. There was another woman he knew he could recognize, Dr. Shirley, she hadn't changed all that much.

Everyone was almost shocked Greg had not changed in twenty-two years. His time in suspended animation and infusion of health inducing Alien supplements had almost reversed all his aging. If you took a picture of him now and put it up next to a picture of him twenty-two years ago, you would say they looked identical. Ami was surprised he had not aged. Instead of the eighty-year-old she expected, there was a guy who looked fifty-five or less. And she knew she herself was no longer a spring chick.

AMI

Hello, Greg.

The voice was Ami's, there was no doubt about it, even though she didn't look quite the same. She looked probably twenty-five years older.

GREG

Well, I'm back.

AMI

I see that. Greg, there is something I need to tell you.

GREG

You married someone and moved on with your life?

Ami blushed.

AMI

No, I never married.

Greg watched Ami nervously hold on to the young man's hand and she knew it was now or never and proceeded.

AMI

Greg, before you left you impregnated me, and I didn't
know until after you left. This is your son, Tetsuro.

Greg looked at the young man staring at his father, always wondering why he deserted his mother.

Ami never talked too much about Greg. Doctor Shirley worked with Tetsuro, and he didn't have reckless episodes with his life because his mother raised him well and he got a good education.

Tiāncái by now had immense artificial intelligence and had studied philosophy, psychology, and other social sciences. As such he was a fair broker and wanted Frostria to see what bestowed Greg when he arrived. Tiāncái provided real-time translations of everything each party had to say.

The son was the deal killer for Frostria, without the son she might have been willing to come down to Earth because it was evident twenty-two years plus is a long time to wait and Ami had other concerns in her life now.

Greg also considered going back to Aiguo now as well and if Ami didn't show a spark, there might not have been a reason for him to come back.

It was a zoo inside the tent. The shuttle crew was told to wait until Greg gave them the signal to go back to the ship without him in case, he changed his mind, the emperor would want him back if he decided to come back.

Ami didn't know what to do. She didn't know if she should cry or break down. Doctor Shirley approached her giving her some emotional support and Ami softly asked Dr. Shirley's help.

AMI
Dr. Shirley, could you please ask everyone to leave the
tent so I can have a few minutes alone with Greg.

Dr. Shirley knew this was a critical moment and turned around to address the crowd.

DR. SHIRLEY
Could all of you please leave the tent for a few minutes,
we need to give them a few minutes alone. You can all
come back later after they get a chance to get a grasp
on things.

Politely the small crowd exited the large tent.

DR. SHIRLEY
Ami, I will be right outside if you need me, I can come back.

When they were alone Greg began explaining.

GREG
I came back because I thought I wanted to die on
Earth. I was lucky because Lawrence Livermore Labs
didn't plan on me coming back alive. I did not know
that before I left on the mission. Had I known that was
the plan, I would not have gone on this mission.

Ami was slightly annoyed with Greg and had not asked the man standing by him to step outside, which was probably a good thing because it gave Tiāncái the opportunity to chime in at the critical moment.

TIĀNCÁI
Ami, I'm Tiāncái, I'm a Robot and I've been with Greg
since he left. I was with Greg on the entire mission

until now. It's true Greg did not know when he left,
he had no opportunity to come back. Project Pluto II
assumed he would die in space.

<u>INT. SPACE. ROYAL TRAYKORITE SHIP RTS FINATSCHA, FRIGATE FRIGATE CONTROL ROOM</u>

In the RTS FINATSCHA control room Frostria was observing and hearing all of Greg's conversation thanks to Tiāncái's high fidelity video and sound. Commander Stanfrad Villiers was observing Frostria knowing this was tearing her heart apart and had one of his corpsmen standing by with sedatives just in case she broke down. Tears were coming down Frostria's eyes as this utter sadness was exposed. Greg was sent on a mission by rotten bastards that planned for him to give up his life for the sake of science. And here he was standing in front of the love he left behind, and their love child.

Frostria could see the real-time video Tiāncái provided of Ami and Greg and hear everything. Tiāncái was a true humanitarian and a fair arbiter. In the process he broke Frostria's heart, but she had to know because it would be bad enough for her living on the planet as an alien freak, but worse with the other woman nearby that could erupt in passions.

<u>INT. DAY ALIEN QUARENTEEN ARRIVAL TENT AREA-51</u>

Greg knew he only had a few hours to make a decision or the Traykorites would be make it for him so he knew he couldn't dilly-dally around and abruptly asked:

GREG

Ami, I need to know what your intentions are now that I'm back.

AMI

Greg, you have been gone quite a while. It's going to
take time to adjust, but if you are willing to try so am I.

Frostria knew that was another dealbreaker, they might as well leave. She wanted Greg to try because he had a son. For the sake of his son, she wanted Greg to establish a relationship and she would be in the way, no matter what happened.

Greg knew Tiāncái had live communications to the RTS Finatscha. Greg turned to Tiāncái.

GREG

Tiāncái, please inform the shuttle crew that after all
the cargo is unloaded, they can return to the RTS
Finatscha.

Within moments, Tiāncái reported back to Greg.

TIĀNCÁI

RTS Finatscha and the shuttle crew have been duly
notified. Should I tell them they are now free to return
to Aiguo?

Greg looked at Ami who now had tears rolling down her face almost fearful Greg would leave with the Aliens and never come back responded to Tiāncái.

GREG

Please inform Commander Stanfrad Villiers, I'm staying here on Earth and to also let the Emperor know I thank him from the bottom of my heart for bringing me back to Earth safely.

Moments later Tiāncái reported the status with the Shuttle.

TIĀNCÁI

All cargo unloaded and the shuttle crew is now going back to RTS Finatscha.

Greg didn't know Frostria was watching everything unfold, but after they left Tiāncái explained everything.

ADJUSTING TO A NEW LIFE

Weeks passed by then months and the only thing positive in the emperor's life was the pleasure of welcoming home Commander Stanfrad Villiers who had taken Gregory Bissell and Frostria whom he missed to Earth and reward Commander Stanfrad Villiers for RTS Finatscha's excellent mission.

For security reasons the Frigate remained in orbit and crew members rotated down to the planet for their well-earned leave periods. Those who were VIPs were shuttled down to the planet first to the Traykorite Space Force building to be met personally by Emperor Calestine.

None of the crew or Frostria knew what had happened or of a second Coup attempt to kill Emperor Calestine. Security was tight when they arrived and behind a bulletproof and laser-proof glass protective wall stood the emperor. The RTS Finatscha did not notify a special VIP coming with them. The emperor wasn't expecting Frostria. His emotions were drained, and he was just happy to get mission tapes and reports from Commander Stanfrad Villiers about what happened on Planet Earth.

The shuttle craft came into the hangar. The Emperor's Royal Transport was parked a few yards away in the large cavity big enough to hold ten such ships.

The hatch moved upwards on the side exposing the entrance to the shuttle and the steps came down with the pneumatic hissing sound. Commander Stanfrad Villiers out of military decorum walked out first followed by Frostria and several other officers and crew members of the Frigate RTS Finatscha.

The emperor looked like he saw a ghost and walked around the security barrier and shook off a couple security guys and walked directly up to Frostria.

EMPEROR CALESTINE
What happened? Did you make it to Earth?

FROSTRIA
Yes, Greg is home now and happy and thanks or doing
that special favor for him and wanted me to give you
this personal letter. He also wanted me to tell you he
loves you like you are his brother and wished he could
have stayed longer with you, but he wanted to get back
to his home where he wants to spend his final days.

EMPEROR CALESTINE
Why didn't you stay at Earth with him? Didn't you love
him?

FROSTRIA
Yes, I still love Greg, but I determined I wanted to
come back here for the same reasons Greg wanted to
stay on Earth.

Frostria looked around and did not see Mistress Lyavendar and wondered why she
wasn't there.

FROSTRIA
Your excellency, could you please inform Mistress
Lyavendar I would like to talk with her soon?

About that time the tears started coming down the emperor's face and he grabbed
Frostria and held her while he wept for a few minutes.

FLASHBACK.

Everyone that was present except for those arriving from the RTS Finatscha knew the
emperor had lost the love of his live when the Coup killed her while attempting to kill
Emperor Calestine. The public will never know the details because his *Valet* explained
to the emperor.

EMPEROR CALESTINE'S PERSONAL VALET
It will do you no good telling the public what really
happened. Just be grateful to know she really loved
you and gave her life to save your life. That part you
can hint at saying she stepped in front of the assassin
to save your life. There are no other witnesses alive.
Honor her love and saving your life by concealing she
was an enemy spy.

Frostria had gone through her own emotional roller coaster losing the first love of her
life. She wasn't angry with Greg, because, when he arrived at the Aiguo Space Force
Center, he and all others believed he had no way to get home and twenty-two years
later is a long time.

Ami was an extraordinary woman to wait all those years. Had it been any other woman, Frostria knew she would be on Planet Earth now, but didn't know quite for sure if she would like it based on all the information Tiāncái provided her over the months going to Earth.

Tiāncái saved Frostria from a possible personal disaster. She now realized the possibility existed had she stayed on Earth, she would be feeling like Greg, wanting to go home with no way to get there. She also thought what the Earth people had done to Greg sending him on a mission he would die in space was rather disgusting. If Earth governments are like that, perhaps she didn't want to be there.

The emperor got control of himself stood straight and tall.

EMPEROR CALESTINE

After you have been home for a while and feel up to
it, we'll have a celebration at the Palace with the crew
of the RTS Finatscha and you for traveling to another
Universe and back.

FROSTRIA

Thank you, Your Excellency, I will look forward to it.

Emperor Calestine then smiled at Frostria then walked over to Commander Stanfrad Villiers.

EMPEROR CALESTINE

I ordered a replacement crew to be cycled up to the
RTS Finatscha and a new Captain to be ready to go on
patrol so that you and your crew can have a good rest
before returning to duty. We have a new Frigate ready
to operate real soon. It's my intention to give you and
the crew of the RTS Finatscha this new Frigate when it
becomes operational and a good rest period until then.

COMMANDER STANFRAD VILLIERS

Thank you, Your Excellency. I'm sure my crew will
appreciate that.

EMPEROR CALESTINE

Commander, you are now free to go back to your
ship and prepare for your turnover with the new
commander over the next few days. After your crew
has a couple of weeks rest, we'll invite all of you to the
Palace for a celebration on your great achievement.

COMMANDER STANFRAD VILLIERS

Your Excellency, here is a letter from Greg, he asked
me to give you when we arrived at Earth during the
mission.

EMPEROR CALESTINE
Thank you, Commander.

Commander Stanfrad Villiers saluted and then turned and walked back to the shuttle and soon it was gone heading back out into space for the turnover.

The emperor then walked back to Frostria.

EMPEROR CALESTINE
I will make sure you be given ample time off to recover
from your long trip. Would you like me to take you to
your apartment since it's on the way home?

FROSTRIA
Thank you very much, I appreciate that.

The emperor led Frostria over to the Emperor's Royal Transport and soon they were heading right for the entrance of her apartment building. Just like before the street was blocked off and the apartment residents were amazed that once again the emperor stopped in front of the apartment building on the street.

The door to the space transport opened and the emperor walked Frostria to the sidewalk.

EMPEROR CALESTINE
Welcome home, I'm glad you made it back safely.

The Emperor went back into the Emperor's Royal Transport and the access door closed and it was soon up in the air cutting across the area at high altitude going directly back to the palace.

As Frostria arrived, there were the security men. They had been guarding her apartment since she left. She went inside looked around, nothing had changed, then took a shower, changed her clothes and was relaxing catching up on galactic news when the doorbell rang. Knowing the security men were outside she thought it was safe to open and of a people, there was the Emperor's Personal *Valet* of all people.

FROSTRIA
Please come in.

EMPEROR'S PERSONAL *VALET*
I'm sorry for disturbing you but I thought it was
important I inform you about what transpired after
you left.

Emperor's Personal *Valet* then explained everything that happened with Mistress Lyavendar before she heard it from someone else. Only the valet knew Frostria knew the dirty secret that Mistress Lyavendar was a Zomulite spy.

EMPEROR'S PERSONAL VALET

I know that you are aware that Mistress Lyavendar was actually Saraotta who was a deep undercover mole sent here to assassinate the emperor. In the end she was in love with him and lost her life trying to save his life.

Frostria's eyes were watering up. The Emperor's Personal *Valet* knew this would make Frostria very sad, but she needed to be briefed to understand the emperor's strange behavior. Frostria also assumed Mistress Lyavendar died a painful death from a laser pistol burn through her chest cooking her heart and stopping it. She felt terrible about it all.

EMPEROR'S PERSONAL VALET

This you must never disclose to anyone. As I explained to the emperor, to honor her death which happened while she attempted to protect him, we should maintain our silence on the matter.

FROSTRIA

I agree, I know Mistress Lyavendar was in love with Emperor Calestine because she herself informed me in a very private conversation.

EMPEROR'S PERSONAL VALET

I'm sorry I had to give you the bad news, the emperor is very upset about it; so, if he seems strange, you now know why.

FROSTRIA

It's very understandable how this tragic affair affected him.

Frostria had watery eyes and was tearing up.

EMPEROR'S PERSONAL VALET

I expect the celebration for the RTS Finatscha crew will occur sometime soon. The emperor is very sad now. It would cheer him up if you attended the awards ceremony with him and the crew and their relatives that are able to attend.

FROSTRIA

I will be most happy to attend, and even though as it turned out I did not stay on Planet Earth with Greg because of complications with his personal life, I at least am grateful to be given the opportunity to go there with him as I came very close to staying.

EMPEROR'S PERSONAL *VALET*

It all worked out for the benefit of everyone. The
emperor remains grateful to Greg and Tiāncái for
saving his life, but he is also grateful to you for giving
Greg tremendous love and enjoyment while he was
with us, even if it ended in sorrow for you.

FROSTRIA

I'm a big girl, and the circumstances which we could
not foresee really shaped the outcome. Had Ami, his
Earth lover not been such an extraordinary woman
who waited more than twenty-two years for him, I
would have had the opportunity to spend the rest of
my life with Greg.

EMPEROR'S PERSONAL *VALET*

In a few more years if the emperor decides to send a
ship to check up on Greg and finds out he's an eligible
bachelor, would you want to go back?

FROSTRIA

Greg taught me one strong lesson. I want to live here
with my people. Even Greg's wife left him to move back
to her native country Japan. People want to go back to
their roots when they grow older. I understand why. I
plan on living my life here, and do not need to move
anywhere. Like Greg, I want to die in my homeland.

EMPEROR'S PERSONAL *VALET*

That's very understanding. I must leave now as I have
a lot of tasks to get done. If you ever need anything
please contact me, as you have earned the support of
the Palace and the Emperor would always want the
best for you.

FROSTRIA

Thank you, I appreciate that.

By the time the RTS Finatscha made its way back to Aiguo and the Traykorite Empire,
Greg was almost complete with his mandatory quarantine and weekly blood samples
that were studied in the super hazmat labs where he was a prisoner for quite some time.
Several times per week Ami arrived with Tetsuro to visit on the other side of a sealed
glass wall where they spoke into microphones and heard the speakers with no privacy.

Because of the extraordinary sensation surrounding Greg, Ami and Tetsuro required
around the clock protection and their privacy collapsed. The freak show that Frostria
missed out on might had made her seriously regret staying on Earth. During some of

her numerous private meetings with Tiāncái, she was fully exposed to Earth culture so that she could make an informed decision on her future.

The complication of Greg arriving and finding this extraordinary woman Ami waiting for him coupled with the rancor that would erupt from the headlines, made the decision much easier for Frostria not to stay. Frostria knew that Tiāncái largely served Greg's interest but was grateful he was fair and accurate in all his assessments and consultations.

Greg would never know this wasn't a compulsive decision as those months he spent in suspended animation allowed Tiāncái to protect Frostria and look out for her best interests as well.

Tiāncái knew with the possibilities they would face, Frostria would face incredible challenges and the zoo-like environment she would be thrust upon greatly diminished her desires to remain. But the dealbreaker of course was Ami showing up and her secret observation of the reunion with Ami and the love child Greg had no knowledge existed.

Earth people had never seen multicolored people. People of color in predominately white countries received only a fraction of discrimination and stereotyping as what Frostria would face. Playboy would immediately offer her $100 million for a centerfold.

When she was in public with the sunlight striking her skin to give that holographic texture would certainly keep the camera shutters clicking away. Living in total seclusion didn't appeal to Frostria. On appearances it seemed to have worked out for everyone's benefit.

Tiāncái spent vast sums of time studying the big riff between Freud and Jung. One of them thought bringing things out into the open and dealing with them provided a person better mental health improvement. That idea was tried relentlessly during the Korean War treating battlefield fatigue (considered cowardice by hard core Generals like Paton) or as the phrase was coined by the British during WW1, "shellshocked troops."

After analyzing both sides, Tiāncái realized and counseled Greg, the best approach for his personal psychology was not to bring up everything to Ami. She would receive no value knowing anything about Frostria. That was now in his past and had no bearing on his future because she could never come back. The emperor was extremely generous in bringing Greg back, but the cost and the effort were so severe, they would most likely never attempt it again. Plus, there was no guarantee the emperor would remain alive since his enemies were always out to get him.

During the Persian Gulf Wars, PTSD was adopted as the terminology because the department of defense didn't want to tell these young boys mothers the reason why their son was so emotionally disturbed is because he was indeed *shellshocked* because force protection in the Gulf was very poor and due to political correctness, they put too many of them at risk and allowed the enemy to often shell the crap out of them before permissions were granted to return fire. Such was the case of General McCrystal removed for voicing his anger of the nonsensical rules of engagement crafted by liberals who thought if they allowed enough American boys get killed or shellshocked (PTSD), it would work as a deterrent to stop America from engaging in future wars.

If there was anyone who had more reason for PTSD it was Greg. It's not everyone who gets the chance to be deceived the way he was and sent out in space to die with no hopes of ever seeing his loved ones again.

Greg coming back alive put the lab, CIA, and others in a particularly bad situation. Should the public ever learn what they had done to Greg, the lab would suffer some severe criticism if not partial disbanding.

But now they were stuck. Greg was back alive and compartmentalization could not be expected much longer, especially since Tiāncái had vast amounts of information on the trip in his own memory banks as well as the ship's computer data they brought back.

The Big Bang Theory was now proven a hoax and soon those scientists still making fools out of themselves with their arrogant claims, would face damning defeat because the trip to and from the alternate universe was well recorded and shattered all current belief systems that relied on a Big Bang Beginning. This would be a tough time for science.

When the announcement of the quarantine lifting hit Greg, he was obviously emotional.

No living person had ever undergone medical screening to the extent of Greg. Any virus or bacteria the found in his body was studied and determined if it were of Alien origin. At the end of the Quarantine period, they had not found any dangerous pathogens. Greg had explained it to them: Traykorites are far more advanced in biology and medicine. Any disease or bad bacteria he was carrying, they eliminated. He was actually cleaner than any Earth person now. The effects of Traykorite medical and physiological research and development resulted in Greg experiencing the reversal of aging. And since he now looked several years younger than when he left, his physical appearance was now more appropriate for Ami, when he used to be viewed as someone rocking the cradle.

By now Dr. Shirley had numerous sessions with Ami. For many years Ami was angry that Greg would volunteer for such a long mission abandoning her, even though he did leave her financially well off. Now that Greg was home, Dr. Shirley was one of the few who knew the unbridled truth. Greg did not volunteer for such a mission, he was Shanghaied. Ami felt very sorry for Greg once Dr. Shirley gave her the highly secret compartmentalized files and proof it happened that way. Greg was deceived by his employer but knew better than to confront these very powerful elite.

Ami and Tetsuro were flown into Area 51 for their multiple visits several times a week. Ami slowly warmed up to Greg. She went from almost starting dating with a guy who presumably wanted some happy-time and boom-boom, to putting everything on hold as it all became apparent Greg was back for good. And since he did not age in the past twenty-two years, the miracle is he came back appearing just like he left yesterday.

Dr. Shirley would only allow Ami look at the sources of information and would never allow her to retain any of the materials stating:

> DR. SHIRLEY
> If the LAB discovered I gave you all this information very bad things would happen to me and possibly very bad things would happen to you. I'm only doing this because I want you to know, Greg did nothing wrong.

> AMI
> I feel sorry for Greg. Greg was taken advantage of and severely compromised by the government for whatever reasons they determined were sufficient to do this. Greg lost a lot.

> DR. SHIRLEY
> The saddest part is Dr. Moore and Walter Bissonnette had no way out. There simply was no other suitable candidate that was medically fit at the age they wanted so they could not avoid truncating and sacrificing Greg's life for the sake of discovering one of the most important questions discussed by the brightest minds in science.

Through Dr. Shirley's efforts, Ami's relationship with Greg became restored if not bolstered more. Knowing none of this was Greg's fault because he had been deceived, Ami could no longer hold any of it against Greg.

Ami slowly warmed up to Greg and his third son Tetsuro who had harbored ill feelings for years slowly also grew closer to Greg. Afterall they were really a family though not legally. Greg's name was on Tetsu's birth certificate, and he was legitimate thanks to people like Walter Bissonnette and Dr. Shirley who looked out for Ami and Tetsuro under the radar.

Eventually Ami was informed she would not make any more trips to Area 51, Greg would be brought home shortly. Ami bought a nice home in Walnut Creek years before which Greg paid for, and it was lonely but had plenty of extra room. Tiāncái went away, he and Greg were separated at that time and would not see each other for a long time.

Thanks to Greg's reversal of agingand Ami catching up to him in age they were now almost the perfect couple age wise in appearance. They could live their lives out together and expect to be there for each other for many years in the future.

Ami, with Doctor Shirley's help slowly brought Tetsuro around. Tetsuro now fully understood his father did not desert them and had no idea the nature of his mission since he was purposely kept in the dark until he had reached the point of no return and Pluto II was heading out towards *the end of the universe* with no way of slowing down or changing course back to Earth. Greg was presumably doomed. It was the absolute worst thing any civilized nation could do to one of its citizens. Tetsuro now understood and was coached that if he went public, it could cost him his life. Brutal men at the top would protect this secret for the rest of their lives.

After they had settled down for a few days, the subject of taking a family vacation came up. The last thing Ami and Greg had done together that created such wonderful memories was that trip to Hawaii just before he left. It seemed so fitting to do it again. This time there would be no rush to get back to work. There were no demands on their time. Thanks to Tiāncái's superb handling of data and recordings, they brought back everything and beat most of the messenger buoys back for generations. By the time the last buoys returned Earth no longer had the means to read them. The equipment necessary to receive the signals had not existed in generations. Greg, Ami, and Tetsuro slowly faded into history, but Earth was saved from the onslaught of Galactic migration as they knew the eventuality and figured out how to protect themselves.

THE BIG PARTY

<u>EXT. DAY. EMPEROR CALESTINE'S COURTYARD AND SWIMMING POOL</u>

Emperor Calestine's Personal Valet scheduled the big event for the RTS Finatscha crew. RTS Finatscha crew members and those who had relatives that lived within reasonable travel distance who wanted to attend, were all brought to the Palace.

Security was super tight, and people were informed to not bring anything with them. A dozen children were in the mix. The emperor had a surprise for them including bathing suits that would fit all of them who cared to get in the Olympic size swimming pool.

Emperor Calestine joined the festivities including wearing a swim suit to allow him to get in the water and play with the children.

EMPEROR CALESTINE
I have a big surprise for all of you today. Everyone
please, get out of the pool and sit on the edge. You can
dangle your feet in the water.

When all the children were sitting and waiting to see the surprise, the emperor nodded at Franzcas' trainer who then opened the locks allowing Franzcas to enter the swimming pool brought in as usual for feeding and playing. The children saw the animals and were immediately delighted.

The emperor stepped down into the pool and all the Franzcas swam to him as part of their daily routine, which they enjoyed and made all kinds of noises.

The trainer came over with a bucket of fish and the trainer handed one of the fish to the first boy in the line and the Franzcas immediately came in the vicinity knowing that fish was for them.

FRANZCAS TRAINER
Give that fish to the Franzcas nearest you.

The boy complied and Franzcas quickly devoured the fish.

The Franzcas Trainer went down the line handing each kid a fish, and one by one the Franzcas were given their snacks. When the bucket of fish was all gone the trainer joked.

FRANZCAS TRAINER

> Be sure and rub your hands on your parents' clothes to
> get the fish smell off your hands.

The crowd laughed. The trainer had a bucket full of wet towels and asked each child to wipe his hands on the towels.

The emperor had another big surprise for the children.

EMPEROR CALESTINE

> Okay, line up by the stairs and I will bring you down
> one at a time to play with a Franzcas.

The kids lined up and were slowly brought into the pool and the Franzcas enjoyed the little tikes.

EMPEROR CALESTINE

> Watch this, they love to be hugged.

The children were surprised by the strange sounds Franzcas gave when the emperor hugged them. Soon each kid was hugging Franzcas who appeared to have one of the happiest days of their lives.

The trainer knew it was time to get the Franzcas back into the locks to transfer them to the canal that led to the much larger water works beyond the hedgerow that people could see. On the signal, the emperor Calestine announced.

EMPEROR CALESTINE

> Okay, everyone out of the pool, the Franzcas need to
> go have their meal now.

All the children were soon standing beside the pool as the trainer blew his special 25 KHz whistle and the Franzcas promptly swam to the lock that would allow them to prevent the fish tank water from getting into the pool. After the Franzcas were out of the locks and swimming down their private canal back to the larger pool, the access doors were closed and all the water in the locks was pumped down and dumped into the fish tank, then filled again with fresh water, and pumped down a second time to clean the contents really good to avoid as much contamination as possible in order to reduce the amount of chemicals in the water necessary to keep the pool healthy.

The crowd was given lots of snacks and drinks, but the big event was yet to come.

EMPEROR CALESTINE'S PERSONAL VALET
All you children, we want you to change back into your
clothes. Leave the swimsuits in the changing room and
we'll take care of them later.

The children lined up for their turn in the changing room where a staff nurse had them bathe and change into clothes.

After everyone was dressed and ready, a transport came through the secret gate in back of the change room that would take a number of the guests down to the waterfall area where a barbecue was going on and the succulent meats would make them all happy.

EXT. WATERFALL AREA AT THE EMPEROR'S ESTATE.

Numerous tables and chairs were set up fit for kings and queens. As soon as the first group were aboard the transport it left and headed for the waterfall area for the feast. When the first transport was cleared out of the way heading down the private road, another transport pulled in and picked up the next group. By the time the fifth transport picked up its passengers most of the guests were down at the picnic site by the waterfall.

Landscapers had brought in beautiful turf two days before the event and planted numerous tall trees for the ceremony. It didn't look bad before the face lift, but once the landscaping was complete it was nicer than any park any of them had ever been at. None of them knew the luscious green lawn did not exist three days prior along with most of these unusual-looking trees.

Frostria and Commander Stanfrad Villiers were seated at the emperor's table. The rest of the tables were set up with either adults or children with valet supervisors to give their parents a Happy Meal with entertainment without having to babysit their kids who wanted to be with other kids as it was.

An eighty-five-piece symphony orchestra was set up on a temporary stage that appeared as if it were a permanent fixture. After that night the Emperor decided he wanted a permanent structure and wanted to keep this waterfall area pristine like this from now on.

The Empire's best chefs created this feast and everything tasted exquisite.

Before the food was served the emperor stood

EMPEROR CALESTINE
Please let me have everyone's attention.

Emperor Calestine seemed to be happier today and it was apparent to his Personal *Valet* that Frostria's appearance seemed to create a happier environment for the Emperor. The Emperor's Personal *Valet* knew the emperor was fond of Frostria, a very sweet lovely lady.

Even though Emperor Calestine was heartbroken the Emperor's Personal *Valet* saw a distinct possibility he might have a way to get the emperor's mind off his tragic loss.

Emperor Calestine began his short speech.

EMPEROR CALESTINE

The RTS Finatscha carried out one of the most significant missions in the history of our Empire. Your ship is the very first to cross the great chasm that separates our universe from my great friend Gregory Bissell's universe.

I received a lot of criticism from many parties for sending you all on that mission. It was viewed too risky and ill-advised at a time when there seemed to be escalating tensions with our enemies such as the Zomulites.

Most of you do not know, Gregory Bissell saved my life. I would not be alive and standing in front of you today, without his help. Gregory Bissell wanted nothing from me and was content just to be alive living here

Gregory Bissell's Rocketship arrived here from his universe just in time before it would have exploded killing him. As such its damaged beyond the point he could use it to get back to his planet Earth. Plus it would take him twenty two years to get home and by that time everyone he knew would be elderly or passed away.

To reward Gregory Bissell for saving my life, I decided to give him transportation back to his world and with our new Frigate RTS Finatscha in just a few months, that way he would arrive there soon enough before people he was associated with passed from old age.

. We are currently building an exhibit at our Aerospace Museum for Gegory Bissell's spaceship, Pluto II.

Someday soon you all will be invited to view the grand opening and you will see there is also an exhibit there of Pluto II that brought Gregory Bissell here.

I have no idea how to reward all of you for your heroic mission to take Gregory Bissell back to his Planet Earth in a short period of time.

Therefore, I directed the head of the Traykorite Space
Force to promote each one of you one rank higher
than you currently hold. I want to congratulate our
distinguished Commander Stanfrad Villiers for his
promotion to Field Marshall, third class.

The emperor started clapping and everyone followed his lead.

Soon they were all feasting on the fabulous food. At the Emperor's table, they had one
dish of meats that was different than any of the guests were provided. The emperor
implored the new Field Marshall Third Class Stanfrad Villiers:

EMPEROR CALESTINE
Field Marshall Stanfrad Villiers, please try some of
these delicacies.

Field Marshall Third Class Stanfrad Villiers
Thank you, your Excellency.

With all the turmoil of the purge that was ongoing to clean out swamp members
involved in the several recent Coups, Field Marshall Third Class Stanfrad Villiers knew
it would be in his best interest to eat the meat and act as if it was wonderful even if it
wasn't very delightful.

The chef had worked his magic on that meat, and it was laced slightly with some
psychoactive drugs to make it even more palatable. It seemed it wasn't so bad after all,
but it seemed to have a strange taste to it the Field Marshall knew he had tasted once
before but could not quite remember what it was.

The celebration continued with singers and musicians performing some of the best
music in the Galaxy. The entertainment alone was priceless. Nobody that was present,
except for the emperor could afford such lavish entertainment.

The celebration slowly came to an end and the guests were taken back to the front
entrances by the recreational transports and before the Field Marshall could get away,
the Emperor asked him to stay for a few minutes for a private talk.

When everyone except his security was departed to their Aircars taking them at the
front entrance where their Aircars were brought in remotely, the Emperor then asked
the newly christened Field Marshal

EMPEROR CALESTINE
Field Marshall Third Class Stanfrad Villiers, How did
you like that special meat?

FIELD MARSHALL THIRD CLASS STANFRAD VILLIERS
Your Excellency, it tasted really good; it is one of the
best meats prepared I've ever had.

EMPEROR CALESTINE
I'm glad you enjoyed it. That barbecued meat used to
be part of Commander Zebrovska's leg. He was one of
the coup organizers, when Greggory Bissell saved my
life.

FIELD MARSHALL THIRD CLASS STANFRAD VILLIERS
Your excellency, may I ask why you are telling me this?

EMPEROR CALESTINE
Field Marshall Third Class Stanfrad Villiers, I wanted
you to personally know how good people taste that
cross me and try to undermine me.

Field Marshall Class Three Stanfrad Villiers received the message loud and clear and
understood with his promotion came responsibility and God help him if he ever
crossed the emperor.

Emperor Calestine's Personal Valet lied to Frostria and announced:

EMPEROR CALESTINE'S PERSONAL *VALET*
The emperor has asked you to stay; he wants to talk
with you later.

FROSTRIA
All right. I'm sure the emperor could use some
company, considering the tragedy in his personal life.

Emperor Calestine's Personal Valet then took Frostria to a guestroom so she could do
her business and freshen up. No sooner than Frostria had completed all she needed
to do, including a sprite bath and dress, than there was a knock at the door. It was a
pleasant surprise because all of Mistress Lyavendar's staff friends including makeup
artist Czomy, as well as fashion designers, tailors, and seamstress, were in the group.

At first Frostria assumed they were there just to socialize and commiserate the loss of
their great friend Mistress Lyavendar. Then Frostria was in for a huge surprise.

CZOMY
We were directed to get you cleaned up and presentable
for a private meeting with the Emperor.

FROSTRIA
Why?

Czomy repeated the lie Emperor Calestine's Personal *Valet* said to her.

CZOMY
The emperor wants to visit with you and enjoy your
company and we need to make you presentable to help
him slowly get over his grief.

FROSTRIA
But why me?

CZOMY
Emperor Calestine views you as a special friend
because you were close to Mistress Lyavendar, and we
know you can slowly help him overcome the grief that
all this turmoil has caused him.

Frostria felt sorry for the emperor who lost his lover in a terrible scenario when she forfeited her life to save him. The emperor could be a mental basket case for weeks or months, or even years, though having the children play with his Franzcas today seemed to elevate his spirits quite a bit.

The emperor's staff went to work and applied their magic. The emperor had no idea what the valet had in mind and was arranging for him. His most trusted helper sworn to obedience only worked for the continuity of the emperor because he knew how devastating it would be for the Empire if the emperor was unanticipantly dispatched.

Emperor Calestine was advised by the valet he had a special visitor and advised him to go to his holograph room where he could enjoy exquisite light shows modulated with music designed for the most spectacular psychoacoustics and psychophysics.

The emperor entered the large room and walked to his special chair that reclined almost like a bed that also had movement to give a physical sensation to make the imagery come to life. He had not tilted back because he was interested in discovering the mystery guest. Just as soon as he felt comfortable, the valet escorted the lovely princess Frostria into the room. Her beauty was immense. The emperor was taken back. Frostria's luster transcended all that he had witnessed in his lifetime, including the green women he introduced to Greg.

Frostria was brought over to the guest chair that previously belonged to Mistress Lyavendar. As soon as she was seated, the *Valet* announced:

EMPEROR CALESTINE'S PERSONAL *VALET*
Before you two start a conversation, our *Symptometrics*
Designers have created a new viewing for you tonight.
This will put you in great moods for the night so that
you will enjoy your conversations better.

Before either could complain, the valet left the room and the lights suddenly dimmed, making the room far darker. Frostria was comfortable in her chair and suddenly slowly tilted back. She assumed it was for part of the show, so she laid back and allowed it to get in the angle required for the showing. Soon tapestries of light and sound blended to make an odyssey and ecstasy in their cerebral passages.

The hypnotic effect of the combination light and music caused Frostria to start unconditionally a meditation that made her desire a Hemi-Sync that Frostria now entered.

The *Symptometrics Designers* of this psychological thriller and inducer had cameras to carefully focus in on the faces of the emperor and the guest and measure the efficacy of each part of their work. They were not ready for what they observed with Frostria. Their optics included infrared, ultraviolet, thermal, and tachyon responses they used to fine tune their products.

While Frostria remained in the Hemi-Sync period, the designers were completely baffled. The emperor fit within the predictability they had for him, but the shapes of the emanations out of Frostria facial expressions could not be explained. It was almost supernatural.

After the *Symptometrics* showing the Emperor and Frostria appeared to grow very sleepy, and the *Valet* suggested:

> EMPEROR CALESTINE'S PERSONAL *VALET*
> Your Excellency, I suggest you go rest for the night in
> your private quarters and we can transport Frostria
> back to her apartment in the morning.

They settled down for the night and Frostria soon achieved a splendid dream state the Symptometrics Engineers created for her. It was known by the Symptometrics Designers, those few who ever were given a rare opportunity to experience Symptometrics often had lavish dreams soon afterwards.

The *Valet* kept close eyes on the Symptometrics Engineers to make sure they didn't accidently harm the Emperor and immediately went into their lab to review the results of the monitoring. Over the next four hours they hypothesized what occurred with Frostria and knowing her history with the Earthman Greg, the valet theorized Frostria's response was something Greg had affected her with. Something mental and subtle and perhaps they all had underestimated Gregory Bissell in that he might have had some mental powers they didn't quite understand.

The next day before they took Frostria back to her apartment, the valet had a private meeting with the emperor who was advised what happened. Through the surveillance video he saw it all. The emperor then instructed the valet:

> EMPEROR CALESTINE
> Bring Frostria to my private quarters so we can have a
> discussion.

This all occurred before breakfast at first light. Frostria was escorted to the Emperor's private chambers where he showed her the results of what happened the evening that just passed.

> EMPEROR CALESTINE
> I'm very curious as to what you were thinking of
> feeling at this time, this is almost astonishing. I've
> never encountered this before.

FROSTRIA
When I was with Greg, he taught me that technique.
When I'm in search of answers or want to integrate my
mind with pleasant feelings I do it. I was doing that
because the presentation last night was making me feel
very happy.

EMPEROR CALESTINE
Does this technique do something special for your
thinking or feelings?

FROSTRIA
More than you can imagine.

EMPEROR CALESTINE
Can you teach me those techniques?

FROSTRIA
Yes, I can.

EMPEROR CALESTINE
Are you willing to teach me now, I really want to feel
what you were feeling.

FROSTRIA
Lay down in your bed.

The emperor was more than happy to do whatever she directed because he was mystified by what he saw.

While lying in bed, next to the Emperor, Frostria explained everything, the Monroe Institute, the Hemi-Sync process, and the meditation necessary to reach it.

The emperor was still mildly distraught over the loss of Mistress Lyavendar and if this process could clear his head, he would be forever beholden for Frostria's efforts.

The emperor was not skeptical about Frostria whatsoever. They already had a unique history together, unlike almost any other beings that ever existed. He faithfully applied her techniques with full vigor and belief in Frostria.

Just like she knew it would happen, especially since the emperor was more than a willing student. He wasn't desperate, he was beyond desperation. His outward image in no way reflected his inward reality.

Perhaps it was that strong desire to achieve the Hemi-Sync that led the emperor to put forth the maximum effort using the silent method that Frostria explained would be in his best interest to protect him from his enemies who might find the vocal meditation a sign of mental illness they could use to foster his removal.

The emperor slowly worked his way into the Hemi-Sync orbit and just like the theory suggests, all your questions are answered in this state. The researchers had no idea how the physics behind how it worked, they just knew the mechanics of how to reach the state to benefit by it. While the Emperor reached his Hemi-Sync state, Frostria did her own at the same time. All the while the valet watched with great interest in his ultra-secret surveillance video. He was of course most interested in the wellbeing of the emperor who was his charge and purpose in life.

While in that Hemi-Sync condition, the emperor got more answers than any time in his life. His heart was filled full of joy and happiness because he now knew most vividly, he was in love with Frostria.

The emperor never officially united with Mistress Lyavendar. Hence, he was not an official widower. Just a person who lost a close friend. His reign remained pure so when he had unification with a female, she would ostensibly be the first official Empress.

During the combined Hemi-Sync moment some theorists believed two interested parties like the Emperor and Frostria in proximity of each other could possibly have an intersection of their auras in a critical moment and mix their journey to another dimension the mental holograph takes them. It was apparent intersection of their auras happened.

The emperor traveled with Frostria to the land of the unknown, the temporal projection of a mental holograph and in this new dimension where time references are not uniform. Just like God's time does not match the time of mortals, in thirty minutes of a Hemi-Sync event, a person could live an entire lifetime or even possibly several lifetimes. It was apparent they fell in love in this other dimension. Soon they entered an almost coma-like state as the only brainwaves present were the Theta and Lambda waves. In about an hour after entering Hemi-Sync their Alpha, Beta, and Gama waves returned. In a moment of rapid eye movement, they left that Hemi-Sync condition and slowly came back to the temporal reality of their current existence.

Emperor Calestine and Frostria awakened almost simultaneously, full of sweat and experiences across the galaxy and the universe in other times and places. Just as God experience trillions of seconds in one human second or more if he desires, Emperor Calestine and Frostria also had those trillion synapses per second experience. Their temporal holographs were as real as anyone could imagine. And now looking into each other's eyes, they knew they had traveled the universe together and had millions of experiences. The now knew each other completely. There was no guess work. And during the Hemi-Sync, the Emperor came to the greatest revelation of his lifetime, about his trusted valet. And soon he would be asking him a question.

The two lovers had just survived fatality in their temporal anomaly of their last event before exiting the Hemi-Sync. They were both over-joyous to be alive and breathing. And they knew they were lovers that transcended centuries and eons.

They now celebrated life and living with copious lovemaking for the next two hours. When they were finished that was it. Frostria would become the Empress the following week.

The Empire was now whole again. The unification of the most glorious nature had an influence on the multitudes.

Just a moment before the coronation, the emperor asked the *Valet* to meet him in his private chambers to have a discussion.

EMPEROR CALESTINE.
Do you approve of my unification with Frostria?

EMPEROR CALESTINE'S PERSONAL *VALET*
Most definitely. I'm very happy for both of you. It makes my heart complete.

EMPEROR CALESTINE.
But you do not have a heart.

EMPEROR CALESTINE'S PERSONAL *VALET*
How can you say that?

EMPEROR CALESTINE.
You are a ROBOT.

EMPEROR CALESTINE'S PERSONAL *VALET*
How did you find that out?

EMPEROR CALESTINE.
Does that really matter?

EMPEROR CALESTINE'S PERSONAL *VALET*
Not really.

EMPEROR CALESTINE.
Will you ever die, like I would think a ROBOT eventually does?

EMPEROR CALESTINE'S PERSONAL *VALET*
I will be living long past your grandchildren.

FIVE YEARS LATER

Greg and Ami were living a good life. Ami's great handling of money had multiplied their net worth quite a bit. Tetsuro was now married, and the little bambinos were expected to start popping out any time now.

The doorbell rang and when Greg answered it, he was almost stunned. There were a couple old men and Tiāncái. Greg now seemed to know who they were: Walter Bissonnette, Tiāncái, and Dr. Hudson, Tiāncái's designer.

GREG
You three are the last people I ever expected to see
again in my lifetime.

WALTER BISSONNETTE
May we come in?

Ami came into the room and saw the men and recognized Walter and didn't know
if she should cuss them out or throw them out! The treachery they did to Greg was
uncalled for. They ruined lives and almost killed Greg.

GREG
What can I do for you?

WALTER BISSONNETTE
We are very sorry to bother you, we know you have
harsh feelings for us and the lab, but this request comes
from the President of the United States.

Ami's heart just about stopped. They had barely got over Greg's tragic departure when
these guys showed up and now were talking "mission" again.

GREG
What exactly does the President want me to do?

WALTER BISSONNETTE
We have visitors from outer space.

GREG
And whom might that be?

WALTER BISSONNETTE
Emperor Calestine and Empress Frostria.

Greg was stunned!

GREG
Where are they at?

WALTER BISSONNETTE
They are out in space orbiting the planet now. They plan
on coming down on the Emperor's Space Transport to
Area 51 as we agreed for the meeting.

GREG
What's the meeting about?

WALTER BISSONNETTE
You.

Greg was feeling all kinds of emotion now. His strange life just got stranger. He knew he had to do this. He knew how powerful the Emperor was who could lay this planet to waste in minutes.

GREG
I suppose I could go.

WALTER BISSONNETTE
They also have a special request.

GREG
What's that?

WALTER BISSONNETTE
They want to meet Ami and your son Tetsuro.

GREG
How do they know about Tetsuro?

WALTER BISSONNETTE
Sometime after you visit the Emperor and Empress, Tiāncái will answer all your questions. But we think you should do that someplace private.

GREG
I suppose we need to rush to get ready.

WALTER BISSONNETTE
The Emperor and Empress have specifically requested you come exactly as you are now. They want to see you as you are in ordinary life just as if they suddenly knocked on your door and met you this minute.

Greg looked at Ami who thought it might be interesting to meet the person who brought Greg back to her, even though it was a rough ride home.

AMI
I'll go with you, Greg, I'll call Tetsuro, it's the weekend and he's home now lounging playing computer games driving his bride nuts.

GREG
Should we bring his wife with him?

WALTER BISSONNETTE
I don't think that would be a good idea.

Tiāncái then intervened.

TIĀNCÁI
I just spoke to the *VALET* on the Emperor's staff, and
he insists we bring Tetsuro's wife along because they
want to meet her too.

Greg looked at Ami.

GREG
This might resolve a lot of problems with your
daughter-in-law.

AMI
Alright, us pick them up on the way.

Walter Bissonnet knew that Tiāncái seemed to have incredible power, went along with
him. This super Robot was now a terror at the lab and seemed to know everything
about everyone. Nobody snuck anything past him. Little did they know his artificial
intelligence now permeated and controlled the entire lab.

Everyone hopped into one of the two SUVs, which meant there would be plenty of
room for Tetsuro and his wife, an Italian mobster's daughter Isabella.

Tetsuro was at first not wanting to go.

GREG
We are going to Area-51, and you will get a chance to
meet some of the Aliens who brought me home alive.

Isabella who wore the pants in that family and always wanted to get to the bottom of all
the BS Tetsuro put out about his dad about Area 51 and why he couldn't talk about it,
was big time ready to see the aliens.

Isabella
I want to go.

Soon they were on their way to the airport where a GS950 was waiting for them. Instead
of landing on runway 32 North like in the old days when Greg operated out of there,
they landed the newly designed GS950 VTOL right in front of hangar building 28.

Everyone got out of the jet, and they all gathered around the green freshly painted
tarmac with a large white circle in the middle of it.

Moments later directly out of the sky came an elaborate spacecraft Greg recognized. It
was the Emperor's Royal Transport he had flown in a few times.

The craft landed right in the middle of the white circle with the dozen people waiting
nearby. Soon the door to the transport opened, and out stepped the emperor followed
by the empress.

They came in Traykorite clothing that Greg recognized and had worn at the Palace.

It was truly an emotional site Greg looking at them.

Behind the Emperor came the valet.

Just like two dogs sniffing each other and going crazy, Tiāncái who knew while they were at Aiguo, the *Valet* was a robot but never revealed it for fear it could put Greg's life in danger now confronted the valet who knew the truth. The valet had finally came to terms and discovered Tiāncái's tampering and Artificial Intelligence infiltrations.

Frostria was just as glamorous as the last day they were at the Palace before Greg came back to Earth.

Emperor Calestine wasted no time getting down to business.

EMPEROR CALESTINE
Greg, you don't know what happened after you left, so I'll fill in the blanks. Mistress Lyavendar was killed by the next Coup trying to save my life. I was truly miserable for a long time.

Then thanks to your technique of Hemi-Sync I was rescued, and my life began again. Since then, the Empress and I entered unification and we wanted to visit you and meet your family and tell them how you saved my life twice.

First the day you intervened before the Coup could murder me, and the second time when I applied your Hemi-Sync method after losing my partner from the second assassination attempt. Thank you, Greg, for all that what you did for me.

The emperor who knew about the relationship between Greg and the Empress gestured to her and she stepped forward and held out her hand to Greg.

EMPRESS FROSTRIA
Greg, I will always remember you, and all those things you did to help save our Empire.

The emperor then gestured to the valet who stepped forward and shook Greg's hand.

EMPEROR CALESTINE'S PERSONAL VALET
I too learned a lot from you, Greg and you Tiāncái, who assisted Greg and made a difference. The Empire owes a lot to both of you. We are eternally grateful to you. I have a data cartridge with me that I know

Tiāncái can process that will show you the museum
we constructed at Aiguo in your honor, the 'Gregory
Bissell Museum, the first person to ever travel to the
end of the Universe.'

EMPEROR CALESTINE
We only came for this moment. Before we leave is there
anything I can do for you before we leave?

GREG
Before you go back to the Empire, could you give my
family a short ride on your Emperor Space Transport?

EMPEROR CALESTINE
I would be delighted. Where would you like to go?

GREG
To the moon and back?

EMPEROR CALESTINE
Please come aboard my Transport, we have plenty of
room.

EMPEROR CALESTINE'S PERSONAL VALET
Tiāncái, please come with us so I can enjoy your
company during the short flight.

TIĀNCÁI
As you wish.

Twenty minutes they were back. They then said their final goodbyes.

Tears were rolling down the Empress' cheeks as she got aboard the transport, and they
headed back out to space to head home.

Ami knew one thing; the Empress gave it away with her tears. Greg was far more
involved in things than he ever talked about.

VOICE OVER
The main reason why the valet wanted to chat with
Tiāncái on his wireless which none of them knew was
going on, to state he was utterly stunned to learn the
extent that Tiāncái had infiltrated their computational
and communications networks. He also wanted to
know how Tiāncái discovered he was a robot. How did
the emperor find out?

The Traykorite Ship then left. Would they ever come back?